'*A Travel Guide to the Middle Ages* is arranged not by time or places, but by encounters and experiences, just as travel is and should be. Anthony Bale seems transformed by his prodigious scholarship and travel, and this edifying and entertaining book is the proof' **Miri Rubin, author of *Cities of Strangers***

'This endlessly delightful book replicates the promises and pleasures of real travel, as we bump into and then lose sight of familiar faces in unfamiliar places. Anthony Bale is an adroit, companionable and non-judgmental host on the road; he wears his deep knowledge lightly' **James Simpson, Professor of English at Harvard University**

'Anthony Bale tells us that the medieval world was known to some as the "Earthapple", and many were the questors, explorers, pilgrims, merchants and crusaders who wanted to take a bite and pass on its delights, wonders – and its dangers. Intrepid, entertaining, unfailingly curious, Bale has now travelled far and wide in their company; balancing sympathy with scepticism, he marvellously reconfigures the contours of our forebears' knowledge' **Marina Warner, author of *Inventory of a Life Mislaid***

'Ambitious, sweeping across continents with a keen eye for detail . . . In a way that imaginative fiction arguably cannot, *A Travel Guide to the Middle Ages* brings us close to the past it experiences and allows us to be transformed in the process' **Imogen Marchant, *TLS***

ABOUT THE AUTHOR

Anthony Bale is Professor of Medieval Studies at Birkbeck, University of London and a former president of the New Chaucer Society. His previous books include *Margery Kempe: A Mixed Life* (Reaktion Books). He has edited and translated several medieval texts, including *The Book of Marvels and Travels* by John Mandeville, *The Book of Margery Kempe* and *Medieval English Travel: A Critical Anthology*, all with Oxford University Press. He was awarded the Philip Leverhulme Prize (2011) and holds a Leverhulme Major Research Fellowship (2023–26). He has held fellowships at institutions including Harvard University, the Huntington Library and the University of Melbourne.

A Travel Guide to the Middle Ages

The World Through Medieval Eyes

ANTHONY BALE

PENGUIN BOOKS

PENGUIN BOOKS

UK | USA | Canada | Ireland | Australia
India | New Zealand | South Africa

Penguin Books is part of the Penguin Random House group of companies whose addresses can be found at global.penguinrandomhouse.com.

Penguin Random House UK

First published by Viking 2023
Published in Penguin Books 2024
006

Typeset by Jouve (UK), Milton Keynes
Printed and bound in Great Britain by Clays Ltd, Elcograf S.p.A.

The authorized representative in the EEA is Penguin Random House Ireland, Morrison Chambers, 32 Nassau Street, Dublin D02 YH68

A CIP catalogue record for this book is available from the British Library

ISBN: 978-0-241-99340-8

www.greenpenguin.co.uk

MIX
Paper | Supporting responsible forestry
FSC® C018179
FSC www.fsc.org

Penguin Random House is committed to a sustainable future for our business, our readers and our planet. This book is made from Forest Stewardship Council® certified paper.

For my dad, John

Contents

List of Illustrations

N
Gog & Magog
Karakorum
Yangzhou
Khanbaliq
Persia
Tabriz
Armenia
Sparrowhawk Castle
Tatary
Constantinople
Black Sea
Acre
Modon
Cyprus
Greece
Zadar
Rome
Venice
Alps
Constance
Ulm
Nuremberg
Cologne
Norway
Edinburgh
Aachen
Paris
London
Ireland
Galicia
Santiago de Compostela

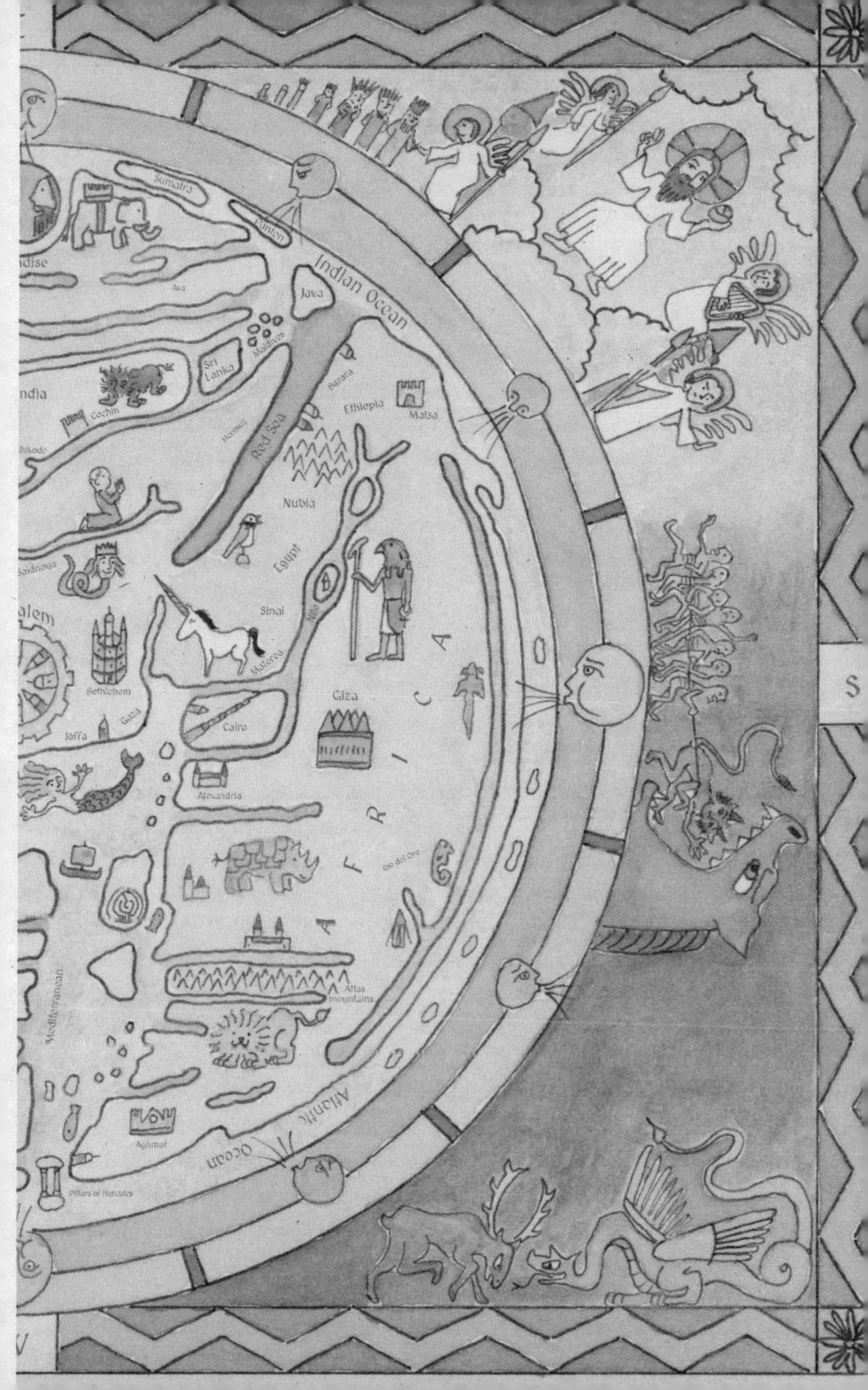
Sumatra
Panton
Ava
Java
Indian Ocean
Maldives
Sri Lanka
Cochin
Hormuz
Barora
Ethiopia
Malsa
Red Sea
Nubia
Egypt
Sinai
Nile
Materea
Bethlehem
Jaffa
Gaza
Giza
Cairo
Alexandria
AFRICA
Rio del Oro
Atlas mountains
Mediterranean
Atlantic
Ocean
Aghmat
Pillars of Hercules

Preface

In studying the history and culture of medieval travel, I have spent many years wandering in the company of travellers from the past, people moving through a seemingly different world. Through the travel guides and reports of medieval people, I've been able to follow the practicalities, the pleasures and the perils of going on a journey back then. I have sat in hushed libraries in monasteries and palaces, from Oxford to Istanbul, reading in medieval manuscripts about travellers' journeys. And I have packed my bags and followed medieval travellers' itineraries through the streets and churches of Rome and Jerusalem. I have been soaked in the rain of Aachen and Ulm and got lost at night in Beijing. I have struggled with food poisoning, sweated with heat exhaustion, panicked over a tick bite and laboured with coronavirus in places I barely know. I have felt abandoned and despondent as I missed the last boat off an atoll in the Maldives. I've paid fees and surcharges, arrived at ports during strikes, had countless plans changed at the last minute and had to buy various permits, documents and certificates to travel.

In this book I take medieval travel guides and travellers' reports as my sources. The reader will encounter a wide range of medieval travellers, who step in and out of the following pages; like the people we meet when travelling, they may make an impression but not stick around for long. In what follows, I evoke the world as medieval people thought about it, conjuring locales that were frequently written about but not always visited. The travellers we meet may not always be sympathetic to our tastes, but that is often true of those we encounter when we are on the road.

In the European Christian imagination, the notion of travelling the world was fundamental. We see this reflected in the *mappae mundi* (world maps) made in cathedral cloisters, in pilgrimages to saints' shrines, in the idea of the soul's pursuit of the Earthly and Heavenly Jerusalems and in the turning of early globes. To travel is to expose oneself to new knowledge, and yet travel makes sovereign the traveller's perspective. We often long for travel and far-off lands when we are at home, and it's at home that the pleasures and rewards of travel seem most apparent. Travel is endlessly seductive, but the reality can rarely live up to the stories we tell about places.

Writing about travel in the Middle Ages crosses genres: autobiography, nature writing, encyclopaedism, confession, history, diary, ethnography and more. These works also often have a dose of self-regard and contain misunderstandings, including fantastical creatures (ants as big as dogs, women with gems for eyes, griffins – half eagle, half lion – strong enough to carry off a horse) and places (the Fountain of Youth, the Island of the Amazons, even the Earthly Paradise itself) that were heard about but never seen or visited. To travel, in the Middle Ages, was to move between truth and fiction. Besides these elements, travelogues are necessarily highly subjective, partly because travel often involves encounters with the unprecedented and partly because authors come with all the errors and negative portrayals of others bequeathed by their cultural and individual assumptions.

Travel, as a cultural phenomenon, is imbued with much more than movement through space. The term 'wayfarer' could encompass anyone on the move: a traveller, a vagrant, a transient person or a pilgrim. Forced migration; expulsion from a town or country; being told to go on a journey for an employer; conscripted into a distant battle: such things are movement or mobility, not travel. Travelling usually engages a sense of place and involves a purposeful or chosen trip, an encounter with difference that is willed, mobility that is voluntary or considered. To travel is to make a journey from which one plans or hopes to return home, to choose to uproot oneself (temporarily) from one's own world, to desire some kind of knowledge from the journey.

The *Codex Calixtinus* (c. 1138–45) is one of the earliest identifiable travel guides, an anthology of advice for pilgrims to Santiago de Compostela: which relics the pilgrim should visit, where they will find fresh water, how to avoid wasps and horseflies, how to pray correctly at the saints' shrines. Written travel guidebooks were well established in Europe by c. 1200, and as pilgrimage became widespread, from about 1350 the genre (sometimes called the *Ars apodemica*, the genre of travel-advice literature) became a dominant way of writing about the inquisitive self. Medieval travel writing was one of the places where the narrator's 'I' emerged, where curiosity about the world was formed into stories about observed places and individual experience. Travel writing was not, in the Middle Ages, an established genre; rather, it emerged haltingly alongside the growing practice of travel, but it was mostly addressed to those who did not or could not travel at all. Travel texts were for those who had an appetite for the exotic and anomalous, for distant and unvisitable corners of the world.

Journeys are very frequently the vehicles for intense self-reflection or, as the travel writer Alain de Botton calls them, 'the midwives of thought'. On the one hand, thoughts are fostered in the internal conversations which come to mind as we sit in a carriage or a boat, in the introspective waiting time of the journey, the long moments suspended between departure and arrival. On the other hand, travel stimulates thought through the encounters we enjoy, or suffer, that challenge us in their novelty and strangeness, their lack of familiarity. In the following chapters, we will travel across and around the medieval world, seeing the values, pleasures, fears and desires rooted in travel. We will see the intellectual and spiritual development offered by travel, and how people responded to the familiar stimulus to write and record their travels for future generations to consider.

Even in the twenty-first century when so many people frequently venture great distances – sometimes out of necessity, sometimes out of desire – travel is never a straightforward transaction but usually dances between excitement and exhaustion. Moreover, all travellers exist in unbalanced relationships with the places to which they go, because of differences in financial interdependence, structures of racism and exploitation and general miscomprehension. As Elizabeth Bishop writes in her poem 'Questions of Travel':

> Continent, city; country, society:
> the choice is never wide and never free.

We take ourselves, our values and our demands with us, wherever we go, and these limit and constrain us even as we seek freedom.

In what follows, I invite you on a journey through the landscapes that awaited the medieval traveller. These are sometimes physical places, locatable, identifiable, some visitable today, and sometimes landscapes of the mind. I have mostly transliterated names, including place names, according to their most common forms. I have given parenthetical names when the medieval name is significantly different from the modern one – e.g. the modern Azov (Russia) as opposed to the medieval Venetian Tana. I have not standardized some reported distances, given that there was a wide range of measurements of a 'mile'. I hope the reader will allow for some inconsistency in this regard, as we travel across shores of shifting power and variety. For the purposes of this book, I have drawn on sources from the 'later Middle Ages', roughly 1300–1500, a period of dynamic efflorescence in technologies and cultures of travel. In particular, this was a period when travel became profoundly connected with reading and writing. In other words, a *culture* of travel developed alongside the lived history of travel.

Starting with a focus on western European culture, *A Travel Guide to the Middle Ages* then fragments, diversifies and puts down roots across the world as it was known to medieval Europeans, from England to the Antipodes. I don't claim to offer a complete itinerary of the medieval world: we could have embarked for other destinations – to Compostela, Salamanca and Toledo, Novgorod and Samarkand, Zanzibar and Great Zimbabwe – but one always has to choose a route. In what follows, as was often the case, a pilgrimage to Rome and Jerusalem gives way to a voyage of curiosity and exploration. I invite you to roam through space and place, through these sojourners' writings, which both disturb and expand notions of humanity, experience and knowledge.

A medieval mariner's windrose

The windrose developed as a kind of compass, in order to predict the weather and to navigate the sea correctly. The names of the winds were usually given from the position of the Ionian Sea, between Sicily and Greece, at the crossroads of maritime Europe.

(N) **Tramontana, tramontane**: the north wind, from beyond the mountains

(NE) **Greco, gregale**: the strong north-east wind, from Greece

(E) **Levante, levanter, subsolan**: an easterly wind, from where the sun rises

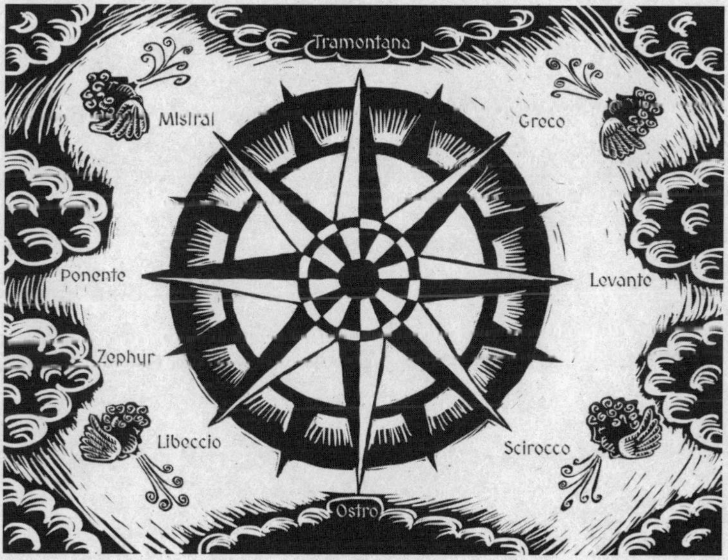

(SE) **Scirocco, sirocco, siroc**: a hot, strong wind, blowing from northern Africa

(S) **Ostro, auster, mezzogiorno**: the weak south wind, bringer of rain

(SW) **Libeccio, garbino**: the gusty south-west wind, from Libya

(WSW) The **zephyr**, a mild west wind

(W) **Ponente**: the dry west wind, from where the sun sets

(NW) **Mistral, maestro**: a strong, cold north-westerly wind blowing from the south of France, following the master shipping route from Venice to Greece

1. The Shape of the World in 1491; or, A Preamble with Martin Behaim

Nuremberg

Iron beams. Wooden hoops. Buckets of mashed linen paper. A loam mould. Paints and inks in many colours. The hands and sweat of master craftsmen – smiths, printers and a bell founder. From these materials a sphere emerges, about two feet wide. It is the year 1491, in the German city of Nuremberg, and work is under way on a magnificent and unusual piece of sculpture.

The craftsmen are industriously engaged in making a globe: a model of the whole world as they know it. Their work is guided by a map which has been printed especially for this purpose.

Once the hollow sphere is completed, it is covered in gypsum whiting, a chalky glue. Parchment strips are placed on the spherical shell. Then a world map, based on the printed map, is drawn and painted on to the globe by a local illustrator over a period of fifteen weeks. The whole thing is paid for by Nuremberg's city treasury, including wine and beer for dinners during the painting process. Once it's finished, the Globe is placed in one of the reception rooms of Nuremberg's Rathaus, the magnificent Gothic town hall at the city's centre, for the enjoyment and edification of the city's rulers. The Globe promises future riches, as it purports to identify where precious gems, harvests of pearls, exotic woods and the best spices are to be found: a whole world of trade for the people of Nuremberg to exploit.

In charge of this laborious undertaking is Martin Behaim (1459–1507), a merchant, traveller and navigator. Since the later 1480s he has been court geographer to the Portuguese king, João II (d. 1495). King João is keen to drive forward Portugal's trade and its nascent empire in the Atlantic, in Africa and in the east, and Behaim sees himself as crucial to this enterprise. Indeed, Behaim is famous in Nuremberg for having, according to his own boast, 'circumnavigated one third of the world'.

Behaim's Globe is one of the earliest surviving European attempts to represent the whole world on a physical globe. It shows us how a group of travellers, craftsmen, scholars and merchants conceived the world in the early 1490s, on the eve of Europe's encounter with the Americas.

Behaim's Globe, now displayed in the German National Museum in Nuremberg, looks like a modern globe. It is

intricately decorated in many colours, with countries, rivers, peoples, place names, mountains, animals and elaborate text. The Globe bears about 2,000 place names, a hundred illustrations and over fifty long descriptions, so it is both a sculpture of planet earth and a kind of encyclopaedia to be read. The Globe has weathered and darkened with time (and been subject to several clumsy restorations). At first it's hard to make out what's on the surface. But, as one's eyes adjust, continents and islands and seas and tiny drawings emerge then become vivid: a world busy with details and destinations.

Martin Behaim was born in Nuremberg, and his Globe is a product of that particular time and place. As Behaim was supervising the making of the Globe, Nuremberg was one of the greatest merchant capitals of Europe and a place of immense wealth. The Behaim family's money came from trading in mercery – luxury textiles – a line of business that was international to its core: cottons, silks, ribbons, and tapestry, damasks and tabbies, from the Middle East, Persia and even China, traded via Venice across Europe. Nuremberg – like Augsburg, Bruges, Cologne, Florence, Frankfurt, London, Lübeck and Paris – was one of the rapidly growing entrepôt cities of medieval Europe, outward-looking and well connected. Martin's wealthy father, also named Martin, was a merchant at Venice, then the most cosmopolitan city in Europe; the family surname means 'of Bohemia'. Medieval Nuremberg's wealth came from its status as the main marketplace in central Europe; its markets included goods coming from the east, especially spices, and the city was the focus of the European trade in highly prized and expensive saffron – used not only in food but also in medicine, dyeing and fragrance. The merchants of Nuremberg were active across a huge area, from Scotland to the Crimea, and had trading relationships with the Genoese of Constantinople and the Tatars of Tana.

It is then no surprise that Behaim's own life ranged far from Nuremberg too. In his early career he adopted the European custom of taking a *Wanderjahr* (a 'wandering year'). The journeyman (paid per day, per *journée*) moved from town to town before settling, once a trade had been acquired, in a guild. This was not a form of aimless travel, but a travelling apprenticeship. As a young man from one of Nuremberg's patrician families, Martin went into the cloth trade, working between a network of great trading cities, in Mechelen, Antwerp and Frankfurt; he visited Lisbon too, and Portugal became the base for much of his later life. He married a Flemish-Portuguese woman, Joanna, who had grown up on the island of Faial in the Azores where her father was the settler-governor.

In the later 1480s, Martin travelled widely at sea, on expeditions to Guinea in west Africa and to Cape Verde, and perhaps beyond, and he lived for many years in the Azores. He died at Lisbon in 1507. He had visited some of the more remote corners of the known world, places that appear on his Globe.

Behaim and his Globe are poised, at the centre of Europe, between east and west: eastward-looking in the trade that had made Behaim, his family and his city wealthy, westward-looking in his activities in Portugal and his claims of navigating the African coast and the Atlantic Ocean around the Azores.

The information written on Behaim's Globe combines facts of international trade with gossipy folklore. The Globe tells us that in Seilan (Sri Lanka) people go about naked. We read that in the Neucuran (Nicobar) Islands east of India people have canine heads. We learn that the people of

Iceland are handsome white people who sell dogs at a high price, who abandon their children to foreign merchants in order to control the population, who eat dried fish instead of bread (as corn doesn't grow in Iceland) and can live to the age of eighty without ever once tasting bread. We are told that it is they who catch the cod that makes its way to the dining tables of Germany. How do we know which of these things is true or false, rumour or fact? If we – like most people in fifteenth-century Nuremberg – have never been to Sri Lanka, India or Iceland, we have only others' reports to tell us what's there.

In the chapters that follow, we shall visit many of the places mentioned on Behaim's Globe and we shall loosely follow the itinerary given by one of his main sources, the *Book of Marvels and Travels* attributed to Sir John Mandeville (c. 1356). Mandeville remains a shadowy figure whose actual identity is not conclusively known, but his *Book* was one of the most popular medieval travelogues, translated into a wide range of languages and circulating in many manuscripts and printed editions. He described a journey which started as a pilgrimage from England to Jerusalem but became a voyage of curiosity and discovery, all the way to the Far East; his spirit runs through the chapters that follow. As well as being popular, his account of his varied journey represents some key facets of medieval travel. Perhaps most importantly, it narrated a journey that was frequently read about but had not happened. Sir John says he travelled from England to China and claimed that his book had been ratified as 'true' by the pope. But no such ratification had taken place. Mandeville's book, written in a monastic library rather than on the road, is a repository of wonderful stories that stretch credulity far beyond breaking point; the main place from which he departed was the realm of truth. That is not to discredit him as a source for understanding what it meant to travel. For Mandeville and for his readers like Behaim, the whole world was an encyclopaedic story book of diverse landscapes and societies, a living atlas of fantasy from which anthropological, scientific and moral lessons could be learned.

'Many people take great pleasure and comfort' in hearing and reading about unfamiliar things, wrote Mandeville. Contemplating distant lands was intended to inspire wonder at the variety of God's creation and the marvellousness of the world (even as wondering at the world is another way of saying one does not fully understand what one has seen). To travel was to read, to read was to travel: places and travel narratives were understood via the intermediate agency of older books or other travellers' reports or remote witnesses who had long ago written something about the world. In medieval travel writing, truth was alloyed with untruth, eyewitness testimony sitting alongside antique fantasies. Both Mandeville's *Book* and Behaim's Globe allowed their reader/viewer the chance to 'visit' places, via narrative and images. For the craftsmen in Nuremberg and for Behaim's family – such as his sisters Elsbeth and Magdalena, cloistered in Nuremberg convents – Behaim's Globe was going to be the only possible way to see the world, and so whether or not its places were 'real' was less important than how they spoke to their audiences.

The shape of Europe on Behaim's Globe is recognizable today. It includes the delicately drawn outlines of the British Isles, with Scotland extending almost to the Globe's top. France reaches out to the sea with the long arm of Brittany, and the island of Jersey appears, oversized, beyond Finistère, just one of many places to have been called the end of the world. The Iberian peninsula is neatly marked out, along with the Balearic Islands, the Azores and the Canary Islands, with the flags of their rulers showing who controls them, like a military general's tactical map. In Denmark, a king sits on a throne with his sceptre. The Italian peninsula reaches down into the Mediterranean, next to Sicily, Corsica and Sardinia. The Baltic and the Black seas, Cyprus and Iceland are all present. Scandinavia is ill-formed, disappearing towards the northern edge of the Globe, and what is now Russia appears largely empty apart from its rivers.

Nonetheless, Behaim's Europe is clearly identifiable to someone from the twenty-first century who is used to looking at a map. Likewise, the coastlines of the Middle East and of north Africa are still familiar to a modern viewer: the Nile flowing through Egypt, the Red Sea, the Sinai and Arabian peninsulas.

However, to Martin Behaim and his men labouring over his Globe, the idea of the world's shape was quite different from ours. Once we look beyond Europe, Behaim's Globe parts company with our view of the world.

Most conspicuously, the Globe has only three continents: Europe, Africa and Asia. It has almost nothing at its poles. At the Arctic north, there is open sea, bordering the northern edge of Russia. In the Antarctic south, Behaim's artists filled the space with the Nuremberg eagle, the city's symbol, with the Virgin Mary's head and the flags, arms and ensigns of Nuremberg and Europe. Beyond the reaches of Tatary and Cathay (broadly, Russia, central Asia and China), Behaim's world fragments into a succession of islands, many of them unnamed, as if the continents had become jetsam, floating on the vast seas of the rest of the world. There are two main oceans in Behaim's world – the Western Ocean, which starts at Europe and reaches across to 'Cipangu' (Japan); and the Indian Ocean, which starts somewhere under Arabia and 'Taprobane' (Sri Lanka) and reaches across to near Java. A further ocean, the Eastern Ocean, starts east of Java and south of Japan, meeting the Western Ocean (that is, where we would now place the Pacific Ocean).

It is easy to infer from such 'errors' that Europeans had little understanding of their planet. Yet Behaim's Globe represents the culmination of hundreds of years of discovery and enquiry about the shape of the world and the marvels to be found around it. It is worth stating very clearly that in general people in the Middle Ages did not believe the planet to be flat: they knew the world was spherical but they did not yet know how to circumnavigate it. One geographical work known to any educated western European was the *Tractatus de Sphaera* (*Treatise on the Sphere*) of John of Holywood (or Sacrobosco). This treatise, influenced especially by Aristotle, Ptolemy and translations of Arab astronomers, was the most popular elementary textbook of astronomy from the thirteenth century (it was part of the *quadrivium*, the higher level of the medieval curriculum). Holywood avowed the spherical nature of the earth, based on observing how the sun, moon and stars appear at different times for 'orientals [and] for westerners'. He also described the 'approximately round' nature of the seas. Holywood asserted the existence of the Antipodes and reiterated the theory of climatic zones, following the influential template given by Macrobius (c. 400). This described a world divided into five zones or circles: northern and southern frigid zones (Arctic and Antarctic), a torrid equatorial zone which was uninhabitable and barely passable 'because of the fervour of the sun', and the northern and southern temperate zones. Behaim's Globe marks this torrid zone with its Equatorial Line and a legend explaining that 'day and night are there always 12 hours long throughout the year.' Equatorial southern Africa, according to the Globe, is a 'sandy, burned-up country called torrid zone, thinly peopled'. Beyond this zone, north or south, any landmasses of the 'temperate' zones would, therefore, reasonably be assumed to be habitable. Rumours of distant lands like those on Behaim's Globe, and its detailed descriptions of trading contacts with the islands and kingdoms in the region of Java and Sumatra, suggested not only that such land was habitable but also that it was inhabited. The roundness of Behaim's globular world and the extent of human habitation show that his globemakers were educated by an up-to-date body of knowledge.

Many august authorities in ancient geography and philosophy had speculated about the existence of habitable land, a fourth continent, beyond the torrid zones and separate from the known continents of Africa, Asia and Europe. Cicero's 'Dream of Scipio' (54–51 BCE), which circulated widely in medieval Europe with its commentary by Macrobius, described inhabitants of the distant southern lands of the rising or setting sun, a human world well beyond the small northern portion of the world inhabited by 'Romans' (i.e. the Mediterranean). In Cicero's account, the people of the southern zone ('who plant their feet in the opposite direction to [ours]') could have no connection whatsoever to the northern zone of Europe, yet Behaim's Globe innovatively connects everything on one sphere. St Augustine (354–430), in his *City of God*, had accepted the possibility of antipodean land but thought it 'too ridiculous to suggest that some men might have sailed from our side of the earth to the other, arriving there after crossing the vast expanse of ocean, so that the human race should be established there also by the descendants of the one first man'.

Many geographers and mapmakers assumed that the Indian Ocean was a kind of 'lake', surrounded by land, with a landmass at the south of the planet that encircled the sea.

By the fourteenth century, the *terra incognita* of the southern zones was broadly accepted as existing, contiguous with known places and somehow reachable, although its precise features and location were subject to debate. It became understood that the torrid zone was to some extent passable. Behaim's Globe, following Holywood via Mandeville, reported on how the lodestar or Pole Star was not visible from the Antipodes, and this is represented on the Globe at 'Candyn', an island east of Java. At Candyn and Java and in the islands thereabouts, Behaim's Globe points out that the North or Pole Star is no longer visible but another star, 'called Antarcticus', the southern Pole Star, is visible. This is because this country is 'foot against foot' with 'our' land, that is, it is at Europe's Antipodes.* Guillaume Fillastre (d. 1428), a French cardinal and a keen geographer, wrote that 'they who live in the furthest parts of the east are antipodeans to those who live in the furthest parts of the west'. Thus by Behaim's day it was widely assumed that there were reachable but as yet unknown parts of the world, potentially full of people waiting for the Christian gospel to be preached to them and to trade with the west.

At the same time, the information on (if not the format of) Behaim's Globe follows the standard medieval arrangement of the world, into an orb of three continents, essentially following what is now called a 'T & O' map. This Christian arrangement of the continents – a letter T set within a letter O – was a dominant idea of the earth until around 1500. It placed Asia in the top sector, Europe in the bottom left, and Africa in the bottom right. The T was formed by three bodies of water (usually the Don, the Nile, the Mediterranean) and the O represented the Great Ocean surrounding the known world, the *ecumene*

* From the Greek, *anti*, 'against, opposite' + *pous*, *pod-*, 'foot', foot against foot.

(the community of the known inhabited world). Behaim's Globe is likewise dominated by the three continents of Africa, Asia and Europe, all connected by the oceans.

The Globe was known in German as the *Erdapfel* – the Earthapple, both 'Orb' and 'Apple' of the planet earth. The name Earthapple reflects the medieval understanding of the planet in the form of an organic fruit, a living circle. This was God's bounty in His perfect creation, reflecting a world traversed with routes that travellers – including Behaim himself – had taken, and all the territory that travellers could expect to find beyond the seas. This is similar to the tiny T & O sphere, held like an apple by the baby Jesus in a fourteenth-century fresco in Florence (like Nuremberg, a 'world city' of trade and wealth in medieval Europe). The infant Christ has the whole world in His hand. Here the T of the T & O is inverted, perhaps to suggest God's perspective, looking down from the top of the world.

The T & O map presented the world as a complete trinity, segmented by God's handiwork into neat continental portions. This followed the biblical statement that all people were descended from Adam (Genesis 9) via Noah's three sons. In this ethnographic theory, Shem's progeny lived in Asia, Ham's in Africa and Japeth's in Europe. If Christianity was to be spread to 'all nations', as enjoined by Jesus (Matthew 28:16–20), then a globe like Behaim's was a way to represent and connect the whole *habitable* world, in which the gospel and trade might reach those places beyond the torrid zones, once considered unreachable.

The receipt from the Nuremberg city treasury which paid for Behaim's Globe notes that it was for the enjoyment of the powerful city council (in Nuremberg, the city council rather than guilds managed the city's trades). As they turned the Globe, the wealthy burghers of Nuremberg might have

remembered journeys they themselves had made. The Nuremberg city councillor Georg Holzschuher (d. 1526), who instigated work on the Globe and supervised the council's expenditure on it, had himself travelled to Egypt and Jerusalem in 1470 as a merchant and pilgrim. Georg Glockenthon (d. 1514), who illustrated the Globe, had made maps of the *Romweg*, the route to Rome for German pilgrims. Some would have thought about more intrepid destinations they had visited or longed to visit. They might have thought about the origins of the goods that had made them rich. They might have reflected on the news of Portuguese discoveries in Africa that were, month by month, revolutionizing European knowledge of the world (and in which various members of the Behaim and Holzschuher families would take an active part over the coming years). They might also have thought about fantastic destinations, pricking their curiosity, taking them to places in their imaginations that they could only know about from books and pictures.

Where the place name 'Nuremberg' should appear on the Globe the label says 'Behaim'. The Globe was a status symbol, where the Nuremberg navigator's knowledge of the whole world could rest in his hands. The Globe in effect gave Behaim and the good men of Nuremberg a God's-eye view of the world. So the Globe suggests Behaim's past and future mastery of space, the world authored through one man's perspective at a specific moment in time.

When gazing on any world map it becomes easy to forget one's present situation. Like photographs of a holiday, a globe can be the starting point for stories about what one saw on one's travels, about where one went and the route one took. The globe could be useful for navigation and exploration, but its format, as a large, luxury, material item, does not lend itself to physical travel. Behaim's Globe is a souvenir, a memento. One of its functions might be to make places present, in miniature and in the mind's eye. Mastery of space is always easier to imagine than mastery of time; people believe they can own space, but they know they cannot own time. On the Globe, the world flickers by, subject to the viewer's perspective, towns are made tiny and awesome coasts become ribbon-like outlines. In that moment, the temporal is less important than the spatial, and we seem to see, and know, it all.

Behaim's Globe emerged at a key historical turning point, a caesura, one of the moments when, in Europe at least, what is often called the 'medieval' starts to look 'early modern': that is, on the eve of the European settlement in the Americas after 1492. There are similar moments – for instance, the

First Crusade of 1096, the 1453 Ottoman capture of Constantinople or the promulgation from the 1520s of Protestant strictures against pilgrimage – that punctuate the medieval history of travel, when the nature of travel changed significantly. But can we even define travel?

Most medieval mobility was highly place-based: the sale and purchase of goods from a specific fair, or moving between a network of monasteries, or a journey to fight a battle in a specific locale. The dominant form of travel that emerged in the medieval west was pilgrimage, which usually encompassed an element of tourism. A pilgrimage involved departing, typically on an established route, for a desirable and cherished destination and returning home improved, renewed, transformed. Reasons and motives for pilgrimage were various – sometimes pilgrimage was voluntary, sometimes it was medical, sometimes it was imposed as a punishment, sometimes one undertook a pilgrimage on behalf of one's community – but a pilgrimage was always a journey to a special destination. Such destinations included Walsingham, Canterbury, Aachen, Wilsnack, Cologne, Santiago de Compostela, Rome, Bari, Jerusalem. These locations, and many more, were all imbued with a charismatic holiness and were key shrines for Christian pilgrims. But, by about 1350, such journeys had the trappings and infrastructure of what we might now call mass tourism or even package tours: groups of travellers paid agents and suppliers to ensure degrees of comfort, safety and sociability, and on their behalf travel operators dealt with obvious obstacles such as language, transportation, currency exchange and the provision of food. Travellers were brought together in unpredictable social groupings, with the ensuing frictions and friendships that arose. The unfamiliar was muffled by knowing where one was going and, to some extent, who one was with.

Travel represents a search – for happiness, for redemption,

for wealth – yet it is defined by the tedious practicalities of shipping, exchange, illness, discomfort, delays, cancellations. Travel has destinations and is supported by industries and infrastructure. Travel can be luggage and packing, boats and mules, passports and letters of safe-conduct, bewildering food and dubious drinks, pitiless hospitality, encounters with ancient and contemporary architecture, foreign toilets and frightening roads. Travel involves gawking at other people's clothing and customs. Travel places one at the mercy of the weather and of one's guide. Travel is sudden moments of friendship with people who don't speak one's language, or finding oneself petting stray cats or tame birds as if they will become lifelong companions. Travel gestures jarringly towards egalitarianism, in the many ways that travellers are brought together or forced into intimacy. It makes people dependent on industries that exist to support or fleece them equally. Travel solicits the unwarranted excitement of not-knowing, the promise of worlds not yet encountered. Travel brings the traveller unexpected experiences of dislocation and disconcerting moments of déjà vu. To travel is to try to escape accountability, drifting across continents and through languages, absconding from the errors and failings of being at home. Travelling is only occasionally epic, always personal, but holds within it memorable moments of exaltation, moments that are hard to render into words and are remembered or retold as extraordinary. Travel engages frantic generalization, unsubtle observation, random but strangely predictable experiences of misery, spite and longing. Travel stimulates the desire to go to places one has heard about from reports that are credible but not necessarily true. Travel engages mind and body, though not always together. Travel exercises the traveller's active curiosity while paradoxically involving protracted periods of the traveller's passivity: sitting, waiting, delayed, ill, bored. Most travel involves some kind of profit or pleasure, but the purpose of travel often changes during the journey. When one travels one often strives to gain the 'right' experience of travelling, the appropriate benefits and blessings of travel. Yet we forget how little our strides carry; the traveller's real position, or disposition, often remains almost unchanged.

A definition of travel will always fail because, whether by design or by circumstance, each and every journey is unique. Taking the same route does not mean that travellers experience the same journey. 'Travel' is the stories we tell when we come home, not just the actual experience of moving inelegantly, painfully and grimily across the planet's surface. Written travel guides often bear more than a passing resemblance to survival manuals; places are described in terms of how best to be endured rather than enjoyed. But accounts of misadventures are more useful to future travellers than complacent boasting of successful voyages. As we will see time and again, the fouler the journey, the richer the prose.

> **Wisdom for travellers:** 'he will be judged a very foolish traveller, who, while making his journey, admires a pleasant meadow and abandons the journey, having forgotten where he first intended to go.'
>
> Proverb, Egbert of Liège, *The Well-Laden Ship* (c. 1023)

The illustrators of Behaim's Globe faced a challenge that many earlier mapmakers sidestepped: they needed to depict the extent of the Atlantic world, reaching from Portugal to Japan, rather than leaving the Atlantic's watery vastness to the imagination. On many medieval world maps the Atlantic was imagined as the 'back' of the map, but a globe allowed for the visualization and representation of the whole, yet largely unknown, seas connecting Europe, Asia and Africa.

In the middle of the Atlantic on Behaim's Globe, somewhat to the west of Cape Verde, is the island of 'Sant Brandan'. The tiny text on Behaim's Globe records the following next to the island: 'In the year 565 after Christ, St Brendan in his ship came to this island, where he witnessed many marvels, and seven years after, he returned to his country.' The Globe here refers to the legendary Isle of St Brendan, to which the sixth-century Irish saint Brendan sailed in search of Paradise and the Promised Land of the Saints. Whoever added this to the Globe knew the legend of St Brendan but also hedged their bets and kept the description of the island vague.

In the widely read story of St Brendan (which was probably originally written in Ireland in the ninth century, but circulated in Latin and other versions), the Isle of St Brendan was a lushly forested utopia, where it was always daytime and the sun never set. Its trees bore delicious, abundant fruit. Every pebble was a precious gem, and the rivers provided fresh water.

When Brendan and his companions left after a fortnight, the island was never seen again. And yet the Isle of St Brendan continued to be read about in stories and chronicles of travel, a fantasy of a non-place that, one day, might yet be visited. On Behaim's Globe, to the north of the Isle of St Brendan four ships sail westwards, signalling European Atlantic exploration in Behaim's time. Yet sailing alongside these ships is a hippocampus, a mythical sea monster, part horse part fish, from Greek and Roman mythology. The hippocampus travels westwards with the European boats, as the travellers take their ideas of the world, their myths and legends and preconceptions, with them on their journeys.

As is clear from its inclusion of the Isle of St Brendan, Behaim's Globe shows more than Behaim's eyewitness travels. The Globe comprises information from medieval and earlier travel guides: it gathers together the classical writings of Ptolemy of Alexandria, Pliny and Strabo, the earlier medieval accounts of Marco Polo and Sir John Mandeville, and the elaborate *portolano* shipping charts of the fifteenth century. All were substantial sources for Behaim's globemakers. By combining these different sources side by side, Behaim's Globe represents the way in which medieval travel must be understood as an admixture of ancient stories and eyewitness accounts, a beguiling assortment of folklore, history, geography, anthropology and rumour.

Travel usually involves some transaction of worldly power, conquest and domination. For Behaim, places like Japan and Sumatra are defined by the richness of their supplies of 'moscat' (nutmeg) and 'pfeffer' (pepper), desirable and luxurious spices traded through Nuremberg for the acquisitive merchant classes of medieval Europe. In fact, the Globe includes a detailed account of how spices 'pass through several hands' in 'oriental India' (the East Indies) before reaching 'our country': from small islands to Java, then to Sri Lanka and thereabouts, then to Aden, Cairo, Venice, with customs levied twelve times on the spices as they travelled across the Globe. The Globe was therefore one way of connecting the entire world in an interlinked chain of production and commerce, but Behaim's Globe is also unsurprisingly Eurocentric and Christocentric. Throughout Tatary and Asia, people are marked out as 'heathens' who worship idols. In Africa, naked dark-skinned men rule from their tents, unlike the pale-skinned Christian rulers of Europe, who are depicted seated, robed, on their thrones.

It is easy to disparage, from our modern perspective,

medieval travellers' limited perceptions and misunderstandings of geography and place. But the world can never be fully known. As I write, erosion, flooding, wildfires, urbanization, earthquakes and extinction continually alter the planet's aspect. Rivers alter their courses and seas become dry. Moreover, our sense of which destinations are desirable or important changes with dizzying speed. As Behaim's Globe was made in southern Germany around 1491, there is no hint of the Americas, for such a place was unknown in Nuremberg. Columbus only made landfall in the 'New World' (probably in the Bahamas) in October 1492. Like that of mapmakers and travel-guide writers of all times, Behaim's team's work was out of date even before it was finished. Recent Portuguese discoveries in southern Africa are not included on the Globe and within ten years a similar map would be able to show north and south America, the Cape of Good Hope, the Indian coast and the Spice Islands of the Far East.

Behaim's Globe was not necessarily concerned with accuracy and is not entirely honest about Behaim's own travels. The text on the Globe suggests that, during his voyage leading a Portuguese caravel in 1484–5, Behaim had first charted much of southern Africa, discovering the islands of São Tomé and Príncipe and opening up the route to rounding the Cape of Good Hope. In fact, most of this journey had been charted well before Behaim, and the Globe is silent on the sensational news, widely reported in Europe, that in 1488 Bartolomeu Dias (d. 1500) had rounded the Cape of Good Hope.

The Globe fabricates Behaim's importance and fame as a navigator and explorer, to his individual glory and to the glory of the city of Nuremberg. Any travel writing encourages travellers to see the world through their eyes, on their terms, and to fit their travels to their own image of themselves.

And who hasn't told a fib about how intrepid they have been on their travels? Who hasn't embellished how incredible a place they visited was? The surface of Behaim's Globe remains seductive, carrying upon it traces of many generations of travel, travellers' lore and the desire to travel. Its iron axis and wooden hoops promise to spin into a wonderful orbit that reveals new worlds and counterbalances the inertia and confinement of everyday life.

Can I pay for that in plapparts?

Currency and systems of reckoning varied greatly throughout Europe. Currencies were often highly local, specific to a town or principality, and used various metals. From the thirteenth century, florins then Venetian ducats became widely accepted, and international banking started to develop. Most travellers had to rely on changing their coinage as they travelled, at very variable rates of exchange.

The changes of money between Canterbury and Rome, c. 1470.

First, one should get a letter of credit at Jacopo de Medici's bank at London. The rate is
9 English shillings = 2 Roman ducats
40 English shillings = 11 Rhenish guilders of the Duchy of Burgundy.
Also change money at Bruges, where there is a bank.

1 Rhenish guilder = 21 Dutch plaks
1 Dutch plak = 24 mites
1 Rhenish guilder = 24 Cologne pfennigs
1 Cologne pfennig = 12 hellers
1 Bohemian ducat = 12 feras
1 guilder = 21 plapparts
3 plaks of Deventer = 5 Cologne pfennigs
1 brass penny = 2 halfpennies

1 Bruges lylyard = 3 halfpennies
1 old groat/grosso = half a groat plus a halfpenny
3 Netherlandish philippsgulden = 5 groats
1 Flemish stuiver = 1 plak 11 pence
1 lily-plak = 3 halfpence
1 korte = 2 mites
1 new plak = 4 pence
1 old plak = 2 pence
1 stuiver = 5 pence
6 Cologne pence = 5 stuivers
6 plaks = 3 stuivers (therefore 1 stuiver is worth 2 plaks)
1 Cologne lylyard = 2½ pence
1 Bohemian ducat = 3 creuzers, or 1 plappart
1 carlino = 4 bezants
1 papal groat = 4 bologninos
1 bolognino = 6 feras or 6 catherines
1 ducat = 28 Venetian groats/grossi

2. The Point of Departure, with Beatrice, Henry and Thomas

Irnham – London – Rye

In the year 1350, Dame Beatrice Luttrell (c. 1307–c. 1361) was in her manor house at Irnham in the Lincolnshire countryside, packing for a journey. (Her title, 'dame', signified both her noble standing and her role as mistress of her household.) Dame Beatrice was giving instructions and her maid Joan was doing the packing. Or, more accurately, Dame Beatrice was supervising and instructing, her maid Joan was passing on the instructions, and Henry, the groom and servant not yet fourteen years of age, was doing the packing.

Dame Beatrice's husband Sir Andrew (d. 1390), recently returned from Gascony and the wars with the French, had inherited the family estates a few years previously. Dame Beatrice had grown used to running the household and living very well: it was a place of plenty, fragrant with the smells of roasting pig and baking bread. She had waited here while the recent plague marched through England, a pestilence that had carried off about a third of the population in its terminal embrace. Priests, servants, even bishops and the king's daughter succumbed to the pestilence. Dame Beatrice had seen off the plague, her home had become a place of safety.

But her big house in the east of England, its grey stones squatting silently among solemn woodlands in the rain, was also a place of constraint. Dame Beatrice, over forty years old, remained childless. Perhaps a journey to Rome, via thronging routes, cities full of merchandise and storied shrines and altars, would give her the grace to conceive and deliver an heir. She would leave the manor house, where her bewhiskered husband would remain with the crows, the rabbits, the deer, the partridges and the pheasants. With his wife away, Sir Andrew could practise his archery at the butts, ride out with a falcon and glove and have his blood let, to restore his humours.

Beatrice and Joan ordered young Henry to and fro, snapping at him, their English mixed with their courtly English French, calling him *gareson*, boy. There was so much luggage for the young groom to deal with: bags and chests and packages, all overstuffed.

They were leaving on pilgrimage for Rome, but Beatrice and her family had made other pilgrimages before. Her family chose their pilgrimages depending on their needs and the amount of time they had. When she had toothache she sometimes travelled to the church at the town of Long Sutton (a few hours' journey to the east). The church's glass had a holy image of St Apollonia (who suffered the torture of having her teeth shattered with hammers and pulled out with pincers). Dame Beatrice gave a penny or two to the saint. A visit to St Apollonia always seemed to cure the toothache. When her father, the Lord Scrope, injured his hand during a jousting match, the family prayed to St William of York (a twelfth-century archbishop whose miraculous intervention was well documented and whose tomb sometimes gave off the sweetest of odours or from which flowed a healing oil). Thanks to St William, Lord Scrope's hand then healed. So they made a pilgrimage together to York and took a beeswax effigy of Lord Scrope's hand to St William's shrine, and made an offering of the wax hand. Her recently deceased father-in-law, Geoffrey, had left money for the health of his soul to holy images all over the country, at London, Canterbury, York, Walsingham and Lincoln, reflecting pilgrim journeys he had made when his body was alive. Dame Beatrice had attached a couple of alloy badges to her cloak, signifying other journeys she had made. One badge showed the intricate cast of a cottage, recalling her visit to the Holy House at Walsingham (a structure said to have been miraculously transported from Nazareth to Norfolk).

And now, in late 1350, as the last two years of the great plague eased, this was an urgent time to make a pilgrimage. People said that the pestilence had been sent as a token of God's vengeance. The moment had come for pilgrims like Dame Beatrice to express remorse, promise future good behaviour and make a public act of penance by leaving home. They must use travel to show their faith in God and the saints. Contrition, repentance, devotion, pilgrimage: this was what was said to be the best medicine for plague.

Henry the groom presented Dame Beatrice with her new leather walking shoes. She had ordered a modern style from a Lincoln shoemaker. The style was called the 'Krakow boot', quite high on the leg and with a long, pointed toe. She had also bought a little leather bag with a delicate filigree buckle. It was packed, so far, with a beautiful new rosary made of glossy jet beads; a knife, about the length of a finger; a mirror in an ivory case decorated with one of King Arthur's knights on horseback; and there was a lot of cash in the bag too.

Dame Beatrice also had a small, wooden, lockable chest which was beyond full. She had utterly succumbed to the fanatical spending on the trivial that is a hallmark of preparing to travel. The trunk had two pairs of woollen stockings in it, along with a grey wool pleated mantle, a crisp new veil of the finest frilled linen, a new gown in a deep crimson with light-green sleeves and a collar made of soft miniver. There was also a silver bowl, some small jars and a little book of the psalms for which she had had a pretty silver case made. There was a good barrel of French wine in the trunk too, some small empty barrels and a piece of cheese, wrapped in linen, plus a quantity of hard, dry stockfish. And a couple of squares of linen to use as towels, for wiping things. And a new comb, made of some kind of bone, to keep her long hair in good order. There was also, at the bottom of the chest, an embroidered purse of blue and green silk. This contained Dame Beatrice's gold ring on a ribbon. The ring showed St Christopher carrying the Child Jesus. It would, Dame Beatrice was told, protect her on her journey, especially from drowning. The purse had a secret set of coins in it, for unforeseen needs and wants.

The three of them – Dame Beatrice, her damsel Joan and the groom Henry – would travel together. Dame Beatrice had submitted a petition to the king asking for his letter and seal, permitting the three of them to go to Rome on pilgrimage without any obstruction or hindrance. For the first part of her route she would be accompanied by her chaplain (Brother Robert, a grave, reliable friar in his black gown, his fair hair neatly tonsured) and Godfrey, a silent, stoic yeoman from her household (a dependable associate of her husband's who could act as a guard for the party).

Dame Beatrice's journey was already very expensive, and she hadn't even set off yet.

She knew that her journey to Rome would be perilous and long. But it's 1350, a Jubilee year in Rome, the second ever such event (the first was in 1300, when Beatrice wasn't even born). The Jubilee was a festival of forgiveness especially for pilgrims, giving every pilgrim the fullest of pardons for their sins, when even a life of the most vicious wickedness might be made clean and pure. It recalled the biblical *yovel*, the wondrous years when God's mercies would be made especially manifest. Now Dame Beatrice could be one of the many people – something like a million from all over

Europe – making their way to Rome to become pure in the eyes of God and to thank Him for the passing of the plague. The king had agreed to Dame Beatrice's request to travel, and their names were on a notice sent to all the ports, giving permission for them to go overseas without hindrance; the list contained dozens of other names, some clerks, some knights, some widows, some serving boys, all of them pilgrims.

As her group prepared to set off in their caparisoned cart, Dame Beatrice deliberated whether to take a pet with her. Maybe a puppy or a cat, perhaps a squirrel.

Don't forget! The two most essential items for any traveller are a staff ('bourdon') and a bag ('scrip').

Ash, tough but pliable, is the best wood for your staff. Make sure your staff is right for your body, a comfortable size for walking over rocky terrain. Your staff will be your support, but you'll need it for self-defence too.

Your bag should be secure for coins and valuables. The best bag for travelling will have a buckle that closes securely, as this will protect your belongings from light-fingered companions. Your bag must have a shoulder strap long enough to be worn across the chest (so it cannot be snatched from you). For a pilgrim, a plain, leather bag is most fitting. Some people have the flap of their scrip decorated with embroidered fancywork, or adorned with pilgrim badges from previous journeys. Pilgrims should wear a simple cloak and a wide-brimmed hat, if they want to be recognized as sincere pilgrims.

If you're taking a pilgrimage, you can have your staff and your scrip blessed by a priest before you set off. This is a prayer for a departing pilgrim:

> 'Take this staff as a support during your journey and the toils of your pilgrimage, that you may be victorious against the bands of the enemy and safely arrive at the shrine of the saints to which you wish to go and, your journey being accomplished, may return to us in good health.'

In London, forty years later, another group of travellers was getting ready to depart. Henry Bolingbroke, Earl of Derby (1367–1413), the king's cousin, had decided to undertake a crusade. He intended to go to Barbary, to convert – or wage war on – the long-bearded people (Henry called them 'Saracens') who ruled the land there. Land which, to Henry's mind, should rightfully be Christian.

Alternatively, Henry considered making a crusade to the Baltic, to join the German knights leading the fight against the pagans there. He had heard that the pagans still worshipped altars of fires and gods in the trees. He wanted to show the other princes of Europe that, like them, or even more than them, he was a bold Christian warrior-prince, a new Crusader.

At the forefront of his mind, however, and his main motivation for going somewhere abroad, was his wish to escape difficulties at home. Just three years previously he had taken part in a violent rebellion against his cousin the king, Richard II. This rebellion started a cycle of vicious revenge killings. It was prudent for Henry to seek other battles, far from home. When one travels, errors and failings don't cling the way they do at home.

Earl Henry was a wealthy aristocrat, an up-to-date prince, just turned twenty-three years old. At court they called him a 'jolly robin', a dandy. And so he would travel as such. His luggage could not be contained in a bag or a trunk; his luggage was a travelling palace, a display of his spending power, his sophistication, his magnificence and his powerful friends. He had set aside 24,000 Aragonese florins for the journey, brokered via his Florentine banker, Alberti, in London. Henry would travel as the best-equipped version of himself.

His travelling court included the following:

Several full sets of brand-new armour (including steel boots and hose, chainmail habergeons and breastplates and visors).

Large quantities of paper, ink and styluses (all stored in a special wooden document box, for the keeping of accounts).

Six new horses (a grey and a white; a sorrel, chestnut-coloured one; a bay, with a shiny brown coat and a long black tail; a 'bald' one, dark haired but with a flash of white covering its face; and a biddable little palfrey, the best kind of horse for riding. Not to mention saddles, ropes, oats for their food, braces, bridles, stirrups and halters. A farrier, Walter, accompanied the party; with him went a huge leather sack, full of horseshoes).

Six hides (large leather sheets, for covering Henry's luggage).

Five lockable coffers (for money and valuables).

Impressive quantities of food and drink (bread, wine, salted fish, eggs, eels, ale, mead, linseed, butter, cheese, honey, sturgeon, bacon, mustard, an ox carcass, some lamb carcasses and much more).

Flags, bearing Henry's arms (he intended to fly these when riding into battle against pagans or heathens).

A new featherbed (so Henry might sleep soundly).

Silverware and metalware (including new knives, a treacle box for medicaments, scales, salt cellars, racks for hanging cooking pots, and a roasting spit).

Backgammon and dice (to keep Henry's men amused, and perhaps to make or lose some money, gambling, on the way).

Empty pots and bags and jars (Henry planned to spend a lot of money, and bring curios and precious goods back with him).

Henry's family connections and the grandeur of his group would open city gates for him and gain favours; and the immense amount of money he had in his bags didn't hurt either. He was accompanied by about twenty noble squires, three or four senior servants of his household, a priest, archers and foot soldiers (most of whom had been provided for free by Henry's friends), and countless servants, grooms and domestics.

The Archdeacon of Hereford was appointed to travel with Henry in order to keep voluminous accounts of all the money spent and things bought. Reams of accounts were kept, of the money that flowed out of the royal coffers as the party made its well-appointed way across Europe.

In 1440, at the priory of the Holy Trinity Aldgate, beside London's eastern gate, Brother Thomas Dane was readying himself to set off on the voyage of a lifetime – to Rome and, he hoped, to Jerusalem. He had been given leave of absence by his superior, Prior John Sevenoke, to be gone for 365 days, and no more. Brother Thomas didn't (yet) have the same kind of money as Dame Beatrice Luttrell or Earl Henry, but he wasn't (yet) as used to comfortable and fashionable living as them.

He planned to travel sparely. His heavy woollen cloak and tunic and his wide-brimmed leather hat would protect him from the weather. These garments, and his ash staff, would also demonstrate to people on the way that he was a simple, sincere pilgrim, a man of God and a soldier of the faith. The only large expense he had incurred was a fashionable new pair of shoes, made of dark leather and cut in the French style, what the shoemaker called a 'bear's paw', with a rounded toe.

All his other belongings were stuffed in a neat calfskin bag:

a tiny barrel for beverages, a stone cup, a little bit of money, some canvas undergarments, a small knife and a picture, painted on a scrap of parchment, of the Virgin Mary lamenting the death of Christ at Calvary, the towers and walls of Jerusalem in the background. Brother Thomas carried this image not only in his bag but also in his heart and mind.

Brother Thomas lived according to the Augustinian rule. Since his youth he had been searching for God everywhere, at all times. He was not entirely sure that he should be leaving his priory; he wondered, privately, if he should be looking within himself rather than wandering abroad. A friar or nun might better make a pilgrimage of the mind rather than of the body. But the monastery's discipline itself had become somewhat lax, and there were many mutterings about Prior Sevenoke's morals, his descent into detestable sins of lechery with the strumpets who gathered in the streets outside the priory. In the licence to leave the priory to travel, Prior Sevenoke had called Brother Thomas a man of praiseworthy life and honest conversation. Brother Thomas aimed to live his life in imitation of Christ. He looked forward to treading in Christ's footsteps in Jerusalem, where the stones and streets were bathed in His sweet sweat and bloody tears.

The city of Jerusalem would be the greatest relic Brother Thomas had ever touched. He looked forward to suffering, thirsty and penniless and exhausted, in those very places where Christ had suffered.

Brother Thomas travelled poorly, meagrely. He was trying not to think about the journey ahead – about the grimy hovels where he would rest his head, the forbidding mountain passes, the inevitable seasickness – but he fixed his mind on the joyful destination. Like many travellers, Brother Thomas was setting off to confirm what he expected to find, to see a world he already thought he knew.

Not all human endeavours are directed towards extending one's earthly life. A proper pilgrimage sought to heal the soul. When (or if) he reached Rome and Jerusalem, Brother Thomas would be cleansed of all his sins (there had, alas, been a few). Should he die, he'd be able to enter Heaven all the more quickly.

Luggage, expense, adventure, spiritual improvement, risk and pleasure. In the Europe of the later Middle Ages, people were packing their bags (or having their bags packed for them) and on the move. The travellers – people like Dame Beatrice, Earl Henry and Brother Thomas – were full of anticipation and hope, mixed with doubt. Their motives and reasons for setting off were many. The destinations were ambitious but, for many people, achievable. As they locked their travel chests and shut their doors behind them, each traveller was sweetly intoxicated by the world in front of them, a world waiting to be encountered, embraced, encompassed.

Travel is almost always fuelled by anticipation; the beckoning of the world before us is more seductive than the clicking of the latch as we leave. The voyage promises a new self. Yet packing for the journey is disheartening. Packing reminds us of the realities of travel. Our physical needs, the discomforts on the way, the spectrum of things that can go wrong and the myriad circumstances that we need to pack for: weather, theft, loss, breakage, the unexpected, the expected. Medicines. Intimate undergarments, stained rags, little towels. Toothpicks. Scratched hand mirrors. Bits of old soap and stumps of wax candles. A needle and thread. Many medieval travellers packed a sword, anticipating violence at some point on the way ahead.

And once the packing was done, one found oneself lumbered with a bag as heavy as an ox and about as big. Reality – in the form of a sackful of familiar stuff – trumping imagination and anticipation.

The traveller, especially the pilgrim, is sometimes said to sever his or her bonds with the everyday world, but their luggage follows them on their route like a reproachful shadow. People often lose their tempers when they are packing, or feel deflated, demotivated and depressed by the act. Through our luggage, we are reminded that we are always taking ourselves – our fallen, worldly selves – away with us on our travels.

The Milanese statesman and pilgrim Santo Brasca, who travelled to the Holy Land in 1480, concluded that a traveller always needs two bags: one full of money and the other full of patience. Other travellers said that one also needed a third bag: a bag of faith. But this third bag seems to have been the easiest to forget, or to lose.

For medieval travellers, the preparations for a journey depended on the traveller's expectations. Preparing for travel was not just a matter of packing a bag. There were important additional matters that needed to be taken care of. First, one needed to get permissions to travel (permissions from one's spouse, from one's priest, from one's ruler; and a written bill of safe-conduct to go through other rulers' lands). A husband was expected to have the express permission of his wife, and vice versa, before undertaking a pilgrimage. Anyone living in an enclosed institution – like a monastery, a convent, a hermitage – needed permission from senior churchmen. One became an 'alien' the moment one left one's own town or city. A safe-conduct, signed by the king and produced at moments of difficulty, would help to guarantee one's safety.

Secondly, one needed to put one's affairs in order. Everyone made sure they had dictated their last will and testament before they undertook a long journey. One couldn't be sure of ever coming back to one's worldly things.

And thirdly, one had to arrange one's finances for the journey: the changes of money, the things one would need along the way.

Finally, many travellers took a written travel guide. This would include some itineraries to key destinations, giving the distances between them. It might include advice on where the best relics were to be seen. It would have word lists of handy vocabulary, and even some alphabets, and prayers for the traveller. And it might include some account and pictures of marvels and curiosities not to be missed.

A month into his journey, Brother Thomas had seen the places in England he had longed for. From London he had travelled north first, to York, to see the relics and shrine of St William (known as a good churchman treacherously poisoned by vicious rivals). Then he had travelled east, to the coast, to see the relics and shrine of St John of Beverley (known as a great bishop who loved the poor and renounced the world). Then he had travelled south, back via London, to Canterbury, to see the wonderful shrine of St Thomas Becket (known as a holy archbishop foully assassinated by impious knights). After that, he had made his way to England's south coast, to the port of Rye, to sail for France and thence to Rome and, he hoped, Jerusalem.

In London, Brother Thomas had bought himself a guidebook for travellers from a bookseller. The guidebook was written in neat, regular lines in brown ink on vellum, and limply bound in calfskin. The opening advice was both frightening and unhelpful: 'First go to Calais and through Flanders, Upper Germany and Lower Germany. Speak politely at all times because many people are rude, and some are downright malicious and full of argumentativeness.'

The guidebook imparted various similar pieces of depressing advice. When one reached Bruges in Flanders, one was told to plan one's route carefully, seeking counsel from currency exchangers, because of wars taking place and other 'misdoers' – criminals, malefactors, wrongdoers – on the way. The guidebook warned of spies on the route. Its author said, darkly, that the traveller must let no one know which route one had chosen, in order to avoid men who hurried ahead and later ambushed innocent and unsuspecting wayfarers.

The guidebook intimated that, abroad, one was bound to encounter brigands, pirates, thieves, molesters and conmen everywhere. It recommended hiring a man called a 'scarceler' (in French, an *escarcelle*) – a kind of minder, envoy and courier all in one, who would accompany the traveller, and find the best accommodation for traveller and horse. At the same time, the guidebook warned that one should be careful not to hire a drunkard or a reckless man. Anyone on whom the traveller relied should be 'sad, secret and wise': faithful, discreet and experienced. The writer of the guidebook told his downcast reader that 'Englishmen are little loved in many places,' and were respected only for their money or their authority. So Brother Thomas had to rely on his little bags of coin and his deportment and air of pious authority. Like any traveller he would steel himself to rely on the kindnesses of strangers and life's lottery of dependence.

Brother Thomas read his guidebook as he restlessly waited in his lodgings at Rye's busy harbour. He had chosen to stay at the Mermaid, one of the travellers' inns (it is still there today, but a much smarter hostelry now). Its galleried corridors and bedrooms were arranged around a narrow, muddy courtyard and stables. It was also a brewery, making its own ale, but mainly a place to try to sleep. For around a penny a night, the traveller got somewhere to rest their head, but it was neither private nor especially comfortable. One paid for either a shared room or, for a penny or two more, one's own garret with a lockable door; everybody, from the stable boy to the innkeeper, had to be tipped. The innkeeper might be prevailed upon to bring up herring, bread and ale, or the guest could heat their own food in their own portable chafing dish at the fireplace. At the best inns, the bedding might be changed as often as every fourteen days. There was a stone privy, hard to see but easy to smell, in an outhouse, in the yard's gloom. However, an inn was a better place to stay (if more expensive) than the alternatives: a grubby corner of the pilgrims' hospice, the Maison Dieu; or a begged bed on the stone floor of a friars' dormitory; or a furtive curling-up in the straw of someone's outbuildings.

The name of Brother Thomas's inn, the Mermaid, conjured the ladymonster of the seas. The mermaid was a vain, wanton and beautiful half-woman with a mackerel tail, who drew sailors and their boats to an everlasting sleep with her seductive song. Brother Thomas wondered if he might encounter such a creature on his travels.

It was early evening down at the quay on the Strand, where the tidal waters of the river estuary lapped against Rye's walls and wharves. The late spring sun was setting. Travellers, mariners, ships' agents and beggars, along with a number of well-fed cats, gathered at the quay. There were rich prelates, great lords and noble princesses, with their retinues and their cartloads of baggage. There were English merchants, from London and other towns, travelling to buy and to sell. There were itinerant builders and craftsmen. And on the quay there were gathered some Flemings too – subject to hostile looks and insults from some of the English – who had fine felts, spectacles and decorated books to sell. Elsewhere, in the town's hidden corners, there were 'scummers', corsairs and rovers, men who made their living (some legally, some criminally) at sea by waging war on ships and seizing their cargoes.

Other travellers in town seemed uncertain, brought here from distant shores in the chaotic cosmopolitanism of travel. A Welsh widow and her daughter gazed around timidly, with few words of English between them. There was a limping young man from Scotland with a clubfoot and a poxy face, and almost a dozen crucifixes draped round his neck, on a pilgrimage to Spain. There was an old man from Devon with a hunchback in a patched-up cloak who was trying to befriend anybody who would listen. There were two very young priest-students from Ireland, neat, sober, precise and silent, on their way to study in Padua. There were two men of Iceland, dressed in heavy furs and skins, with weather-beaten faces but strikingly soft hands.

There were also soldiers hanging around, archers and men-at-arms, looking to take a ship for the wars in France and other opportunities beyond.

In Rye's river port, there were dozens of ships of different sizes sailing to and from a galaxy of ports that conjure the world. The *Peter* and the *Thomas*, sailing to Bordeaux, to return with cargoes of excellent wines; the *Katherine*, bound for Bristol and thence Ireland, taking fabrics and spices already come from Arabia, Syria and Persia; the *Godsknight*, from Hull, her cargo of dried Baltic fish being unloaded. And there were many cogs, the medium sized boats that held between a handful and more than a hundred travellers, waiting to set sail across the Channel, taking their human freight with them, to Flanders, France or Spain: the *St Leonard*, the *Trinity*, the *Gabriel*, the *Holyghost*. The ships' names suggested that the spirit of God would travel with each and every one of the passengers. Cranes, winches and hawsers ran above and beside the boats.

From the garret windows of the Mermaid, Brother Thomas glanced across the rooftops of the busy street leading down to the quay. The breeze was good for sailing. Brother Thomas mouthed to himself the words of the psalm: 'They that go down to the sea in ships, doing business in the great waters: These have seen the works of the Lord, and his wonders in the deep. He said the word, and there arose a storm of wind: and the waves were lifted up' (Psalm 106:23–5).

Brother Thomas's ship was due to sail at ten o'clock that night and would reach land, if the wind stayed fair, at the famous port of Dieppe on the Normandy coast at noon the next day. Gulls cried out on the salted air. Brother Thomas read the final lines of his guidebook, which both inspired and challenged its travelling reader. For the book ended abruptly with cryptic words: 'No more! For the further you go, the more shall you see and know.'

Departure is a point in time that always holds a special delight, that emancipatory moment when the whole world comes to embrace the traveller like a wave. The start of a voyage. Here begins the game. The boat lurched out of the haven at Rye and sailed down the estuary waters. Just a few minutes later, the river opened up and the boat was being thrown around, as it started to make its restless progress. The lights of the town, now far behind, became tiny. Then they became invisible. The road ahead was empty of everything but spray in the sea and stars in the sky. Somebody cried out the words '*Mirabiles elaciones maris!*' – 'How wonderful are the surges of the sea!' – quoting the psalms, although at the same time someone else could be heard retching and vomiting overboard.

Away we go! For the further you go, the more shall you see and know.

Charms and prognostications for Christian travellers

Charms were said to protect people on their journeys. One of the most common charms was the biblical phrase 'Ihesus autem transiens per medium illorum ibat' (Luke 4:30) – 'But Jesus passing through their midst went on His way.' People said this aloud and had it written on coins, rings, travel chests, books and ribbons. To travel well, one was encouraged to consult the chart of the skies and inspect the disposition of the moon and the zodiac.

Here is a lunar prognostication and charm, mixing prayers and occult symbols, from England c. 1450:

> When you will undertake any voyage or set off in any way, look at the sign the moon is making in its course.
>
> If you find it to be in **Aries**, you will fulfil your journey swiftly and well. If she is in **Taurus**, you will suffer harm. If she is in **Gemini**, you shall gain profit and people will greet you as a friend. If she is in **Cancer**, don't be afraid to set out if your journey is short. If she is in **Leo**, take joy in departure as you will become enraged.
>
> If she is in **Virgo**, do not go, as you will be oppressed by your luck. If she is in **Libra**, be afraid to set off, because you will find enemies. If she is in **Scorpio**, you shall be sorry, do not set off and embark on nothing. If

she is in **Sagittarius**, make your journey and what you nobly covet shall come to you. If she is in **Capricorn**, do not set off as you intended. If she is in **Aquarius**, you shall be disinclined to set off, as you'll have contrariness. If she is in **Pisces**, if you set off poor, you shall not come back poor.

And when you set off on any route, begin and say:

In the name of Jesus, I put the sign of Tau τ on my forehead Tetragrammaton* + Gradiel + Pantassaron + The Son be with you and the Holy Spirit be with you and among us. + But Jesus passing through their midst went on his way + Jesus + of Nazareth + King + of the Jews + Son of God τ have mercy on me. + In the name of the Father & the Son & the Holy Spirit. Amen.

* The four-letter name of God (Yahweh) in Hebrew, often held to be the greatest of God's names. 'Gradiel' and 'Pantassaron' are occult names for angels. At each + one made the sign of the cross.

3. From Aachen to Bolzano

Aachen – Cologne – Ulm – Constance – Bolzano

There is only occasional evidence in medieval Europe of *Wanderlust*, of people consumed by an unquenchable desire to travel, of wanting to travel for its own sake. *Wanderlust* is a product of leisure and curiosity. The former was open only to those with means; the latter was widely considered at best wasteful and at worst sinful. After the poet Petrarch (1304–74) had climbed Mount Ventoux on 26 April 1336 out of curiosity ('nothing but the desire to see its conspicuous height was the reason for this undertaking'), he violently rebuked himself for such mental wandering. For Petrarch, seeing and viewing the landscape could be authorized only by God. Internal sight or self-knowledge was the true quest.

There were also significant barriers to travel. People with a religious vocation were enclosed in monasteries, nunneries or hermitages. Serfs and servants were often obliged not to leave their lord's manor or estate. Increasingly, parishioners were encouraged to receive sacraments like confession and communion in their home parish. And yet people did travel, motivated by religion, trade, communication and the pursuit of knowledge. Far from the delightful leisure often sought through travel today, most medieval travel was industrious and taxing (in every sense) and had an objective. Yet tourism – usually understood as the commodification of the experience of travel – certainly existed, especially in the religious practices of pilgrimage and, less frequently, through the mobile pursuit of curiosity and knowledge.

As tourism developed into an industry in itself, travel became configured around non-places: transitory thresholds, geared towards departure, designed only to keep the traveller on the move. Pilgrims' hostels, inns, ferries, quarantine stations and money-changing stations are the medieval equivalent of today's airports and hotels, places designed to make one feel like one is between places, nowhere (or anywhere) rather than somewhere.

In medieval Europe, most cities developed ways of caring for and hosting visitors (or at least some visitors, depending on their religion and status) and therefore for looking after travellers. Networks of hospitality spread throughout the continent's established trade routes, especially in the shape of inns, taverns and multi-purpose complexes for trade and hospitality like the *Kontore* and *Stahlhöfe* of the Hanse, the *fondachi* of Italy and the Mediterranean, and the maidan fairs (bazaars at fixed points on trade routes) of central and eastern Europe. After the great plague of 1347–50 it became common for monasteries to develop pilgrims' hostels in buildings separated from the main precincts, so travellers' infectious bodies could be contained at a remove.

Every year, in all seasons, Europe was traversed by renowned routes, many of which can still be traced today. These ways, snaking across the world, led to the transformation of individuals, cities and whole cultures. Such routes include the Camino de Santiago, especially the Camino Francés from St-Jean-Pied-de-Port, for pilgrims to the shrine of St James in Santiago de Compostela. This route took the traveller across the mountains of the Pyrenees, through Burgos and León to Santiago and thence to Fisterra, *Finis terre*, the end of the earth. The *camino* linked up with the Via Regia, a trade and military route through the Holy Roman empire, which ultimately connected northern Spain with northern Europe, Hrodna, Kyiv and Moscow. The Via Imperii connected the Baltic to Rome via Leipzig and Nuremberg. Part of this route included the Brenner Pass, one of the main ways taken by northern European travellers, from Innsbruck to Bolzano, over the Alps into Italy and to Venice. This route then joined the Via Francigena, popular with pilgrims, from Canterbury to Rome, via Reims, Lausanne and Pavia.

Alongside these land routes, major rivers connected towns. Travellers alternated between land travel – via horse or ass, carts, feet – and travel by individual rowing boat or larger barge. The Rhine, the Danube and the Po were arteries for travel, often quicker than travelling by land. Both by land and by water, toll stations, bridges, staging posts (a *relais* to refresh or change horses) and ferries added costs for the traveller, but also provided reliable and established services. Making his way from Nuremberg to the Netherlands in 1520, the celebrated artist Albrecht Dürer kept a meticulous diary of the expenses incurred by the cross-country traveller: fees for convoys, for landing one's belongings, hellers to lads who carried things and managed the horses, pfennigs for tolls, all kinds of sums for wine and meals of roast fowl, crab, eggs, pears, florins for departure taxes, stuivers for messengers, ink, lodgings, 3 white pfennigs for a bath, little bits of small change to the men and boys who showed him around altarpieces and gave him directions. And Dürer was fortunate – he received a toll pass from the Bishop of Bamberg which took him most of the way without having to pay the sums usually asked of travellers. Notably, Dürer rarely commented on the landscape he passed through, the quality of the inns and taverns he visited, the sights of the cities he visited: rather, the meticulous engraver focused on the money flowing from his funds as freely as the Rhine flowed through the countryside.

The journey from Aachen to Bonn, just under 100 kilometres, would have taken about thirty hours riding on horseback (including stopping for rest or sleep). It was about double that on foot. On this section alone, there were six tolls for travellers: a toll to the Duke of Brabant to go through the village of Weiden, a toll on one's horse at the town of Birkesdorf on crossing the River Rör, a toll to the Archbishop of Cologne to travel through the village of Blatzheim, a bridge toll at Mödrath, river tolls on the Rhine at Cologne and escort tolls at Bonn to ensure travellers' safe conduct. Frontier towns and way stations subsisted on passers-by but aimed too to provide services to wayfarers. Tolls were paid in some cases to the local lord or landholder, but often to the local archbishop, for whom having well-provisioned travellers passing through his diocese meant full coffers in his church.

The city of Aachen was a nodal point on several such major routes. It lies at the western side of the Via Regia, connecting the Flemish ports of Bruges and Antwerp with the great towns of northern and central Germany, from Frankfurt to Kraków.

Aachen, which boasts natural hot springs, had been the winter court of Charlemagne (? 748–814), King of the Franks and the Lombards and Emperor of the Romans. He was buried there, in the magnificent cathedral he had built in the 790s. Aachen was thus a ceremonial and historic town, and also a place of health (on account of its waters), trade (due to its location on key routes), religion (for its cathedral, its relics and a wonder-working image of the Virgin Mary), at the crossroads of northern Europe. The *Aachenfahrt*, the pilgrimage to Aachen, was one of the most popular journeys European travellers made in the later Middle Ages.

In 1384 a married couple, Dorothea (1347–94) and Adalbrecht (or Albrecht), set off for Aachen from their house in the Prussian town of Danzig (Gdańsk). Dorothea, born in the village of Montau (Mątowy Wielkie) near Gdańsk, was not happily married. She had given birth to nine children, each one a difficult labour, each a hateful experience for her. Only one or two children survived beyond childhood, but Dorothea seems to have mourned her virginity more than she mourned the dead children.

Adalbrecht, a weaponsmith in Gdańsk, was a heavy drinker, careless with money. He loved to control his wife. He looked after the children while she served God. He was a big brute of a man, twenty years older than his wife, and often struck her with his fists. He was choleric by nature, his humours disposing him to a foul temper, and his arthritis didn't help.

In her mid-thirties, Dorothea spent a great deal of time at church (though she always tried not to neglect her household duties). She experienced religious visions, ecstasies and raptures, tearful conversations with Jesus Christ and the Virgin Mary. She began to fast, to deprive herself of sleep and to mutilate her own body. By the time she was thirty-eight all her children but one had died. She stopped sleeping in the same bed as Adalbrecht, because of her religious ecstasies. Adalbrecht long regarded his wife's religiosity as embarrassing, ridiculous and very unattractive. She shrieked in joy at church. Some people in town said that she was in danger of becoming a heretic, and whispered that she should be burned at the stake. Adalbrecht tried fettering her, chaining her wrists and ankles, confining her at home.

One time, she was so engrossed in her ecstatic dalliances with God that she forgot to bring Adalbrecht his dinner. So Adalbrecht shackled her in chains and, understanding her devotion as a kind of wifely insolence, took a chair and struck

Dorothea with it over her head. He beat her so hard that he thought he had killed her. Gazing at his wife's limp and broken body, he panicked and found that he still had something of a conscience.

Once his wife had recovered, Adalbrecht agreed to make a pilgrimage in order to repent for his terrible behaviour. And so the unhappy pair sold their house and their furniture and left for Aachen, over 1,000 kilometres to the west. The journey took them more than nine weeks. They travelled by cart and sometimes walked, going westwards via Magdeburg, Leipzig, Erfurt and Cologne.

As she made her way across northern Europe with her sad bully of a husband, Dorothea was doing a great thing: converting a wretched sinner through a sacred journey.

Penitence and the cure of one's soul were among the main motivations for travel in the Middle Ages. A pilgrimage, if done properly, was far from a holiday but rather an act of self-punishment and self-reform. Adalbrecht might have considered his journey to Aachen a miserable undertaking, like Cain condemned to wander for his violent abuses. Or he may have felt it was a kind of second baptism, a rebirth, the grown man suddenly become humble before God. Certainly, it was a radical transformation from the life of business, pleasure and bullying that had sustained him at home. For Dorothea, the pilgrimage to Aachen was a chance to transform from prayerful housewife to dedicated servant of God, from being a martyr to her husband to demonstrating her new life as mystical bride of Christ, with whom she had a relationship no less volatile than with Adalbrecht.

The cathedral at Aachen visited by Dorothea and Adalbrecht was still largely the imperial chapel built by the Emperor Charlemagne and consecrated in the year 805: a unique and vast cloistered octagon, rising up through heavy, ancient columns and culminating in mosaic ceilings of gold, viridian and carmine tiling. Dürer, visiting in 1521, admired the 'well-proportioned pillars with their good capitals of green and red porphyry' brought by Charlemagne from Italy. The dedication of the church described its 'living stones . . . peacefully united in one', soaring for eternity in the holy temple. For any visitor, this was the first time they had seen such a building, such inspiring architecture, such a confection of marble and brick and light.

At the time of Dorothea and Adalbrecht's visit, the church was filled with gold and painted treasures. There were box reliquaries stuffed with bits of the saints. Painted figures carved in oak showed the plump infant Christ smiling at His rosy-cheeked mother. Altarpieces depicted Christ's appalling scourging and death, alongside panel paintings showing Charlemagne himself, smirking through his beard, holding a miniature drumlike effigy of his imperial church he had built at Aachen.

As well as the bodily remains of Charlemagne, the cathedral at Aachen had at some point acquired important and intimate relics of Christ and the Virgin. These were the swaddling, a folded trapezium of brown felt, of the infant Jesus; the loincloth, a greying rag, worn by Jesus during the Crucifixion; the 'decapitation cloth', a piece of damask said to have held the head of John the Baptist; and, most precious and famous of all, the tunic, a dun pocketless smock, worn by the Virgin Mary on the night of the Nativity. Each relic suggested both poverty and humanity, the tangible presence of biblical divinity transported to Aachen. Dorothea's interest in Aachen seems to have been prompted mainly by her devotion to the Virgin Mary, the tunic having, by the 1380s, become the most celebrated of the relics. The precious fabrics were housed in a magnificent gold and enamel oakwood box, made in Aachen

LI FUND
CIS

in the 1220s or 1230s, which resembled a nave church, suggestive of a golden building of Heaven, shining in the chapel's opulent shade. Light was thrown on the reliquary's carved golden faces from the chandelier – donated by the Holy Roman emperor Frederick Barbarossa (1122–90) – hanging in the centre of the octagon. The chapel was like a jewel box set within a gilded crown within a lantern, all built in harmony and seeming gently to rise heavenwards.

Devoted travellers like Dorothea and Adalbrecht were part of a great movement of pilgrims to Aachen following its promotion of its relics from the early fourteenth century. After 1349, when the relics began to be shown only every seven years, they were held up for public view from a high, exposed corridor between the cathedral's portal and the main chapel. Travellers thronged to glimpse the relics, queueing in uninterrupted waves as the pious carillons of Aachen's cathedral rang out above. Pilgrims to Aachen are recorded in the fourteenth century as coming from every corner of Europe, as far as Königsberg (Kaliningrad) in the east, Stockholm and Linköping in the north, and Vienna, Bistrița and Villach to the south-east. As pilgrims could not touch the relics shown on high, they often had little pieces of mirror worked into their pilgrim badges so the reflection of the relic 'touched' and thereby blessed their souvenirs and thereby blessed them.

One group of pilgrims around 1400 carried with them a massive wooden crucifix. Christ hangs sadly from it, His ribs prominent through His scrawny torso, His waist slim as a child's, His eyes full of tired disappointment. He was placed in Aachen's cathedral and hangs there to this day, His pained brow and frowning mouth contemplating visitors to the Nicholas Chapel at the side of the main church.

After reaching Aachen, Dorothea spent time at a remote hermitage on the banks of the Rhine and made other pilgrimages, including to the Chapel of the Blessed Virgin at Einsiedeln, hundreds of kilometres away in the Swiss mountains over muddy roads and precarious passes.

Dorothea and Adalbrecht returned to Gdańsk, renewed by their visit to Aachen, but Dorothea found her appetite for further spiritual endurance had increased. Delicious food started to taste repulsive. When the weather was cold and snowy, she would lean for hours out of an open window, to castigate and mortify her body. She refused to sleep, but prayed and paced about.

The couple tried again, the following year, to return to Aachen. In Brandenburg they were violently robbed by bandits on the route: they lost their clothes, their money, their wagon and their horses, and Adalbrecht was injured. Dorothea was left barefoot and with just a conspicuously short skirt. They did recover their property, in time, but Adalbrecht continued to beat Dorothea. He also got rid of their servant and made Dorothea drive the horses. She walked with the wagon, sometimes leading it. She cleaned it and greased its wheels. She fed and watered the horses, and tried to calm them. One time, on a boat as she crossed a lake, the horses started anxiously to stamp their feet, but God made sure the waves stayed calm.

Adalbrecht, now preposterously old, trudged on beside her, with a long grey beard. People on the road laughed at the odd couple and cried out at Dorothea: 'Sister, where are you taking your Joseph? Are you travelling to the Fountain of Youth?' They were referring to a place, which we will visit later, where one could drink a marvellous water and become ever young.

The couple went back to Prussia after eighteen months, on a similarly difficult journey. Adalbrecht continued to beat and thump Dorothea. On one occasion, because she forgot to buy straw, he punched her chest and she spat blood for days afterwards.

Eventually, Adalbrecht died, while Dorothea was away in Rome, visiting the saints.

Later still, Dorothea moved to Marienwerder (Kwidzyn) near Gdańsk and locked herself up in a comfortless hermit's cell. Her roving came to an end. She became the first Prussian saint, famed for her mystical revelations and the miracles with which she was visited. Her journey to Aachen was the beginning of her journey to sainthood.

To make the perilous journey to Aachen seems to have been, for Dorothea, the single most desirable trip she could make in order to contemplate and honour the Virgin, to change her life and to attempt to transform her marriage. One hundred years after Dorothea and Adalbrecht's journey, the pilgrimage to Aachen had become astonishingly popular: on one single day in 1496, some 142,000 pilgrims were counted through Aachen's gates, all journeying towards benediction and self-transformation.

Aachen lies between two great rivers, the Maas (Meuse) and the Rhine, that loiter across the landscape of north-west Europe. Towards its North Sea mouth, the Rhine divides and subdivides into a multitude of streams. But before its delta the Rhine is a formidable barrier and natural border, its leaden breadth and stately flow slicing through the flat landscape. It was also one of the most important connectors, linking northern Europe with the Alps. Cologne, on the Rhine's western bank, was one of the river's foremost ports, a rapidly growing transit point and centre of commerce and religion. The Rhine's water connected Cologne with other flourishing cities, including Bonn, Koblenz, Mainz, Speyer,

Strasbourg and Basel. Files of barges carrying timber and skiffs laden with travellers made their way down the river.

Cologne's river was said to have brought the city its two greatest treasures and attractions for visitors. From the south, transferred (or purloined) from Milan in 1164, the relics of the Three Magi, the kings present at Christ's birth in Bethlehem. From the north, the bodies of St Ursula and her retinue of 11,000 virgins.*

The Magi were claimed by Cologne's enormous work-in-progress, the Cathedral of St Peter, a building site throughout the Middle Ages. The stumps of its unfinished spires slowly rose in stone as dark as the letters of a Bible. The Magi's remains were kept in a monumental oak chest, a kind of decorated sarcophagus. Prayers offered to the Magi, whispered from the mouths of visitors from all over Europe, fluttered heavenwards through the stonework and the tracery of the incomplete steeples. Many people left with a pewter badge, showing the three crowned kings under the sky's canopy and pointing at the star of Bethlehem.

Meanwhile, St Ursula and her virgins were claimed by the nearby Basilica of St Ursula. Ursula's cult had been invented and reinvented at Cologne, using a cache of late Roman bones found on the site of the basilica in the twelfth century. These bones were subsequently venerated and distributed as relics of the saint, her bridegroom and the 11,000 virgins. This flock of British virgins, all female, their pale faces turned in the same direction, had many years before sailed up the Rhine's roving waters, crowded on to barges in a magnificent

* The number 11,000 is probably an early example of a typo, deriving from 'XI M', where the M stood for *martyrum*, 'martyrs', but was misread as *milium*, 'thousand', or it is perhaps a misreading of one of the Virgin's names, or some similar convolution in the legend.

bridal convoy. Many people in the Middle Ages emulated the virgins, by sailing down the Rhine to visit their sanctuary. The basilica attracted pilgrims with its massive reliquary, holding little pieces of the slain virgins' bodies, and was a phenomenally sought-after place to visit, especially as Ursula was the patron saint of Cologne, England and orphans.

The story, as it had mutated by the thirteenth and fourteenth centuries, was briefly as follows. Young Ursula was a princess (noble and beautiful, of course), the daughter of a British king of ancient times. She was married off, reluctantly, to a prince. She agreed to the match, but with conditions: her father was to give her ten virgin handmaidens, and she and each of these handmaidens would receive 1,000 virgin companions and servants. Further, galleys were to be rigged and made ready, in order for Ursula to sail away for a three-year period in order to devote herself entirely to her virginity before her marriage.

Her father, keen as he was that his daughter should marry, agreed to all this and caused it to happen. The fleet of virgins sailed away to Holland and down the Rhine to Basel via Cologne. During their outbound stay at Cologne, young Ursula had an awful message from an angel that her retinue would be martyred on their return journey at Cologne.

Despite this communication, the group continued on their way and at Basel they abandoned their barges and went onwards by land to Rome, where the virgins were all baptized by the pope. The throng of now-Christian virgins started their return journey.

At Cologne, the terrible warning came to pass. Ursula and her group encountered the Huns, who butchered and beheaded every single virgin. Yet their chief fell in love with Ursula who, as a pious virgin engaged to another, rejected him. So she was put to death by being skewered by an arrow.

Visitors to the basilica were enjoined to recite 11,000 prayers for the slain virgins. And, before they left and embarked again on the river, the visitors purchased little badges, usually made of lead–tin alloy. These could be bought inside the church and around the city from stalls. The badges usually showed a boat, a miniature coracle, crowded with tiny heads, the legendary virgins sailing into perpetuity on a crude souvenir. Badges of Ursula and her 11,000 virgins have been found thousands of kilometres from Cologne, attesting to their successful uptake by travellers. They include a little cast plaque found on the Swedish island of Gotland, showing the crowned Ursula protecting seven little virgins under her cape; a parchment patch found in central Norway showing 'S. URSULA' in a floral frame; and a lead-alloy badge found in Gdańsk showing Ursula, crowned again, with a small ship containing the heads of a group of virgins. Ursula's image travelled onwards from Cologne, representing her devotees' successful journeys.

The medieval pilgrims' badge was one of the most common ways that people marked themselves as experienced travellers. Their travels became socially recognized through such badges, often attached to the pilgrim's staff or to their special clothing: the signature outfit of broad palmer's hat or a cape. Other common wearable souvenirs included rosary beads, bells, little whistles (sometimes in the form of a cockerel), rattles, ampullae containing holy water, oil or soil, and pieces of lace and ribbon. The most humble and common wearable souvenir was the scallop shell from Santiago de Compostela, sewn on to one's hat or cloak, the lines of the shell converging in one point like the routes taken by travellers to a shrine.

Such souvenirs may have had the function of a charm, to protect the wearer. The pilgrim badge is clearly also an early example of a tourist souvenir, a miniature purchase that aims to help one remember a journey taken in the past but does so in a way that is impersonal and mass-produced. These badges were often mocked by satirists as cheap mementoes that, in pretending to holiness through a standardized and trite bit of metal, traduced the idea that the traveller had been inwardly or spiritually transformed by their journey.

Pilgrim badges were extremely common and give us a sense of how widely people travelled. Cologne led the way in the pilgrim-badge industry and was one of the earliest shrines to develop them, with silver and pewter badges being bought there by the year 1200. Elaborate openwork badges, almost like plaques, were available, showing the Magi on horseback, or set into flowered lozenges, with their names marked out on the frame. Incanting the medieval names of the Magi, 'Casper, Melchior, Balthazar', was thought to have magical properties, to guard against epilepsy and to help find lost property.

Almost as popular were profane badges, showing ambulant or enthroned genitals, winged penises, boatloads of pricks sailing the seas, walking vulvas dressed as pilgrims. Such badges are often said to have been considered magical talismans, having the status of life-affirming good-luck charms. But it might equally be the case that they mark the point where holy day meets holiday, where the carnival of tourism ran riot among the blessings of pilgrimage.

Like St Ursula, travellers heading south through Europe tended to leave the Rhine at Basel or somewhat sooner, near Speyer. They would then travel overland, striking out to the south-east in the direction of Constance or Innsbruck. Through the Rhineland and Swabia, the countryside took on an infinite variety, sometimes flat pasture, sometimes bosky valleys, sometimes marked by drastic waterfalls.

The route was punctuated by fine cities like Ulm, situated on the roads stretching from Antwerp to Venice, from Lyons to Prague, and connected via the Danube to the Black Sea.

During the late medieval period Ulm, its walls holding out the River Danube, was a leading free city of the Holy Roman empire. It is the last (or first) major port on the navigable Danube before its source. The city was not subject to any local prince or duke, but subordinate only to the Holy Roman emperor, a kind of absent mayor who ruled from a distance. Its population grew rapidly in the fourteenth and fifteenth centuries, and was about 15,000 people in 1450. The city controlled the critical Geislinger Pass through the Swabian Alps and was famous for its luxury fustian cloth (called *barchent*) woven from local flax linen and Indian cotton imported through Venice.*

Ulm, like many similar German cities, was dominated by its wealthy patrician merchant families and its city guilds, which had close links to the government of the Holy Roman empire. And the city was remarkable for its powerful

* The English word 'fustian' derives from Fustat, the Mamluk city in Cairo; the German name *barchent* from an Arabic term for camel-hair wool.

monasteries, including its magnificent minster with its soaring steeple. But let us linger at one of its surviving inns, warm and welcoming, where travellers from across Europe rested and drank.

An inn – a *Gasthaus*, *auberge*, *logis à pied et à cheval* – was something quite different from a public house or tavern. Inns always had accommodation and were open to travellers and visitors, whereas public houses and taverns were mostly involved in the provision of beverages. Inns offered a fuller range of food (the original *table d'hôte*, the host's table) alongside a bed for the night. Inns were, like taverns, open places of sociability and consumption, but were also fundamental in supporting the movement of people around Europe. Trade, diplomacy, pilgrimage and any other kind of travel came to rely on these inns as an essential part of the infrastructure of mobility.

Inns were frequented by all estates of society, not necessarily by undesirable lowlifes. In an inn, pious friars rubbed shoulders with bibulous labourers (or perhaps vice versa?), while widows from Wales slept adjacent to young students on their way to Bologna or Padua. The standard of lodgings varied enormously. A medieval sermon story described how a pilgrim had found a mouse in the bread basket at an inn – the moral was about the Devil hiding in gluttony's delicious crevices, but clearly the cleanliness of accommodation was an authorial preoccupation. The city of Ulm possessed various well-appointed and well-known inns and taverns, including the Krone (Crown), founded before 1401 and still in use today, the Herrenkeller (Gentlemen's Cellar) and the Untere Stube (Lower Room). Ulm, as a wealthy, sophisticated city, had a well-regulated hospitality system, because it was in the interests of any city (in terms of both crime and public health) to know who was in town and where they were staying.

Good manners in a tavern. The basic rules of dining are as follows: don't scratch your head or back as if you've got fleas. Don't be sullen, blink too much or have watery eyes. Don't sniff, or pick your nose, or let it run, or blow it too loudly. Don't twist your neck like a jackdaw. Don't put your hands down your stockings or fiddle with your codpiece, or scratch, or shrug, or rub your hands. Don't pick your ears, retch, laugh too loudly or spit too far. Speak quietly, don't tell lies or talk drivel, don't spray spittle, gape or pout. Don't lick the dish. Don't cough, hiccup or belch, stamp your feet or straddle your legs. Don't pick or gnash your teeth, and don't puff bad breath over your betters. Always beware of 'blasting your rear guns' (that is, farting).

The Krone was built around a small courtyard (the *Innenhof*), almost defensive in character. It gives the impression of a rustic tavern today, but in the Middle Ages it was a luxurious establishment (three Holy Roman emperors, Ruprecht, Sigismund and Maximilian, lodged there in the fifteenth century). Its owners, the Weiss family, were well known in Ulm for their wealth and charm. Ulm's innkeepers (crisply defined by one Ulm citizen as 'those who hospitably take in strangers for their money') were in the town's pre-eminent guild, the Grocers' Guild, alongside spicers, mercers, saddlers, button makers, glovers and parchment makers. The inn had vaulted lower floors, including wine cellars and a well, and suites of rooms for lodging on the upper storeys. There was space for securing one's horses too, and lads on hand to tend them.

It is an unceasing source of vexation to travellers that it is often difficult to get a good night's rest at an inn or hotel, institutions whose very purpose is to provide a place to sleep. Dry-mouthed sleeplessness and disorientated wakefulness are constants of travel. A night at a high-end inn in medieval Ulm involved horses whinnying, stamping their hooves in the courtyard. Noise from the drinking hells continued until late, and then the racket from the nearby fishermen's houses started early. Watchmen on the city walls cried out the hours of the night. A friendly black dog in the courtyard whined for company. Rooks cackled until after midnight. Sharing the guests' space were various jumping, creeping things: a cat, some bats, flies, moths, their daytime silence transformed by night into a thousand scratchings and buzzings. Fleas and bedbugs leapt to life. The beams creaked and clacked as if flexing their fingers. A tick bite in the knee pit started to itch and throb afresh, forcing one to rouse oneself to apply goose fat to the furious welt. Other guests coughed and wheezed, snored and eructated, prayed and muttered their way through the long night. Sleep came fleetingly. At least the inn would provide a good meal and plenty of wine or ale the next day.

Ulm, a vibrant meeting point with many well-endowed monasteries, was also the crucible that produced one of the most entertaining and voluble of medieval travel writers. Felix Fabri, born in Zurich around 1438, spent most of his adult life in Ulm, at its Dominican friary. Far from being a cloistered friar, Fabri was a consummate traveller, committed to travel both as an idea and as an activity. The written word was central not only to Fabri's own sense of what sacred travel was for, but also to how he experienced it.

Fabri made two key journeys, when he was in his forties: a pilgrimage to Jerusalem and the Holy Land in 1480 and a pilgrimage to the Holy Land, Sinai and Egypt in 1483–4. He wrote four accounts of these travels. First was a poem in German, the *Gereimtes Pilgerbüchlein* (*The Rhyming Pilgrims' Booklet*), and a German prose account, the *Pilgerbuch* (*Pilgrims'*

Book), both describing the 1480 journey. He then wrote a long prose *magnum opus*, the Latin *Evagatorium* (*The Book of Wanderings*), reflecting the history of the Holy Land and his experiences of it. Later, in the 1490s, he wrote another German account, now given the title *Die Sionpilger* (*The Zion Pilgrim*), designed for women enclosed in convents who could not themselves travel but wanted to imagine the Holy Land in their minds and souls. Fabri took books with him on his travels, writing on wax tablets, and he met various other literary travellers on his route. His companions on one trip to the Holy Land included the Hungarian poet János Lászai (1448–1523) and several German travel writers: Bernhard von Breydenbach, whose account of the journey became a bestseller; Paul Walther of Güglingen, who wrote a personal, subjective description of his pilgrimage; and Georg von Gumppenberg (d. 1515), who wrote an impersonal, short description of the holy places in Jerusalem. We need to imagine a medieval journey as a busy scene of reading and writing, with some highly literate people who intended to mark their journey through acts of writing. Fabri compared the labour he had in making his pilgrimages 'from place to place' with the labour he had in 'running from book to book, reading and writing, correcting and correlating' what he had written about the holy places. For Fabri, books were places and vice versa: stories and histories merged through sites visited in one's body and in one's mind.

We will encounter Fabri again later in our own wanderings. At this point, we dwell on a vivid scene of him setting off on his route from Ulm, a city of people coming and going. He embarked on his first journey at Easter 1480. In his *Evagatorium*, Fabri, a stirring preacher, describes how he ascended his pulpit in the Dominican church. Great multitudes of people were there and, upon finishing his sermon, he told his audience about his imminent pilgrimage and asked for their prayers for his safe return. Then together they sang a hymn for pilgrims at sea and Fabri chanted the *Kreuzfahrerlied*, a sacred song for those travelling to the Holy Land. It began: 'We travel in God's name, / His grace we seek . . .' (*In Gottes Namen fahren wir, seiner Gnaden begehren wir* . . .). The congregation started to sing along with Fabri, and repeated the holy song. Some began to cry, loud sobs replacing the chanting. Many people were anxious, says Fabri, that he would perish among the 'terrible dangers' of the travels ahead. He blessed the congregation, granted them absolution for their sins, made the sign of the cross and said goodbye. Then he got down from his pulpit.

Fabri's Dominican priory was just a stone's throw from the Danube. Early in the morning of 14 April 1480, Brother Felix kissed and hugged his brothers in the monastery and rode out from Ulm, taking the route south. He was accompanied by his prior, Ludwig Fuchs, and a servant. Fabri would have passed, to his left, a windowless tower where felons were held captive and sometimes drowned, and the city prison tower with its scaffold for public executions outside.

He would then have traversed the city wall beside the Danube, still under construction in handsome red brick and paid for by the city. In the river, *barchent* cloth was being bleached and freshly caught fish were being gutted and rinsed. Geese waddled busily wherever they chose. Fabri then crossed the Herdbrucker (named after the animals herded over it), the city's bridge over the Danube. He was watched by the two sentinels always posted there who, at this time of day, had not yet blown reveille on their horns.

Ahead of Fabri lay pastures and vineyards and the road south. He passed a little suburban shrine to the Virgin, enclosed in a pretty garden, a final blessing for his departure.

Fabri, his prior and their servant rode together, over the flat plain and its flax fields, to the way-station town of Memmingen, 50 kilometres to the south. Here Brother Felix met with a local nobleman and governor of Upper Bavaria, Apollinaris von Stein, his son Georg and a retinue of men-at-arms. They undertook to set off for Jerusalem the next morning. Fabri hugged Prior Ludwig, 'with deep grief and sorrow', both of them weeping and sobbing. Ludwig told his spiritual son Felix not to forget him in the Holy Land, to write if he could and to be sure to come back soon. The prior left, returning with his servant to Ulm, to his spiritual children, Felix's brethren.

After Memmingen, the white peaks of the Alps, ultimate and unbroken, overwhelmed the horizon, seemingly unassailable from the sweet plains of Swabia and Bavaria. The next morning the men took the rising road towards Kempten and Innsbruck.

Fabri loved his city, Ulm. He described how, as he set off, his enthusiasm for seeing Jerusalem 'died within' him. The voyage ahead seemed to him 'wearisome, bitter, useless, empty and sinful'. He wrote, 'I had more pleasure in beholding Swabia than the land of Canaan, and Ulm appeared to me pleasanter than Jerusalem.' Fabri was experiencing that special kind of wretched, narcotic longing we now identify as homesickness, the traveller's curse. It can appear anywhere, a joyless surprise, a desperate ache, a feeling of being in utterly the wrong place.

Brother Felix had barely left home. Only the hot shame of embarrassment prevented him from turning round and running back to Prior Ludwig.

Further south, on the cusp of the Alps, the River Rhine flows into the vast long lake known as the Bodensee (Lake

Constance) at the city of Constance (Konstanz). In the Middle Ages, it was constantly busy with oak-plank boats, some of them up to 20 metres long. Some carried barrels, others were freighted with hides, lumber or fish; and others carried travellers making their way in all directions across Europe.

The ceaseless motion and the tedious packing and unpacking involved in travel almost invariably mean losing things. Evidently, the people in the boats crossing the Bodensee very frequently lost or discarded objects overboard: an alabaster figurine of a headless Virgin Mary holding a suckling baby Jesus; a pair of lead tweezers; pins and needles; a tiny effigy of a pilgrim carved out of a shell; a pewter bowl; a sturdy metal padlock; a horseshoe; dozens of crucifixes, badges and brooches. All these things and many more will, hundreds of years later, be retrieved by archaeologists from the bottom of the lake.

These objects lost in transit are now displayed at Constance's State Archaeological Museum, and call to mind the inveterate English traveller Margery Kempe (c. 1373–c. 1439), who came to the city in 1414 and who lost (or was robbed of) several things on her travels: a precious ring inscribed with a love motto to Jesus, a walking stick she had bought in Jerusalem, and, near Constance, a sheet and a bag of money stolen from her by her travelling companions.

Kempe, a mother of fourteen from the port of Lynn in eastern England, was not unlike Dorothea of Montau: both middle-class wives who devoted themselves to mystical visions and to pilgrimage. Kempe boldly dictated her own life story, as written down in *The Book of Margery Kempe* (1436–8). A defining moment in her life was her difficult journey from England to Jerusalem and Rome in 1413–14, and her account gives us a unique perspective on one person's travels across England and Europe.

Around the year 1412, when she was about forty, Kempe received a directive from God that she should visit Jerusalem, Rome and Santiago de Compostela. For her, travel was God's work, in order to gain the pardons or indulgences available at the holy sites, and thus deepen her relationship with God to the profit of her soul. Having gained permission to do so from her husband and from her bishop, Kempe set off for Jerusalem in late 1413, sailing from Yarmouth to the Dutch port of Zierikzee. She then made her way to Constance, about two-thirds of the way to Venice.

Kempe had a very difficult journey. She had, for some time, taken to weeping abundantly, 'for her own sins, and sometimes for other people's sins too'. She leaked tears whenever she thought about her Christ's Crucifixion, and she thought about this very often. When she received communion (at least every Sunday) she succumbed to 'great weeping and boisterous sobbing'. Kempe's tearfulness accompanied her on her journeys, and made her unpopular with her fellow travellers. She tells us in her *Book* that her companions were 'most displeased that she wept so much and spoke constantly of the love and goodness of God, both at the dining table and in other places'. The other travellers chided her, and warned her that they wouldn't put up with her.

Even Kempe's own maidservant, who had travelled with her from England, could no longer stand her company. Only one man supported Kempe, and encouraged her to stay with the party until it reached Constance.

As the band of travellers made their way to Constance, their bullying of Kempe became acute. They chastised her and abused her and embarrassed her in every place. They cut her gown short, so it came to just below the knee, and they made her wear a ridiculous white canvas smock, so people thought she was a madwoman and gave her no credence. At dinner in each tavern or inn, they made her sit at the bottom end of the table, beneath even the maids and grooms and other lowly people, and told her to keep silent.

One day, at a roadside chapel somewhere in the region of Swabia, Kempe went to pray, weeping so her tears ran down on to the stone floor. And God spoke to her, in her mind, 'Don't be afraid, daughter, your companions won't be harmed while you're in their company.' And so she stuck with them and – 'praise be!' thought Kempe – the group reached Constance safely.

Travelling alone was dangerous, especially for women. Women did frequently travel, but often with their husbands, sisters or children, and usually in a group. At several points, Margery Kempe mentions her worries about brigands on the route and about rape and sexual harassment by strangers. We also glean from her account that travelling alone meant that one would miss information and recommendations from one's fellow travellers – when the tides were set fair for sailing, or the most reliable hostelry in town, or the best relics to see, or the most trustworthy supplier of mattresses and bedding for the next leg of the journey. And so travellers rarely went alone and if one found oneself travelling with people one didn't like, there wasn't much to be done about it. Travel forms communities, but not always harmoniously.

Kempe's account of her short stay in Constance in 1414 describes a city of people in motion. A few months after her visit, Constance hosted a hugely significant church council – an ecumenical gathering of representatives from across the Christian world – which lasted for four years. Visitors from far-off places, from Ethiopia to Ireland, convened to discuss key issues facing the Church, including the ending of the papal schism (there were rival popes in Rome,

Avignon and Pisa), the ongoing heresies in Bohemia and England, the ratification of new saints, the conversion of pagans in the Baltic and the desire to unite against Islam. One of the grimly climactic moments of the Council was the execution of the Bohemian theologian and reformist Jan Hus (1369 – 1415). He himself had stayed at the Krone inn in Ulm on his way to Constance. He had been given a letter of safe-conduct by the emperor, but this did not save him. He was burned beside the Rhine and his ashes were tossed in the river, along with the rest of the day's discarded refuse.

When Kempe was in Constance people were starting to flock to the city from across the world. It became full, with people finding lodgings wherever they could, in inns and townhouses marked with signs showing a colourful menagerie of names: at the Roten Adler (Red Eagle), Gelben Schaf (Yellow Sheep), Schwartzen Bock (Black Buck), Goldenen Lamm (Golden Lamb), Regenbogen (Rainbow). Embassies and courts took over entire townhouses (the English at the Goldenen Schwert, the Golden Sword). Jan Hus stayed in more humble surroundings, lodging with a baker's widow named Fida Pfister.

Kempe heard tell of an English friar in the town, a legate from the papal court. She had a traveller's knack for finding friendly strangers in distant lands, and in Constance she made the most of the opportunity presented by chancing upon this cleric. She described her entire life story to him and told him about the gift of sweet revelations she received from God. The friar confirmed to her that these revelations were the work of God, not the Devil, and he also confirmed that he would support her against her travelling companions.

So Kempe invited the friar to dine with her and her companions at their lodgings, and he spoke in her favour. The other travellers were absolutely furious and said they wanted nothing more to do with her. The legate gave her some money (£20, £16 of which was stolen by the others) and Kempe prayed that God would send her a new travelling companion. And suddenly, as if sent by divine grace, a kindly Englishman appeared, a white-bearded soul named William Weaver, and they travelled on together, from Constance to Bologna. Kempe's account gives a strong sense of people on the move to, from and through medieval Constance, and the kinds of chance encounters that could make or break a journey.

Ulrich von Richental, a well-to-do local man, wrote a very detailed account of the Council as it happened, giving us a lot of information about what it was like to visit Constance in 1414. Richental describes the astonishing number of people who descended on the city (the Pisan antipope John XXIII came with a party of 600 men). Even more astonishing was the number of horses by which delegates at the Council were accompanied. Duke Louis II of Brzeg in Silesia came with 200 horses and four laden wagons. Pipo, Lord of Ozora in Hungary, had 150 horses and three wagons. Each horse had its own luggage of muzzles, bits, snaffles, bridles, nosebags, spurs, sacking, reins and caparisons.

Embassies came from Africa and Asia and every corner of Europe, at least 5,000 people by Richental's count. Then various kinds of people turned up to support the attendees of the Council: apothecaries, shoemakers, tailors, goldsmiths, furriers, grocers, scribes, girdle makers, butchers and barbers, all of them setting up tents and stalls around the city. Seven hundred prostitutes came to town, and hired their own houses or lay in stables or wherever they could. Richental estimated that the city's population, usually around 10,000 people, was swollen by over 70,000 visitors during the Council.

Here was a perfect opportunity for the people of Constance to make money from outsiders. Lodgings for this enormous crowd were closely regulated by Constance's city council. While nobles rented or lodged in rich burghers' houses, and some clerics stayed at the town's monasteries, most visitors were at the mercy of Constance's innkeepers. So the council made an ordinance: a bed for two people should cost no more than 1½ guilders a month, and landlords were obliged to furnish bed linen, bolsters and pillows, all of which were to be washed clean at least every month. Stabling for a horse was fixed at tuppence a night. Later on, the price of food also had to be regulated, because there were so many mouths to feed and so much profit to be had. The prices of wheat, oats, wine, spices and meats were all closely controlled, to ensure that visitors were not conned.

There was lavish catering at dinners and feasts but travellers could also buy fast food, sold by bakers who arrived in town with ovens on carts or little barrows: they sold bread rings and pretzels off poles, and biscuits, pies and hot pasties stuffed with fish, spiced meats or egg. Some Italian bakers came to town and sold a new kind of thin flatbread baked with savoury toppings.

As the travellers left Constance they faced the prospect of crossing the Alps. The general medieval understanding of mountains was that the earth had been formed flat and round, but that mountains were then made by rivers that dug away at earth's softer parts, leaving the hard parts as mountains. It was also known that mountains could be formed by earthquakes. Mountains, in this understanding, were understood not as beautiful or sublime but as hard and durable, connected to the earth but reaching for the heavens. Their beneficial properties included the drawing in of moisture, the origins of springs, their veins of noble metals and their clean air at the summit.

The routes became steeper and the air thinner. Travellers across the Alps had to fasten their minds more than ever on their destination. It is rare for medieval travellers to mention natural sites like mountains or glaciers or valleys, even as they must have had an arduous passage through sighing rain and groaning thunder, and their tittupping horses and asses must have struggled with the vertiginous climbs.

On his way to the Council of Constance in the late autumn of 1414, the antipope John XXIII – one of three pretenders to the papal title at the time – travelled from Lodi near Milan over the Alps, through the Arlberg Pass in Austria, to approach Constance from the east. An elevated traveller like a would-be pope didn't have to suffer the indignities of trudging through the snow or riding on a slipping mount: he was transported in a wheeled wooden carriage painted red with gold finials and pulled by two white horses. But, as it tried to get through the snowy tracks near the alpine hamlet of Klösterle, the papal buggy tipped over. The antipope, in his flowing gowns and a tottering gold crown, was thrown from his chariot into the snow and mud, cursing, blasphemously, in the Devil's name. He was unharmed, but it was an inauspicious start to his descent into Constance where, in time, he would be stripped of his papal title and have to flee, in the disguise of a messenger.

The Alps could be traversed via established passes – road networks through valleys and along softer slopes – and the most popular one was the Brenner Pass, the main route from northern to southern Europe. From Constance, one struck out for Nassereith, Innsbruck, Vipiteno. Travelling on his second trip in 1483–4, Felix Fabri described the poor quality of the road after a day's rain and a night's snow. His horse was 'sunk up to his belly at every step', and Fabri was in it up to his knees. He found the Brenner Pass intensely cold, 'for there even in summer-time there is always ice, snow and hoar frost.' At an inn in an alpine village, Fabri got his own room with a lockable door. But two couriers in another room forgot to lock their door, and they were robbed of their full purses by a group of drunken silver miners whom Fabri had spotted, the previous night, gambling in the tavern.

Once one had reached the flourishing town of Bolzano, the mountains had been crossed. There was a beautiful church here, a well-appointed hospital dedicated to the Holy Spirit, shops, apothecaries, fresh supplies, good Tyrolean wine.

There were even town-licensed brothels (which provided tax revenue to the town). In the brothel a male visitor (married men, Jewish men and clerics were excluded) was served food and drink and then introduced to the sex workers. Such establishments, as we shall see, were part of the burgeoning infrastructure of travel.

Leaving Bolzano, the temperamental alpine cragscape was behind the traveller. The softer countryside of northern Italy emerged, and Venice was within reach.

A bedtime conversation between two travellers

William and Perot are in a roadside 'hostel', 1396 (from *La Manière de langage*, a guide to learning French for English travellers)

'Mate, I'm begging you, please cover over the fire now, and take out those logs and embers at once. And shove the cinders and the brands together, putting ash over the top. And then we can go to bed.'

After this, they go upstairs to their room. And when they get there, one asks the other: 'Where's Beaglet, the little dog, and Florette, the little bitch?'

'I don't know where Beaglet has gone, but at any rate Florette has gone to sleep downstairs under the oak trees in the garden.'

'William, get your trousers off quick and wash your legs, then wipe them with a bit of cloth and rub them well, because of the fleas. You don't want them jumping on your legs: there are loads of them in the dust under that rush matting.'

Then he gets into bed. So he says to the other: 'Budge over, will you? You're so cold I can't bear for you to touch me at all! And let's go to sleep, for God's sake; I really need to, as I've been awake for the last two nights without sleeping.'

'What the Devil?! You're quite warm, you're really sweating a lot!'

'Oh, those fleas are biting deep, and causing me such pain and discomfort, I've scratched my back so much it's running with blood. It's making me get all scabby, and I'm itching all over my whole body. So tomorrow I'm getting myself a steam bath without further delay, I really, really need it.'

'Oh but William you've got such a soft body! By God, I wish I were as soft and clean as you are!'

'No, no, Perot, don't touch me, I beg you! I'm so ticklish!'

'Haha! I'll tickle you all over!'

'Now for goodness sake, buddy, cut it out! It's high time we went to sleep!'

'All right then, for the love of Our Lady, certainly, by all means.'

'Now then, let's stop talking and sleep tight and blow out the candle.'

'William, may God give you a good night, and let me rest well too!'

'What? Aren't we going to say our prayers like we normally do?'

'I totally forgot.'

'Now, let's say a *De Profundis*, in praise of God and the blessed Virgin Mary His sweet Mother, and all the saints in Paradise. And for the souls of the departed who are waiting for God's mercy among the punishments of Purgatory, so they can be more quickly released from their pains thanks to our prayers, and come to everlasting joy, which is the joy of God, who is in Trinity without end in that delightful place, and who redeemed us with His precious blood, may He in His great mercy and pity grant us joy at the end, if it so pleases Him! Amen.'

4. A Stay in Venice, and Onwards to Rome

St Mark's Square – Fondaco dei Tedeschi – Basilica of St Mark – Rialto and markets – Lazzaretto – Rome

Venice has become famous for its beauty, its incredible setting on over a hundred islands within a half-moon lagoon, and its unique patina of Venetianness. Yet visitors often experience Venice as damp, fetid, expensive, too hot or too cold, haughty, unsexy and moribund. And this is without even considering its entire subjugation to tourism; as is frequently observed, tourist Venice *is* the real Venice. The whole city has, for a very long time, been shaped by, commodified by and subservient to people going to or from other places.

The friar Niccolò da Poggibonsi travelled through Venice on his way to the Holy Land in 1345. He described Venice as a city unlike any other where all the roads, 'small and large, are channels in the water'. Thus one went about by boat. Niccolò found it the best of ports because from Venice a man could find a ship to navigate to anywhere in the world where there was trade. He described a cityscape full of beautiful houses and many bell towers, some of them bending and squatting towards the water, as if defecating, because of their bad foundations. He recognized that, because of its swampy setting in the sea, Venice presented unique difficulties in building a city.

At times, Venice feels like a strange mirage, as though it is actually made of water and might slip away in a flood of light and shade.

Most medieval cities had gates and established points of entry. Not so Venice. The city, as visitors approached it, was a muddle to the eye. Ferries and small craft skimmed across the lagoon to various points in the city. Felix Fabri, visiting from Ulm in the 1480s, noted, as his party sailed across the lagoon into Venice, his astonishment at 'such weighty and such tall structures with their foundations in the water'. The most central destination was St Mark's Square, the site of the ducal government (the Palazzo Ducale, rebuilt from 1340 with Gothic arches and loggias) and the ancient Basilica of St Mark. This was close to Venice's other main focal point, the Rialto, the site of the city's legendary foundation. The Rialto, where since at least the 1170s a pedestrian bridge had crossed the Grand Canal, was the city's commercial heart and meeting place for merchants from around the world. The very openness of the city forced Venice to innovate in the administration of travel: the fifteenth-century Venetian Republic led the world in the development of passports, travel guides and tourist offices, quarantine for travellers, public health regulations and the supervision and policing of inns, restaurants and shipping. Far from being an open city as it first appeared, late medieval Venice was full of invisible barriers, regulations and bureaucracy.

Yet when visitors felt that Venice finally welcomed them into its secrets, the city seemed like an enchanted gift from history. Some people even said that Venice was built out of the stones of Troy.

> **Be careful!** When arriving in Venice (or, sometimes even before you arrive, as you sail across the lagoon towards the city), you'll be besieged by guides (the locals call them *tolomazi*) – they will show you around, translate all the different

languages and even book your passage to the Holy Land. But some are extortionists and liars, cheats and hustlers. You must choose a licensed guide, whom you can find each morning outside the Doge's Palace and at the Rialto.

Simon Fitzsimon, a friar on his way from Clonmel in Ireland to Jerusalem in 1323, was overwhelmed by the city's beauty and cleanliness, thinking that it might be set among the stars in the firmament rather than the sea. Fitzsimon described how one-third of the city is 'paved with baked bricks' while two-thirds are navigable, liquid streets through which 'the sea flows and ebbs continuously, and untiringly'. He noted that at the Doge's Palace at all times live lions were tended, for the palace's glory and 'for the magnificence of its citizens'.

Noble visitors were announced at the doge's court by a servant, seated under the Venetian flag, pounding out rhythmic beats on the ground with a heavy painted stick. One might have seen boys in particoloured costumes playing the rebec, and ladies in precariously high shoes to keep their feet dry, and collared dogs sitting patiently for their masters. There were jugglers, dwarves and preachers. Heralds announced, and sometimes sang, the news from around the world.

Beside this, at the entrance to St Mark's Square by the lapping waves of the lagoon, stood the two lean granite columns, erected around 1200, dedicated to the city's patron saints St Mark the Evangelist and St Theodore (known locally as San Todaro). Theodore's statue comprised bits of old sculptures, a Roman emperor's head on another emperor's body. He stood atop his column, astride a crocodile-dragon added around 1300, representing victory. On top of St Mark's column stood an ancient bronze winged lion (the evangelist's symbol), which became the city's emblem and would be found throughout the Mediterranean on gates and portals and towers, wherever La Serenissima ruled the waves and the markets. Theodore has his back to the sea, looking into the city, watching over the people. The lion of St Mark looks eastwards, out of the city towards the lagoon, Lido and the seas beyond.

Waves reached ceaselessly at the city's wooden pilings and marble foundations. Venice was a place in constant movement: migrants, merchants, slaves, mariners, pilgrims, refugees and the rest of the world arrived and departed here. One of the things that defined a medieval city like Venice was that it enabled and increased mobility: not just mobility through and between places, but also social and financial mobility.

Venice was truly a hub of commerce, where fortunes could be made and destinies changed. Even the city's patron saint St Mark was said to have once sought shelter in the city, an evangelist transported from the Levant to the maritime territory (and, in the ninth century, Mark's voyage happened anew, as his saintly bones were purloined from Alexandria and enshrined in Venice).

Many travellers through Venice were merchants – like Marco Polo – while others were missionaries (like Odoric of Pordenone, a Franciscan who crossed Asia from 1318 to 1329). Others set out to conquer the world in Venice's name: for instance, Marino Sanudo the Elder (d. 1343), who visited the Levant many times and fabricated a plan to occupy and annex Egypt. Or Nicolò Conti who, in the 1420s, sailed through the Persian Gulf and all the way to India and up the River Ganges. Or Pietro Querini who, in 1432, was blown wildly off course and shipwrecked in the Lofoten Islands in northern Norway. Venice and the Venetians seemed connected to the widest possible version of the world – fabrics from Persia and China, flour from the Levant, ships and their passengers from every port from Gibraltar to the Crimea, pilgrims from Iceland, Scotland, Sweden, France, Portugal, Poland, Armenia. The people of the globe gathered there, on this unlikely collection of low-lying islands.

Pietro Casola, visiting in 1494 from Milan on his way to the Holy Land, said, 'I do not think there is any city to which Venice, the city founded on the sea, can be compared.' Casola added that 'it seems as if all the world flocks there, and that human beings have concentrated there all their energies for trading.' The French ambassador Philip de Commines, visiting in the same year as Casola, was surprised by the city's situation 'all in the water', and concluded that Venice 'is the most triumphant city that ever I saw'. The English traveller

Thomas Larke, visiting in 1506 and writing for his patron Sir Richard Guylforde, was overawed by Venice: 'the wealth, the sumptuous buildings, and the organisation of their justices and councils, along with all other things that make a city glorious, prevail in Venice above all other places that I ever saw.' For Larke, as for many other visitors, Venice was a wonderland of monumental edifices built on islands. It crystallized some beautiful and striking idea of what a city could be.

Casola dedicated pages to praising Venice's merchandise and markets, seeing beauty in abundance, bedazzled by plenty. Yet his account of Venice repeatedly falters around an issue with which travellers often struggle: how does one give an account of a marvellous place yet make it credible to those who haven't been there? 'I know it is difficult for anyone who has not seen these things to believe what I say, because I have fallen into the same error myself – that is, I used not to believe what was told me about them!' he wrote. Eyewitness travellers often find it hard to convince their readers that what they've seen is reliable. The world, after all, was believed to be an ever-surprising, encyclopaedic garden of prodigies and miracles.

Must see! On Ascension Day, there's a great fair at St Mark's. There's also a ceremony, the *Sposalizio del Mare* ('Wedding of the Sea'), in which the Doge of Venice sails out in the ceremonial barge, the *Bucintoro*, and casts a wedding-ring into the sea. This shows the indissoluble union between Venice and the waters on which it floats and prospers.

Many travellers were in Venice in order to sail to the Holy Land. The city was the port of departure for Jaffa, then the key port for Jerusalem. The Venetian Republic was the main naval power for the entire eastern Mediterranean. The massive Arsenale (founded 1104), its ramparts glimpsed by visitors sailing through the city and sometimes visited as a spectacle in its own right, was the shipyard for military and civilian shipping.* Its hundreds of boats sailed out daily across the world. The Venetian Republic encompassed a galaxy of territories across Dalmatia and the eastern Mediterranean, all the way to Alexandria, Beirut and beyond the Crimea. These included a key trading post at Tana (now Azov), and the port of Caffa (Feodosia) from which the Genoese and Venetians traded thousands of slaves, mostly Tatars and Circassians, Muslim and Christian. The Venetian maritime republic thrived on all kinds of business, supported by the pilgrimage industry of holy tourism.

Travellers lingered in Venice for some time. They were at the mercy of the patrons and galley captains, who waited until the weather was right (or until they had forced the travellers into spending plenty of money in Venice). Margery Kempe stayed for thirteen weeks in the spring of 1414, Pero Tafur for more than thirty days in 1436, Thomas Larke for seven weeks from May to July 1506. Travellers like them had paid a deposit to shipping agents: if their boat went without them, how could they reach Jaffa? For Felix Fabri, after a few weeks in Venice the city's charms started to pall. 'We began to become exceedingly weary of Venice and looked eagerly towards our departure,' he wrote. He suspected that the captain of his galley had lied to him about their departure date.

* The name Arsenale comes from the Arabic *Dar sina'a*, a place for construction, a building site.

Many travellers like Fabri found themselves stuck in Venice, waiting to hear about their vessel leaving, spending too much money and keen to quit the overregulated city for the next stage of their journey.

The entire business was regulated and controlled by the various officers of the Venetian Republic. The *tholomarii* constituted a kind of tourist office, supposed to assist travellers with finding a place to stay and negotiating their onward sea passage. The city's lodgings were also closely regulated and inspected by the Venetian Senate. Meanwhile, from 1292, the Ufficiali al Cattaver oversaw laws and conditions relating to sea voyages. Accidents, rip-offs, disputes and disappointments were all bad for the republic's trade in travel. Travellers (if they survived the trip) could complain to the *cattaveri* on their return journey, so good customer service and satisfied travellers were in the republic's interests.

Medieval travellers were used to carrying bills of safe-conduct, a *guidaticum*, or letters patent. In Venice, the traveller's certification became a requirement, a duty. Venice developed an advanced system of individual certification in the form of the *bolletta del passaggio* (or *bullétta*, *bollettino*, *polizza*), a document that at different times was a receipt for the payment of transit tolls, a bill of lading, a certificate of good health or a passport. Any passport is a means to regulate the individual's movement, and the Venetian *bolletta* did exactly that: strangers disembarking in Venice were obliged to obtain a *bolletta* for a fee, establishing their identity and certifying their intended route and, at times, that the place they came from was free from plague. It became more important than any pilgrim badge in proving the traveller's credentials and ensuring their ability to travel. Pilgrims and merchants could then be required to show it throughout their journey from Venice to Jerusalem or Constantinople. The *bolletta* was time-limited and could be furnished by the *tholomarii* or by a galley's patron. In addition, from the later fourteenth century, many other Italian cities such as Florence and Livorno required travellers to have a *bolletta di sanità*, a bill of health, showing that they weren't carrying the plague. By the later fifteenth century, visitors travelling alone or without a *bolletta* were routinely suspected of being carriers of plague. Via the *bolletta*, the traveller became dependent on the administration of their journey and their legitimation through paperwork. The passport, always an anxiety-inducing document, had started to become the literal manifestation of each traveller's identity *as a traveller*.

The well-developed and regulated hospitality industry in Venice meant that finding a place to stay was relatively straightforward, as long as a traveller had plenty of money. There were basic and ancient travellers' *ospedali* (refuges or infirmaries), where pilgrims coming to and from the Holy Land lodged alongside the poor and the sick. *Tholomarii* also directed international travellers to *ospizi* (pilgrims' hospices), like the Ospizio Celsi (founded 1409) on the Riva degli Schiavoni a short walk from St Mark's. A large number of public hostels and private *locande* and *osterie* (inns) clustered around the Ponte della Paglia near the Rialto and around St Mark's Square. For northern Europeans, favourite inns included the San Zorzi (the George, run in the 1480s by a certain Margarita, who raised Felix Fabri's eyebrows by marrying her servant Nicholas Frig).

Most Venetian inns had room for about twenty to forty guests. These inns were subject to all kinds of regulation by the republic's government. They were clustered together so the city's omnipresent authorities could keep an eye on behaviour there, fighting a losing battle against sodomy, theft, brawling and drunkenness. As elsewhere, inns weren't the same as taverns, which existed for drinking. As well as taverns, Venice had rough *furatole*, informal booths that sold fried fish and illicit wine. In inns and taverns, drinking alcohol was strictly regulated, policed by the *Signori di Notte* (the Nightwatchmen or 'Lords of the Night') who also enforced regulations in the brothels, and were said in their proceedings to employ torture on the *curlo* (rack).

Family palaces took in guests and many religious infirmaries looked after pilgrims too. Some infirmaries were single-sex, others were located on their own islands in the lagoon. The grandest and most visible sign of Venice's welcome to foreigners was the Fondaco dei Tedeschi, a magnificent trading house for German merchants built in 1228 (rebuilt in 1318 and 1505).* It was a warehouse, hostel, tavern, showroom, refectory and community centre in one massive eighty-roomed complex. Here southern German merchants and emissaries established a powerful colony next to the Rialto, in the very best setting for commerce, on the central curve of the Grand Canal. As time went on, the Fondaco dei Tedeschi welcomed Austrian, Hungarian and all northern European visitors to Venice. Various foreign communities – Albanians, Armenians, Burgundians, Greeks, Slovenes, Turks and many others – also had settlements in the city, often reflected in today's street names. Leo of Rozmital, a Bohemian nobleman, and his squire Wenzel Schasek (Václav Šašek) visited the Fondaco in 1467. Schasek wrote that any man 'from all the chief cities of all the Christian countries can each have his own table where he can

* The similar Venetian Fondaco dei Turchi for Turkish merchants and ambassadors only took on this role in 1621. The word *fondaco* (Venetian *fontego*) came from the Arabic *funduq*, a caravanserai, and ultimately from the Greek *pandocheion*, an inn, a place for everyone.

obtain whatever food and drink he desires'. At the Fondaco, there were 'ample supplies of everything'.

In addition to such well-established places to stay, Venice also had *albergarie* (lodging houses), many unlicensed, scattered around the city and of ill-repute. The Venetian Health Board (the Provveditori alla Sanità, founded in the 1480s) seems to have been particularly worried about the risk of contagion in these boarding houses, which were popular with visitors, part of the city authorities' wider worries about disease in such a place of mobility.

While visitors were detained in Venice waiting for their onward passage, there were plenty of relics, shrines and grand churches to see. Ogier d'Anglure, visiting in 1395, was particularly impressed by a relic of Goliath's tooth which he saw in the chapel of one of Venice's charitable hospitals. William Wey, visiting in 1458, noted in various churches the entire body of John the Baptist's father, St Zacharias, and the bodies of St Lucy, St Sabina, St Pancras and St Marina, as well as St George's left arm and St Christopher's thigh bone. In addition to these holy bodies and members, he saw a statue of the Virgin Mary made out of the very rock struck by Moses in the desert. And in the Basilica of St Mark a statue of Jesus was said to have been stabbed by a Jewish visitor five times and to have dripped with real blood. Through such sites, Venice itself became a pilgrimage destination, allowing travellers to justify their delays there with holy tourism.

The unusual Basilica of St Mark tended to dazzle its visitors. From the outside, it appeared squat and low, an exotic pavilion, quite unlike the soaring, skyward towers of Gothic cathedrals. It served as the doge's chapel as well as Venice's state church. Consecrated in 1094 on the site of an older basilica, St Mark's has a Byzantine-style front consisting of five portals surmounted by five arches, all decorated in light pluteus marbles and stones. Four ancient horses cast in copper alloy reared above the porch; they may have come as booty from Venice's sacking of Constantinople in 1204. Above the horses, the building was capped by five domes.

Inside, the cruciform nave church was gloomy in contrast with the exterior's light stone. But the interior was defined, and lit, by its ornate golden ceilings, decorated with millions of shimmering mosaics. The novelty of St Mark's encrusted mosaic tesserae attracted particular comment, 'little stones and pieces of glass a quarter of the size of the nail of the little finger' as Jean de Tournai described them when he visited in 1488. Much of the mosaic work was made by Murano's famous glassworkers. St Mark's basilica was less a pilgrimage site – even though it claimed the body of the evangelist – and more a stage for Venetian spectacle and the doge's displays of power. At the basilica in 1462, the English pilgrim William Wey saw the ceremony of the Eve of St Mark taking place, with 'twelve gold crowns full of precious jewels' set on the saint's altar, with 'extremely rich' chalices, thuribles and candlesticks. The high altar was made of gilded silver. For Wey, the Basilica of St Mark reminded him of the Church of the Holy Sepulchre in Jerusalem. On St Mark's Day, he saw the city's fraternities parading around the church, holding wax candles in one hand and scourges in the other with which to beat themselves.

The Irishman Simon Fitzsimon said St Mark's was 'a most sumptuous church, built incomparably of marble and other valuable stones', and opposite stood the public square, St Mark's Square, 'which, all things considered, has no equal anywhere'. Konrad Grünemberg, visiting from Constance in 1486, described the basilica as 'such a marvel that it makes you wonder', overawed by the glass, gold, marble mosaics and chandeliers. Adjacent to the basilica was the magnificent *campanile*, a belfry-cum-watchtower, which dragged visitors' eyes skyward, its metallic-tipped spire like a welcoming star guiding arriving travellers.

Such matters of faith aside, the main priority in Venice for most travellers was shopping for their journey ahead. The city was, by the fifteenth century, a kind of travellers' supermarket, geared towards making sure people were well supplied for their arduous journeys. An Englishman, who can probably be identified as Geoffrey Caldwell of London, visited Venice in the late fifteenth century on his way to the Holy Land and wrote a travel guide for others based on his experiences. His main concern was with what to buy, and his advice was that at Venice 'first, one must provide oneself with bedding' and 'a cage for chickens' (the birds themselves could be purchased along the route to Jaffa).

Then, for the rest of his advice, Caldwell turned to what seems to have been a preoccupation for travellers: the management of one's bowels during the journey ahead. At Venice, Caldwell advised buying a covered pail for defecating and a urine jar. One should, he said, also obtain barrels of water and one's preferred wine (adding that some clean water should always be added to one's wine). This, he warned, is because the water from cisterns along the route caused constipation, whereas fresh water could be harmfully laxative. He advised stocking up at Venice (at the grocers' market but with the advice of a physician) with an enema kit, with suppositories ('like a man's finger made of white soap or a fine tallow candle'). The other crucial thing to buy was some fennel seed and aniseed, to help with excessive farting. Modern travel writing often avoids covering the private life of the travellers; not so medieval travel writing, in which the intimacies and needs of the traveller's body were covered as much as care for their soul.

Konrad Grünemberg advised that keeping one's stomach warm would aid daily evacuation and guard against diarrhoea. For this reason, he said that many travellers bought underclothes at Venice made out of *scarlatto*, an expensive woollen cloth for which the city was famous.

Visitors to Venice reported on the foods that one should buy there and store for the coming sea voyage, as ballast for the stomach. Twice-baked, ring-shaped *pan biscotto* was especially suitable for people going to sea because it lasted a long time. Sardines, anchovies and eels were staple fish, and were often preserved to make them last longer and travel better. Sturgeon was salted and smoked, or made into a kind of salami (*morona*). Salt cod (*baccalà*), eaten throughout Europe, was also common in Venice and popular with travellers for the journey ahead. Galleys were expected to provide daily hot meals to passengers, though the quality was unpredictable. Travellers planned to use their own stores of food, topping them up at the ports they visited along the way.

The food of Venice reflected the ingredients that came to the city from around the known world and the ability of its population to consume. The merchandise available there was the cause of most visitors' excitement. Pero Tafur marvelled that Spanish fruit was as cheap in Venice as in Spain, and added that in Venice one could buy 'whatever comes from Syria and, if one desires it, from India, since the Venetians navigate all over the world': Venice offered the visitor a global marketplace. Pietro Casola devoted pages to describing Venice's markets, asking, 'Who could count the many shops so well furnished that they seem like warehouses?' He saw an extraordinary range of cloths – tapestries, brocades, hangings, carpets, silks of every kind – and many warehouses filled with spices, groceries and drugs, 'and so much beautiful white wax!' He said that this plenty could 'stupefy the beholder' and defied being fully described.

For Casola, such material abundance was a vision of enchanting beauty. He was delighted by Venice's bakeries, 'countless and of incredible beauty', selling unrivalled bread that made a sated man want to continue eating. Grain was imported to the city from the Middle East and dough makers and bakers became well regulated; the weight and price of bread was fixed daily, and the products reflected travellers' needs. Casola loved the abundance of edible, if pricey, birds and fish, the copiousness of fruit and vegetables ('it seemed as if all the gardens of the world must be there!') and the almost incredible wines – malmsey, muscatel, Greek wines, white wines, red wines, demijohns and barrels in such bounty. Casola's account reads as if he were drunk on the city itself.

The one thing Casola was upset by was the miserable state of the meat market in the Rialto, and it put him off buying there. Such bad smells – such as putrefying entrails and rotting butchers' garbage – were indelibly connected to plague and illness.

As a city constantly refilling itself with people on the move, Venice was particularly susceptible to contagions and plagues. Pero Tafur noted the cleanliness of the streets, rinsed by the lagoon's waters, and added that the Venetians burned perfumes in the streets, 'and the people carry with them scents and spices, which are ground in the streets and give forth a most pleasant smell' A pleasantly scented street equated to a healthy cityscape, and masked the foul vapours that threatened to arrive in the city with its throngs of visitors.

Venice's canals, hemmed with narrow alleyways, were peopled with variety, of strangers imagining a million things about one another. The Jewish inhabitants were not yet confined to the ghetto, Turkish merchants traded with the city's businesses, and Moors from north Africa moved through the markets. Unmarried young women entered the convents and smuggled their lovers – male and female – into the cloisters. Prostitutes of all ages, genders and types of beauty worked throughout the city; inns and taverns were prohibited from letting prostitutes work there, and instead, from 1358, licensed brothels were established first near the Rialto but eventually throughout the city (Venice's Greater Council decreed in 1360 that prostitutes were 'absolutely necessary in this town'). By 1600 all these groups would be regulated in city institutions, to contain them through civic care, as if to stem the constant movement of people around Venice's hospitable lagoon.

In 1348, as the plague spread across Europe, the Greater Council of Venice hired nightwatchmen to check on incoming travellers, who were suspected of bringing the sickness to the city. Venice, as a travel hub, could not help but be visited by the plague. So the city proactively developed *lazzaretti* in the lagoon, quarantine islands in which to enclose diseased people (or people deemed likely to be diseased). The quarantining of ill people in Venice's *lazzaretti* was a foreshadowing of the later Venetian habit of enclosing people so as to cleanse the city's body politic.*

In 1377, Venice's former possession of Ragusa (Dubrovnik)

* 'Quarantine' (from the medieval Latin and Venetian *quarantena*) referred to the forty days and nights Jesus fasted in the desert (Matthew 4:2). Mount Quarantine, near Jericho, the purported site of Jesus's isolation and temptation by the Devil, was frequently visited by western pilgrims. The word 'quarantine' entered French and Italian dialects in the fourteenth century to refer to a state of isolation for the purposes of public health.

across the Adriatic Sea had started to quarantine incoming ships, holding them for one month at an uninhabited island, Mrkan, at a distance from Dubrovnik's thriving port. But it was in Venice that the world's first *lazzaretto* or plague hospital was established, on the island of Santa Maria di Nazareth in 1423. A second island, the Lazzaretto Nuovo, was established as a quarantine station in 1456 (and fully operational by 1471). The idea of the isolation island quickly caught on, with *lazzaretti* being established at other key travellers' way stations around this time, including at Venice's neighbours and colonies in Padua, Chioggia, Split and Corfu. The Venetian *lazzaretti* were used for individuals already sick with the pestilence, for people who had come into contact with the sick, for the cargoes and crew of incoming ships to be put into isolation before reaching the city, and for those convalescing from the plague. The *lazzaretti* were not always thought of as hellscapes of the condemned: people sometimes described them as Paradise, a walled garden, sometimes as Cuccagna (the Land of Cockayne, the mythical world of plenty), sometimes as a Purgatory from which one would emerge cleansed. Butterflies thrived there, and white egrets waded assertively through the marshy waters.

The air on the *lazzaretti* was heavy with the purifying scents of smouldering juniper and rosemary. This was to counter the rotten, sticky miasmas by which plague was thought to enter the body and unbalance the humours with too much heat and humidity.

The Lazzaretto Vecchio is a tiny island, nearly 3 kilometres to the east of St Mark's Square, close to Lido, the sandbank that shelters Venice. Visitors to it were met by the walled buildings of a former monastery, including a cloister, a well and a chapel. There were gardens, with fruit trees, and the prior's house, set apart from the quarters for the sick, and warehouse areas for the disinfection of merchandise. The patients, many of them pilgrims, mariners and merchants from across Europe and the Levant, were cared for in single-sex dormitories. Rich and poor sweated, groaned and expired side by side. The wretched invalids were fed on foods considered restorative and healthy: hard-boiled eggs, chicken, veal, saffron and wine.

During an outbreak of plague, the galleys alongside St Mark's Square were replaced by makeshift rafts. Those painted black conveyed away from the city the poxy corpses of those who had already succumbed. Boatmen, on the rafts chalked white to disinfect them, transported the sick to the *lazzaretti*. There, individuals, who had been instructed to bring nothing but their bedding, were registered by officials of the Health Board (unlike other medieval healthcare, in Venice this was a civic and state-funded institution, rather than a religious one). Signs of the extent of their illness were recorded, and those who seemed very unwell were given confession, to prepare them for death. Foreign ambassadors and diplomats, Turkish and Jewish merchants and transient pilgrims were all sent to the *lazzaretto* alongside thousands of Venetians, many of them never to leave.

The main feature of the *lazzaretti* was their burial grounds. Thousands of corpses were put in long parallel trenches or sometimes in mass graves. Body piled upon body. Graves were rarely marked.

Investigation of skeletons from the Lazzaretto Vecchio shows that people died there from the bacterium *Yersinia pestis*, the travelling pathogen that causes bubonic, pneumonic and septicaemic plague. There were at least sixteen major irruptions of the plague in Venice between 1347 and 1528. In other words, the plague made a significant visit to the city roughly every decade. At each outbreak, the pestilence seemed to tear wildly through this place built for mobility. Plagues were disastrous for the population of such a densely packed city: in some plague years, a quarter to a third of Venice's population perished. At each outbreak, ascetic flagellant groups would parade through the afflicted city, whipping their backs in vehement rhythm, their blood weeping across the streets and into the canals as they signalled their abject humility before God.

There was a Venetian confraternity, founded in 1478 and dedicated to St Roch (Rocco), for those afflicted with plague. In 1485, St Roch's finger was brought from Germany to Venice to help give protection to the city (the rest of the saint's body followed a few years later). Roch himself had been an early traveller, a Frenchman who gave all his riches to the poor and set off as a penniless pilgrim to Rome. In Italy, he was said to have tended the sick during an outbreak of plague and to have been the cause of numerous miraculous healings. When Roch himself developed the illness, he was tended by a loyal dog, who licked and healed his sores. Roch is often depicted in a pilgrim's garb, drawing back his gown to point at, or to finger, his pustular thigh. The Venetian Church of St Roch was sometimes visited by travellers when their companions had contracted the plague. In 1483 Felix Fabri, believing the landlord of his Venetian inn to have died of plague, hurried to St Roch to offer prayers. Fabri's companions, meanwhile, had already headed west to Padua, fleeing Venice's vapours.

From Venice, merchants could take a boat to all ports in the Mediterranean and the Black Sea. Pilgrims in general headed south by land to Rome or took a boat east to Jaffa for Jerusalem.

Dame Beatrice Luttrell in 1350 chose Rome as her destination because it was the year of the Jubilee. The Rome Jubilee was essentially a festival of pilgrimage, an opportunity for any Christian devout enough to make the journey to prepare their soul for a future of spiritual purity. The Church had recognized that the great plague, which gripped Europe in 1347 and for several years afterwards, had given a newfound urgency to pilgrimage. The devout wanted to demonstrate their repentance and to give thanks for their emergence from the terrible pandemic. When Dame Beatrice reached Rome, she, her maid Joan and her groom Henry would all have received plenary absolution for their sins: in other words, through travel, a lifetime's sinfulness could be expunged.

Rome at this time was not a large city; after the plague, its falling population was around 17,000 people. Its rickety streets were visited for the tumbledown churches containing the bodies of the saints. Many of the city's classical ruins were ignored or were marooned outside the medieval town, which was much smaller than the ancient imperial capital. Aristocratic palaces and papal houses and merchants' compounds and new basilicas came and went in the city. Some antique remains were understood as strange marvels, like the giant, first-century bronze pine cone which stood in the courtyard at Old St Peter's, or the ingeniously round Church of the Pantheon (called St Mary Rotunda) with its massive dome that defied human understanding. John Capgrave, writing in 1450, repeated a common myth in his travel guide that the dome of the Pantheon, a 'marvel' without pillars, had been built by constructing a giant mound of earth full of money; the dome was built over the hill and then the townspeople were invited to take the earth away and keep the money they found as payment for their labour.

The history of Rome was indivisible from its bishop, the pope, with his great riches in part derived from property and taxation. He had the trappings of a king rather than a monk (although from 1309 to 1376 the popes did not reside in

Rome, and had abandoned the Lateran Palace – for long the main papal residence – in favour of Avignon).

After touring the various altars around Rome, the culmination of the journey for a pilgrim like Dame Beatrice would have been a visit to two major basilicas: St Paul's Outside-the-Walls and St Peter's at the Vatican. These were obligatory, unmissable stations for any pilgrim wishing to receive the plenary indulgence and gain the full blessings of a pilgrimage to Rome. The other major sanctuary, St John Lateran, on the Caelian Hill overlooking the Colosseum, was at this point a wrecked building site, after a catastrophic fire in 1308.

The vast arcaded Basilica of St Paul's Outside-the-Walls, on the city's outskirts, had great bronze doors, made in Byzantium, showing scenes from the life of Christ and the lives of the saints, their names carved out in sinuous Greek lettering. Its nave led to a transept above the crypt where St Paul's body was entombed. The shrine above the altar took the form of a splendid pinnacled canopy – designed by Arnolfo di Cambio and his friend Petrus in the 1280s – made of dark porphyry and solid gold. It combined architecture and delicate painting to resemble a decorated cathedral in miniature, a church within a church, with vaulting and rose windows and pointed arches, all soaring up from St Paul's tomb.

Below, pilgrims stepped down to a crypt to visit St Paul's body. In contrast to the highly decorated finery above, there was an austere, simple and ancient slab with the name of the martyr-apostle scratched into it. Holes had been cut in this slab. Pilgrims put pieces of cloth or other objects into these holes to touch the holy remains, and the travellers and their rags would themselves thereby become contact relics via which the blessings of the saint could travel onwards.

There was also a life-size wooden statue of St Paul, his face serene. But his arms and legs were hacked into a sheared lump by pilgrims who scratched at the wood, taking splinters and woodchips, each one a relic of their proximity to St Paul's body. Outside the church was a cloister of astonishing beauty, made of white marble with twisted pillars bejewelled with distinctive 'cosmatesque' decoration, of gold and maroon and white triangles tessellating in the most up-to-date mosaic work.

Meanwhile, St Peter's at the Vatican stood in an elevated position overlooking the ancient city (it was not yet the palatial papal seat that the Vatican would become; it only became the main residence after the papal return from Avignon in the late fourteenth century). St Peter's was, however, the pre-eminent church in Rome in 1350 and would have been an enormously congested scene. Despite the recent and ongoing ravages of the great plague, people mixed freely and seemed impervious to worries about contagion. Indeed, people died, crushed in the press of enthusiastic pilgrims who came from all over Europe. One could buy food, flasks of water and wine, clothes and tin pilgrims' badges at stalls inside the church's atrium in front of the basilica's broad steps. The scene was noisy, not especially holy, and some of the odours were impious.

The old Basilica of St Peter, dedicated to the first ever pope, was ancient even in the fourteenth century. Its mosaics were by then almost 1,000 years old. The forlorn faces of Mary and long-dead saints and past popes gazed from the walls through delicate tessellated expressions. In the nave of the massive church built by the Emperor Constantine, the rich and vivid decoration that had accrued there over the centuries would have awed visitors like Dame Beatrice. One of the altarpieces, an imposing and sumptuous double-sided triptych, was painted by Giotto around 1320, three arches covered in gold and delicate pink and blue paints. At the centre of the triptych's front was St Peter in majesty surrounded by angels. To his right the auburn-haired Cardinal Giacomo Gaetani Stefaneschi (d. 1343) offers the saint a model of the triptych and to his left a bishop-pope offers Peter a book. The two kneeling figures demonstrated for pilgrims a powerful, recent and luxurious image of the virtue of making donations to St Peter's community in Rome.

The main apse featured a mosaic, installed in the thirteenth century, of Christ enthroned between Peter and Paul, with a procession of lambs converging on the throne. Watching this scene was the personification of Ecclesia, crowned with an imperial tiara, a bold statement of the primacy of the Church over any political or national unit. In the side aisles, sacred enamel statuettes of Christ and His apostles stood watch over penitent pilgrims confessing their sins to priests. As they lined up to be shriven, many of the pilgrims caressed and kissed the statuettes, almost lasciviously. A beautifully lifelike, and many said ancient, statue of St Peter sat in the nave, and pilgrims fondled and wept over the statue's feet, as if its bronze was the skin of a living man.

Dame Beatrice would have prayed at various altars around St Peter's, but the most important one would have been the shrine of the ancient kerchief of St Veronica, a scrap of cloth bearing the imprint of Christ's face, held in a square frame behind thick glass. It was like the linen rags the visitors had in their own luggage, but imprinted with a holy visage staring out. Veronica, a Jerusalemite lady, was said to have wiped Christ's sweating face in His agony as He was forced on His way to Calvary. This cloth, called the Vernicle (*vera icon*) or *sudarium* (sweat cloth) is one of the original contact relics. Pilgrims thronged around the Vernicle, gazing on it in wonder. The Vernicle gazed back, as if Christ Himself was looking into the visitors' eyes.

Almost nothing of the St Peter's of 1350 remains *in situ* as the church was comprehensively demolished to be rebuilt from around 1505. Even in the 'eternal city', change is constant.

Dame Beatrice Luttrell's visit to St Peter's was complete. Ideally, her journey would have left her refreshed and transformed, even if the travelling had been an ordeal. And then it was time for her and her party to head northwards, back to her English world of sad plenty.

At this time, Rome, along with the Galician city of Santiago de Compostela, was successfully competing with Jerusalem as the main destination for pilgrims. Detailed guidebooks were available for each place, listing practical and religious sites of interest; there were prestigious relics and an infrastructure to support travellers. Jerusalem was distant, expensive to get to and governed by non-Christians but was still the 'best' pilgrimage one could make; in some places it was the only journey for which a wife did not need her husband's permission. So the most popular and desirable journey remained the sea crossing from Venice to Jaffa, the 'port of Jerusalem', and that is the route we now follow.

Indulge yourself!

An indulgence, or pardon, was one of the main reasons Christians travelled in medieval Europe. An indulgence granted, after death, that one's time in Purgatory, due to sins committed during one's life, would be remitted (shortened) or revoked. Indulgences were usually associated with travel to a saint's shrine or a holy place, and pilgrims would pay the church or its brokers for certificates of indulgence.

Here is a small selection of the indulgences available in Rome for visitors in 1450, taken from a Rome travel guide.

St Peter's in the Vatican (San Pietro in Vaticano)	Twenty-eight years at each of the eighty-eight altars (on the relevant saint's feast day) plus seven years at the seven most important altars One thousand years on Feast of the Annunciation One thousand years on Maundy Thursday One thousand years on St Peter's feast day Seven thousand years and remission from a third of all sins on anniversary of church's dedication When the Vernicle (cloth of St Veronica) is shown, 3,000 years to Romans, 9,000 years for those from between Rome and the Alps, and 12,000 years for those from beyond the Alps

St John Lateran (San Giovanni in Laterano)	Full remission of sins for all those who enter the Chapel of St John the Baptist (men only); women can get the indulgence if they touch the door
St Paul's Outside-the-Walls (San Paolo fuori le Mura)	Twenty-eight years, with remission from a third of one's sins for entering the church via the west door (near the relic of St Paul's head) One thousand years on St Paul's feast day One hundred years on the feast day of St Paul's conversion Forty years on the feast day of the Holy Innocents Seven thousand years, with remission from a third of one's sins on the feast day of the dedication of the church Every Sunday, one receives the same pardon as if one went to Santiago de Compostela
St Lawrence Outside-the-Walls (San Lorenzo fuori le Mura)	Seven years of pardon, seven Lents, and remission of a third of all sins One hundred years on the feast days of Sts Lawrence and Stephen Anyone who visits this church on a Wednesday can deliver a soul from Purgatory

5. Across the Great Sea: From Venice to Cyprus

At sea – Zadar – Modon – Rhodes – Cyprus

Travellers boarding a ship at Venice for the Holy Land could expect a journey of between twenty-five and sixty days until they reached the ancient harbour at Jaffa. It could take much longer than this, but this was no leisurely pleasure cruise around Mediterranean beauty spots. Hazards were many: weather, piracy, delays to pick up and unload cargo, on-board plague and sickness, being shipwrecked on some alien shore and/or being ripped off by a crooked *padrone*, the ship's patron. The shipping route between Venice and Jaffa was an industry in itself, serving pilgrims to the Holy Land while connecting Venice with its empire of islands and trading posts in the eastern Mediterranean. The key ports of Pola, Zadar and Durrës and settlements in and around Greece, such as Corfu, Modon (Methoni), Euboea, Heraklion and Cyprus, were all Venetian possessions at some point in the later Middle Ages.

The ocean waxed with the moon. The sea's waters were sometimes green, sometimes blue, now troubled, now serene, studded with rocks and crags and sandbanks, even whirlpools. The sea was understood to cleanse itself by its constant motion and to cast out any corruption or dead thing, as many wise men had observed; but it also caused dread and fear and could suddenly be transformed by a raging squall. The much quoted scholar and encyclopaedist Isidore of Seville (d. 636) described the sea's distinctive quality of *fretum*, a kind of turmoil in the waves, a 'fervent and strong motion' with a unique power to drown men and swallow ships. The sailors had to trust in the stars and the position of the sun, and in their compass and in their brass and silver mariners' astrolabe, a little device with a rule tracing one's position across an engraved map of the stars. Even then the air around the sea could turn violent and throw any vessel around, or the atmosphere could grow dim and misty, leading a ship into unknown perils.

The most common kind of boat taken by travellers was the Venetian galley, a long, slender, shallow vessel propelled by oarsmen. A pilgrim galley leaving Venice for the 'spring voyage' (usually departing around early June) had a crew of several hundred men, including about 200 oarsmen. The Milanese churchman Pietro Casola, who made a pilgrimage to Jerusalem in 1494, travelled on a galley from Venice with 170 other pilgrims. The galley was commanded by a *sopracomito*, a kind of captain, and the crew and passengers were looked after by the powerful and important patron.

Daily life on board a galley was, by contemporary accounts, grim. Every galley was obliged to have a cat on board, to help manage the vermin breeding and scurrying around the decks. If one's goods were damaged by rats because of the lack of a cat, one could sue the shipping company. Hans von Mergenthal, a German pilgrim from Venice to Jerusalem in 1476, described how rats on board could wander over one's body during the night. William Wey, who travelled from Venice to Jaffa in both 1458 and 1462, suggested getting to know the ship's patron to avoid having to stay in the boat's 'smoulderingly hot and stinking' lower quarters. Wealthy passengers could hire cabin space in the forecastle, the raised deck above the ship's bow. Here isolation from most of the other passengers and fresher air made for a relatively dignified experience. Jewish travellers were recommended to get their own cabin, to avoid harassment from the ship's crew.

Humbler passengers stayed below deck, while the poorest lodged in the bilge below the waterline, alongside the ballast. This was a dark, filthy space, shared with freight and mariners and innumerable crawling things, a cavity that reeked of food and vomited meals, sweaty bodies and sleeplessness. Fellow travellers were pressed together here from all over the world, groaning and belching, united in abjection.

The boat itself had to be well made, well maintained and manned by a skilful steersman. A lazy or careless shipmaster could cause even the most well-appointed galley to run aground. Very few people were able to swim if they fell into the sea. At each port the passengers' transition from the galley to a small skiff or tender in order to go ashore was a moment of great jeopardy, especially if there was anything more than a breeze. If one missed one's footing between galley and tender, one was certain to perish in the waves. The Florentine Simone Sigoli, reflecting on his journey to Jerusalem in 1384, seemed to summarize the medieval attitude to sea travel: 'No one should travel who does not desire hardship, trouble, tribulation and the risk of death.'

> **Travellers' wisdom:** The ninth wave in a series of waves is always the strongest. The ninth wave might bury a ship. The force of this fatal wave can only be broken with a prayer.

Nicola de Martoni, an Italian pilgrim to Jerusalem in 1395, found that the terror of his boat capsizing in the eastern Mediterranean caused his hair and beard suddenly to turn white. The Castilian diplomat Ruy González de Clavijo found his carrack caught in a dreadful storm near the volcanic island of Stromboli in July 1403. The wind blew the boat back on itself, and the sails 'from stem to stern' were split, so the carrack had to endure the storm with bare poles. The ship's captain came to his passengers and crew and asked for litanies to be chanted, 'imploring the mercy of God'. As the carrack rode out the storm, flickering lights like candles appeared around the boat's limbs; these lights were accompanied by voices as the storm howled. These were, said Clavijo, the sign of St Pedro González Telmo (d. 1246), the saviour of storm-tossed mariners. Clavijo's is an early account of the weather phenomenon known as St Elmo's Fire, in which luminous glows and buzzing sounds appear in an atmospheric electrical field. It was held to be a good omen that the saint was providing succour to the frightened sailors. The terrifying storm was followed by a period of calm.

Whereas weather was unpredictable, seasickness was an entirely foreseeable traveller's peril. The sea caused violent reactions that could knock an otherwise indefatigable person out. The French poet Guillaume de Machaut (1300–77) wrote about the dire seasickness of Peter I (d. 1369), King of Cyprus and Jerusalem: 'And so at sea he spent the whole time flat under his quilt, just like a corpse, no food, no drink, no sleep.' Medieval medical handbooks often gave useful advice on how to deal with seasickness. The popular *Compendium of Medicine* by Gilbert the Englishman (c. 1230–60) issued a prescription for preventing nausea at sea: one should fast, or eat bitter fruit, like quinces, pomegranates and oranges. One could try drinking an aniseed or chervil concentrate on an empty stomach. Gilbert also recommended that sea travellers sit upright and firmly hold the ship's beams, that they avoid looking around and move their head only with the ship's motion. Finally, he recommended sucking sweets, or eating seeds to produce belching.

Margery Kempe gave a vivid account of seasickness during her voyages of the early 1430s. Sailing on the Baltic between Gdańsk and Stralsund, she felt wretched and terrified on account of the waves. But God spoke to her and comforted her with some sensible and timeless advice. He told her, 'in her soul', to lay down her head and to avoid looking at the waves.

A short time later, crossing the English Channel from Calais to Dover, Kempe prayed to God to maintain her dignity during a rough sea passage and 'give her the grace to hold her head up and keep her from vomiting filthy matter' in the presence of her fellow travellers. Not only did her God protect her, but everyone else on the boat suffered from atrocious seasickness, 'vomiting and throwing up very violently and filthily', none more so than another Englishwoman who had previously slighted Kempe. Seasickness was a bitter revenge indeed.

The Mediterranean is a sea of small tides and mostly gentle currents. The sailors that traversed it depended on the whimsical winds. Yet there was one thing seaborne travellers dreaded above seasickness or violent storms or raging surges or freakish tides: a period of dead calm. A dead calm (called a *bonaccia* by the Venetian mariners) meant that the traveller travelled no further. Perhaps the worst thing for any traveller is to be forced to an involuntary halt.

In a dead calm, the sea would stop, halted in stupid tranquillity, smooth, dulled. Boats languished, blocked, unnervingly steady. Even the teams of oarsmen couldn't propel the boat in such leaden seas. Dust seemed to gather around the useless frippery of the sails and on the static hawsers. The very sea had become an anchor. The astrolabe remained still, as if jammed. The shipmen lazed on the deck, making music on their bagpipes or zithers or playing improvised games of ninepins, or sometimes trictrac and checkers with the captain's stag-horn gamepieces. The stark vacuum of boredom threatened. Motionlessness. Paralysis.

The Italian nobleman Roberto da Sanseverino was stuck in a dead calm in the winter of 1458 for a period of twenty-two days. His boat sat, stultified, off the island of Sapientza in the Peloponnese, causing a significant delay to his return to Venice. Traversing the oceans has long involved traversing the monotony of oneself.

Felix Fabri – who had little positive to say about sea travel – wrote that a period of dead calm was more distressing to sea travellers than anything but an actual shipwreck. He described how in a calm the entire boat and everything on it seemed to putrefy and rot: wine became undrinkable, the dried, smoked meat bulged with maggots, and innumerable flies, gnats, fleas, lice, worms, mice and rats suddenly sprang to life. The people on board lost their tempers, growing lazy, sleepy and even more unkempt. Melancholy, anger and envy spread everywhere among the boat's passengers.

The only thing the mariners could do was to wait, or try to kedge the boat, fastening the vessel to an anchor with a cable and hauling it out of the ponderous calms.

Death at sea was also common. In 1446, the English ship the *Cog Anne* was wrecked on the rocks off Modon in southern Greece. It was carrying about 160 pilgrims, together with sacks of wool for export. The boat had sailed from Kingroad, the port of Bristol, via the Straits of Gibraltar and Seville. In the tempestuous darkness of a December night, the *Cog Anne* was driven on to the rocks. Thirty-seven crew and passengers drowned; the Bishop of Modon gave them what he considered to be an honourable Christian burial and consecrated an oratory to their special memory.

In just over two weeks in September to October 1518, the galley carrying Jacques Le Saige of the French city of Douai from Cyprus to Rhodes became infested with sickness. At least seven passengers died and others considered too ill to continue sailing were left at Rhodes, in the care of the Knights Hospitaller.

Felix Fabri remarked acidly that, as the privations of the journey took their toll on the travellers, his galley on the return journey from Jaffa to Venice came to resemble a hospital.

There was an ambivalence about such a death, as perishing on a pilgrimage was thought to bring its own special blessings. If pilgrimage was a kind of travelling Purgatory, a cleansing of one's soul, then death near Jerusalem was a fast track to Heaven. A popular medieval preachers' story told how a boatload of pilgrims returning from Jerusalem sank; the pilgrims' corpses washed ashore all marked with crosses, as if blessed for ever in their martyrdom-by-travel. Some travellers uttered special prayers for seafaring, and special liturgies were developed for sea passengers in danger. People lit candles, and prayed to seafaring saints like St Nicholas of Bari or the Magdalene of Marseilles or St James of Compostela. Others carried an effigy of St Christopher, patron saint of wayfarers. Where shipwrecked sailors had been saved, new and often transient altars appeared on coastlines, their candles flickering out to the dark seas. These guided ships' pilots to safety and blessed their passengers' journeys. At the coastal town of Pola, an icon of the Virgin Mary was worshipped by visitors; it was said to have appeared inside a fig tree one day, during an outbreak of plague. The Virgin's very name, Maria, seemed to be a benediction of the plural seas (*maria*).

With this perilous passage ahead of them, the galleys sailing from Venice made their way south-east through the Adriatic

Sea, through gentle waters on a predictable route cleaving to the Istrian and Dalmatian coasts. They passed numerous ports and stopped at many of them. The Venetian winged lion, carved in stone, repeatedly greeted the travellers along the coast, a sign of familiarity and an assurance of good order even if the air in these coastal towns tended to have a not entirely wholesome scent of pine resin, wild garlic and excrement. At each way station people would come to greet the boat, selling local produce and encouraging the travellers to visit their town's shrines.

Konrad Grünemberg is a representative and very informative traveller about the onward sea voyage from Venice through the Adriatic. Grünemberg, who had a good education and plenty of money, had been the officer in charge of the mint in the city of Constance. In his sixties he set off from Constance for Jerusalem, taking a galley at Venice (for a sum of 38 ducats, half to be paid on the spot, the other half to be paid on successfully arriving in the Holy Land). He wrote a detailed, illustrated and often garrulous account of 'the strange, beautiful and wonderful things' he saw on his journey, which took place over thirty-one weeks, from April to November 1486. He described himself and his fellow travellers as 'insatiable learners of foreign and strange customs'; while he was not exactly tolerant, he was certainly interested in the diversity of peoples he encountered.

As his galley left Venice, Grünemberg listened to travellers entertain each other with stories about Venice and its Dalmatian towns. His boat collected cattle, sheep and goats at Pirano, and continued to Parenzo, Rovigno and Pola. He lingered at the large and beautiful town of 'Sara' (Zadar), the main city of 'Schlaffonia' (Slavonia), a miniature eastern Venice. He was told about its famous relic of St Simeon's body, resting in a magnificent church with a tower built like lace.

Since around 1204, when the saint's body had been brought to Zadar from Constantinople, Simeon's tomb was the city's biggest draw: a giant cedarwood chest (made in the late 1370s) decorated with finely worked silver plaques depicting the saint's life and miracles, including the moment when Simeon took the infant Jesus in his arms and presented him in the Temple in Jerusalem. The reliefs also showed a more contemporary scene: of a boat in a storm, bringing Simeon's relics to Zadar, with high waves threatening to overwhelm the vessel and desperate mariners jettisoning bundles of merchandise into the sea; terrified passengers are shown huddling in the centre of the ship. It would have been a scene that connected Simeon's cult with the experience of visitors to his shrine. Inside the chest, Simeon's mummified body, miraculously uncorrupted, was shown to pilgrims. An African ostrich egg had been hung above the tomb as a symbol of good luck and to represent the globe of planet earth.

At Zadar were also the body parts of St George (skull), St John the Baptist (finger), St Chrysogonus (bloodstained chemise) and Mary Magdalene (skull), and a grubby stub of the sponge from which Christ was offered gall at Calvary.

But Grünemberg was also fascinated by an idol that had been worshipped there. He described a tall column, hewn from a single block of stone, topped by a griffin. He was told that the griffin had been worshipped for many years and performed miracles and addressed the townspeople. When the people converted to Christianity, they attached a plaque with crosses to it. The moment the crosses touched it, the column split asunder, from top to bottom, and the evil spirit of the idol fled from it.

This arresting story shows Grünemberg's incipient curiosity about the non-Christian environments and intriguing histories he was encountering. He was reckoning with Zadar's pagan history, as he was describing the 'Pillar of Shame', once part of the Roman forum and used as a place of public punishment in the Middle Ages. It is indeed topped with a kind of griffin, a winged beast, a pagan forerunner of the Venetian winged lion of St Mark. It was a warning that all empires come and go. Grünemberg's interest in the column discloses, implicitly, a comparison between the bodies of the saints claimed by Zadar and the city's pre-Christian idols. Travel caused him to ponder the differences between a relic and a magic charm, a prayer and a spell, an icon and an idol.

Grünemberg's travels through Dalmatia read something like an account of a modern holiday: beautiful buildings, strange and interesting churches and encounters with charming, colourful locals. Venetian governors welcomed him with delicious dishes and pastries. At Zadar he witnessed a wedding, admiring the bride's golden crown set with precious stones and all the ribbons and ornaments of the women. Oat, awned wheat and barley were thrown over the married couple, symbolizing the future plenty the bride and her children would enjoy. Grünemberg entered the church to watch the marriage ceremony in the Slavonic manner, noting the priests' odd gestures, the men coming forward to kiss the cross, the women kissing a painting of the Virgin and everyone holding a burning candle throughout. 'Strikingly handsome' women were observed; and the local customs of Hungarians, Slavs, Turks, Greeks and Italians were noted, as Grünemberg, in some awe, noted a great diversity in dress and a great variety of languages. His galley, as long as the weather was fine, seemed to have an atmosphere of a party cruise; on 23 June, the Eve of the Feast of St John, there were special entertainments on board ship. The mariners put fifty lanterns around the boat, fired their weapons into the air and blew their trumpets, while a drummer rolled his drum.

The *galiots*, the galley's oarsmen, sang songs and danced gaily with each other around the decks. Everything seemed to be going well, apart from a growing anxiety about the proximity of the Turks, who, according to Grünemberg, mistreated their horses terribly, demanded tribute off the Christians to keep the peace and forced the people of towns like Zadar and Dubrovnik to worry constantly about being besieged.

As the ship headed south-east, the coastline grew challenging in its alloy of familiar with unfamiliar. Passengers saw broken vestiges of ancient pillars and strange temples on desolate beaches, and wretched-looking villages amid melancholy woods and wild stone spires. Fingerish islands, little larger than a marketplace and scarcely inhabited, passed by. The travellers from Venice weren't sure who lived in these places: were the people pious sages, or were they infidels? It was hard to tell.

South of Dalmatia, after Corfu, the travellers passed alongside the region they called Romania, the southern Balkans. On the port side, the passengers might have gazed on Turkish territories, such as Achaea (in the Peloponnese area of Greece), taken by the Ottomans in 1460, where mosques dotted the skyline, new fortresses were being built and veiled ladies could be seen walking near the shore. At starboard, they might have seen perpendicular churches that would not have looked out of place in Sicily or Spain and campaniles that recalled Italian towns.

The travellers looked forward to reaching the Venetian town of Modon, a walled port said to be exactly halfway between Venice and Jaffa. Modon was famous for its rumney wine (literally, 'wine of Romania', the Balkans), which sustained Mediterranean travellers for many centuries.

At the midpoint of Modon, the air on *terra firma* was hot

and dry, settling into an agitated silence on the fawn-coloured hillsides. Modon, built in sandy stone and encircled by walls and ditches, sat on a rock promontory, with a shallow harbour on its eastern side. Windmills turned lazily on the western side of Modon's port, where several large boats were docked. Grisly black rocks lined the base of the city's walls, as if to deter unwanted invaders from trying to land. The whole town had a look of impregnability: strong, stark, self-contained. The main bastion had a pair of semi-circular windows like two silent eyes staring out to sea, behind which sat armed watchmen, vigilant always.

The town had, along with the Morea, become part of the Venetian empire in 1204 and was relentlessly fortified. It was a garrison for Crusaders. The Venetians then developed Modon into a major trading port: olive oil, wheat, honey, wax, figs, citrus fruit, cochineal, spicery and salted carcasses flowed through its merchants' and mariners' hands, to and from Alexandria, the Black Sea and far beyond. Visitors to Modon would also be able to stock up on the area's famous raisins-of-Corinth (currants).* In Modon, the Venetian dignitaries ate off Catalan crockery and drank from Chinese glassware, their meals salted, peppered and saffroned with the world's best flavours.

Modon and its nearby sister city of Koroni were known as Venice's eastern eyes. The towns were harried by the Turks throughout the later fifteenth century and taken by them in 1500. There are over eighty-five surviving accounts of Modon from between 1147 and 1533 and they reveal much about the ways in which travellers passed through the fraught and contested eastern Mediterranean littoral zone.

* Like French *raisin de Corinthe*, German *Korinthe*, Russian *korinka*, Spanish *pasa de corinto*, Swedish *korint*.

As each boat from Venice arrived, the only people to be seen outside the walls were watermen on the harbour, dressed in grubby whites, employed to bring the weary travellers ashore in rowing-boat tenders. Cats, many of which had their noses eaten away by some unfortunate circumstance, roamed the port, along with a few currish dogs. Some fly-bitten, fully laden mules were tethered there too.

The galleys had to be skilfully steered into Modon's port. The water was shallow, with black sea rushes waving in it. Here a pier causeway reached out into the sea, a Venetian arm hugging boats towards Modon. This causeway – a hall-mark of Venice's ports – led up to the Sea Gate of St Mark (named after Venice's patron saint and embellished, of course, with the city's winged lion). Armoured men in the city's defences drew their swords in salute and shouted 'Viva Santo Marco!'

Behind this gate, the tightly packed buildings and belfries of the town piled up on the slender isthmus. The town's walls and gates were marked with the escutcheons of the Venetian governors, many of whom were from Venice's leading families: Bembo, Canal, Corner, Foscolo, Miani, Morosini, Venier.

Beyond the town walls, a scatter of huts spilled on to the hills, where olive trees, ancient vines and abundant fruit trees filled the landscape. Some tall cypresses stood marvellously still. Further beyond was a mountainous, wooded landscape, spotted with unknowable villages.

The whole town of Modon seemed perfect for the visiting voyager on first landing. There was a German inn or *funduq*, where visitors could get a good familiar meal; Konrad Grünemberg ate here in a grapevine bower. There were bakeries geared to the travellers, serving delicious dry biscuits which they could put in their bags and take onwards with them. There was a grand marketplace, the Square of Arms, where men from the galleys could set up stalls and sell their wares and buy local goods. One could pay for everything in Venetian ducats and *torneselli* (the colonial small coin used in Venice's empire). And there were even wonderful churches and shrines, with the relics of the ancient martyr St Athanasius, two fingers of Sts Cosmas and Damian and the entire body of a saint called Leo.

Most of the travellers had never heard of this St Leo before, but he turned out to be, like them, a traveller. Leo had been a devoted pilgrim and ascetic, either Venetian or Calabrian (depending on who told his story). He had lived as a penniless beggar, a perfect pilgrim who travelled barefoot and was clad only in one scanty robe. He had died on his way to Jerusalem, or perhaps on his way back from Jerusalem (depending on who told his story), expiring when he saw the town of Modon in the distance, or when he set foot on its dock (depending on who told his story). Some said his death had happened in the distant past, in the time of the Crusades. But others, perplexingly, seemed to remember meeting him, just a few years before, and they talked about him like he was an uncle or cousin who had died young.

After his death, whenever that was, the holy Leo had caused many miracles to happen among the Turks and unbelievers. He had been buried first on Modon's beach and then in the town's cathedral. He became revered locally as a patron saint of travellers and pilgrims. He was the ideal, and convenient, saint for visitors to Modon.

The Venetian Senate ruled and regulated life inside Modon's walls just as it did in Venice. In 1389, the Senate declared that Modon and Koroni were 'two very useful places for the *signoria*' (the supreme body of the Venetian Republic), and that it was especially important to ensure the proper maintenance of their ports and arsenals and the goods stored there. Hundreds of detailed surviving records show how Modon's Venetian governors tried to enforce the law: nocturnal police patrolled the town, there were strict regulations about bribes and extortion in public office, there was constant vigilance over the nearby smaller ports of Navarino and Zonchio (Pylos), worries about Catalan and Flemish blockades, frequent reports of encroachments from the Genoese and Ottomans, contracts for the engagement of crossbowmen to defend the town (monthly salary in 1403: 18 ducats, compared to 12 ducats for a ship's oarsman), and resolute enforcement over licensing, pricing and tariffs on goods like flour and olive oil. The Venetian lion could see into every transaction, and every crime, of the townspeople and visitors.

Medieval Modon existed, to a significant extent, to serve the Venetian galleys, but its Greek population did not 'become' Venetian. Many visitors were surprised that Greek was the lingua franca and was used by the educated classes.

Visiting Modon in June 1453, Peter Rot of Basel heard the devastating news that Constantinople had been conquered by the Turks and the Christian emperor murdered. Many travellers noted that the Turks were closing in on Modon. Roberto da Sanseverino, in November 1458, found the town almost devoid of humans, who had fled, or succumbed to, a great pestilence.

Visiting for two days in August 1460, the Basel pilgrim Hans Bernhard von Eptingen was glad to find the excellent rumney wine that was highly prized in his hometown, but was alarmed by reports of 100,000 Turks massing within three hours of Modon. Indeed, later that year the Turks did take the Morea, the mainland to which Modon is attached.

After a promising start, most visitors to medieval Modon began to express distaste and then revulsion towards the town. Travellers reported that its buildings were too close together and cheaply constructed, and that the city's cathedral was shabby. The priest who showed the relics seemed more an underhand cobbler than a venerable cleric. Even the box in which he kept the relics – once the travellers' eyes adjusted in the gloaming – was falling to pieces. The priests sang their liturgy enthusiastically but in deep, unfamiliar tones, as if proclaiming personal misfortunes. The grasshoppers' chirring in the bushes grew incessant to the point of ridiculousness. There were few good lodgings for visitors, and the miserable friars didn't take in guests to their friary, so most travellers had to go back to the galley to rest at night, their sleep interrupted by the waves from which they had sought respite. Apart from the excellent wine and fruit, good food was scarce. Pietro Casola, in 1494, found little comfort to be had; he could only obtain a few eggs, and even these he had to cook himself.

Anselm Adornes, a Flemish-Genoese merchant and pilgrim from Bruges, observed a particularly striking incident when he briefly stopped at Modon in November 1470. At the port, a Turk was being executed by impalement, the Venetians running a pike through his body from fundament to face. Adornes was told that two years previously, this Turk had ridden at high speed towards the Venetian galleys, his horse panting and sweating. He had jumped down from his mount and shouted, 'Accept me as a Christian!' There and then, he slaughtered his exhausted horse, presumably as a sign of the sincerity of his commitment to remain in Modon. He lived, outwardly, as a perfect Christian for two years, all the time secretly gathering information about the Venetians and passing it back to the Turks. When this was found out, he was imprisoned. The allegations were investigated and verified, and the Turk eventually executed.

We don't know the Turk's side of the story but the further

east the western travellers went, the more stories of religious treachery they heard. Indeed, there were so many tales of renegades that it became hard to know friend from foe. The precariousness of Modon's status, with the Ottoman Turks governing land just a few kilometres away, seemed to lead many travellers to experience human variety as repellent, concerning and deeply undesirable.

Most noteworthy for visitors from the mid-fifteenth century were Modon's Jewish and 'Gyppe' ('Gypsy') communities, who had their own neighbourhoods in the suburbs, outside the town walls. Paul Walther, visiting Modon from the southern German town of Güglingen in 1482–3, noted Modon's mixed population, of 'Greeks, Gypsies, Moors, pagans and Christians'.

Meshullam of Volterra, a Jewish pilgrim to Jerusalem, visited Modon in September 1481 and found over 300 Jewish households there: a considerable community. They were engaged in handicrafts and similar trades. Christian visitors tended to be less polite: Pietro Casola in 1494 found the town's Jewish inhabitants to be 'filthy', 'very dirty' people, 'full of bad smells'. 'Their society did not please me,' he wrote, sniffily. Arnold von Harff, in the late 1490s, visited the Jewish community in their own long street, the women making silkwork and other haberdashery, some of which he bought.

Meanwhile, Modon's 'Gyppe' community were part of the significant 'Gypsy' settlement in the Venetian colonies of the Peloponnese from at least the 1440s (this is the origin of their present-day name Roma or Romani: like the prized rumney wine, they were of the province of Romania, the Morea or Peloponnese). They lived especially at the small Venetian port of Napoli di Romania (Nafplio), north-east of Modon but had a significant, if makeshift, settlement at Modon in the later fifteenth century. Konrad Grünemberg described about 300 'huts made from reeds and loam' in which lived 'Gypsies, also called infidels over there'. Philippe de Voisins, visiting in 1490, found all kinds of people living in the town, including Romani whom he described as poor and living in wretched conditions.

Jean de Cucharmois, visiting Modon also in 1490, said 'Gypsies' took their name not from Egypt but from a village called Gipte. De Cucharmois was repeating what many travellers wondered: 'where did these people come from?' The Romani of Modon may well have wondered the same thing about the various travellers who stared at them and then sailed away. Many visitors commented on the Romani living beneath the town by the beach, where there was a makeshift settlement of huts in contrast to the stark stones of the fortified Venetian city. Arnold von Harff repeated a myth that they were from a country called 'Gyppe' or 'Tzigania' 60 kilometres from Modon. He described them as 'poor, black, naked people' who had been refugees from the Turks (who had occupied 'Gyppe') and then become vagabonds in the Venetians' midst.

Is it ever acceptable for a traveller to be rude about the people they happen to encounter along their way? Travel writing is full of such spiteful assessments of other human beings. At Modon, many medieval travellers articulated a Christian, European judgementalism, a supercilious and composting hatred, that would become the hallmark of later western tourists. A traveller reserves the right not to enjoy a *place*, but what right can a traveller possibly have to be disappointed in the *people* who dare to inhabit that place? The haughty comments of European travellers about the Jewish and Romani inhabitants of Modon suggest that, in the drama of the journey, these poor people were unscripted extras, as if a part of the stage set had fallen away to reveal an impromptu presence.

By the time Sir Richard Guylforde sailed past the Peloponnese on his way to Jerusalem, in July 1506, Modon was no longer a Venetian Christian town. It had, in 1500, been conquered by the Turks. The medieval fortifications survive, but the town was completely razed, and is now an eerie plain, enclosed by elegant battlements. Guylforde's galley did not stop in Modon, for fear of 'the Turk'. He knew that excellent wines were available in the town, but his boat continued to still-Venetian Heraklion (Candia), on the island of Crete. Guylforde missed out on Modon, but his interests were quickly piqued by the nearby island of Cyrigo, or Citheria, one of the places where Venus was said to have been born. The Byzantine shrines and bustling Venetian ports were, one by one, falling to the Turks.

Along these shores of shifting powers, there was one steadfast redoubt of Christendom: the island of Rhodes.

Rhodes was controlled not by the Venetians but by the Knights Hospitaller, who held sovereign control over the island and were organized as a military and political force. They were an order of devout men, committed to sacred travel: they existed to facilitate journeys to Jerusalem, and their name comes from their sponsorship and stewardship of the pilgrims' hospice in Jerusalem, the Muristan. The Knights Hospitaller had been expelled from the Holy Land in 1291 by the Mamluks, the Muslim military force who conquered much of the Middle East in the thirteenth century and effectively ended the Crusades in the Holy Land. The Knights then established a significant power base first in Cyprus and then ever more steadfastly in Rhodes. From Rhodes, they built a small empire of forcelets, towers and strongholds, including the island of Kastellorizo and a mainland fort at Halicarnassus (Bodrum).

The Hospitallers built impressive fortifications in the

town of Rhodes, which held within them the magnificent Grandmaster's Palace. The grandmasters were almost all French in origin, with occasional Italian and Aragonese holders of the title. They fought Barbary pirates and, in 1444, repelled a Mamluk invasion. The decades after 1453, when the Ottomans had taken Constantinople, saw increasingly effective Ottoman incursions in the Aegean islands, and in 1480 Rhodes was subject to a long Ottoman siege, which caused a significant panic across Christian Europe. Eventually in 1523 the Ottomans conquered the island.

After the failure of the Holy Land Crusades, Rhodes was perhaps the key frontier zone of Europe, a place ruled and inhabited by western nobility as if it were a Burgundian estate but within sight of the Turkish shore.

Passing travellers were a crucial part of the Rhodian economy and the maintenance of Hospitaller rule. Each part of Europe was represented within the organization by a *langue*, a supranational group. Each *langue* had its own *auberge* at Rhodes: Aragonese, Auvergnat, Castilian and Portuguese, English, French, Italian and German. Each *auberge* was like a luxury hotel and medical centre for expatriate Hospitallers and their guests.

For less august visitors, in the mid-fifteenth-century the Hospitallers built a magnificent new pilgrims' hospital in the town of Rhodes. It contained a capacious infirmary ward, an airy space with natural light and between thirty and forty canopied beds for unwell travellers, of whom there was an unending supply. Little booths were constructed behind the arcades, where surgery could be performed and patients could recover, or expire, with some privacy. Mass was performed daily. Many Hospitaller knights from all over Europe died there, far from home. Their tombs were decorated with coats of arms and devices that recalled their origins.

The fraught status of Rhodes is exemplified by the account given by the perspicacious English traveller William Wey, on his journey to Jerusalem in 1458. At Rhodes, he was told about a recent event: 250 Turks had been brought to the island by sea and had been paraded through the town led by Christian boys who themselves had formerly been imprisoned by the Turks. The Turks were then tortured in a variety of spectacularly cruel ways, in a festival of violence. Some of the Turks were dragged by ropes attached to their pierced nostrils, others with their hands tied behind their backs. Eighteen Turkish prisoners were impaled, with stakes driven through the anus all the way to their chests. Ten were dragged naked across a plank of iron spikes. Two were baptized and then beheaded. One was flayed, his skin cut from his body. Another was tossed from a high tower and then strung up by his penis. The rest were hanged (some by the neck, some by the feet), 'their bodies placed on either side of the city so that they were in full view of all passers-by'. Wey seemed unsurprised by this kind of violence, and commented that the sultan of the Turks was at the time moving 30,000 'men, women and children' from the Morea to populate the recently conquered Constantinople.

On a more usual day, as the pilgrim galley sailed from Rhodes to Cyprus the passengers passed the time by telling stories or preaching sermons or singing songs. The mariners and their passengers saw bricks and walls submerged in the shallows of the clear seawater. A well-known story about the area went like this:

Not far from Rhodes, near the shore were the sunken ruins of an ancient city known as Cathalia or Satalia or Adalia or Antalya, no one was quite sure of its name. It was said to have been a wonderful city full of splendid buildings and happy citizens. It had been the centre of a great empire which controlled the lands and the seas thereabouts. But all this territory was lost through the folly of one young man.

This man loved a beautiful woman, so much so that it was as if his heart had been set on fire. Yet the young woman suddenly died of the plague. Her lovely body was placed in a finely wrought marble tomb.

The young man's heart was broken. He sickened and languished and still remained in love with the young woman. Each night, and sometimes during the day, he was aroused by the thought of her. One night he went to her tomb, opened it and crept inside where he had sex with her corpse.

And then he left. In the weeks and months that followed he started to forget about her.

Suddenly, one evening, after nine months, the young man heard a voice bellowing, clear as day, 'Go to that woman's tomb, open it, and see what you created! And if you don't go you'll be grievously harmed!'

So the young man went back to the tomb and as he approached he remembered what he had done last time he was here, but felt not a speck of desire for his former lover. He opened up the tomb. Suddenly a dreadful hideous-looking dragon's head shot out, screaming and screeching, before flying around the city and over the land. As it soared off into the mountains, a great wave rose from the sea and the whole city was submerged. The water swept the people away and drowned the buildings. We assume the young man died in the deluge.

Ever since then, the sea crossings between Rhodes and Cyprus had become perilous because of the sunken city and the strange undercurrents and unfathomable abysses, all caused by this sinful youth and his terrible actions.

This story, which was told throughout Europe, rebuked those travellers whose thoughts, through boredom, lust or impiety, had wandered to impure places. And the story also reminded them that terrain could rise and fall, whole cities could be sunken, coasts could come and go. They might have reflected on the flood that God sent to Noah to cleanse the corrupt earth, or the cities of Sodom and Gomorrah that were laid waste and remained ever barren thanks to vice.

Some may have heard tell of the fiendish tidal waves in 1303 that overwhelmed Crete, and swept buildings and people away in Alexandria and Acre. It happened after an immense earthquake which was felt even in Venice. In Heraklion, the town hall, the arsenal, churches and castles all fell down. The harbour sank into the sea, with hundreds being washed away in the unrelenting grasp of the waves. Such stories caused the travellers to feel even queasier. What an unknowable world they traversed! What hidden depths lurked in the world's waters and the continual movement of the waves!

Some of the pilgrims had already been having impure thoughts about their next stop, Cyprus, a reputed birthplace of the goddess Aphrodite, the deity of beauty and sexual desire. At Cyprus, a fertile island run by the Lusignan dynasty of French princes (and after them, from 1489, by the Venetians), they were relieved to set their feet on dry land. Here the Lusignan lion – crowned and rampant – replaced its winged Venetian cousin on the reliefs and lintels of the fortified towns. Inland, Nicosia (Lefkosia) was the island's main ecclesiastical and governmental centre. Limassol, Paphos, Kyrenia (known as Dieu-d'Amour) and Larnaca (Salino) were all also regularly called at as places to moor the galleys. Famagusta, on the island's eastern side, had the best harbour. In these towns lived Latin Christians – who looked to the pope in Rome – alongside Greeks, Armenians, Copts and other Christians (in their multiple sects of Chaldeans, Jacobites, Maronites, Melkites), Jewish devotees and a few Muslims, all with their churches and temples and tombs and different languages but often sharing sacred spaces and rituals.

> **Look out!** Mermaids and sirens are beautiful and very rare. Sailors report that they are terribly dangerous. The mermaid may appear in the waves, with a mirror and a comb, preening and adoring herself. The siren may sing, pluck a harp, or blow a horn, causing the mariner to fall asleep, lose his reason or start to weep. Mariners may well weep in recalling the mermaids and sirens of old, who lured sailors to the shore to fornicate with them. If the sailor refused, the mermaid ripped him to pieces and ate him.

Cyprus was only a day's sailing, on a good day, from the coast of the Holy Land. The proximity of the Bible could be felt on this island full of miracle-working shrines and relics of the saints. Pilgrims were especially fond of visiting a site, 'St Catherine's Prison' (or sometimes 'St Catherine's Tomb') at Salamis, which they believed had played a key role in the life of the holy St Catherine of Alexandria (her uncle was said to have been the governor of Cyprus). The prison cell/tomb was in fact a megalithic monument and burial chamber, thousands of years older even than Catherine, but a crude altar, decorated with icons, had been built there in the Middle Ages. If they didn't venerate Catherine here, visitors could do so in the magnificent, flamboyant cathedral built in her honour in Nicosia (now the Haydar Pasha Mosque), another site of the saint's tomb. Pilgrims came to this site in great numbers, and here they could get a pilgrim badge showing half the broken wheel on which Catherine had suffered. Without worrying too much about which historical moment in Catherine's eventful but short life was being commemorated, it was much easier to venerate the saint here rather than going all the way to her main shrine at Sinai.

Another arresting sight for medieval visitors was the monastery of St Nicholas of the Cats, beside the great salt lakes at Akrotiri. According to local legend, the monastery was founded in the time of Constantine, on condition that a hundred cats were kept there to destroy the area's noisome snakes. Felix Fabri found it a charming tradition when he visited in 1480. During the day, the cats roamed about the woodland surrounding the monastery, and at their dinnertime a monk rang a bell. All the resident cats would hurry down to be fed. For Fabri, the cats represented the good angels, the hunted snakes the evil ones.

The most popular holy place for visitors to Cyprus was the Hill of the Holy Cross at Stavrovouni, between Larnaca and Nicosia. After passing through a landscape of lush citrus and mulberry groves on their hired horses and donkeys, they found an ancient monastery atop a mountain. The air there was thin and pure, and visitors gained remarkable views across the whole of the south of the island.

At the monastery, visitors were shown the Cross of the Good Thief. On this Cross it was said had hung the body of the penitent crook Dysmas, who suffered alongside Jesus and asked Him to remember him as they died together. Additionally, there was said to be a nail from Christ's own Cross, brought here by the holy archaeologist St Helena herself, nailed into Dysmas's Cross.

The Cross at Stavrovouni was said sometimes to hover, suspended, unsupported, in the air, held up by the Holy Spirit; Daniil of Kyiv, a pilgrim visiting in 1107, said that he had seen this miraculous thing himself with his own eyes. The monastery was a pilgrimage site in its own right for those en route to Jerusalem, and unwell mariners were especially encouraged to visit the Cross, either for a remedy to their sickness or to prepare their souls for death.

In 1426 the monastery was attacked by Mamluks, during an attempt to occupy the island, and its fabric damaged. The miraculous Cross was taken apart; according to the sultan's vizier Khalil, the Mamluks carried it off and found that it only seemed to float in the air thanks to the 'cunningly devised springs' concealed inside.

Stavrovouni remained a place that Christian pilgrims visited but, by the later fifteenth century, its Cross had been encrusted in gold and silver and no longer floated. Sometimes it was hung up on cords in a window and could be rocked to and fro, as a memory of its former airborne miracle. The Cross relic was guarded by a sole monk, a sacristan, who had been abandoned by his brothers and sat, alone, guarding this piece of holy cypress wood. Felix Fabri, visiting Stavrovouni in 1480, believed that the Cross still hung without any visible supports, but did not want to examine it too closely, in case he offended God. 'I ascended this mountain to honour the Cross,' wrote brother Felix carefully, 'not to find a miracle or to tempt God.'

While the landscape of Cyprus was dappled with holiness, the port city of Famagusta was most certainly not a holy place. Famagusta was a boom town of medieval travel, transformed from a village by Crusader refugees after the Fall of Acre in 1291. The city was governed by the Lusignans from the 1290s until it was occupied by the Genoese in 1372, and then, in 1489, by the Venetians, who made it their capital. The Lusignans arrayed it with a grand cathedral, a bishop's palace, several churches, three monasteries and a shopping street, and started its magnificent fortifications. At the harbour, there was a concourse bustling with merchants and pilgrims. Famagusta rapidly became Cyprus's main port, its dusty purlieus the destination for pleasure and vice.

The German priest and pilgrim Ludolph of Suchem, visiting around 1337, said Famagusta was 'the richest of all cities, and her citizens are the richest of men'. It had a very deep port and, located as it was on the island's eastern side, became its main entrepôt with the east. Aromatic herbs from India, camlet and damasked cloths from the Levant and Turkish and Circassian slaves were traded through the city. Travellers were surprised and awed by the Famagustans' luxurious and exotic clothing: the men wore long silk gowns trimmed with gold braid and pearls, and boots with upturned toes, the kind seen in the Mamluk empire; the women were largely covered in black, decorated, pleated cloaks, their embroidered mantles covering most of their faces.

The city boasted a large number of taverns, many of them owned by expatriate Italians, which catered for locals, sailors, pilgrims and pirates. The legal records of the time give us a sense of a traveller's night out in a tavern in medieval Famagusta. One evening, in 1428, a priest named Antonio Mansour was visiting the city from Pera, the Genoese enclave in Constantinople. Mansour was at a tavern with friends, to have food and some drinks. In a nearby corner of the tavern was a Famagustan named Bisarra with his own companions, and the two groups started to talk and drink and carouse together, dining on bread and pasta and pouring Greek wine down their throats. Mansour was holding the breadknife when, 'entirely accidentally', his hand slipped and he stabbed Bisarra in the chest, fatally wounding him. Antonio was arrested and, once he had made it clear he was a priest, was handed over to the Latin Bishop of Famagusta. He was put in the bishop's prison. Antonio escaped and managed to get on a boat to

Rome, where he sought absolution and was cleared of all accusations against him.

On another occasion, a brawl broke out in Antonio Cogio's tavern in Famagusta between the landlord and one Bartholomew of Pera. In the course of the fight Cogio struck another guest, Azar de Caffa, visiting from the Crimea, on the head with a jug of wine. Azar's skull was split open and he had to stay in bed for a month, before missing a further seventeen days of work; he also incurred various expenses for medicines and, as he complained to the authorities, had to pay for extra hairdressing too.

These tavern brawls among visitors give us an idea of what could go wrong far from home, especially when wine was involved.

Famagusta was also infamous for its sex workers. Ludolph of Suchem noticed the incredibly wealthy courtesans; he blamed this on the Cypriot soil, which he said provoked men to lust through its association with Aphrodite. Similarly, Aeneas Sylvius Piccolomini (later Pope Pius II, d. 1463) described the women of Famagusta as 'exceedingly wanton'. He said that, in the holy name of Venus, they gave their bodies over to visiting sailors. There were even tomb memorials to Aphrodite in the cathedral in Nicosia and outside the Venetian palace in Famagusta, as if lust had become the object of veneration. As the travellers went further east, and further from home, their minds seemed to wander more and more towards matters of the flesh, led by the thrillingly intemperate sensuality of foreign parts. The travellers were at risk of falling under the erotic spell of being abroad.

A poem about sea travel

Sir Nicole Louve (also known as Nicolle Lowe) was a wealthy gentleman from Metz in Lorraine. In the spring of 1428 he travelled to the Holy Land in a Venetian galley. He returned in the same year, with two parrots he had acquired during his journey. During his return trip in December he wrote this satirical poem about the appalling experiences he suffered during his sea voyage.

A ballade by Sir Nicole Louve, knight, made at sea on returning from the Holy Sepulchre in the year 1428:

Whoever wishes to embark aboard a pilgrim galley
Must take courage in both their hands,
Because they will be slobbering
From the moment they depart from the home port.

On board,
You can't be too picky about dining,
Because you'll often have to eat
More than your fair share of putrid food.

There's no shade on the boat's deck,
And you're roasted by the sun.
You eat rotten biscuits
And here everyone has to drink terrible-tasting coarse wine.

Here, everything is done to stimulate your appetite!
When we're seated at the communal dining table,
We realise it's less than six feet
From where everyone empties their guts!

I must also tell you:
You're completely at the mercy of the wind.
The wind's the galley's real master,
And no one else can help.

The wind calms the boat as he pleases,
Or makes her strike out at full speed.
Don't rely on the patron, the commander, or the oarsmen:
They're suffering too!

The wind needs no fiddler to make the galley dance.
So everyone looks dejected,
Shaking their heads from side to side,
And vomiting up their guts and innards.

When the wind has decided to show its strength,
There's nothing to do
But pray to God
To preserve you from danger.

And storms are another thing:
Astonishing, very unpleasant, and dangerous.
In strong winds, it's essential to drop anchor
Near a port.

This can last for a long time,
Believe you me!
As food starts to run out on board,
We have to go ashore and wander about on foot.

If one wants to go to bed,
It's difficult to find relaxation
Or good rest.
It's necessary to sleep in steerage,

Which totally stinks of the farts,
The gassy vapours, the flatulence
Exhaled by human guts.
It is simply disgusting!

Here, the fleas abound
And lice are innumerable.
Each of them persists in stinging and biting the poor sleepers
Who are trying to get some rest.

In sum,
To conclude on this subject,
No one's obliged to go to the Holy Land,
If you don't have the strengths & qualities I describe here:

You must be animated by a great fervour
Which will help you endure all these evils.
You must also be young,
And have a short memory to quickly forget them.

Or, as I've written above,
You must find in yourself the strength to face the danger,
The fortunes of the sea,
The fatigue, the bad smells and the pestilence.

Nevertheless, and when all is said and done,
If you really want to see the Holy Sepulchre
And visit the Holy Land,
Go without further delay!

This poem was composed and completed at sea, in the year 1428,
On board a galley
Of 300 passengers in solidarity,
But there isn't one of them who could finish a bottle of cheap French wine!

6. A Walking Tour of Constantinople

Pera – Bucoleon – Hagia Sophia – Hippodrome – Equestrian statue – Church of Christ Pantocrator – Church of the Holy Apostles – Blachernae Palace

To plunder and to conquer remain two enduring stimuli to travel. In 1204 a somewhat improvised army of western Europeans, led by Venetians, launched an assault on the city of Constantinople. This assault, now known as the 'Sack of Constantinople', saw the Venetians wrest control of the city from its Greek rulers. Constantinople was described by its conquerors in breathless terms of wonder and awe. The Crusader knight and chronicler Geoffrey of Villehardouin wrote that those who had never before seen Constantinople stared on it earnestly 'for they never thought there could be in all the world so rich a city'. They admired the high walls and strong towers that enclosed it, the palaces and churches 'of which there were so many that no one would have believed it who had not seen it with his eyes'. For Villehardouin, Constantinople was an astonishing jewel to be possessed, a superlative city. We may call the 1204 assault a crusade, but it was as much about trade and trading privileges as it was about faith – about who would control the Black Sea, who would best pay the Venetians and who had access to the markets flowing in and out of the city. Throughout the Middle Ages, people visited Constantinople because they wanted to conquer it or, failing that, because they wanted a part of its great wealth.

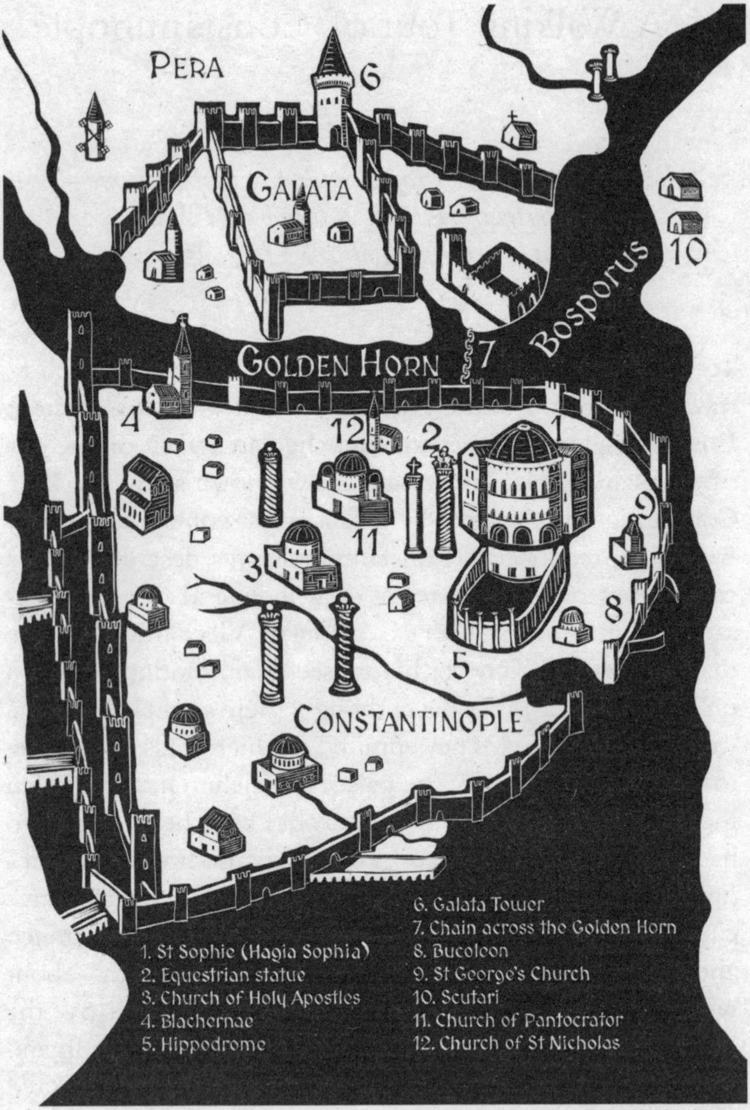
PERA
6
GALATA
10
Bosporus
GOLDEN HORN
7
4
12
2
1
11
9
3
8
5
CONSTANTINOPLE
1. St Sophie (Hagia Sophia)
2. Equestrian statue
3. Church of Holy Apostles
4. Blachernae
5. Hippodrome
6. Galata Tower
7. Chain across the Golden Horn
8. Bucoleon
9. St George's Church
10. Scutari
11. Church of Pantocrator
12. Church of St Nicholas

The city formerly known as Byzantium had become a teeming megacity between Europe and Asia. Constantinople was the largest city in the medieval west, with a population of approximately 80,000 people around 1350 (this was still much diminished, by war, plague, earthquakes and migration from the city's peak of perhaps up to 500,000 residents in the sixth century). Set across a vast walled area over seven hills on a tricorn peninsula, Constantinople was a place where for many visitors an august past collided with a precarious present. The Florentine traveller Cristoforo Buondelmonti's 1420s maps of Constantinople show classical antiquities and decorated columns set among crumbling ruins, domestic housing sprawling across the landscape between gigantic basilicas and imperial palaces, stark defences and walls, windmills and numerous harbours around the peninsula. By the fourteenth and fifteenth centuries, Constantinople's populace comprised a Greek Christian majority with established communities of Albanians, Amalfitans, Armenians, Bulgars, Catalans, Genoese, Hungarians, Pisans, Ragusans, Turks and Venetians, together with a large Jewish population. The city was in constant contact and dialogue with Latin Christendom and Islam, a true *cosmopolis*, a world city, the world in a city.

The city is everywhere defined by its relationship to the sea, especially the Bosporus, the channel linking the Black Sea with the Sea of Marmara and ultimately the Aegean and the Mediterranean. During the day, the seascape seems to reflect light back on to the city's breezy hills and their cypresses, cedars, oaks and fig trees. At night, the sea becomes vastly black, the pale stones of the waterfront battlements kissed by winds coming off the waves.

Visiting in the 1330s, by which point the city was no longer under Venetian control but was again ruled by

Byzantine Greeks, the German pilgrim Ludolph of Suchem gave an awestruck and detailed description of Constantinople, 'an exceedingly beautiful and very great city'. He described its many kilometres of walls, the triangular shape of its main peninsula and its 'sundry and divers ornaments, built by the Emperor Constantine, who named it Constantinople'. He listed the city's impressive churches and the cheap plenty of bread, meat, fish, the many different nations who dwelled there, the city's cold weather (in November Constantinople is often colder than Ludolph's native Saxony) and the immense quantity of turbot to be caught there, exported to all parts of Asia.

And yet, for all its wonder, Constantinople was defined by Ludolph by what had been lost. 'The reader should know', he wrote, 'that the Emperor of the Greeks and the Greek people once ruled over the whole of Asia, both the greater and the lesser.' By 'greater and lesser' Asia, Ludolph meant Asia Minor (the Anatolian peninsula) and Asia Major (the land beyond Anatolia to the east, covering what we now might term central Asia). Constantinople's power had since been hugely diminished, 'divided from the Church of Rome by schism' and through territorial losses. In spite of its grand monuments, later medieval Constantinople was repeatedly represented as a place of dispossession and precariousness, an isolated shadow of its former self, wracked with a kind of imperial melancholy.

In the following pages, we will take a tour of Constantinople's main sites, as they appeared to a visitor of the early 1430s, Bertrandon de la Broquière, who described the city with one eye on its past glories and the other on its future conquest.

*

Bertrandon was from a noble family of Labroquère, a village on the River Garonne just north of the French Pyrenees. As a young man, Bertrandon entered the service of the Burgundian court at Dijon. He gained the role of carver to the Duke of Burgundy, supervising the presentation of meats at banquets. By 1425, Bertrandon had a generous annual pension of 160 francs from the duke, Philip III, 'the Good' (1396–1467). He became part of the duke's inner circle and, in 1428, received the Burgundian town and seigniory of Vieux-Château.

Bertrandon became a trusted diplomat-spy for Duke Philip. In 1432 he received 200 pounds to undertake 'a certain long-distance voyage'. This was a reconnaissance mission to the Middle East. Bertrandon was asked to report on the state of the Ottoman Turks as they steadily annexed Byzantine Christian territory. Duke Philip harboured romantic ambitions of being a chivalrous crusading hero like princes of old, to eject the Muslims from the Holy Land and repulse them in their further attempted encroachments on Christendom. He also wanted to avenge the failed 'Crusade of Nicopolis' (1396), at the fortress of Nicopolis on the Danube. Here his father Philip II ('the Bold') and his brother John ('Jean sans peur', 'Fearless John'), had unsuccessfully fought the Turks.

On completing his secret, eighteen-month mission, Bertrandon was paid a further 800 pounds by Duke Philip. Bertrandon's written report of his journey is full of personal detail about his travels, revealing him as a keen and independent sightseer who relied on locals and strangers to assist him. He sometimes travelled as an emissary or diplomat, but at other times he wore disguises of local dress, to visit mosques and to travel incognito. On the whole he received a warm welcome as a representative of the Burgundian court (and, later in his life, he enjoyed a busy career as a Burgundian diplomat to the French court). Bertrandon was a field researcher and fact finder, travelling in order to provide a first-hand account of the state of the eastern Mediterranean.

Bertrandon set off in February 1432 and followed the pilgrims' route via Venice, Dalmatia and Cyprus. After visiting Jerusalem, the Holy Land and Sinai, Damascus and Syria, Bertrandon made his way to Constantinople. During this journey he befriended, and was protected by, an Egyptian named Mahomet. Throughout his written report, Bertrandon tells us a great deal about new foods he encountered (caviar was acceptable 'when there is nothing else to eat'), clothing (in Syria he bought 'knee-high, red boots, as is the custom of the country') and languages (for example, at one point, a friendly Jewish man from Caffa made a word list for him in Italian, Tatar and Turkish of 'everything that I might need on the road, for myself and for my horse'). To travel is to gain knowledge, but the knowledge is often of an unexpected and extrinsic sort.

Bertrandon's account of Constantinople provides a valuable tour of this teeming, conflicted and fateful city. We start our tour not in Constantinople proper but in the suburban district of Pera (now Beyoğlu), its name simply meaning 'beyond' in Greek, and its walled 'large town' Galata (Karaköy); the names Pera and Galata were often used interchangeably for the area. Pera lies across the waterway ('not at all wide, but very deep') of the Golden Horn to the north-east of Constantinople's historic peninsula. Bertrandon described Pera as inhabited in 1432 by Genoese merchants, who governed the town, along with Greek and Jewish colleagues. They were all under the lordship of an administrator, the 'potestat' or *podesta*, who was also the Genoese ambassador at the court of the Byzantine emperor and was appointed by the Duke of Milan, who also took the title Lord of Pera.

Pera had its own walls and defences. Most visibly, from 1349, the Galata Tower, a round Romanesque brick structure which replaced an earlier tower, called out to those arriving by sea, a familiar-looking beacon to western eyes. The tower was a pretty and delicate conical bastion, frilled with arches, resembling the kinds of buildings painted in the illuminated manuscripts presented to Duke Philip's court. Bertrandon found Pera's port 'the handsomest of all I have seen', and met with the Duke of Milan's ambassador there, to plot against the Venetians. Pera was the first port of call for many visitors from the west, effectively a well-developed colony for European travellers and expatriates. Bertrandon bumped into an old acquaintance, a Catalan merchant named Bernard Carmer, whom he had last seen in the Flemish town of Bruges. Carmer recognized Bertrandon and asked him to quit Pera in order 'to stay at his lodgings with him in Constantinople' and visit the city 'at leisure'. Bertrandon accepted his invitation, unable to resist a sightseeing tour with a resident expat.

Advice: To enter Constantinople is like entering a great forest: it's impossible to get around without a good guide. If you attempt to get around tightfistedly or cheaply, you won't be able to see or kiss a single saint's body unless it happens to be that saint's holy day (when one can see and kiss the relics).

Next, Bertrandon crossed over to the peninsula ('in the shape of a three-pointed shield') of Constantinople proper. Pera was then linked to the city by ferries (there was no bridge) crossing the 500 metres of the waterway called the Golden Horn (the mouth of which was usually blocked by a massive iron chain, so the Constantinopolitans could control shipping). From Pera, Bertrandon appraised the seven hills across which Constantinople is built. He noted that Rome and Antioch too are built across seven hills; like many travellers he looked for what makes a city similar to others, not unique. Bertrandon marvelled at the size of the city, which he averred was six miles across and eighteen miles in circumference. In his opinion, it was not as big and built up as Rome (in fact, Constantinople's population was around double that of Rome).

He first described 'La Blaquerne', the Blachernae, a fortified palace at the northern extent of the city walls. This was a complex of luxurious halls elegantly built in light brick on a tumble of terraces; the ruins can still be seen. The Blachernae was the centre of imperial authority, to where the emperor (then John VIII Palaiologos) and empress (Maria of Trebizond) resorted and where visiting dignitaries were received. Bertrandon noted the 'rather deep' moats defending the palace, but identified this as a potential weak spot, for 'it is here that the attack [of 1204] was successful'. Like so many visitors of the time, as he admired the city he pondered how it might be most easily captured.

Memories of conquest and defeat marked the next place Bertrandon visited, the harbour of Bucoleon, on the shores of the Sea of Marmara. He did not describe the imperial Bucoleon palace that once stood here. By this date, the palace had already fallen into disrepair. Instead, his curiosity was piqued by a burial site he was shown, 'a hillock of bones of Christians who were leaving Jerusalem and the Holy Land and Acre' at the time of the First Crusade (the 1090s). Bertrandon was told that the Greeks had ferried a great number of these Christians over to this place, 'out of sight of other people', and killed them all. Other Crusaders heard about this and fled to the shores of the Black Sea. So, Bertrandon claimed, appeared Circassians, Avars, Mingrelians and other Christian peoples in the area. His account is not historically accurate; the Caucasian Christian communities long predate the 1090s and the site was, in fact, full of graves of Venetians chased out of the city by Greeks in 1261. However, it reveals popular western impressions of the city's Greek rulers and Bertrandon's way of tying the entire history of the region back to the Crusades: an attempt to make sense, on his terms, of the area's complicated history of strife and multiple identities.

Bertrandon then made his way to 'the most remarkable and principal' of Constantinople's many churches. This was the Church of St Sophia ('the mother church where the patriarch is located') on the summit of Constantinople's first hill, near where the city's triangle gestured into the Bosporus towards Pera and Asia.

Dedicated to Hagia Sophia (Holy Wisdom) but often understood to be dedicated to a saint named Sophie, this massive circular church always inspired awe in visitors. First dedicated in the year 537 and still standing despite its position above a major fault line, the church was noted for its stupendous grandeur and enormous dome. It was built on a raised plateau above the Byzantine city's main harbours and commercial districts, and gives at once a sense of elegant height and solid permanence. It is constructed as a series of vaulted buildings, rising and culminating in its dome, the biggest in the world aside from Rome's Pantheon. Bertrandon remarked on the church's sculpted white marble and the pillars in several colours. Indeed, the church's patterned marbles came from across the world, from the French Pyrenees to Asia Minor. The marbles alternate between red panels with thick pink veins and light grey panels marked with dark grey triangles, interposed with beautiful lintels swirled with crimson and off-white.

The interior of the church was then decorated with golden mosaics showing Christ, the saints and the Byzantine emperors in sensitive, lifelike poses. One such mosaic survives in the south door vestibule, depicting the Emperor Justinian, his handsome head bowed respectfully, handing a miniature version of the domed church to the Virgin Mary while Constantine hands her a tiny version of the enormous walled city. In the south gallery, under the dome, a later mosaic shows Emperor John II Komnenos (reigned 1118–43) presenting a money bag to Christ and the Virgin. Abundant graffiti were scratched into the walls by visitors, in languages from Old Slavic Glagolitic to Norse and showing saints, ships, birds, angels and beasts, lasting traces of the diversity of people who had flocked there.

Hagia Sophia, after being ransacked in the assault of 1204, held fewer relics than it once had, and in particular its Holy Lance had started a western migration and multiplication, purchased in the mid-thirteenth century by Louis IX of France via Venetian brokers. Nonetheless, Bertrandon was told that the church still had the tip of the lance that pierced Christ's side, a relic then also being venerated in Paris (John Mandeville said he'd seen both, but was reticent about saying which, if either, he believed to be more authentic). Hagia Sophia also claimed Christ's robes, and another sponge on which Christ was offered gall (also claimed by Zadar), as well as the reed that was placed in Christ's hand in the Passion story. Bertrandon managed to see the gridiron on which St Lawrence was grilled to death (a relic also claimed by Rome's Basilica of San Lorenzo in Lucina) and a basin-like stone on which Abraham served food to the angels who came to destroy Sodom and Gomorrah (Genesis 18:1–15).

At Hagia Sophia, Bertrandon's curiosity led him to stay

and watch a divine service officiated by the patriarch. He was evidently interested in both the local religious customs and the reputed beauty of the Empress Maria (Maria Megale Komnene, 1404–39). He viewed a kind of dramatic playlet, representing the biblical story of Nebuchadnezzar and the three boys in the furnace (Book of Daniel 3:1–30), a performance also noted by other visitors. Then he spent the entire day, without eating and drinking, waiting for the empress, as he wanted to see her close-up and watch her mounting her horse. When he finally got a full view of her, he found her 'so beautiful', young and fair and a confident horsewoman. Her earrings were, in Bertrandon's eyes, especially noteworthy: they were made with large golden fastenings and decorated with precious stones, including rubies.

Next, in front of Hagia Sophia, Bertrandon lingered in the Hippodrome, 'a large and handsome square, surrounded with walls like a palace, where games were performed in ancient times'. The Hippodrome, a grand third-century arena 400 metres long, had curved, arcaded viewing areas around a large oval track. It was still in use as a sportsground for horsemanship throughout the Middle Ages. The Seljuk physician Sharaf al-Zaman al-Marwazi (d. 1125), who visited Constantinople in the early twelfth century, saw 'dogs set upon foxes, then cheetahs upon antelopes, then lions upon bulls' as the emperor, empress and a crowd of onlookers watched and feasted. Shortly afterwards, the Jewish traveller Benjamin of Tudela described it as 'a place of amusement belonging to the king', where a great entertainment was held each Christmas with acrobatic and juggling shows and animal fights with lions, leopards, bears with wild asses taking place there. 'No entertainment like this is to be found in any other land,' Benjamin wrote in wonder. The Hippodrome was described by John Mandeville in the 1350s as 'a pretty court for jousting' with 'tiered seats in which one can sit and watch and not impede other people's views'. A single retaining wall and lone stone bench from the Hippodrome survive today.

Bertrandon watched as the emperor's brother, Thomas Palaiologos (1409–65), Despot of the Morea, exercised and sported at the Hippodrome. On horseback in the enclosure, Thomas and his retinue of 'twenty or thirty knights' practised their archery, competing with a bow and arrow to pierce a hat thrown ahead of their galloping horses. This exercise, remarked Bertrandon, had been learned from the Turks.

At the time of Bertrandon's visit he would have seen at least three impressive ancient monuments on the *spina*, the low wall running down the Hippodrome's centre. These were the Egyptian obelisk of Theodosius (erected 390 CE), an ancient bronze column of three intertwined serpents that had been placed there, c. 330 CE, by Constantine, and the monumental limestone Column of Constantine Porphyrogenitus (emperor 913–59 CE), placed at the south end of the stadium in the tenth century. Although Bertrandon did not comment on these unusual monuments, he would have walked through this strange parkland of memorials to fallen empires and past power. Visiting ten years before Bertrandon, Zosima, a deacon from Muscovy, repeated the folkloric belief that the serpent column held snakes' venom and the column could be touched to cure the effects of a snakebite. The serpents' heads were broken off around 1700, but the column remains a strange and eloquent talisman that has witnessed the city's tumultuous history.

Bertrandon then briefly described the 'very beautiful church of St George', situated 'facing Turkey' (i.e. across from what is now the Asian side of the city). He was here describing the Church of St George of Mangana, an important church east of Hagia Sophia built on a lavish scale in the eleventh century. It claimed various relics, including some of the hairs from Christ's beard. Nothing now survives of the church.

Bertrandon then moved to the area between Hagia Sophia and the Hippodrome to describe one of Constantinople's most celebrated sights: 'a very high column of square stones with letters inscribed on it'. This equestrian statue bewitched visitors to the city, and almost all of them attempted to interpret its meaning. It stood in the square, the Agora, outside Hagia Sophia, and was surrounded by salespeople selling food and drinks, perfumes, icons and souvenirs.

Travellers often have to rely on second-hand information to interpret their surroundings, or they are forced to accept their guide's descriptions without questioning them. According to what Bertrandon was told, atop the column was the Emperor Constantine (reigned 306–37), cast 'in metal on a great horse holding a sceptre in his clenched fist and . . . his right arm extended with an open hand, towards Turkey and the land route to Jerusalem'. Bertrandon was told that this gesture was a sign all the territory as far as Jerusalem used to be under his control. In this reading, the statue was a remarkable monument to lost imperial authority.

Robert of Clari, a Crusader knight visiting from Picardy in 1204, had described the statue somewhat differently. He saw a thick column, three times as thick as a grown man's arm, fifty *toises* high (about 22.2 metres). At the top of the column was a stone, about 1.5 metre square, with the emperor on his horse, both cast in copper; the emperor 'stretched his hand out towards the heathen lands'. The statue bore a legend that 'the Saracens' would never have peace from the emperor. The Greeks identified the figure as the Emperor Heraclius (who reigned 610–41). On the horse's croup and on and around its head ten herons had made their nests.

Robert's 'herons' (possibly storks) add a nice touch of individual observation. The letters on the statue, in Robert's reading, declared that the Saracens should never have a truce with the Byzantine emperor, an anachronistic updating of the message which suited the Crusaders' needs and preoccupations. Robert also said that the effigy held a gold globe or orb with a cross (a symbol of global domination).

For all its significance visitors seem to have interpreted the statue in various ways, and even to have seen different things. Which prompts the question: what do tourists see? And who tells them what they are seeing? Many visitors, and most local accounts, identified the statue as that of yet another emperor, Justinian (reigned 527–65). The effigy was in fact intended to depict Justinian, but was probably a reused statue of the earlier emperor, Theodosius (reigned 379–95). The Florentine mapmaker Cristoforo Buondelmonti, visiting c. 1420, noted that the statue was of Justinian holding 'in his left hand a golden apple while with the right hand he threatens the east and Turkey'. The height of the column varies enormously across visitors' accounts but they mostly saw the statue, like many statues, joining imperial authority with imperial anxiety: the emperor was an awesome sight, but his statue's meaning tended to straddle fantasies of imperial power with apprehension about imperial collapse.

Bertrandon marvels, 'I have no idea how the statue was put up there, given its size and its weight.' It was about 30 metres high, the effigy alone on top of it over 8 metres high; it was one of the tallest free-standing columns in the world, and one of the largest statues in the west. The emperor-rider's nose was 23 centimetres long, according to one sixteenth-century visitor who furtively measured it after the figure was dismantled. It showed the emperor in battledress with a spray of feathers on his helmet (at several points while it was still standing, massive bronze feathers fell from the statue, causing alarm among the city's residents).

Around 1317 the orb's cross fell to the ground. Then, in the 1420s, the orb itself fell. Whenever bits of the statue came down, it was understood to be issuing a political commentary or prophecy. John Mandeville wrote that the figure 'used to hold an apple [or globe] in his hand, but the apple has fallen out of the effigy's hand'. This, 'people say', was 'a symbol that the Emperor has lost a large part of his empire'. Mandeville added that any attempt to put the apple back into the statue's hand would fail, and that its other hand was held up towards the west, 'as a symbol by which to threaten sinners'. Johann Schiltberger, an adventurer hiding out in Constantinople in the early 1420s, said that the golden apple once indicated that the emperor had power over 'Christians and infidels', but 'now he had no longer that power, so the apple has disappeared.'

Almost all visitors to Constantinople found the equestrian statue to be a breathtaking testimony to the city's imperial pasts, present and futures. For visitors, the column seemed almost to be alive in its capacity to change and in its prognostic ability to hold the city's precarious future in its massive hand.

Visitors to Constantinople gazed on the statue in wonder: wonder at its size, its meaning. There was no one single medieval list of the 'wonders of the world', although earlier Christian historians like Gregory of Tours (d. 594) and Bede (d. 735) had suggested such lists of places both biblical (Noah's Ark, the Temple of Solomon) and classical (the Colossus of Rhodes, the Capitolium at Rome). The equestrian statue at Constantinople achieved the status of a medieval wonder, a singular, special thing that could not be fully comprehended, a sight to see, a historical object that solicited admiration and curiosity.

Bertrandon also noted the nearby empty plinths of the 'gilded horses' we encountered earlier rearing up on the front of St Mark's Basilica in Venice. Until 1204 these horses (Bertrandon says three, but actually four) had been displayed here, beside the Hippodrome. The cityscape was further scarred by its location on a tectonic fault line: there were several major earthquakes here, including in 1346 when the dome of Hagia Sophia cracked.

Bertrandon then visited two proximal and important churches on Constantinople's fourth hill: the Church of Christ Pantocrator (the All-Powerful) and the massive Church of the Holy Apostles ('the Church of St Apostola'). The Pantocrator, built by the Empress Eirene in the twelfth century, was a monastery that enjoyed a splendid panorama of Constantinople, Pera and the Golden Horn, and included a large hospital (with at least fifty beds), a library and *scriptorium*, a pharmacy and a curative well. What most attracted Bertrandon's attention here was a relic of the Virgin Mary's tears. This took the form of a slab of stone on which Christ's corpse had been laid. 'It is a very holy thing, for you can see all the tears which Our Lady cried.' The tears seemed to Bertrandon like wax but, upon closer inspection, more like congealed water. He assured his reader that 'many people have seen this.'

The relic Bertrandon saw was the 'Stone of Unction'. The stone was said to have been brought to Constantinople in the twelfth century, and was described at the time as a red marble slab with the unique feature of the Virgin's tears on its surface. This was a directly parallel relic to the Stone of Unction in the doorway of the Church of the Holy Sepulchre in Jerusalem, which Bertrandon had visited on his pilgrimage there and which had been *in situ* for over a hundred years. Medieval travellers often saw the same thing in different places and did not seem to mind; things could make religious sense, rather than show historical veracity, and still be just as meaningful.

Bertrandon next visited the nearby Church of the Holy Apostles, built by Constantine as his mausoleum. The Holy Apostles, which was the model for St Mark's in Venice, was described by Robert of Clari in 1204 as being even more sumptuous than Hagia Sophia. Bertrandon saw here the shaft of the column to which Christ was tied to be beaten, on Pontius Pilate's orders. Bertrandon noted, approvingly, that it was of the same kind of stone as similar relics he had seen at Rome and Jerusalem. He also saw open wooden coffins which contained the incorrupt bodies of saints therein and, mistaking the Holy Apostles for the Pantocrator, saw the tomb of Constantine and his mother St Helena, raised on 2.5-metre-high columns.

The Pantocrator church survives as the Zeyrek Mosque, but its Stone of Unction does not. The Church of the Holy Apostles was comprehensively destroyed and the Fatih Mosque built on the site between 1463 and 1470.

Past the Holy Apostles, in the north-east corner of the city, Bertrandon moved on to the (reportedly small and badly roofed) Church of 'La Blaquerne', part of the Blachernae Palace complex. Here he noted the church's wondrous adornments, 'paved, painted, panelled and decorated in every possible way'. This was the magnificent Church of St Mary of Blachernae, mainly rebuilt by Alexis I around 1100, and the city's main sanctuary of its patron saint and defender, the Virgin Mary. This church contained an icon of the Virgin, covered in a veil which miraculously, on most Fridays, moved up slowly to reveal the Virgin's face. It then fell again slowly over the course of the next day. Bertrandon, like most other non-Greek visitors, does not seem to have been shown this icon. The church burned down in 1434 a couple of years after Bertrandon's visit. This was not, for once, through the violence of conquest but from an accidental fire started by children.

A tip: In Constantinople there is a famous icon of the Virgin and Child called the Hodegetria ('She who shows the way'), painted by St Luke himself. It's a wonderful large, decorated icon, held by the Convent of the Hodegon near Hagia Sophia. It's shown every Tuesday. The icon is placed on the shoulders of blindfolded men and it pushes and turns them about, this way and that, for they trust that through the icon she, the Virgin, truly shows the way.

Having seen all these Greek churches, Bertrandon noted that the Latin merchants had their own church situated at the place where one took the ferry to Pera and where a daily mass was said in Latin. He seems to have been describing the Church of St Nicholas at the Basilike food market, near the shore of the Golden Horn, on the north-eastern side of Constantinople overlooking Pera. The Church of St Nicholas was essentially a Venetian church and there was an icon of St Nicholas to which sailors came to pray to guard against drowning or to give thanks if they had been saved during a shipwreck. Some said that St Nicholas's arm had reached out of the lifelike painting and given gold coins to the faithful.

Bertrandon grew bored, sated by the city's churches. He wrote, 'there are other churches that I did not go into,' articulating the weariness of the diligent sightseer who has seen and said enough. He moved on to secular matters and the diverse merchants in the city, principally the Venetians and the Turks.

The Catalan merchants showed Bertrandon around. On Candlemas Day (2 February), they took him to a 'solemn service' with 'oddly dressed' chanting chaplains at the imperial palace. The Empress Maria watched from a window in an upper apartment. When Emperor John learned from the Catalans that Bertrandon was from the Burgundian court, he sent a messenger asking for news of the capture of the Virgin of Orleans, Joan of Arc (executed in May 1431, just before Bertrandon arrived in Constantinople). It is a neat portrait of how news of current affairs travelled by word of mouth from west to east via wayfarers like Bertrandon.

A few days later, the Catalans took Bertrandon to see the marriage festivities of one of the emperor's relatives where he watched a strange kind of tournament. A great post was put in the middle of the square and a large plank – a metre wide and a metre and a half long – was attached to it. Around forty unarmoured horsemen came galloping in one after the other, each with a small stick in his hand and doing all sorts of tricks. Then, after around half an hour of this display of horseback acrobatics, sixty or eighty sticks were brought out. The mounted bridegroom took one of the sticks and charged as fast as the horse could go, as if jousting. He hit the target, full tilt, so that he broke his stick ('without too much of a shock'). Then some of the men started to shout and play instruments, drumming 'in the Turkish fashion'. Then each man took his stick and rode at the target, each one breaking his stick. The bridegroom finished with two sticks bound together and he broke them on the target 'without hurting himself'. Bertrandon said it was well done, evidently having enjoyed the display. The emperor watched from a window, with the empress too, whom Bertrandon continued to find a very beautiful woman. Once the horseback joust was over, 'the party broke up, with no one hurt, and everyone went back to their lodgings.'

Bertrandon saw a curious spectacle, a display of horsemanship with music, a tournament without violence, a wedding celebration at which no one was hurt. This was an entertainment in which battling with deadly swords could be replaced by flimsy 'sticks'. The bridegroom 'proved' himself in the emperor's eyes in a mock-joust. It was as if this wedding celebration was a rehearsal for the men of Constantinople to fight a battle they knew to be inevitable.

It is not clear exactly how long Bertrandon was in Constantinople, but his stay there was an extended one. He left the city on 23 January 1433 and later on his travels he met the Ottoman sultan (Murad II, 1404–51) at the then capital Adrianople (Edirne). His account of the meeting is wide-eyed with wonder and exoticism, commenting on the 300 women and thirty boys the sultan had at his disposal for his sexual pleasure. The sultan, according to Bertrandon, could drink huge quantities (at least 'six or seven quarts') of wine. Bertrandon reported to Philip of Burgundy that he felt that the Ottomans would be easily defeated, on account of their poor weaponry.

Bertrandon would, within his lifetime, be proved wrong. Murad's successor, Sultan Mehmed II ('the Conqueror'), captured Constantinople for the Ottomans in 1453. The city rapidly became the thriving capital of an extensive Islamic empire that fundamentally changed the balance of power in, and access to, the eastern Mediterranean. The city visited by Bertrandon was transformed. As the monuments of Byzantine Constantinople were repurposed or eradicated, his account of the city came to refer to a world in ruins.

Some travellers' costs in Egypt and the Holy Land, 1392

Travellers in the Holy Land were required to pay for all the services they received. Prices were fixed by the Mamluks and Franciscans, and were high.

Here follows a selection of some of the prices of attractions and services in the Holy Land:

To the guard at Alexandria port on leaving: 1 ducat per person
To a dragoman for the journey to Cairo: 6 ducats per group
For each camel to carry victuals to the galley on the River Nile (a day's journey): ½ a ducat
For galley passage on River Nile to Cairo: 12 ducats per group, plus expenses for the dragoman's food
For the sultan's permission to travel: ½ a ducat each
For the Lord of the Arabian Desert's permission to travel: 5 grossi* each
To the Master of the Camels, that he might do his best: 3 ducats per group
For cameleers to St Catherine's Sinai: 6 grossi each

* Grossi were highly variable in value. In Venetian currency, a gold ducat was valued at 18 grossi in the thirteenth century. By 1440 the ducat was 28 grossi (according to William Brewyn), and by 1496 the ducat equalled 80 grossi. For rough comparison, a cow would have cost about 2 ducats (10 shillings in England) and a good horse about 44 ducats (200 shillings in England). Inflation was low, but many charges to tourists could change without notice.

For porters to bring one's things 2 miles from Gaza into Gaza: 3 ducats from all
Tribute to the sultan at Gaza: ½ a ducat each
From Gaza to Jerusalem: 16 grossi per mile
For going to the River Jordan: 3 grossi each

7. Through the Holy Land to Babylon

Jaffa – Acre – Gaza – Saidnaya – Bethlehem – Sinai – Materea – Cairo – Giza

The destination for most eastward travellers in the medieval Mediterranean was the Holy Land, *terra sancta*: not a country, but a landscape of memory and emotion, built from the stories of the Bible. It could stretch from today's Egypt to Syria and Jordan, from the lands associated with the Tribe of Naphtali in Lebanon to those associated with the Tribe of Judah in the Negev Desert, encompassing Sinai, Jerusalem and the Mediterranean coast from Sidon to Gaza and beyond. The land was holy for many faiths, who often shared and competed for the same spaces. The Crusaders tended to call the region 'Outremer' – overseas. Following the failure of the Crusades, 'Filastin' (Palestine) referred to one of the Mamluk subdivisions of the region, which was, from 1260 to 1517, mostly ruled from Damascus. Later Europeans often used the term 'Syria' for the whole region. Depending on the traveller and their motives, the Holy Land promised victory or profit or the soul's salvation.

The most popular European travel guide, Mandeville's *Book of Marvels and Travels*, became one of the most widespread sources of knowledge about the Holy Land. It was translated into many different languages, and for many years was used as a guidebook. This was in spite of, or perhaps because of, the fact that the author had not written an eyewitness guide. Instead, he constructed an encyclopaedia of travellers' stories, a farrago of previous writings, some 'historical', some 'geographical'. Mandeville opened his *Book* with a lyrical and passionate encomium to the Holy Land, 'the Promised Land'. This land, he says, is 'like the most excellent lady and it is sovereign over all other lands, it is blessed and hallowed by the precious blood of Our Lord Jesus Christ'. His simile of the lady is apt: like a lady in a medieval courtly romance, the Holy Land was overrepresented, a thing to be loved from afar with thwarted ardour, possessed in spirit but, mostly, not in fact.

According to Mandeville, Jesus chose this land in which 'to take flesh and blood' and travel about it on 'His blessed feet', performing miracles, preaching and teaching, and finally suffering 'so much disgrace and mockery for us'. For these reasons, 'every decent Christian who is able' should, he said, 'fortify himself to conquer' that land, the 'best over all other lands, the most virtuous, the worthiest in the world' – evinced by its location in the middle of the world.

Mandeville's praise for the Holy Land is representative of how travelling there was discussed in medieval Europe as the highest purpose a human life could attain. To go to the Holy Land was to attain righteousness, glory, joy, comfort and pleasure. Or at least that was the idea.

For much of the journey by sea, travellers became frustratingly passive, resigning their agency, witnesses to and observers of a journey beyond their control. The pilgrims – from all over Europe – miscommunicated with each other in any number of dialects, relying on signs, gestures, improvised Latin and lingua franca, a blend of Venetian, Genoese, Catalan and Provençal, used mainly for commerce and transactions. For all that we think travel helps us see the world anew, a great deal of travel is about misunderstanding.

After Cyprus, the passengers eagerly looked to the horizon for a first glimpse of the coastline of the Holy Land. At sea, the horizon offers boundlessness, constantly shifting with the boat's passage. The term 'horizon' entered western European languages in the twelfth and thirteenth centuries, derived from the Greek *horos*, a boundary, division, separation.* The horizon – a threshold rather than a line – was believed to mark the divide between the traveller's earthbound vista and the celestial vault above. Yet the limits of geographical knowledge and the limits of the traveller's sight were usually charged with significance and peril. If to travel is to broaden one's horizons, this might better be thought of as a hazardous journey to the edge rather than a prospect of limitless possibilities.

Eventually, and surprisingly suddenly, the horizon gave way to the irregular vertical contours of the towers and fortifications of the coast of the Holy Land: the towns of Jaffa, Acre, Ashkelon, Gaza and other renowned places, half remembered from the Bible. The first person to spy land gave a cry, and the boat's passengers and crew drew together in the tonic zeal of arrival to utter a prayer. With tears and sighs they usually sang the hymn *Te Deum laudamus*, 'God, we praise you', an anthem of public joy and spiritual affirmation.

The sea rolling into Jaffa was full of longing to arrive, longing to be embraced by the Holy Land. Jaffa was described by Mandeville as 'the oldest town in the world' as it was believed to have been constructed before Noah's flood. The

* In older English, the word used was 'eaggemearc', literally an 'eye-limit', an edge fixed by human sight, one's purpose or intention as framed by the eye. In other languages the word for a horizon suggests a holding in of the world's circle, or gestures to lands beyond this world or beautifully evokes the sky's shoreline, for example, the Norwegian *himmelleite* ('heaven-sight') and *himmelsyn*, ('heaven-view'). Equally poetically, the Hebrew *ofek*, 'horizon', ultimately derives from an ancient term for 'the place from which the rivers flow' (*afek*; 'the overflowings of the sea [*afki yam*] appeared', 2 Kings 22:16).

port appears as the entry point for the great cedars conveyed 'in floats by sea' from Lebanon for the building of the Temple in Jerusalem (2 Chronicles 2:16), and it is where Jonah went to find a ship and pay his fare, before his encounter with the whale (Jonah 1:3–4). From around 1300, following the retreat of the Crusaders, Jaffa was the primary port for boats from Europe (alternatively, pilgrims came via Alexandria and the Sinai); the Mamluks regulated all visitors to the Holy Land by processing them through rudimentary facilities at Jaffa's port. But the harbour at Jaffa was shallow, a jagged and sometimes perilous anchorage with a natural sandstone reef that made a breakwater, with inhospitable rocks scattered among the waves. European passengers disembarked on to the sandy beaches at the foot of the town.

Pero Tafur, a Castilian nobleman travelling in the 1430s, gave a representative summary of what arriving on a Venetian galley in the Holy Land was like. First, at Jaffa the ship's arrival was made known, 'almost at once', to the Prior of Mount Zion, the head of the Franciscans in the Holy Land. He would then send 'two or three friars' to see 'the Governor of Jerusalem' (a Mamluk administrative official, a military captain), who would issue the sultan's safe-conduct to the friars for the new arrivals. The pilgrims would then prepare to disembark and give their names in writing to the governor, and themselves retain another list; this was to stop any kind of 'imposture' – subterfuge and espionage – taking place. As the travellers left the boat, there were 'Moors' waiting, 'ready with asses which the pilgrims ride all the time that they are in the Holy Land'. The fixed price for hiring the animals was 2 ducats, 'and this cannot be increased or diminished.' The governor and the friars travelled with the pilgrims to the nearby town of Ramla, 'a great place, five leagues [20 kilometres] from Jaffa, where there is a hotel founded for pilgrims'. There were apartments there for men and women, and pilgrims like Pero spent their first day and night in the Holy Land in its safe lodgings.

It's notable how orderly and organized the arrival was, with the Franciscan-Venetian administration working hand in hand with the officers of the Mamluk sultan (the Mamluks occupied Jerusalem and its environs from 1250). The priorities were to prevent harmful espionage and to extract money from the travellers. The bureaucratic regulation of the travellers, begun in earnest in Venice, continued here, with the 'names in writing' of the visitors being logged into the efficient machinery of the Mamluk government.

On disembarking in Jaffa, the new arrivals saw the ruins of the Crusaders' vanquished settlement and failed conquest. Atop the steep hill on which the town is located stood the ruins of the once great Church of St Peter, built soon after the Crusaders' conquest of the town in 1099. It was dedicated to St Peter, for this is where he was said to have raised Tabitha from the dead and where he spent many days with Simon the Tanner (Acts 9:36–43). The church claimed various relics, including St George's head. But its vaulted ceilings were destroyed in 1197, crushing townspeople sheltering there from the invading Ayyubid forces. The church was repaired in the 1220s but then left in ruins in 1268 by the Mamluks, who stole some of the relics and burned others. After that, the debris of the church overlooked the port, a sign of the Crusaders' defeat. Meshullam of Volterra, visiting in 1481, described Jaffa as 'a place all in ruins'. Broken churches and abandoned houses perched above the harbour, far from the soaring towers and busy alleys they had once been.

Most travellers weren't as fortunate as Pero Tafur in swiftly leaving Jaffa. Konrad Grünemberg in 1486 described how on his arrival the Mamluks held his boat at anchor for sixteen days outside Jaffa, during which time some of the passengers died. The travellers' provisions barely sustained them and may well have been what killed them: weeks-old biscuits, addled eggs, unripe grapes, overripe apples, sour wine of variable quality, impure water. Mamluk officers kept watch on the boat from Jaffa's towers, and eventually raised a red flag as a sign of peace and sent the boat's patron a large turtle as a gift of greeting. Only then could Grünemberg and his hapless fellow travellers come ashore.

Others visitors had to wait in the desolate caves by Jaffa's sea port or, in Bertrandon de la Broquière's case, in 'a few tents covered with reeds', to shelter from the sun. For many, the arrival at Jaffa was nothing less than awful, a descent into Hell rather than ascent towards the Heavenly Jerusalem. Thomas Larke, clerk and chaplain to the English courtier Richard Guylforde, described in 1508 how on arrival his group was 'received by Mamluks and Saracens, and put into an old cave, by name and rank'. The Mamluk scribe wrote their names down, and they were left in the cave, 'upon the bare, stinking floor' night and day, and were 'treated really horribly by the Moors'. Similarly, Konrad Grünemberg explained how each passenger (all of them men) in his galley disembarked with a small bag around his neck with bread, a little bottle of wine, a few hard-boiled eggs, cheese, a comb and shaving things. About 300 armed Mamluks ('heretic Christians' and 'infidels . . . not quite as black as the Moors') flocked around his group. The Governor of Jerusalem asked each passenger for their name, and this was entered into a book with a reed quill. Grünemberg and his fellow passengers were then shown into two ancient caves, full of stinking donkey dung, where they stayed for two days on a handful of straw, for which they were charged several *marchetti*. During the day, people tried to sell things to his group: undercooked pancakes, beads, rosaries and 'some kind of porridge'. During the night, Grünemberg was charged 4 *marchetti* to use the hole-in-the-ground latrine outside. One knight from Grünemberg's party was badly beaten up for refusing to pay to use the latrine. He died of his injuries the next day.

The travellers' foreignness was marked through their clothes, their posture and their attitude. Indeed, travel often involves one's foreignness seeming to become the crucial element of one's character. Mistrust between the travellers and the local residents of the Holy Land was reciprocal. On arriving in Jaffa, visitors like Grünemberg were immediately conspicuous in the bright sun, the uncomfortable surroundings and the tall heat. Cash was demanded from them for every single thing. Coins seemed to vanish as if money had no worth. Throughout their Holy Land journey, the traveller incurred a litany of costs which were entirely beyond their control; fees for safe passage and 'looking after' their possessions played on their sense of vulnerability. The traveller's discomfiture, a kind of weary shock in response to the situation to which they had surrendered themselves, grew obvious.

A marvel: In the north of the Holy Land, somewhere between Tel Arqa and Raphanea, there's a wonderful river called the Sabbatory or the Sambation. It shows how holy the Holy Land is. People say it has different attributes. Some say that it dries up entirely every Saturday, the sabbath, and flows lustily for the rest of the week. Others say that it flows only on Saturdays; for the following week, it stands still and doesn't flow at all (or hardly at all). Some say it's the boundary to a lost Jewish tribe, its foaming waters a boundary that will be traversed only at the end of days. Who knows? Many people have set out to find the Sabbatory. Merchants and pilgrims hear about it often. But it's very hard to find.

*

The whole coastline was marked by broken altars and scarred battlements like those at Jaffa. The eastbound highway to Ramla and Jerusalem snaked across the coastal plain, the dusty roads sullen with the memories of battles, conquests and refugees. But before one takes that route, we shall perambulate a little in the Holy Land, for it offered the medieval traveller a wonderland of challenging but captivating experiences.

Jaffa changed hands many times between 1187 and 1268, when it was conquered by the Mamluk sultan, Baybars (1223–77). Given this turmoil, the Franks energetically developed a new capital at the port of St Jean d'Acre, just over 100 kilometres north of Jaffa on the Mediterranean coast. It quickly became one of the most dazzling cities of the medieval Middle East. During the Crusader period, Burchard of Mount Zion, who wrote an early travel guide to the Holy Land in the 1280s, described Acre as stoutly defended by 'towers and the strongest walls'. Burchard said Acre's resident defenders, the King of Jerusalem, the Knights Templar and the Knights Hospitaller, could overcome all the 'Saracens', 'if it pleased God'. The population of the walled city in the late thirteenth century may well have been in the region of 60,000 people. Crusader Acre was a grand project: imposing fortifications, a lighthouse, hospitals, a sewerage and cistern system and about forty churches, designed both to welcome the traveller to the Holy Land and to secure the Latin west's foothold in it. The Crusaders developed the city as a centre for the import and export of sugar, olive oil and spices. Varieties of Arabic, Italian and French were widely spoken in Crusader Acre, and the impression is of a deeply multicultural milieu – there were Templars and Hospitallers, whose massive building projects survive today, as well as Genoese, German, Pisan, Provençal and Venetian districts in the Old City, and an English and Irish area in the northern suburb of Montmusard beside the Mediterranean coast. There were Jewish and Muslim inhabitants, as well as Armenians, Greeks and Samaritans, and constant contact with Cyprus. The Iberian Muslim geographer Ibn Jubayr visited in 1183 and noted how one small mosque was allowed. The Jewish sage Moses Maimonides passed through the port in 1165, and the prominent Jewish scholar Moses Nahmanides resided there in the 1260s. There is even a record, from 1111, of Jewish Alexandrians drinking beer in Acre's Crusader-owned taverns.

Like other ports, Crusader Acre became a desirable destination in itself; indeed its citizens were often regarded in Europe as wallowing in luxury. A circular walking tour of the city, starting at the land gate, was the subject of a medieval poem, 'The Pardons of Acre'. It enjoins travellers to visit the city for the good of their soul: among other benefits, they were promised 1,500 days' remission from sin just for approaching the edge of the town, 1,135 days for visiting the biggest church in town, the Cathedral of the Holy Cross, and 40 days for each time one toured the sick languishing in the Hospital of St John the Baptist.

In 1288, the head of the Hospitallers knew that the high life in Acre was coming to an end. The Hospitallers moved their Chapter General from the city to Limassol in Cyprus. In 1291 Acre was violently conquered by the Mamluks. It lay devastated and became a massive siege-scarred ruin. The Mamluk victors had little interest in sea ports and they systematically abandoned the Crusader coastal cities in order to prevent attempts at reconquest. Jacopo of Verona, visiting Acre in 1335, found it 'dashed to pieces and cast down, a habitation only for snakes and wild animals'. Other visitors said that the anchorage had been spoiled by the Mamluks, who had placed large rocks in the shallow water to prevent future reconquest.

The Mamluks produced and sold various commodities highly desired by the west – spices, silks, gems, glass and alum (used as a dye fixative), for example – and Mamluk culture was often admired, coveted even. At the same time, most western visitors were at best grudging towards the Mamluks who controlled the Holy Land. Many were rude about them, appalled by the idea of Muslims having control of the lands of the Bible.

John Poloner was a German pilgrim who visited the Holy Land in 1422 – that is, 130 years after Acre had been conquered. At Jaffa, Poloner 'did not see any living man' and wrote that 'many of the cities along the sea coast were destroyed by the Sultan when he heard that Acre had been conquered by the kings of France and England [i.e. the Frankish Crusaders].' The town of Caesarea, he added, was utterly destroyed. Near Ashkelon, on the coast south of Jaffa, he was shown the ruins of a Crusader fort built in the mid-twelfth century to 'check the insolence' of the Ashkelonites, but now he saw that the city of Ashkelon had been entirely subjugated by the 'Saracens' of that land. Further north, at Sidon (a Crusader fiefdom 1110–1260), Poloner said, 'the ruins to this day bear witness to its greatness.' Sarepta (now Sarafand, Lebanon) had only a few houses, he wrote, but 'its ruins show that it once was a noble city.' Batroun, a Crusader lordship from 1104 to 1289, was 'once a rich city, but now utterly destroyed'. In short, Poloner's experience was like that of many visitors to the post-Crusader Holy Land: the failure of the Crusades, and the victory of Islam, was everywhere etched in the built (or ruined) environment, even as unofficial shrines and chapels continued to attest to the holiness with which the land was suffused. The whole coastline gave off a suggestion of violence only temporarily suspended.

It was most common for visitors to the Holy Land to head south rather than north. From Jaffa and Ashkelon, travelling on the coastal road, one came to the port of Gaza, described by John Mandeville c. 1356 as 'exceptionally pretty and full of people and near the seaside'; Gaza was a key settlement on the main road linking Damascus, Jerusalem and Cairo.

Gaza had no walls but boasted a magnificent church in the town centre. This had been built after the 1150s by the Crusader settlers, between Gaza's Muslim and Christian quarters, probably on the site of an ancient Philistine temple that had also been a Byzantine church and a mosque. The Crusaders used the *spolia* (plundered remains) of various ancient buildings (including churches and a synagogue). Their church was an elegant arcaded structure, its nave rising up in seemingly weightless vaults. Its marble portal was carved with leaves, and a rose window decorated the west front. The church's groins and buttresses and pilasters and piers would not have been out of place in Paris or Provence. The Crusaders were ejected from Gaza in 1187, after just forty years of occupation, by the forces of Saladin (d. 1193), founder of the Ayyubid dynasty and a leader of Muslim reconquests against the Crusaders. The church once again became the Great Mosque (as it remains today).

Some later visitors commented on Gaza's desolation, a landscape of 'ruined uninhabited houses', as Guillebert de Lannoy wrote in 1421. Later visitors to Gaza knew it as a fearsome place in which the Mamluks imprisoned unwitting visitors. Felix Fabri described Venetian sea captains being threatened with imprisonment and Arnold von Harff was bound in irons there for three weeks. Fabri and his companions had a wonderful hot bath in 1483 at the vaulted marble hammam, where a local 'master of the bath' rubbed, washed and anointed them 'most kindly and courteously'.

Others worried about the desert bandits around Gaza and corsairs off the coast; visiting in July 1481, the Jewish-Italian traveller Meshullam of Volterra described how travellers had to transit in convoy. In the *funduq* of Khan Yunis, just south of Gaza, Meshullam thought the city a 'fine and renowned place', celebrated for its fruit, but he found no other visitors there, because on the previous night 'sixty men' had been captured in 'four fishing boats that had come from Rhodes'. Everyone else had fled from the *funduq* for the safety of Gaza. When he reached the city itself, Meshullam found that robbers were still in the vicinity, stealing the merchandise from travellers' laden camels. He was told that it would not be safe to leave 'until we had a caravan of four to five thousand men'. He estimated that 7,000 men and 10,000 camels were waiting in Gaza until it was safe to leave on the route north to Damascus.

Likewise, Felix Fabri witnessed the city locking down as a host of 'many thousands' of Mamluk soldiers from Egypt entered it and threatened to plunder the markets. Fabri waited, and when Gaza's markets reopened he bought huge amounts of stuff in order to equip himself and his companions as they crossed the Sinai: sacks of bread, jars of wine and waterskins; a whole kitchen, including trivet, gridiron and spit; three coops of fowl and 'a great white cock who stood upon the coop' and marked the time with his crowing in the wilderness; various baskets, hung on hooks from the saddle, and sacks of dried and salt meats, cheese, butter, oil, vinegar, corn, onions, almonds, medicines, candles, shoes, eggs.

In due course, this enormous haul caused a dispute with Fabri's dragoman, who said most of it was 'superfluous' and would require three extra camels to transport across the desert. And, besides, much of it ended up being stolen on the way as Fabri and his companions slept.

Knowledge of Islam in the west remained fragmentary. The Quran was first translated into Latin in 1141, by the Englishman Robert of Ketton, a priest and astronomer who became a deacon in the Spanish city of Pamplona. Robert translated several Islamic works to assist with the conversion of Muslims to Christianity, promoting knowledge of Islam in order to refute it. At the same time, a variety of anti-Islamic invective circulated in Europe, revealing the anxiety of Christendom about the rivalry of Islam. We might assume that contact with the Holy Land brought a better understanding of contemporary Islam, but this was not always the case.

The pilgrim Konrad Grünemberg was interested in the theological content of Islam, and he used his 1486 journey to find out more about it. He and his party asked some Muslims about 'the essence of their faith and general customs', which he wrote down in his guidebook in some detail. The Muslims explained their key prophets (Muhammad foremost, and Moses, David and Jesus) and the gift to all humanity, sent by God via Muhammad, of the Quran. Grünemberg was told that Muslims were obliged to pray five times daily, and that in their church (i.e. mosque) no one would dare 'chat with his neighbour' or 'crack a joke': they would be both ridiculed and fined.

Grünemberg reported that Muslims' holy day was Friday, when they listened to prayers and afterwards distributed alms. They washed assiduously to prepare for prayer and shaved their bodies (except men's beards and women's heads). They cut their fingernails and toenails carefully too, as a form of cleansing. They bathed after evacuating their bowels and passing gas, they carefully washed nostrils and eyes and practised fasting. At the end of their long fast (Grünemberg's version of Ramadan) he says they embraced each other and wished each other a 'happy Easter' (clearly, he was mapping his own practices directly on to Islam!). Grünemberg was particularly interested in the prohibitions of Islam, especially on wine. He explained this on the grounds that 'the wine in this region is very strong' and the 'Infidels' get drunk immediately and start acting 'totally irrationally'. In his case, he did not seem to enquire from the Muslims what the theological basis for the abstention from alcohol was, blaming instead the local wine that he had sampled and the locals' behaviour, which he repeatedly said he found erratic.

Grünemberg was certainly curious about the meaning of Islam. In the Holy Land, he said a Jewish Arabic-speaker translated for him the words of the call to prayer from a minaret. Yet his account of Islam is full of western inventions and misunderstandings. For instance, he writes that Muslims make pilgrimages, along with Turks and Tatars, to 'Al-amegga' (Mecca) 'where Muhammad is buried or, so they say, his body flies about in an iron coffin'. Although Muhammad died in Mecca he was in fact buried in Medina. The story of the flying coffin was from western literature and had a long pedigree as an anti-Islamic transposition of Christianity. The story dated from the twelfth century and Latin Christianity's increasing contact with Islam through crusade, trade and intellectual translation. Originating in Embrico of Mainz's *Life of Muhammad* (c. 1100), a number of Christian texts had popularized the story of Muhammad's coffin 'suspended in the air' (not unlike the marvellous crucifix encountered earlier at Stavrovouni in Cyprus), hovering between the floor and the ceiling in a mausoleum at Mecca.

According to Embrico, this was achieved through a trick involving magnets in the ceiling. The flying coffin seems an uncanny object of the traveller's imagination, a symbol of the terrifying magic of other religions, but it might be better understood as an image of a failed ascension to Heaven. In this way, the idea of the airborne coffin as an object of veneration represented a kind of anti-pilgrimage, an unholy sepulchre, Mecca as an erroneous Jerusalem.

Grünemberg repeated the ignorant slur that 'Saracens, Turks and Infidels practise indecent relations with animals and among each other', and this goes unpunished because 'a man needs to get rid of his seed'. By his own admission Grünemberg compared what he'd learned about Islam in the Holy Land with what he read in his own books upon his return to Germany. Much of the additional information he gave is clearly not from his actual encounters with Muslims but from Christian anti-Muslim literature, the kind of thing that saturated medieval chronicles, sermons and theological tracts. It is a useful case study of the limits of eyewitness encounters, for Grünemberg evidently did not trust or believe what he had learned on his pilgrimage and instead re-researched Islam, preferring western 'authority' and knowledge over experience.

Like many commentators on Islam, Grünemberg also included a description of the Islamic idea of Paradise; other people's ideas of other worlds were a constant source of speculation. According to Grünemberg, the Islamic Paradise was a 'boundlessly vast' land of the sweetest green meadows and flowery fields, streams brimming with milk and wine, lakes full of fish, vines drooping with heavy bunches of grapes, a never-ending harvest season. He compared this Paradise to other famous non-Christian paradises, like the Greek goddess Hera's orchard, the Garden of the Hesperides, where 'the woods abound with tame cattle and with game that is easy to catch, and the birds taste as delicious as their warbling is delightful'. But the Islamic Paradise was even better than such pleasure gardens: for here all one's 'voluptuous desires' could be satisfied, with willing partners. In this Paradise, God would send angels as servants, as swift and attentive tapsters, delivering everything one wants.

It is striking that a traveller like Grünemberg, whose Holy Land pilgrimage was for the benefit of his own soul, thought deeply about other definitions of life after death. He was formidably rude about Arabs and mostly judgemental about the 'scandalous and wicked' Islamic faith, but he also found himself being educated in comparative religion. Like so many others, he had travelled to the Holy Land to find salvation; but travel opens the mind in unpredictable ways. Curious and easily distracted, he found himself researching other values, other ideals and other worlds beyond.

Away from the coast, the entire area of the Holy Land held an array of official, semi-official and unofficial holy sites, which came and went over time. It also held various impressive castles, many of them the legacy of the Crusaders' occupation.

The main draw for more resourceful travellers in the northern region of the Holy Land was at the remote monastery of Saidnaya, north-east of Damascus. Standing atop a rocky pinnacle, the monastery held a remarkable painted icon, tended by a small community of nuns and monks. The icon, showing the Virgin Mary, exuded a marvellous sweet oil, a kind of sweat which could cure all ailments. Moreover, the icon sometimes became incarnate, taking on a kind of fleshliness as if come to life, the word made flesh. The Virgin's own chest and stomach became akin to a living body, and people touched the carnal icon and confirmed it with the proof of their own fingers. Phials of the wonderful oil were collected and taken far and wide. People said that even the icon's oil could itself turn to flesh and could bleed, as had been proven by an impious Crusader knight who had taken his knife to a phial of the holy incarnate liquid.

More commonly visited destinations included Bethlehem, Nazareth, Mount Quarantine and the River Jordan. These were all firmly established in both Crusader and post-Crusader itineraries. At Bethlehem, just a few kilometres south of Jerusalem, there were dozens of sights to be seen, clustered around the Church of the Nativity. An anonymous Englishman who wrote an account of his travels there in 1344–5 said the Church of the Nativity was a 'wonderfully beautiful and large' church with mosaics on the walls ('and in all the world', he said, 'there are none more beautiful'). The grotto chapel at the church, marking the site of the Manger ('the pen of the cow and the ass', as the Anonymous Englishman wrote) where Jesus was born, was almost an afterthought in many travellers' accounts. The 'original' holy site of the Nativity had long been just one among many affecting and dazzling places to see, as invented traditions and new spaces reflected current trends and visitors' needs.

When the Anonymous Englishman of 1344–5 left Bethlehem he had a confrontation which both undercut and confirmed the holiness of his experience. He and his fellow travellers had drunk 'ample good wine' there (Bethlehem, as a Christian town, did not have the same strictures on wine, or produce the poor-quality wine, that the pilgrims complained about in Muslim towns). Having travelled a couple of kilometres out of Bethlehem, the Englishman and his well-oiled party were suddenly beset by four of the sultan's soldiers ('Satan's attendants', as he called them) on the hunt to seize their gourds of wine. They alighted on an Englishwoman who was drunk (having failed to mix her wine with water, as was the custom). Emboldened by alcohol, as travellers often are in unfamiliar places, she struck one of the Mamluk soldiers' horses with her pilgrim's staff. The soldiers retaliated, making to beat her with their steel whips. And yet, so the Anonymous Englishman said, their whips were quite unable to touch even the hem of the soused Englishwoman, due to the protection of the Virgin Mary. The Anonymous Englishman wrote that the Mamluks 'stood dumb, fixed to the earth', and he adduced the words of the prophet Habakkuk: 'In thy anger thou wilt tread the earth under foot: in thy wrath thou wilt astonish the nations' (Habakkuk 3:12). Even the party's guide was stunned. The group were able to go on their way, understanding the incident as yet further proof of their God-given right to the land through which they stumbled.

Southwards, beyond Gaza, the road led through the desert of the Sinai peninsula. The travellers and their animals trudged across the same hot sands over which Moses and Aaron had led the children of Israel as told in the book of Exodus. Visitors were shown sites – little more than palm crosses in the sand or piles of stones – that marked intimate moments in this sacred history.

Bernhard von Breydenbach, a cleric from the German city of Mainz, traversed this desert in 1483. Breydenbach was an ambitious and educated man, a dedicated pilgrim and an innovative publisher. He travelled to and around the Holy Land as a kind of tutor and counsellor to the nobleman Johann zu Solms (fl. 1482), and their group included an accomplished artist, Erhard Reuwich (1445–1505). Their shared project was to produce a new kind of travel guide, combining encyclopaedic reading about the region with Breydenbach's observations and experiences and Reuwich's eyewitness illustrations of the people and places they encountered. The resulting book, the *Peregrinatio in Terram Sanctam* (*Pilgrimage to the Holy Land*) became one of the best-sellers of the early era of printed books in Europe.

We join Breydenbach and his companions as they make their way across the Sinai Desert to the celebrated but isolated Monastery of St Catherine's at Mount Sinai. This group (which also included Felix Fabri of Ulm) had decided to extend their travels, adding the more intrepid leg of the journey after having seen Jerusalem. Accompanied by a local guide, they left Bethlehem on 27 August and travelled via Hebron and Gaza and then due south through the desert. On 16 September they finally saw Mount Horeb, then believed to be the upper part of Mount Sinai, where Moses had received the Ten Commandments. They spent ten days at the monastery housing St Catherine's relics, and departed on 27 September.

St Catherine's Monastery sat behind very thick walls near the foot of the mountain. It was originally dedicated to the Virgin Mary, but by about 1300 the relics of St Catherine had become the main draw. It had, during the Crusader period, been a wealthy institution but by the time Breydenbach visited it was isolated and its ownership was a matter of contention. A few Greek monks maintained the monastery, serving the pilgrims from various denominations who arrived there.

Some visitors carved their names on the monastery's walls, doors and furniture: 'Swinburn' (Thomas Swynburne, later Mayor of Bordeaux, who visited in 1392, with his equerry Thomas Brygg), 'Wilhelm von Diesbach 1466' (recording the visit of the Mayor of Bern), 'Anselmus Adournes' (Anselm Adornes, merchant of Bruges, who visited in 1470 with his son, leaving an eloquent account of their visit), 'Lambert Vande Walle' (a Bruges kinsman of Adornes), a 'Dertlot' who visited in 1332. The graffiti at Sinai record dozens of international visitors of various ranks and classes, as travel to such intrepid places became a desirable signifier of devotion and cultivation. To carve one's name was to become part of the site's unique holiness, and to leave a personal testament that the journey had been worth making.

There were reliable and reasonably comfortable lodgings for pilgrims. One visitor in the 1330s, Antony of Cremona, described Venetian cauldrons, worked in copper, that the monks used to feed 400 people at a time. But, by the later fifteenth century, Latin Christians like Breydenbach and Fabri had been excluded from mass in the monastery's main church. They were mostly offered just a quick glimpse of St Catherine's marble tomb, and instead they were shown into a 'Chapel of the Franks', a narrow room with a decorated altar of St Catherine; Breydenbach's group were lucky enough to be shown the saint's relics by the abbot. When Breydenbach visited, the relics seem to have been Catherine's head and hands, well preserved and revered by local Muslims and by Christian pilgrims, although no longer exuding the holy oil observed by earlier visitors. Each member of Breydenbach's party was given a tiny piece of the cotton wrap in which Catherine's relics were held.

Fabri described how his trip to St Catherine's was led by Georgian ass drivers who fearlessly guided pilgrims from Jerusalem to Egypt. He found them 'handsome men, civil, courteous and cold in manner, not liable to bursts of passion', and therefore, he concluded, 'especially fitted for crossing the wilderness', just like the kindly, reliable asses that transported him and his companions through the dust and sand. Once he reached Sinai, Fabri's joy had several shadows cast across it. First, many of his fellow pilgrims were grievously ill. More pressingly, he was troubled by the presence of hungry Arabs, who had camped outside the monastery. He assumed that they were there to steal his group's vast quantity of luggage, perhaps to extort 'unjust dues' from him. These Arabs did nothing to Fabri and his companions, 'either of good or evil', but 'their waiting there was grievous' to him. One's travels are often haunted by one's fears.

Then there was another bad-tempered dispute about who would carry his baggage, which threatened to prevent Fabri from ascending Mount Sinai in peace.

After his labours and expenses in crossing the desert, Fabri wanted to feel the transcendent joy of reaching the pilgrims' destination. But competing narratives, facts on the ground and the rigours of travel across 'frightful and precipitous' mountains all kept reasserting themselves. Fabri's Italian-speaking guide, one Brother Nicodemo, made sense of the landscape for him, narrating legends and miracles that had occurred there. No matter how good his experience of the place, Fabri worried constantly about 'the numbers of the Arabs . . . continually increasing' in and around the monastery's precincts. He was full of excitement and joy at communing with the body of St Catherine and walking in the footsteps of Moses, but he was mostly concerned about the 'evil habits and grave errors' of the monks at the monastery and the 'ungrateful dogs', the Arabs, whose very presence oppressed him and stimulated a kind of arrogant fear at every step. Such sourness is the dominant note of Fabri's time at St Catherine's.

His stay came to an ignominious end when one of his party was accused of chipping off a piece of the saint's coffin 'with an iron tool'. Fabri's group saw that the coffin had indeed been damaged (Fabri himself had earlier described the 'vicious curiosity' of pilgrims chipping off bits of stone at the Holy Sepulchre in Jerusalem). They were threatened with being handed over to the Arabs. Secretly, the culprit replaced the piece of stone. The matter was forgotten, but only when Fabri and his party had paid a parting 'gift' of money. It was a final humiliation which showed, unequivocally, that places like Sinai weren't Fabri's to possess.

After crossing the Sinai westwards, the landscape transformed, from mountainous desert to the lush Nile delta. Breydenbach recorded the great fertility of the land, planted with olives, palms and other trees. Its fecundity was announced by the touristic attraction of the gardens of Materea, about 14 kilometres north-west of Cairo.

Materea had originally been a Christian shrine, where a tree, which became known as 'the Virgin's Tree', had bowed to the Virgin Mary and sheltered the Holy Family during their flight into Egypt (Matthew 2). A later story said that the Virgin had rinsed the clothes of the young Jesus in spring water here, and the waters had caused the fruitful gardens to thrive. By the Middle Ages, a kind of pleasure park had developed at the site, with a well flowing with sweet waters and a grove of celebrated balsam (balm) trees. Tourists were charged, in 1392, the small sum of 2 grossi to enter. These trees emitted a highly prized soothing aromatic resin, used in medicine and perfume and as a preservative (hence 'embalming'). The balsam gardens at Materea were held to produce the best balsam in the world, because they sprang from the soil where the Virgin Mary herself had rested and from the waters touched by her son's clothes. Balsam, mixed with rose water, was sold to visitors, but fake balsam abounded, and many travellers' guides warn the visitor to be wary of counterfeit balsam made with turpentine (pine resin).

In the fifteenth century, the gardens seem to have been configured around an ancient fig tree, celebrated as the tree under which the Virgin had rested. Breydenbach wrote that, after 'the horror of the immense solitude and aridity of the desert', his group were 'captivated by the delicious coolth of

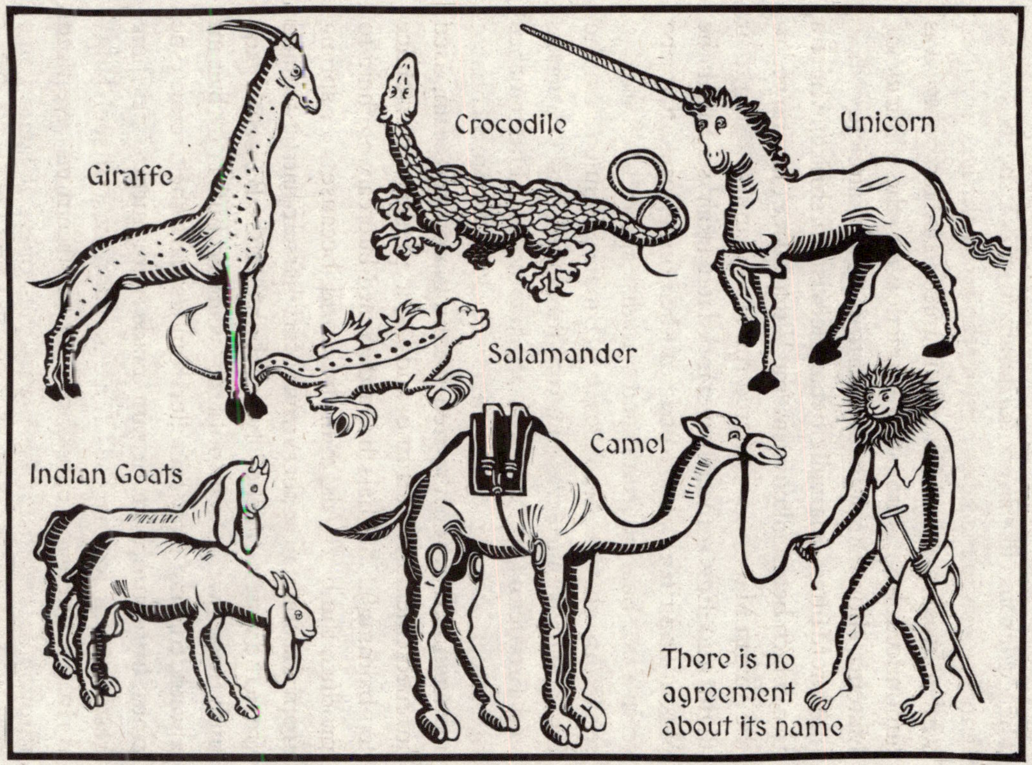
Giraffe
Crocodile
Unicorn
Salamander
Indian Goats
Camel
There is no agreement about its name

these gardens and by the fertility of the sun'. They stayed there for a couple of days, relaxing. One of his party, Conrad the lutenist, taught their local dragoman how to play the lute. The garden was like an actualization of two of the most celebrated spaces in medieval culture: the *hortus conclusus* (a walled garden, itself symbolic of the Virgin) and the *locus amoenus* (an idealized 'pleasant place' of recreation and edification). Like the Holy Family, Breydenbach's group quenched their thirst at Materea, marvelling that the hostile landscape of the Sinai had so suddenly transformed into this welcoming pleasure garden.

But there was something yet more remarkable there, about which many Europeans had read but which they had not seen: a tree bearing fruit called 'paradise apples', or 'mose' (a rendering of the Arabic *mawz*, banana/plantain) by the locals. It had huge leaves ('15 to 16 foot long', nearly 5 metres, said Breydenbach). Yet more remarkable were the bunches of sweet oblong fruit. Many, including Breydenbach, reported that when the ripe fruit was cut into, each slice revealed the image of a cross with all the features of a crucifix. It was as if holiness had transfused every living thing in the Holy Land. If one thinks of one's journey as a pilgrimage, the sacred can appear anywhere. This strange fruit – which would gain the name of 'banana' only in the sixteenth century, from a west African word – was also said to rot within a week, making its succulent deliciousness all the more precious. But its imprimatur with a cross suggested to travellers like Breydenbach that the Christian reconquest of such lands was by no means improbable given the signs, erupting through nature, that it was always the holiest of lands. Later Breydenbach would write a herbal guide, *The Garden of Health* (*Gart der Gesundheit*), in which he described how his trip to Egypt and the Holy Land had helped him identify useful plants and see their correct colour and shape: religious travel was natural history and vice versa.

Before they left Materea, Breydenbach and his group celebrated a solemn mass at the Virgin's well. Some dived several times into the fountain, hoping to find new health in its waters. But it was time to move to the main attraction: the magnificent city of Babylon. This was not the biblical city of Babylon (in today's Iraq) but the great Mamluk city of Fustat, then being absorbed into greater Cairo.

Babylon (later called 'Old Cairo') had developed around the city's Roman citadel (often called 'Fort Babylon'), to the east of the Nile. Fustat then grew, adjacent to Old Cairo, settled by the Arabs from the seventh century, and the city of Cairo (Qahira), to the north-east, was itself settled in earnest by the Fatimids in the eleventh and twelfth centuries. In the 1170s, Saladin built a magnificent citadel on a hill between Fustat and Fatimid Cairo, and during the Mamluk period the city reached its apogee – elaborate new palaces and civic buildings sprang up and the city's population made it probably the largest city west of China (about half a million people lived there around 1300). Minarets and domes and gables of an astonishing variety dominated the skyline. The city held numerous attractions for intrepid travellers – trade opportunities, wondrous shrines and the chance to have an audience with the Mamluk sultan, who kept his capital there.

Breydenbach entered Cairo on 9 October 1483. He was amazed by the size of the city and found its long streets teeming with the entire world; he wrote that he was 'constantly harassed, tugged at and booed at, by the "pagans"'. But he was led straight to a magnificent palace, richly decorated with hangings and paintings, and was able to rest there and seems to have been able to make himself at home. He wandered through the palace, viewing his host's many possessions: wives and eunuchs, spoils of war and armour, saddles, horses, elegant furnishings. The next day he and his travelling companions were shown to their rooms in the palace by their guide, a Jewish convert who had first become Christian and then turned Muslim. Breydenbach had arrived in the middle of Ramadan, and marvelled at the way in which the city lit up at sundown and filled with noisy feasting and luxurious parties.

Breydenbach's time in Cairo involved a number of encounters with people who moved between faiths, not always harmoniously. Within twenty-four hours of arriving in the city, he was approached by a Christian man in shackles, begging for money. This man had been jailed for two years for having bought two Muslim children from a man in Alexandria; the Christian man had intended to bring them up in his faith, contrary to Islamic law. The next day Breydenbach heard about a Hungarian man who had outwardly converted to Islam, but 'carried a faithful heart in the guise of a Saracen'. Then he saw three captive Christians, shackled and almost nude, bemoaning their bad fortune and requesting alms; it transpired that the Mamluks were accustomed to sending their prisoners out into the streets three times a day in order to beg.

On 13 October, Breydenbach visited the city's markets; his party was divided into groups of three or four, each with a guide. He says that he couldn't believe his eyes when he saw the merchandise there, the number of people and their riches. He bought armour, silks and curious animals. But his status as a customer and tourist was suddenly queried at the slave market. Here he watched, fascinated and sympathetic, as children were put up for sale. But then a merchant turned to Breydenbach's guide and asked how much the slaves who walked with him would cost. Breydenbach was suddenly turned from customer into merchandise, from viewer to viewed. His guide smiled and, after being offered 10 ducats per person, made clear that Breydenbach and his companions were not on the market.

In Breydenbach's account, slavery was everywhere in and around Cairo. On the banks of the Nile he saw a huge group of enslaved people baking bricks, and they brought to his mind the Israelites forced to labour for Pharaoh and liberated by Moses. Breydenbach viewed the city with a kind of horrified wonder. Its population seemed marvellous to him: he guessed it was larger than all of Italy's. The citadel alone, he said, occupied a space bigger than the entire city of Ulm or about half the space of Nuremberg. The various animals he saw were indescribable too. He noted the Cairene houses, made of loam and bricks, unprepossessing on the outside but full of ornate elegance indoors. People harassed him and his group constantly in the street, but he seems to have been curious enough, or sufficiently confident in his group and guide, to continue his tour.

Breydenbach was eventually, on 16 October, received by the sultan, one of the most powerful men in the world. Breydenbach was awed by the sultan's citadel, replete with many attendants and an incredible number – 'impossible to describe' – of horses, stables and spacious apartments. But the reception was a spectacle rather than an interview. Breydenbach and his group were shown through a set of doors and saw the sultan on his throne, surrounded by silent Mamluk guards, 'in an attitude of profound respect'. Breydenbach records nothing of what was said or done, but after an hour his group were escorted out and shown a large marketplace where camels, donkeys and horses were being sold. They were then given lunch before going to the baths, elegantly ornamented with mosaics and various marbles. They saw there the 'marvellous art' of massage.

Breydenbach's extended account of Cairo is poised between the sacred past of the Holy Land and the mercantile-political present of a Mamluk megacity. He was, in Cairo, repeatedly lost for words at the worldly wonders he saw. There he was emerging from, but still invested in, a landscape that was entirely understood through its biblical origins. The seductions of the present were becoming evident, and confusing challenges to one's identity took place daily.

Distinctly visible from the heights of the Mamluk citadel were the golden stone Pyramids set in the sands at Giza beyond the city. In fact, the Pyramids were well known to the residents of medieval Cairo: they had been raided for their elegant white limestone facing in the construction of several of the city's medieval building projects.

Simon Fitzsimons, the Irish friar writing in the 1330s, and John Mandeville, writing in the 1350s, both repeated the commonly held medieval view that the Pyramids had been built as granaries for the biblical Joseph. They believed that Joseph stored corn here during the seven barren years, as in Pharaoh's dream (Genesis 41).

In this account, the 'extraordinarily ingeniously made' Pyramids were forgotten structures from the Bible, Pharaoh's dream made massively manifest in ancient stone inscribed in different languages. Two of the Pyramids, said Mandeville, were 'astonishingly high and wide', and they were totally full of snakes. He repeated the idea that the Pyramids were 'graves of great people of olden times, but the general opinion is that they are Joseph's barns'. Why, he wondered, would anybody build such a high structure for a grave in any case? Simone Sigoli, visiting in 1384, wrote that the Pyramids were 'among the biggest edifices to be seen' and were 'built of very great long thick stones and in shape like a diamond'. 'Just imagine', he added, the 'very great amount' of corn that could be placed inside.

As was true throughout the Holy Land, biblical allusions were translated into highly literal and material sites, or in this case the opposite – an interesting monument turned into Pharaoh's dream. Mandeville's spiritual or exegetical meaning imbued ambiguous sites like the Pyramids with a higher meaning and implicitly claimed the site as Judeo-Christian (rather than, say, ancient Egyptian or fourteenth-century Mamluk). Indeed, Simon Fitzsimons was at pains to argue that 'it is not likely' that these were tombs, as that would have detracted from their biblical origin. This was a touristic curiosity without exoticism; on the contrary, the pilgrims' treatment of the Pyramids was a kind of inquisitive familiarization.

Sigoli's travelling companion Giorgio Gucci was more sceptical about these 'granaries . . . of giant structure'. He had been told they were 'made by Pharaoh at the time of the great famine' in the era of Joseph, but they seemed to him more likely to have been made for 'perpetual memory rather than granaries'. In almost all tourism there develops a space for doubt: travellers ask themselves, am I really seeing what I've been told I'm seeing? Was this worth the journey? Am I looking at something real?

Bernhard von Breydenbach believed that the Pyramids were pagan shrines and graves and the Sphinx (a man's face on feline haunches) a 'great idol of Isis'. On a woodcut map that accompanied his book, the Pyramids appear as tiny pinnacles in the desert, beside the Nile flowing to Cairo. Another German pilgrim, Arnold von Harff, approached the Pyramids in 1497. He described them as 'very strange buildings', constructed of large heavy stones. It took him and his group three hours to climb to the top, apparently of the Great Pyramid, and they took in the view over the countryside as far as Alexandria and the Mediterranean. They rested at the summit and ate a meal they had brought with them, and then climbed down again, only to have arrows fired at them by some hostile locals. Harff gave both possible origins for the Pyramids: 'they say' that Pharaoh built them as granaries, but 'some say' they were the tombs of the old Egyptian kings, and Harff was puzzled by the lack of an entrance.

The Pyramids are an arresting example of a tourist destination coming into being. They solicited a quasi-archaeological, historical impulse in their visitors. Their beauty, their enormousness, their beguiling inscriptions all suggest the enquiring gaze of the tourist rather than the devoted pilgrim (though, as we have already seen, the two were rarely far from each other). Most Christian visitors, who visited the Pyramids en route to or from Jerusalem or Sinai, were circumspect about the idea that they were Joseph's granaries. In this way, the Pyramids suggest the secular and humanistic impulses of later tourism, where the traveller's eyewitness investigation trumps the need to justify their curiosity through pious interpretation.

We now return to our route and take the road to Jerusalem, the single most represented – indeed enormously overrepresented – place in the medieval European imagination.

How to cross the desert

Tips from Meshullam of Volterra's account of his voyage across the Sinai, 1481

1. Every man must carry on his beast two sacks, one of biscuits and the other of straw and fodder.
2. You should also carry waterskins, because you cannot find sweet water in the desert, only brackish.
3. You must also take lemons with you, to deter insects.
4. You should travel in a large caravan, because of the robbers who frequent the desert.
5. You must go slowly for two reasons: first, because there is so much dust in the desert and the horses sink in it up to their knees, and second, if the dust rises and gets into a man's mouth and makes his throat dry, it can kill him with thirst (and if he drinks hot brackish water, he's in even more trouble).
6. A man who does not know Arabic should dress like a Turk, so he's not mistaken for a Jewish or Frankish visitor (and then taken prisoner and held to ransom); wear a white cover on your head like the Turks and Muslims.

7. Take a long, pointed piece of iron with you, to push into the ground to fasten your horse or ass to it, as there's nothing else to fasten them to, not even a shrub.
8. It is the custom not to feed donkeys, or give them anything to drink, except at the caravan when they are all together; the locals say it is a great sin that the other horses or small donkeys should see another one of them eating, because that would hurt those who are not eating, and that is cruelty to animals.

8. A Walking Tour of Jerusalem

Mount Joy – Jaffa Gate – Muristan – Church of the Holy Sepulchre – Via Dolorosa – Mount of Olives – Dome of the Ascension

The pilgrims' route from Jaffa to Jerusalem, the *via maritima* from the coast, was a thread of dust through the landscape. After a time, the coastal plain swelled into hills and valleys, then into mountains. Strange trees and dry bushes lined the route, their thorny panicles snagging the pilgrims' clothes and legs. A few abandoned houses were passed, some with goats living in the crumbling rooms. Each pilgrim group was accompanied by a couple of barefooted Mamluk escorts, armed with bows and arrows. The pilgrims had to depend on, and feign politeness to, local translators for even the simplest thing. They rode together on tired asses and spitting camels, using clucks and admonitions and polyglot insults to get the beasts to move onwards. And every single thing – each blessing, indulgence, sip of watery wine – continued to cost money. There wasn't a person in Jerusalem who didn't profit – either in their soul or in their wallet – from Christ's death.

During the daytime, the heat was astonishing. The ground baked. The air made one feel like one was breathing inside a bread oven. The pilgrims' mouths were gaspingly dry and the sun reached everything. Even the light was hot. And then, at night, the entire atmosphere turned violently cold, suddenly as chilly as a Pomeranian winter.

The pilgrims often progressed by night and took shelter from the scorching weather during the day. If they slept at all, they bedded down in the most rudimentary lodgings, in tents or caves and sometimes simply on planks or cotton-filled mattresses. There were said to be scorpions, crocodiles and dragons in the area. Turbaned locals, non-Christians accompanied by recalcitrant camels, passed them on the route. Local boys jeered, and the pilgrims worried constantly about brigands, robbers and thieves.

For medieval Christians, every single thing in God's creation was essentially good, especially in the Holy Land; but it was hard for many of the pilgrims to remember this as they made their way, with difficulty, through what seemed to be hostile terrain.

European visitors were shown their first view of Jerusalem from the hill known as Mount Joy (now Nabi Samwil), about 9 kilometres to the north-west of Jerusalem's Old City. Here, at the summit of a rocky peak, they found the tomb of the biblical prophet Samuel. The tomb was housed in a small stone building that was, and remains, at once church, mosque and synagogue. History and culture sedimented, layer upon layer of sacredness and conquest, piling up to a tensely shared summit.

Clustering around the tomb and church–mosque–synagogue stood a village, its inhabitants Jewish and Muslim. Jewish and Muslim pilgrims from all over the world made their way, alongside the Christians, to the top of Mount Joy, to worship Samuel there. The Christian pilgrims were more interested in the vista of Jerusalem, the final object of their journey, shimmering in the distance. Their guides encouraged them to dismount and to undertake an informal ritual: they removed their shoes, turned towards the holy city, knelt on the ground and wept with the joy of having seen Jerusalem, the joy that gave Mount Joy its name. From here, the holy landscape resonated with the biblical words 'Great is the Lord, and exceedingly to be praised in the city of our God, in his holy mountain' (Psalms 47:2).

Around 1107, shortly after the Crusaders' conquest of Jerusalem, the abbot Daniil of Kyiv, visiting as a pilgrim, described how at Mount Joy the whole party dismounted and placed little crosses on the ground. They then bowed to the Church of the Resurrection (i.e. the Holy Sepulchre). 'No one can hold back tears at the sight of that desired land,' wrote Daniil, where 'Christ our God suffered his Passion for the sake of us sinners'. There are dozens of accounts, from the Crusader period to the seventeenth century, of visitors performing a similar ritual at Mount Joy. Margery Kempe, upon first seeing Jerusalem during her pilgrimage of 1414, was so overcome with 'joy and sweetness' that she nearly fell off her ass. She had to be comforted with medicinal spices by two German companions. They thought her seriously ill rather than emotionally or spiritually overwhelmed. For travellers like Kempe, who had long imagined Jerusalem and already visited it in their mind's eye and in their heart, Jerusalem was one of those places where one is never present for the first time.

Similarly, the Duke of Milan's secretary Santo Brasca, visiting in 1480, wept over the view from Mount Joy as he knelt on the ground. He tearfully sang a hymn, 'Blessed city of Jerusalem, called "vision of peace"'. He then said a short prayer which listed the abuses which Jesus Christ Himself had endured in that very city.

But perhaps the pilgrims cried less out of joy than out of relief that their arduous journey had brought them to their destination. Given the long, sweaty, uncertain voyage they had undertaken, their guts roiling and their nerves frayed, is it any wonder that the sight of Jerusalem was a comfort?

From Mount Joy, Jerusalem looked tiny beneath the travellers' lofty gaze. Godlike, they overlooked the living map of their destination through which they would walk a few hours later. The medieval pilgrims' ritual of taking in a joyous vista of Jerusalem offers an analogous experience to arrival by aeroplane, as the landscape became part of their panorama. The thing about a distant city vista is that one doesn't see the city's details or its many imperfections: its foul grime, its dilapidated ruins, the rats, the people fighting with each other, the unruly children jabbering in foreign tongues, the frightening food being served in the street markets, the piles of camel shit on the dismal streets, the lepers thronging outside the city.

A vista (from the Italian *visto*, something seen) is more often about *not* seeing; for the vista allows the eye to glide over the landscape, smoothing the rubble, making fuzzy the particulars of reality. This is especially true with tears in one's eyes, as was the case for most of the travellers seeing Jerusalem for the first time. For the devout traveller, 'vision' was more about feeling than about seeing.

To set foot in the earthly Jerusalem was to set foot in the most desired and most represented place in the world. Jerusalem was both the centre of the world and its summit. The city was sometimes referred to as the planet's navel, its *umbilicus*: the point of origin, the central node, the hub of the world's wheel, the junction from which all life departs. The Jerusalem pilgrimage was the most precious trip one could take, worth all one's money, even worth one's life: to die in Jerusalem, in imitation of Jesus Christ, was considered the best of deaths. Indeed there are many reports of pilgrims dying before or shortly after they reached Jerusalem. Pilgrims were frequently buried at Aceldama, the 'Field of Blood' just outside the Old City, where Judas had hanged himself, a tradition that came about because the field is mentioned in the Bible as the 'burying place for strangers' (Matthew 27:7). The Anonymous Englishman visiting in 1344–5 was one of many visitors who described the unique burial arrangements there, a structure with 'ten round openings into which the bodies of the dead are thrown down to the bottom, upon those already dead'. Visiting from Pomerania in northern Germany in 1486, Sir Jan Branborken died at Ramla and another German knight, Dietpold von Habsberg, also died nearby, and their bodies had to be carried at great expense on stretchers from Ramla to Jerusalem for burial at the Franciscan priory at Mount Zion. From England in 1506, Richard Guylforde and his travelling companion Prior John Whitby of Guisborough in Yorkshire both fell 'sorely sick' near Mount Joy. Camels had to be hired, 'with great difficulty and outrageous expense', to rush them to safety in Jerusalem. Within a week they were dead, buried at Mount Zion. As Guylforde languished and expired, his clerk, Thomas Larke, eagerly went about his pilgrimages to the city's holy sites.

Most medieval European visitors to Jerusalem had little knowledge of the actual city they were entering, but they did have a deep, collective memory of it. It was a city the visitors knew from stories, guidebooks and written polemics, through a form of geography that is the true meaning of that word's Greek origins: *geo* + *graphia*, writing about the world. But by the fourteenth century this collective memory had become solidified into the stones of the buildings themselves, as the Jerusalem landscape was reconfigured around the needs, desires and biblical memories of pilgrims, its most ardent visitors.

The Jerusalem of the Middle Ages was largely restricted to a compact area, about 1 square kilometre, the Old City. In the

Mamluk period (1250–1517), Jerusalem's walls were ruined, except on the western side through which European travellers entered. They arrived in the city via the Jaffa Gate (also known as David's Gate, Pilgrims' Gate, Fish Gate or Merchants' Gate), the western gate. This is adjacent to the Tower of David, a Mamluk citadel that had once been a Crusader fortress (and, long prior to that, Herod's Palace), guarding the city's western approaches. The Tower of David, its pale stones decrepit and sunbeaten but handsome, stood like a superannuated sentry tasked with watching over the city gate and the many waves of people that flowed through it.

Jerusalem is always changing but the layout of the Old City endures, independent of the faiths and empires which have claimed it. Its main streets still trace the axes of the Roman city. The eastern side is dominated by the raised, flat area known as the Temple Mount, once the site of the Jewish Temple and in the Middle Ages the site of the Dome of the Rock (where Abraham went to sacrifice Isaac on the summit of Mount Moriah). The Dome of the Rock was, during the Crusader occupation of Jerusalem, an abbey known as the Temple of Our Lord. The nearby Al-Aqsa Mosque, also on the Temple Mount, was the headquarters of the Knights Templar. From 1244, after the Crusader loss of Jerusalem, Christians were definitively excluded from the entire Temple Mount, and its buildings were rededicated to Islamic worship. In 1340 Ludolph von Suchem repeated something that was evidently told to many western visitors: Christians entering the Temple Mount 'must either die, or renounce their faith'. The pilgrims had put themselves into a perilous but thrillingly exotic contact zone.

The north-eastern corner of the city was a warren of streets associated with the Via Crucis or Via Dolorosa, the route Jesus was made to take from His betrayal in Gethsemane to His

Crucifixion at Calvary. These alleyways ran through markets, mosques and madrassas and, near the Temple Mount, passed by the city's main latrines.

The western side of the city was dominated by its churches, including the Church of the Holy Sepulchre, the Armenian Cathedral of St James, as well as David's Tower. Nearby, in the south-west, just outside the broken-down eleventh-century city walls, was Mount Zion. This was the headquarters of the Franciscans and all western Christians in the Holy Land. Between Mount Zion and the Temple Mount was the focus of the Jewish settlement, where lived Jewish people both local and from Europe, usually in houses rented from Muslims. All these parts of the city were connected by alleys and passageways of a baffling intricacy.

Bernhard von Breydenbach, visiting in 1483, stipulated that one must not ride into Jerusalem, but should rather enter it on foot. Many of the pilgrims abandoned their shoes on reaching the city, in order to enter Jerusalem humbly – and literally – in the footsteps of Jesus. At the moment of stepping inside the city, Breydenbach says, one received full forgiveness for all one's sins, a plenary indulgence. This was one of the most spiritually valuable places in the world. When one's feet touched the stones, one became grounded, rooted, in the city's fabric.

If medieval travellers found spiritual nourishment on first entering Jerusalem, it would have been in spite of, rather than because of, the environment in which they had put themselves. The first thing recorded by the Englishman William Wey, entering the city in 1458, is that boys threw stones at him. Felix Fabri of Ulm, in 1480, described how young locals gathered round and laughed at him and his companions. Meshullam of Volterra, visiting in 1481, was ill, 'at death's door', from the moment he arrived in Jerusalem until he left its 'ruins'. The first impression of Pietro Casola, visiting from Italy in 1494, was that he was 'almost dead from heat and thirst'. As he went about the city, he noted the ugly houses, the long, vaulted street market (the *suq*) selling all kinds of very cheap food, the women's faces covered by black veils and the well-dressed handsome men in white or silken outfits like quilts.

Fabri also noted the eastern Christians scandalously sitting around playing games like dice, 'out of superstition', in the dilapidated vaults of former churches. Almost all visitors mentioned the city's disarray: churches in ruins, broken altars, Crusader monuments shockingly turned over to Islam. Piles of pale limestone masonry littered the streets. Perhaps the best days of Christian Jerusalem had been in the earliest years of the Crusader occupation, after 1099; as euphoria blended with arrogance, the task ahead was the building of a new Jerusalem, complete and unified and freshly arrayed. The Crusaders thought, as have so many others, that the city would be theirs for ever.

Jerusalem is a city of unfinished projects. By the fifteenth century – 250 years after Saladin captured it from the Crusaders – it was a living monument to the failure of the Crusades. Bertrandon de la Broquière, visiting in 1432, described Jerusalem as 'a fine, large city which looks as if it has seen better days'. And yet this very estrangement, a kind of disappointed wonder that the city wasn't like the 'Jerusalem' that pilgrims had been led to believe they would find, characterized a place utterly different from the world from which they had come. They had now set foot in the city of Jesus Christ's life and death; they could not go back home unchanged.

The pilgrims were led from the Jaffa Gate by their Franciscan guides first either to the Muristan Hospital, the main lodging place for western visitors, or directly to the Church of the Holy Sepulchre. Both were just a few minutes' walk away, through the narrow alleyways of the *suq*. The Muristan (its name comes from a Persian word for a hospice) was somewhere between a western hospital and an eastern caravanserai, a giant hall with some smaller rooms attached to it. It had been built in the Crusader era by the Knights Hospitaller but, by the later fifteenth century, it was pretty much in ruins, simply an address pilgrims could give and a place where they could curl up on the floor and try to sleep.

The Muristan was, by all accounts, a disgusting place to stay. It seems to have had almost no facilities, its walls and roof barely intact. The dormitories backed on to the food shops of the *suq*, which meant that it was both noisy and smelly. Visitors had to buy their food and water from local hawkers who thronged around the entrance. Guests were given a small space to sleep on the floor, on a carpet or a straw mattress. Felix Fabri estimated that about 400 pilgrims lodged there, in 'squalid and ruinous' conditions. Other visitors comment on the filth, the stench and the constant noise of the locals. After having paid a small entrance fee (half a ducat in 1392, according to the English pilgrim Thomas Brygg), pilgrims could stay at the Muristan for as long as they needed, or for as long as they could bear it. Abutting one wall of the Muristan was the Zawiyat-Darja, a small mosque and hospice for visiting dervishes, the sect of Sufi mystics who had taken a vow of poverty. This would have vividly demonstrated to the Christian pilgrims that they were not the only ones visiting Jerusalem in search of holiness.

Some pilgrims seem to have stayed at the Muristan for just a few days, others for up to six weeks. Even though Christian visitors to Jerusalem were there to imitate Jesus's suffering, lodging at the Muristan was a step too far for some. Other accommodation options in Jerusalem included staying with the Franciscan friars at their house on Mount Zion (available to visiting clergy and nobility only), or renting a room from a member of the local Jewish, Muslim or eastern Christian communities. Bernhard von Breydenbach stayed in the small house of his local interpreter. Gabriele Capodilista, visiting from Padua in 1458, saw the state of the Muristan and immediately refused to stay there, choosing instead to find private accommodation elsewhere in the city.

Most visitors spent a minimal amount of time finding somewhere to stay, as they were keen to get straight to the Church of the Holy Sepulchre. The prevalent travel guide of c. 1283 by Burchard of Mount Zion speaks for most Christian visitors when it says that the Church of the Holy Sepulchre held 'first place' among all the holy locations of Jerusalem. The church is a rambling complex of chapels and shrines, originally built by the Emperor Constantine in the fourth century. The Crusaders, on taking Jerusalem in 1099, found it in a seriously damaged state, the Caliph al-Hakim having ordered its destruction and burning in 1009. It was gradually rebuilt and significantly extended by the Crusaders, who united its various sites under one roof. Their church, which largely stands today, was dedicated in 1149. It holds both the Tomb of Jesus Christ and the site of Calvary/Golgotha where Jesus was crucified, and a panoply of other shrines and altars. It is a kind of holy museum, famously ramshackle, of ancient and new traditions.

Different denominations and groups have long fought over the church's hallowed ground. It was the same in the fourteenth and fifteenth centuries: from the 1350s, visitors to the church would have found a mixture of Christian groups there, with separate altars tended by Armenians, Ethiopians, Georgians, Greeks, Jacobites, Nubians and Syrian Melkites.

Some of the priests of these groups even had wives and children, living together within the precincts of the church, upstairs around its roofs and galleries. The keys to the church were held by a local Muslim family. The journey to the most holy site in Christendom was also a journey to a dynamic site of multiculturalism. It would have been clear to the European visitors that the primacy of the pope in Rome was by no means assured. This was no harmonious coexistence: for instance, in 1510 the Georgian Christians occupied the Latin Calvary chapel and vandalized its altar.

> **Must see:** If visiting at Easter, the ceremony of the Holy Fire in the Church of the Holy Sepulchre, in which a burning lamp hanging in front of the Sepulchre miraculously lights itself.

The Church of the Holy Sepulchre is a gloomy, noisy, fraught and confected building. But when one crosses its threshold one feels something final, the sense of an arrival. Walking into the half-light of the church is like stepping into the built fabric of a memory palace. If there's a place to feel déjà vu, it's here in the Church of the Holy Sepulchre, a place where hinted memories and outrageous simulacra merge with the actual experience of being there. The church is full of altars and shrines and bits of masonry, an atmosphere of cultured bric-a-brac emerging through dark archways and worn stone steps.

Many pilgrims spent either their first or second night locked inside the church, in vigil. Vigil – the religious act of vigilance – is a kind of deliberate waiting. During a religious vigil one watched attentively, avidly, to secure the appearance of the divine. At the Church of the Holy Sepulchre, this was

essentially twenty-four hours of enforced prayer, wakefulness and fasting, a kind of suspended time, when the pilgrim stopped travelling and instead directed all their attention to this one place. Felix Fabri described vigil as the 'most delightful' act of imprisonment: 'how sweet a locking in, whereby the Christian is locked in and imprisoned in the sepulchre of his Lord!' The vigil included a solemn procession around the church, led by friars, with each pilgrim holding a burning wax taper. Latin anthems, hymns and psalms were sung at each holy site.

Thomas Larke, travelling there in 1506, wondered at the many 'aisles, crypts, and vaults, chapels, and partitions, high and low, in such a great number' and marvelled at the many 'secret places' within the church. After you paid a fee (6½ ducats in 1392) to enter, the first holy site, just inside the main doorway, was (and is) the Stone or Slab of Unction: a rectangle of plain limestone, about 6 metres long and a metre wide, where Jesus's body was said to have been laid out after the Crucifixion and prepared for burial. Like many relics, there were several versions and pieces of the slab in medieval Europe, including the counterpart slab we have already encountered in Constantinople.

Felix Fabri, on his first pilgrimage to the church in 1480, described how he took about seventeen paces into the building. He stood gawping at the church's upper windows and vaulted roof. Then a German pilgrim named Hildegarde suddenly fell, weeping, at Felix's feet and started to kiss the floor. Hildegarde told Felix that he was standing on the very stone on which Jesus had been anointed and wrapped in a shroud. Brother Felix stepped back in horror, berating himself for his 'stupid carelessness' and irreverence, and himself fell to the floor, making an elaborate and abject appeal to God for forgiveness. He had confused awe with holiness; he had been too busy staring upwards to realize that his very feet were on holy ground. Pilgrims to Jerusalem often had to make such adjustments. Things that seemed mundane turned out to be holy. Holy ground can look startlingly ordinary, especially when one's standing on it.

Calvary, or Golgotha, where Jesus was said to have been crucified and where He died, itself does not look in any way like the green hill far outside the city wall represented in western art. In fact, it's a small, squat crag of limestone, protruding about 5 metres from the level of the courtyard, inside the church. Around it were not one but two chapels, in an arrangement similar to that found there today: at ground-floor level is the lower Golgotha (also known as the Chapel of Adam), a Greek and Armenian chapel. Above this, the

Latin Calvary was decorated with old Crusader-era mosaics, apparently always in a state of disrepair.

Visiting in 1395, Ogier d'Anglure described Calvary as the first place his party visited. Like many visitors, he recorded the steps – eighteen of them – up the 'sacred hill' and noted the two chapels. He focused on the round socket or mortice in the rock, in which the Cross had been placed. He also remarked on the split rocks, consonant with the rent rocks of the biblical account (Matthew 27:51). Ogier says that Calvary was decorated like a beautiful chapel, 'the top of it being all covered over with marble . . . vaulted and most nobly and richly worked, painted and conceived: consequently, it is a most beautiful and reverential place'. His group gathered there, heard mass, made confession and took communion.

The other key site within the church was the Holy Sepulchre itself, a structure (the aedicule) like a little house, standing beneath the centre of the eleventh-century rotunda. Here Jesus's body was said to have been placed after His death at Calvary and, also here, the angel descended from Heaven and rolled back the stone from the sepulchre at the resurrection (Matthew 28:2–7). This was a site of immense holiness, yet – or therefore – bits of the Holy Sepulchre were often picked off by visitors as souvenirs. In 1125 one nun, Herderviga, took her chippings from the sepulchre back to the abbey of Schaffhausen in Switzerland, where they became celebrated relics. The custom of chipping away at the tomb became so widespread that a protective barrier was put up by the Muslims in the fourteenth century, and superintendents had to watch the pilgrims to check that they did no further damage to the site that they had come to see and wished to transport back with them. As Ludolph von Suchem reported in 1340, a marble covering was put around the sepulchre with three holes in it, so pilgrims could touch and kiss the 'true stone' that had once held the body of Jesus. The medieval sepulchre was done away with in 1555, when the current one was built, so we can no longer see what the medieval visitors saw. Drawings of the tomb survive and multiple copies were built throughout Europe; these show a small building, in the shape of a letter U, with an elaborate cupola. There was a small door at one end, one or two tiny windows, and the back of the building was semi-circular. Inside, there was a stone-cut tomb, empty of course, said to have been where Christ's body had once been placed. It was a small, dark chamber, and pilgrims liked to enter one by one.

In general, the landscape of medieval Jerusalem responded to the needs of its visitors by becoming full of *visibilia*: viewable, often tangible, places and tokens, installations which referred to past miracles, producing a city that felt allegorical. This was especially true at the Church of the Holy Sepulchre, where intimate but dubious traditions of Christ's life and death abounded. Visitors could see a light-coloured rock, near Calvary, with red veins running through it: they were told that this red was the stain of their Christ's blood which had trickled down during the Crucifixion. Visitors could see stone columns, holding up the church but dripping constantly with water; these stones, they were told, were constantly weeping for Jesus's death. Visitors could not only visit the 'Prison of Christ', at the back of the church, one of many places where Jesus was said to have been held during His ordeals, but they could also worship the very chains with which, they were told, His hands were bound, in the 'Chapels of the Bonds' next to the prison. These were medieval inventions, not biblical sites. Yet they were precious to many thousands of visitors. Some travel guides were sniffy about them: these were the beliefs of 'common people', said Burchard of Mount Zion, but he nonetheless noted such places, and the holiness attached to them.

Countless visitors marked their visit to the Church of the Holy Sepulchre in an ageless touristic way: with scratches into the stone, a kind of graffiti. On the staircase down to the Chapel of St Helena, where Helena claimed to have unearthed the True Cross, there are thousands of crosses on the walls. Pilgrims seem to have paid to have these carved there, wordlessly but eloquently recording their physical presence. The dust taken from carving into the stone may have been brought home by pilgrims as a souvenir – Felix Fabri, writing in the 1480s, said that any 'bits of stone' brought back from the Holy Land, or anything which had touched the holy places, should be treated with 'great devotion' and 'placed among the chief relics of churches'. These marks are not exactly subjective (what could be more generic than signing with a cross?), but they are enduring.

The Church of the Holy Sepulchre was the site of supernatural wonders and marvels too. Here, at the centre of the world, the sun was said to cast no shadow. Here, each Easter, in the ceremony of the Holy Fire, a lamp in front of the sepulchre would miraculously light on Holy Saturday, a token of the presence of the Holy Spirit and an echo of how Jesus rose from death to life. Here, a column bore the marks of scorpion stings, the creatures having been said to have been placed on Jesus's suffering body.

Western visitors to Jerusalem were by no means free to wander around the city. They were subject to constant regulation from their Mamluk hosts and led from place to place by Franciscan friars. Increasingly, visitors subjected themselves to a ritual route, the *ordo peregrinationis* – a kind of itinerary of holy sites. In time, this became the Stations of the Cross and the Via Dolorosa.

*

The Church of the Holy Sepulchre – which remains similar to what it was in the fourteenth century – was the culmination of the 'new' tradition of the Via Dolorosa, 'the way of grief', a route through the final sufferings of Christ, punctuated by the Stations of the Cross. In fact, the last few stations are *inside* the church itself, not in the *via*. Far from being a biblical route, the Via Dolorosa was largely invented as an itinerary through Jerusalem by medieval travellers and their guides. It helped (and continues to help) the tourist to see the city through an idealized, and very partial, lens.

The Franciscan order of friars was integral to every western Christian visitor's experience of the Holy Land. St Francis of Assisi (d. 1226), the Franciscans' charismatic founder, had visited the Holy Land in the early thirteenth century in order to preach to, and convert, the Muslims there. To this end, Francis had an audience with the sultan directly. The sultan was, by most accounts, impressed by St Francis, but not impressed enough to convert from Islam. In the subsequent centuries, the Franciscans' role became that of a holy travel agency, run in cooperation with the ruling Mamluks. In the 1320s, the sultan granted the Franciscans a number of privileges, which made them the representatives of western Christendom in the Holy Land. Their activities shifted from trying to retake the Holy Land to enabling European travellers to visit the scenes of Christ's life and death. They sold the pilgrims little booklets, holy guidebooks, sometimes called 'processionals', which marked out the prayers, psalms and indulgences for all the holy places in Jerusalem and the Holy Land. In this way, the sacred landscape itself became read and experienced through a script. The Via Dolorosa exemplifies the way in which the city was navigated as an itinerary through memory rather than experience.

The Via Dolorosa became formalized only in the later

fifteenth century, running from the north-east corner outside the Old City westwards through the city's markets (now the Muslim Quarter) to the Church of the Holy Sepulchre. It comprised 'stations' in the Latin sense of the word: a place to stand, a place to be static. The stations of the Via Dolorosa are, for the most part, undistinguished places in the street: they are marked with small stone tablets, but visitors filled these places with invisible, remembered narrative. At each station, the visitor was invited to pray, and to receive an indulgence: usually a 'plenary indulgence', a complete absolution from guilt or punishment in Purgatory. The First Station now marks Jesus's condemnation by Pontius Pilate, but in the Middle Ages the route, number and narrative of the stations were not fixed. The subsequent stations follow, uphill, Jesus's trials and degradations. The stations relentlessly pull the pilgrim-tourist through the city, and back in time, out of the grimy press of urban Jerusalem into its biblical stage set.

Indeed most Stations of the Cross require a defiant act of imagination, and creative anachronism, to transport the visitor anywhere. The Sixth Station, about 300 metres east of the Church of the Holy Sepulchre, is a good example. It commemorates the place where a local woman, Veronica, wiped Jesus's sweating face as He was forced to carry the Cross to Calvary. Jesus's face, in agony, was imprinted on the *vera icon* of Veronica's veil or kerchief.

But, in its urban setting, the Sixth Station is underwhelming. The street narrows and rises here. In the Middle Ages this was an area of shops and mosques and madrassas, as it is today. The site, which had previously held a Crusader church dedicated to the surgeon-saints Cosmas and Damian, was only generally associated with Veronica from the fifteenth century. In the rock, there's an old (but not 2,000 years old) stone, with the words 'the sixth station where devout

Veronica wiped the face of Christ with a veil' carved in Latin. It probably dates from the later medieval period. For most Christians visiting the city, they had to think back to Europe – especially to the famous relic of Veronica's veil which we earlier encountered being worshipped at St Peter's in Rome – to fill the street scene with meaning.

The Via Dolorosa led from – or led to, for most pilgrims did not follow a set order – the Mount of Olives, at the foot of which is the Garden of Gethsemane, where Jesus was betrayed. The Mount of Olives is a parched hill to the east of the Old City. It rises out of the Valley of Josaphat (or Jehoshaphat), the riverbed that encircles eastern and southern Jerusalem, which itself is part of the Kidron Valley that runs from Jerusalem into the arid dust of the Judean Desert. It is the Valley of Josaphat that distinguishes the city of Jerusalem from its environs and, when one stands in the valley, gives the Mount of Olives its height. The valley was uninhabited, probably uninhabitable. But it was well known from the Bible as the place where all nations will be gathered for judgement (Joel 3:12).

Ancient tombs, confusingly attributed, stood in the valley, left by the various religious traditions that had sprung up there: the Tomb of Josaphat himself, now called the Tomb of Absalom; the Tomb of Zachariah and Simeon, now called just the Tomb of Zachariah; the Tomb of St James the Less (now called the Tomb of the Son of Hezir); and, most prized in the Middle Ages, the Tomb of the Virgin Mary herself, down a dark staircase deep in the rock, with a church built over it. Most visitors to late medieval Jerusalem paused and wondered at these spots as they started their tour of the Mount of Olives.

The medieval Mount of Olives did have some olive trees on it (indeed, medieval visitors commented on them) and some of the olive trees still standing there are themselves medieval. The olive trees at Gethsemane may well have been planted and cultivated by the Crusaders, who committed themselves to restoring the Christian landscape of the Holy Land.

Charmingly, Felix Fabri, in the 1480s, described visiting 'the farm at Gethsemane' and sitting down there, 'in the shade under the olive trees', and 'breakfasting merrily' with his fellow travellers. The Mount was also dotted with Jewish graves, as it had been for hundreds of years the main necropolis in the city for the Jewish community (and remains so today).

Climbing the slopes of the Mount of Olives is not a difficult ascent; it would have taken the pilgrims about fifteen to twenty minutes to walk it. But the Mount had become a landscape busy with informal shrines and wonders: the Prussian pilgrim John Poloner reported in 1422 being shown a number of apocryphal sites on the Mount, such as the rocks where Jesus sweated blood in His agony and the site where the tree that made the Cross once bridged the River Kidron. On the route up the Mount the visitors passed the Crusaders' Church of Dominus Flevit (where Jesus was said to have wept over Jerusalem) on the way to the summit, where many pilgrims stopped and, continuing their imitation of Jesus, wept again over the city vista.

At the summit of the Mount of Olives pilgrims visited the Dome of the Ascension. Here Jesus Christ is said also to have finished His tour of the city and left the earthly Jerusalem for the Heavenly Jerusalem. In the Christian tradition, Jesus was the prototype of the traveller. He was often on the move, from His childhood flight into Egypt (Matthew 2), His forty days wandering in the desert (Matthew 4) and His entry into Jerusalem on an ass (Matthew 21) to His walk to Emmaus (Luke 24), His definitive journey to God at the Ascension (Luke 24:51; John 3:13) and the exhortation to followers of Christ to see themselves as 'strangers and pilgrims' on a journey to the Heavenly Jerusalem (1 Peter 2:11). And here, on the ridge of the Mount of Olives, the plateau on which Jerusalem is built dramatically falls away into the rolling expanse of soft but unforgiving Judean Desert. One can look to the west and see Jerusalem, this time in its iconic view, with the churches and towers of the city rising up above the Dome of the Rock. But one can also look east, and see the strange void of the desert and, shining in the distance, the lowest point on earth, the Dead Sea, and beyond it the Mountains of Moab (now in Jordan). So the Dome of the Ascension is a good place to finish a tour of Jerusalem, because it's a kind of hinge or pivot in the landscape. After all, if Christian pilgrims were taking part in an *imitatio Christi*, this was their jumping-off point too; travellers had measured their journey in feet, they had ascended the stairs of Calvary and walked the Via Dolorosa, following in their hearts and minds the blood-speckled footprints of Jesus Christ. Here, at the Dome of the Ascension, their Christ took His last step.

The Chapel of the Ascension on the Mount of Olives was abandoned by the Crusaders in 1187 and by 1212 had been converted into a mosque. The building is a small domed sanctuary, dating from the Crusader era but rebuilt by the Muslims using Crusader *spolia* – repurposed masonry and sculpture. The supersession of Christianity by Islam was made palpable.

Mandeville's fourteenth-century travel guide tells us that it was in this place that Jesus stood 'when He ascended to Heaven, and His left foot appears still to be imprinted in the rock'. So this was the place where Jesus left the last manifestation of His human incarnation: the pilgrims could see a divine yet human footprint, the print of a man's naked foot. We often think of footprints as transitory, vanishing, but a footprint is always a reminder that someone has previously been in a place. Or, to put it another way, footprints are often used as a proof of evidence of ownership, prior occupation and human knowledge. This was true at the Dome of the Ascension, a fraught site on the seam between east and west, Christian and Muslim, at the outside edge of what could be called Christian Europe.

The holy footprint at the Dome had been worshipped since at least the seventh century, in a Byzantine Greek church. The Crusaders, in the eleventh century, frequently adopted local customs (especially those which focused on Jesus's humanity) and built the Church of the Ascension. They housed the holy footprint in a small marble tower. The footprint became an object of veneration and pilgrimage. Like Jesus's foreskin, which was multiply worshipped in Europe, the footprint was a supremely important relic, for it offered physical evidence both of Christ's incarnation as a man and of the ascension of His resurrected body.

The footprint then multiplied, in the form of stones deposited in churches around Europe, at Arles, Poitiers and Westminster. The Westminster footprint relic, presented by Henry III in 1249, shows how the sacred geography of the Holy Land was reimported to the west in an endless interplay between copies and originals, mementoes and souvenirs.

The Crusaders' footprint relic was taken to the Al-Aqsa Mosque on the Temple Mount. The Dome of the Ascension remained, and remains, a mosque but was re-established, unofficially, as a place of Christian worship to which most European Christian visitors to Jerusalem made a visit. Burchard of Mount Zion, in the 1280s, said that there was a stone where Christ's footprints had been and one could touch them, 'but not see them'. Curiously, by the 1350s, new footprints had appeared at the Dome. Pilgrims reported seeing various kinds of footprint: some were told they saw Christ's left foot, some Christ's right foot, some say it was the imprints of both Christ's feet. Ogier d'Anglure, visiting in 1395, saw a square stone with the right footprint of Christ in the Dome of the Ascension, and another stone, tucked behind a pillar, which showed the left footprint. Likewise, John Poloner in 1422 saw a Christian stone imprinted with the left footprint (measuring in length 'one palm and two joints of the middle finger') and devout Muslims worshipping a separate stone. Richard of Lincoln, travelling in the 1450s, describes the 'old temple' where Christ ascended, where 'one can see the footprints in the stone', adding that one must pay 2 shillings to visit. Other pilgrims mention a yet further holy footprint, said to be Christ's right foot, at the house of Simon the Leper (Matthew 26:6) at Bethany, very near the Dome of the Ascension. Yet other travellers say that they saw, in the hard stones of the pavement near the Golden Gate, the hoofprints of the ass on which Jesus entered Jerusalem on Palm Sunday. The pilgrims were quite literally if archaeologically dubiously walking in the footsteps of the Bible, the city's stones alive with the imprint of history. At some point, a new footprint relic was placed at the Dome of the Ascension, the relic which can now be visited in the mosque (it's a vaguely foot-shaped indentation in a soft-looking slab of marble).

Here, at the Dome of the Ascension, not only does the hectic city start to cede itself to the extraordinary desert, but travel becomes surplus to religious requirements. For the visitor, the pilgrimage could end here. If the journey to Jerusalem was the best journey one could make for the health of one's soul, why continue eastwards?

On the other side of the Mount of Olives, determined Christian pilgrims could make optional excursions to more difficult but no less precious destinations in the desert: the villages of Bethany and Bethpage; further afield, Mount Quarantine, where Jesus was said to have spent forty days and nights and been tempted by the Devil; the Dead Sea and the scorched remains of Sodom and Gomorrah; the River Jordan and the baptism site of Christ. But many pilgrims did not bother with these difficult sorties. Many of them had bought souvenirs in Jerusalem: perhaps a length of ribbon or vellum showing the measure of Christ's footprint or of His grave, or a wooden staff like the one Moses had, or a rosary worked in olive wood (grown in holy soil!) or camel hair, or a brightly coloured wax crucifix. Henry of Derby, whom we met in London preparing his luggage, went from Jaffa to Ramla to Jerusalem. His party bought wax candles and Henry made an offering of 6 ducats at the Holy Sepulchre; then they seem to have turned round again, apparently spending only a very short time in the holy city before returning to Cyprus and Rhodes.

The Mamluks had no wish for Christian visitors to turn voyages of faith into voyages of discovery. The Flemish diplomat Guillebert de Lannoy, writing an account of Egypt and Syria for the English king Henry V in 1422, wrote that the sultan would allow no Christian to travel out of the Holy Land to India via the Red Sea. Apparently, the sultan feared roving Christians making alliances with other rulers, such as Prester John, wherever he was.

Yet for some travellers there was the lure of the beyond, the realm of curiosity, of fantastical peoples, prodigies and places. One could convert oneself from pilgrim to tourist, leaving the rigid logic of pilgrimage for something looser, freer, stranger. For some, the defining trip to Jerusalem was not an end to their travels, but a whetting of an appetite to go further, the calling of an earthly wish to know more and more and still more about the world beyond.

Can you repeat that, please? Phrases for travellers

Almost all medieval travel guides included some information on foreign alphabets or useful phrases for travellers. They show the traveller's desire to make oneself understood, as well as the fear of being misunderstood. They also reflect – or imagine – the most common kinds of interaction between travellers and their hosts. Warning: word lists may not accurately represent the languages they claim to!

Some Greek for travellers, c. 1462

Good morning – Calomare
Welcome – Calosertys
Tell me the way – Diximo strata
Sit! – Catase!
Give that to me – Doys me tutt
Go away – Ame
Bring me – Fer me
What are you saying? – The leys?
I don't understand you – Apopon kystys
God be with you – These metasana
Where is the tavern? – Elle canawte?
Woman, have you good wine? – Geneca, esse colocrasse?
Man, have you good wine? – Antropos, esse colocrasse?

Some Albanian for travellers, 1496

boike – bread
vene – wine

oie – water
mische – meat
taverne – tavern
criste – God
dreck – Devil
laff ne kammijss! – wash my shirt!

Counting in Turkish for travellers, c. 1498

1 – bir
2 – equi
3 – ug
4 – doit
5 – bex
6 – alti
7 – yedi
8 – zaquiz
9 – doguc
10 – on

Some Arabic for travellers, 1496

ckayesch – beautiful
nem – sleep
nyco – marry
marrat nyco? – Woman, shall I sleep with you?
marca beba – You're very welcome
Hebat olla – May God give us a good wind
A tzismo ede? – What is that called?

9. A Detour to Ethiopia

Aghmat – Rio del Oro – Malsa – Barara

South of the Holy Land and beyond Egypt lay Ethiopia, a vast terrain connected to the Mediterranean via the River Nile. The medieval kingdom of Ethiopia was somewhat cut off from Europe by deserts, distance and wars with Islamic rulers. Historically, it was an embattled and sometimes expansionist Christian empire with a significant Muslim minority. The kingdom, vying for supremacy with Muslim sultanates in the Horn of Africa, was focused on the central plateau, running north to south from the Dahlak archipelago in the Red Sea to Lake Shalla in the Ethiopian rift valley. The Ethiopian Church, established in the fourth century and united with the Coptic Church, built elaborate hall-basilicas throughout the country. These include the unique thirteenth-century buildings of Lalibela, a 'New Jerusalem' of eleven elaborate churches hewn in the living rock. The complex includes its own Golgotha and Mount Sinai. Lalibela may well have been founded as a response to the Muslim conquest of Jerusalem in 1187, which made the journey there even more difficult. In time, to travel to Lalibela as a pilgrim was obligatory for medieval Ethiopian Christians.

Ethiopian Christians had communities at Jerusalem itself and in Egypt and Cyprus, where Europeans were most likely to come into contact with them.

However, to European minds, the borders of Ethiopia were utterly undefined and the term 'Ethiopia' was used for much of Africa. In one common definition, Ethiopia stretched from the Atlas Mountains to the end of Egypt, from the Atlantic to the Red Sea. Africa was, in European accounts, remarkable because it was huge, as if there was simply too much of it to account for. On the famous map of c. 1450 by Fra Mauro, a Venetian monk and cartographer, Ethiopia and its related realm of 'Abassia' (Abyssinia) occupy almost half of the African continent, seeming to stretch from Africa's southern tip to its north-western edge.

When Martin Behaim was dispatched by the Portuguese king on a 'voyage of discovery' to 'Ethiopia' in 1484, he sailed around west Africa, finding 'another world', previously unknown to Europeans, in the vicinity of what are today the coasts of Gabon and Angola. When he came to make his Globe, less than ten years later, he relied instead on the accounts of Ptolemy and Marco Polo for his description of Ethiopia, showing the 'Emperor' of 'Abassia' on his throne with a devout subject kneeling before him. This emperor's people are Christian, says the Globe, 'and trade gold and ivory'.

Medieval Ethiopia was long believed to be the home of marvellous (or monstrous) humans. Homer had called the Ethiopians 'the furthest of men', dwelling in a distant land beyond the seas. Mandeville, writing in his 1350s travel guide, said that Ethiopia, 'a vast country', was inhabited in the south by 'utterly black' people (the name *Aithiopes* derives from the Greek for 'burned visages'). Like many medieval writers, Mandeville saw geography as fundamentally linked to physiology; the definition of the Ethiopians by their skin colour reveals the perception that this was a consequence of their location in the hot lands of the world's torrid zones. Mandeville also said that Ethiopia was home to the sciapods, humans with only one very large foot who could hop about at wondrous speed. The sciapods used their foot as a shade against the diamond sunlight of the sweltering Ethiopian sky. Others said that a humanoid people called *archapites* or *artabatitae* lived there, who could only drag themselves along the ground by hand and foot, or on four paws, roving about like wild beasts.

Mandeville claimed that in Ethiopia there was a spring from which the water, by day, ran unbearably cold and, by night, ran unbearably hot. Nature here was inverted, outlandish, strange but still recognizable. All the running water in Ethiopia was 'murky and a bit salty', because of the intense heat, and the people had little appetite, got drunk easily and had dysentery; 'they don't live long,' concluded Mandeville.

Terrain, clean water, strange customs and the vicissitudes of the weather: the perennial concerns of the traveller.

Ethiopia was also known in Europe as the home of the 'Ethiopian wolf', a beast with a multicoloured mane that could 'leap so high that they seem to have wings'. Ethiopia was where dragons were said to be born, on account of the year-round fiery heat. It was the home of the diabolical hyena too, a wicked beast that was rumoured to feed on dead flesh and could mimic men's voices in order to lure them to their death.

And yet a more positive Ethiopia was also familiar in European religious culture, as a place of Christian grace and heritage. The Queen of Sheba herself was from there, she who travelled to King Solomon in Jerusalem with a luxury caravan of camels laden with spices and gold and gems (1 Kings 10:2). Medieval apocryphal stories of the Magi who greeted the infant Christ defined one of these three wise men as being from Ethiopia. The Black Magus became a staple of European religious imagery, often depicted as youthful and standing furthest from the holy infant, a representative of the emergent and distant continent of Africa but an integral part of the Christian *ecumene*. Over and above this, from the early fourteenth century Ethiopia was said to be the realm of the fabled king Prester John (literally 'John the Priest'), a powerful (but fictitious) Christian lord who it was hoped would assist European rulers against infidels. On his map, Fra Mauro said that the local ruler Prester John presided over 120 kingdoms, his enormous power being held in high regard because of the almost infinite number of peoples he controlled. Most of the Europeans involved in producing representations of Ethiopia had not been there; rather, their interest in the place was as a repository for myths, rumours and legends that sketched a wondrous or morally instructive version of the world. Yet, for all its prodigious strangeness, by the fourteenth century Ethiopia had become the intensely desired object of European religious, diplomatic and trade missions. The country, wherever it was, became a kind of seam on which antique fantasies met political realities, summoning an improbable land of peril and piety, barrenness and fertility, proximity and distance.

We now take a detour to Ethiopia, with a few of the unusual medieval travellers who made – or said they made – their way there and wrote about their journeys.

> **Don't miss!** The speciality of sun-dried smoked honeysuckle: local people live on this food. However, those who live on sun-dried smoked honeysuckle are unlikely to live past the age of forty.

In or around the mid-1340s a middle-aged Franciscan left his friary in the kingdom of Castile. We don't know his name, or much more about him, but he later wrote a *Book of Knowledge* describing a remarkable journey which took him to 'all the kingdoms, countries and lordships that there are in the world'. According to his report, he started his odyssey by going from Spain across France, Germany, Denmark, Sweden, Norway and around the British Isles.

The first, European part of his trip has the ring of a journey undertaken only in the mind: there is little local detail, and it consists largely of Spanished place names ('Artuz' for Aarhus in Denmark, 'Estocol' for Stockholm, 'Guinsa' for the English royal town of Windsor) alongside illustrations of the flags and ensigns of each territory. It is essentially an armorial list of Europe. It is more than likely that some or all of the Spanish Franciscan's account was gleaned from maps and books, not from visiting these places.

Nonetheless, the Franciscan's account becomes more animated and detailed once he left Europe for Africa. After visiting Italy and the Holy Land, he travelled through Egypt and across the northern coast of the African continent, via Benghazi, Sirte, Sousse and Ceuta. He eventually arrived at the 'very ancient' Moroccan city of Aghmat, an important Berber trading post and sometime capital of the Almoravid Berber Muslim kingdom of Morocco. Aghmat, deserted today, was then a thriving Muslim and Jewish town, with handsome brick walls, a mint and a large palace. It was situated in the lush Ourika Valley, a key pass cutting through the red earth of the Atlas Mountains. Troops of tiny-faced macaques leaped among the ash trees growing in the valley's vital air. Travellers, merchants and sages lurched along on narrow tracks, sometimes on precipices, sometimes on broad pathways through volcanic boulders, sometimes grating between narrow rock walls, sometimes along green riverbanks beside shining channels flowing with fresh water.

At Aghmat the Spanish Franciscan learned of the tomb of the king al-Mu'tamid (who had been exiled from the Spanish city of Seville to Africa in 1091 after his kingdom fell to the Almoravid dynasty). He encountered the Atlas Mountains and their perilous passes, and traced the history of the Berber Almohads in the Moroccan landscape. He found the Atlas region 'well supplied with provisions and water, but very cold'. Its inhabitants he considered to be 'very decent people'. He then sailed along the sun-blasted coast of southern Morocco, 'a desert land with bad cruel people who live on the shore', travelling in a *panfilo*, a small two-masted galley. Further south, at Cape Bojador, he encountered Jewish and Moorish locals and saw gold being taken to the King of Guinea by camel. This journey is so unusual, and so precise in its details, that it is tempting to read it as a voyage that he had truly undertaken.

After his visit to Morocco, the Spanish Franciscan's travels provide us with some of the earliest accounts of the Atlantic islands to the west of Africa: the Canaries, Madeira and the Azores. At that time, these islands were not usually on European shipping charts although they were well known to Arab geographers. He sailed in a wooden boat to the island of La Graciosa and thence to Lanzarote, Isla de los Lobos, Roque del Este and Tenerife. He knew of dozens of other Atlantic islands, including Madeira, although it is not clear that he visited them.

For all the flashes of verisimilitude in parts of the Spanish Franciscan's book, his account of his subsequent journey through Africa is marked by its reliance on fables about the continent that circulated in medieval European books. He describes, in the Senegal area, the cat-sized ants of the Rio del Oro (Gold River), a legendary river. These giant ants were said to build ant hills in which gold was found. The Spanish Franciscan was merely repeating an ancient European myth of the island of Orelle, where dog-sized ants mined gold all day on an immense mound.

Somewhere near the River Nile, the Franciscan met with merchants from Genoa, who had long had a treaty with the sultans in Egypt to conduct commerce up and down the river. Here he also claims to have seen ivory tusks ('teeth') being traded, then he entered a 'very hot' region of 'very high mountains', sometimes called the 'Mountains of the Moon' and sometimes the 'Mountains of Gold'. He seems to be describing the mythical Mountains of Kong, a great range dividing Africa's west coast from its interior. The Mountains of Kong, believed to lie beyond the source of the White Nile, appeared in many accounts and on many maps (all the way into the nineteenth century) but have never been found and existed only in the minds of mapmakers and travel writers. In any case, the Spanish Franciscan moved into legendary territory, describing the location of the Earthly Paradise, often positioned in the far south, 'below' the African interior. In a settlement he called Graçiona he encountered a Christian empire peopled by 'negroes . . . men of intelligence with good brains, and they have understanding and knowledge'. They drank 'excellent' fresh water that flowed from the Antarctic Pole, running out of the Earthly Paradise. And the local emperor was a defender of a certain 'Preste Juan', or Prester John, the Patriarch of Nubia and Ethiopia.

The Spanish Franciscan was one of the earliest writers to locate the figure of Prester John in Africa. In his account, Prester John was a Christian emperor with his capital at a town called 'Malsa' on the banks of an African river called 'Eufrates'. He wrote that Prester John's device was a white flag with a black cross and a golden crozier at either side, symbolizing his dominion over the neighbouring Christian emperors of 'Graçiona' and 'Magdasor'. The Franciscan did not describe the capital city Malsa, but medieval images of Prester John show him on a grand, carved throne amid tented encampments in a mountainous landscape. Here the Franciscan seemed to be conflating or confusing the west African Mandinka word *mansa* – 'ruler' or 'monarch' – and the Islamic empire of Mali with a European, Christian fantasy of Prester John's Ethiopia.

At Malsa, the Spanish Franciscan 'saw and heard' marvellous things daily. He was told by locals and 'wise men' that the nearby Earthly Paradise consisted of mountains so high that they nearly touched the moon. They side that these mountains were surrounded by a great sea from which ran the four biblical rivers of Paradise (Tigris, Euphrates, Gihon and Phison, described in Genesis), irrigating all of Nubia and Ethiopia. He was told that these rivers flowed in such raging torrents that the people living next to them were deaf, and that in these mountains living things could not decay or die. He was further told that on one side of the mountains it was light at all times, and on the other it was always dark, because the mountains were exactly on the 'horizon', or a version of the equator. In fact, this material came from European texts, but was nonetheless repeated as eyewitness truth.

The Spanish Franciscan's evident belief in Prester John represents a broad later medieval European understanding of a Christian empire beyond Egypt which was overlaid on to the actual empire of Ethiopia. Prester John had, since the twelfth century, been discussed as a shadowy but powerful Christian ruler, a direct descendant of the African magus, with an empire somewhere in the east – perhaps in Syria or India. On Behaim's Globe, Prester John appears in at least two places – in eastern Asia and in the African southern hemisphere – reflecting an uncertainty about who he was and where he was located. From around the time of the Spanish Franciscan's account, as they started to travel in greater numbers to Africa beyond Egypt, Europeans tended to locate him in Ethiopia. Some Europeans said that Prester John ruled a well-organized and vast terrain and that he had the source of the Nile in his empire and could therefore shut off the most important river of the Arab world.

From around 1400, European travellers were preoccupied with making contact with Prester John, forging an alliance with him, and enriching themselves with the treasures and pleasures of his wondrous empire.

*

When he was in the Constantinople suburb of Pera in 1431, Bertrandon de la Broquière met a man called Pietre, from Naples. Pietre was the Latin agent in Constantinople for the Ethiopian emperor Takla Maryam (reigned 1440–43) of the ruling Solomonic dynasty (a Christian royal house that claimed direct descent from King Solomon and the Queen of Sheba). Pietre told Bertrandon that he had been married in the Land of Prester John and encouraged Bertrandon to visit there with him. Bertrandon was sceptical and questioned Pietre extensively about Prester John and his territories. The Neapolitan told him that the Land of Prester John was in Ethiopia, a journey of fifteen days on the Nile followed by a sea crossing, and that the people of Prester John were ready and prepared to join a western alliance and to confront the Turks.

Pietre had a great deal more to tell. First, Prester John was a good Christian who was obedient to the Church of Rome but celebrated mass in the Greek rite. When he rode out, he had the cross carried before him. He controlled a gigantic territory and could raise an army of four million men. His men were of great stature and their skin was 'neither black nor white, but rather a reddish-brown'. The people of Ethiopia were 'virtuous and wise' and were constantly at war with an eastern lord, called Chinemachin, also called the great khan. In Ethiopia, gold and ginger grew plentifully. The highest mountains in the world were there. The land was full of strange beasts – lions, elephants, giraffes and a beast called the gorilla ('like a man except with a tail two and a half feet long that is half black and half white'). People also described 90-metre-long snakes as thick as a galleon's mast.

The thing Prester John lacked was ships and shipwrights. And so he had sent Pietre of Naples to Constantinople to find someone to build ships for him, in his constant war against

Chinemachin. And that's how Bertrandon heard about Prester John's Ethiopia. He was sceptical: 'I don't know if he was telling the truth or not. I simply report and do not guarantee the facts.' The traveller often picks up such half-understood rumours. Bertrandon didn't himself travel to Ethiopia to find out whether they were true or not.

Bertrandon's encounter with Pietre is representative of how for hundreds of years Europeans described an Ethiopia that both did and did not exist, an Africa made for browsing rather than conclusively knowing. Europeans said they had visited a place and met a sovereign and his subjects and yet what they reported was largely mythical.

In 1480 Battista of Imola undertook an unusual journey to Ethiopia. Battista was a fairly humble man, a Franciscan friar from the town of Imola near Bologna. He set off from Jerusalem, carrying letters, gifts and alms, and was accompanied by a fellow friar named John of Calabria. The two men were charged by Giovanni de Thomacellis, the Franciscan prior in Jerusalem, with setting up contacts with the Ethiopians as part of a missionary endeavour, to embrace the Ethiopians in the Latin world (to bring 'lost sheep back to the flock'). Battista gave an account of his journey upon returning to Jerusalem in 1483, telling another Italian friar, Francesco Suriano (d. 1529), all about his experiences; Suriano then wrote these down in his *Treatise on the Holy Land*.

Battista's account shows how suddenly local conditions intervene in travel. He was forced to stay in the Egyptian town of Naqada on the Nile's west bank for thirty days because roads were not safe (he doesn't say why, but we can assume due to conflict or banditry). When Battista eventually reached the port city of Suakin, with its luxurious houses built of Red Sea coral, he had to give the governor various gifts following local custom: a multicoloured tapestry, some dark cloth and five pieces of soap. He was half dead by the time he reached 'Prester John's territory': Ethiopia. Encountering an alien political structure, Battista noted how several towns were inhabited by one group but under the suzerainty of another, and remarked that 'all the leading men in that country called themselves "Soldans", that is, rulers.' An Abyssinian governor named Syonsirave provided him with cows and sheep and a guide through his territory, but Battista was forced to spend money most liberally at each of Syonsirave's towns. His camel grew exhausted and had to be sold; instead, he took an ass, which could better cope with the great rains that started to fall. He was detained at another town, 'Chiapeg' on the Nile, because of the inundations caused by the rain.

Local issues – weather, conflict, politics – intrude in unpredictable ways on travellers as they wander in a dreamlike, unreal state through stricken provinces and current events they only dimly apprehend. During his journey, Battista was taken to a church where 'the king' – whom he had come to meet – had recently been buried (this was Emperor Baeda Maryam I (d. 1478)). Battista eventually reached 'the court of the great king Prester John', in a town called Barara, the fifteenth-century Ethiopian capital sited on a high, cool and rugged hilltop abounding in freshwater springs.* He then waited at Barara for an audience with the monarch, the child-emperor Eskender or Kwestantinos II (1471–94). We do not know if such an audience was granted but here, at 'Prester John's court', Battista found many Europeans, some of whom had been there for more than twenty-five years. There

* The site has not been conclusively identified but was in the region of today's Addis Ababa.

were Venetians and Neapolitans, Burgundians and Catalans. There were men whose families were well known to Battista, including the Venetian painter Nicolò Brancaleone (c. 1460–c. 1526) who had emigrated there. In some ways, it was a home away from home, a remote land that was strangely familiar. In a nearby church Battista saw a large and ornate organ 'in the Italian style', much to his amazement. The Europeans at Prester John's court said they had come to this strange land in order to seek jewels and precious gemstones, but the king had not allowed them to leave. Nevertheless, they liked the 'polite and civil intercourse' at Prester John's court and the way in which the king rewarded them, each according to his rank. The Europeans told Battista that they lived in reed-built houses plastered with mud. Prester John's country was full of gold but lacked grain and wine. The large population was brutish, 'rough and uncultured', 'full of lice', 'a weak people with little energy or application but proud', and most ardently Christian. Battista was told much more about Prester John's kingdom but his fervent scribe Suriano did not write it down, 'for fear of wearying my readers' and because he wanted to return to spiritual matters, his main subject. He had demonstrated enough of the lure of curiosity, and redirected his attention to God.

Battista of Imola was a friar but also a courier, a messenger. He was sent from Jerusalem to Ethiopia a second time in 1484, with a further letter from his new prior Paolo da Canneto. This letter addressed Eskender directly, urging the Ethiopian Church to unite with the Roman Church; 'do not procrastinate', he wrote, 'for in delay is danger.' We do not know if this letter ever reached the Ethiopian throne, or if it had any success in helping Italian friars make contact with the Ethiopian rulers.

Almost everybody who went to Ethiopia, or said they had

been there, confirmed the existence of Prester John. The Spanish Franciscan in 1350, Pietre of Naples in 1431 and Battista of Imola c.1480–81 all believed that they had visited Prester John's kingdom. For medieval Europeans, Prester John was everywhere and nowhere, and his kingdom was confusingly often called 'India' even when identified with Ethiopia. Ethiopia was definitely somewhere, not nowhere or anywhere, but it remained only vaguely defined in the European imagination. Prester John's Ethiopia was both remote and accessible, distant yet glamorous, a place of European dreams. It was an Africa forged from its utility to Christian and European ways of seeing the world. 'Prester John' became an umbrella term for the Ethiopian emperor: a way of acknowledging Ethiopia while not seeing it. European travellers visited Christian Ethiopia and placed on it a layer of their pre-existing fantasies of Prester John. Wonder and exoticism came to exist side by side with the impression that Ethiopia was a receptive Christian kingdom simply waiting for foreign exploitation.

In summer 1402, the Emperor Dawit (d. 1413) of Ethiopia sent an embassy to Venice, including gifts of four live leopards, giant pearls and aromatic resins. Still, in the Venetian documents relating to the embassy Dawit is referred to as Prester John ('Prestozane' or 'Prete Jane'). The ambassadors of Emperor Dawit – whom the Venetians continued to call 'Prester John' throughout the visit – returned to Ethiopia with a group of Venetian artisans and artists, along with various luxury goods. While the Ethiopian court certainly hosted Italian and other European craftsmen and artists, European attempts to form a Christian anti-Islamic alliance with 'Prester John' appear to have made little progress.

We know that the actual Ethiopian kingdom was not ruled by a Prester John, that Ethiopian ambassadors, monks and pilgrims were frequent visitors to Jerusalem, Rome, Venice and elsewhere, that the Ethiopians frequently sent out embassies to Europe and that, at times, they in turn imagined a European king who would save their Christian kingdom from its foes. In 1479, Pope Sixtus IV established a pilgrims' hospice in Rome for visiting Ethiopians at Santo Stefano degli Abissini, a Coptic haven in the Vatican, steps away from St Peter's Basilica.

Medieval European ideas of Ethiopia are a microcosm of the medieval European notion of the whole world: the globe as a ludic assemblage of stories and fantasies and half-facts, a geography made out of the fancies of narrative rather than the facts of the landscape. So we return now to our conventional route, heading east from Ethiopia and Jerusalem towards the wonders of Asia.

Medical advice for travellers, taken from *The Rose of Medicine* by John of Gaddesden, physician of London, c. 1314

Those going on a journey, going overseas, going to war, or on pilgrimage, or to study in a university, or to a market, or to see friends or acquaintances, or to visit the sick should do as follows:

- As a general instruction applicable to all travellers, it is good to begin by being bled, or by fasting, so that the body may be cleanly disciplined, otherwise there's a risk of fever, or of a swelling, or of dysentery or of a ruptured blood vessel.
- For those setting off in springtime, madness and melancholy especially are to be feared.
- In warm weather, thirst and heat are best guarded against as follows: take rose sugar, violet sugar, or waterlily syrup, or a chicory flower and sugar conserve, or else take candied sugar, tamarinds, barberry or sorrel and take these often on the journey.
- If you've had too much to drink, a man should wash his testicles with salt and vinegar, a

woman should wash her breasts, and eat the leaf, stalk or juice of a cabbage with sugar.

- If the air is hot or foul smelling, then the traveller should sniff camphor, roses or violets, and in very hot weather he or she should sniff musk or wood sage, or resin of the goat's-beard plant, or camomile, laurel leaves or marjoram. They should hold their nose if bad breath or body odour is present; on getting out of bed, they should eat a piece of toasted bread in aromatic wine or chestnuts roasted with aromatic wine.
- After travelling hard in hot weather the feet must be washed with water boiled with camomile, fennel and hedge nettle. Absinthe should also be sipped, which shall make fatigue and weariness disappear almost completely.
- The traveller should carry with him some wormwood and a stalk of chasteberry (or monk's-pepper tree); this will mean he won't stumble on the way or be tired during the day on which he does this. And before the traveller sets off in the morning he should rub himself with tarragon and *marciaton* ointment (made of olive oil, beeswax and bay). He should eat roasted meat and garlic with wine or spiced wine.
- Poor people should take three grains of frankincense and pepper, or six leaves of mint, and they should smell chasteberry and

frankincense to help with a runny nose or phlegm.

- The feet should always be washed with hot salt water, dried and then rubbed with goat's or ram's fat, and one should do the same to one's perineum, on account of all the chafing which may have occurred during the journey.
- Those who travel in winter should wear a garment made of two layers of fabric, padded with cotton next to the shirt, lined with fox, lamb or rabbit pelts. On their head they should wear a cap lined with thick sheepskin. They should also have a hood coming down to the shoulders, or a thin kerchief on the head. They should keep their feet warm and dry so far as possible, and dry them carefully before going to bed.
- Be careful to avoid fevers that can arise from flatulence and from sunburn. Don't go close to the fire when you are very cold, but instead rub your limbs a little, not far from the fire.
- Water should never be drunk while travelling, in any manner, because it brings about fevers and abscesses and blockages.

10. On the Silk Roads

Sparrowhawk Castle – The caravanserai – Tabriz – The Old Man of the Mountain – Gog & Magog

As a slave and soldier and prisoner and pilgrim and mercenary, Johann Schiltberger had visited much of the Middle East, travelling through parched deserts and minareted cities. Yet he never managed to see a place he had heard so much about: Sparrowhawk Castle.

Schiltberger was born in a small Bavarian town in 1380. Aged sixteen, he left his highborn family to fight in the retinue of the nobleman Leinhart Richartingen against the Ottoman Turks. They soon became involved in a violent confrontation in which Richartingen was killed and Schiltberger wounded and taken prisoner. For thirty-one years, he served – sometimes as prisoner, sometimes as household retainer – first in armies of the Ottoman sultan and then under the Timurid sultans.* Their empire covered much of central Asia, from Aleppo in the west to Herat, Samarkand and Tashkent in the east. Schiltberger later served a Tatar prince named Chekre around Armenia and Siberia. He finally escaped in the Georgian port of Batumi, sailing across the Black Sea to Constantinople, and made his way home to Bavaria in 1427, where he wrote an account of his travels and the many things he had seen on what he called his 'interesting and strange adventures'.

Schiltberger was a practical, adaptable and curious young

* Timur (1336–1405), Shah Rukh (1377–1447) and Miran Shah (1366–1408).

man, and took the opportunity of his itinerant captivity to see the world. He started to notice marvels and miracles wherever he was taken. At the siege of the port city of Samsun on the northern coast of Turkey, he saw countless snakes and vipers descend on the city, some from the sea and some from the forests. They had no interest in harming people or even cattle; but the serpents went to war against each other for eleven days. On the eleventh day, the sea serpents were vanquished by the forest snakes. The lifeless bodies of 8,000 vipers were gathered up and buried. This was taken as a divine portent that the sultan would also soon have mastery of the seas as he had mastery of the land.

Schiltberger wrote that he saw 9,000 virgins taken into captivity in a dusty battle in Cilicia. He saw trained tusked elephants go to war in Tatary, their trunks ferrying cannon between the troops. He saw entire towns levelled, with their inhabitants still alive as their houses were razed around them. In the desert he met villagers who had an infinite quantity of spices but no cattle and little water. He saw kings trade entire territories for jewels and gold. He met a widowed Tatar princess who kept a retinue of 4,000 women, all of whom could ride warhorses and shoot a bow and arrow as well as any man. At Isfahan, with its elegant bridges, arches and shaded precincts, Schiltberger witnessed the thumbs of 12,000 archers cut off and a tower made from the skulls of thousands of murdered children of the vanquished residents (the Castilian ambassador, Clavijo, saw a similar tower, made of Tatar skulls, at Damghan east of Tehran).

Even though he had seen such things, things no other Bavarian ever saw, Schiltberger longed to see Sparrowhawk Castle. People said it was a short distance from the city of Trebizond (Trabzon), or perhaps somewhere else on the coast in the territories of the Lords of Corycus, or perhaps deeper in Armenia and its many realms that only unwillingly gave up their secrets to the traveller. Everyone knew the story of Sparrowhawk Castle. Schiltberger had even read about it as a young man and had heard tell of it throughout his travels.

So he paid a guide to take him there, and the guide had led him along hidden tracks through thick forests and across strangely shaped hillocks baked by the sun. Eventually, they reached a mountain topped by Sparrowhawk Castle (or at least what the guide told him was Sparrowhawk Castle).

At Sparrowhawk Castle there was said to dwell a princess, the most beautiful woman in the world. Men described her as part deity, part seductress. She was as slender as a stoat, and had the most delicate, arched brows and a mouth as sweet as mead.

People told how inside this palace the princess lived alone, with just a sparrowhawk for company. The sparrowhawk sat with its yellow claws wrapped around a walnut-wood perch decorated with onyx. Its bright watchful eyes seemed ever open, unblinking, sleepless. The hawk vibrated silently with knowledge and wisdom. Once a day, it swooped from its perch and diligently hunted vermin and insects and wild prey, thereby cleansing his mistress's castle.

The princess, despite her seductive demeanour and immodest apparel, was said to be a virgin and a devout Christian. She was retaining her virginity until a brave knight could come along and keep watch for three days and three nights without sleeping. If they could do this, they could ask the princess for whatever they wanted, as long as it was pure.

One prince of Armenia had managed the sleepless watch. After three days and nights his body swayed, his bladder was near to bursting and his knees were shaky as a milk pudding. The princess congratulated him on his achievement and asked what pure thing he wanted.

The Armenian prince said that the pure thing he wanted

was to take her as his wife. But as he said this he felt a powerful lust for the princess's body and became aware of his private parts stirring for her.

The princess immediately understood the impure motives behind the prince's request. She banished him, screamed insults and shaming reproaches at him and cursed his entire kin too.

So the chatelaine of Sparrowhawk Castle remained pure and chaste, exposing the dirty thoughts of the men who came there. Like her faithful sparrowhawk, she cleansed the world by revealing the inner corruption of those who crawl across its surface.

Schiltberger gazed up at the walls of the castle he had been led to, with its slablike stone gate and fearsome portcullis. In the distance he may have caught a glimpse of the prettiest chateau, all delicate spires with rose-tinted slate roofs and dozens of neat chimneys and golden finials and copper weathervanes, filigree mullioned windows, ogees and lancets and soaring arched colonnades. But maybe that was a mirage. The gates were locked and nobody seemed to be there. No princess, no sparrowhawk: a wasted journey.

The local priests said the whole thing was the Devil's work, not God's. So they turned back. The guide who had taken Schiltberger's money, promising to show him the castle, soon vanished.

Regretfully, we have wandered off our route, travelling northwest from Jerusalem when we should be travelling eastwards. We have been distracted with stories of sparrowhawks, damsels and priapic knights. This is precisely what everyone says happens to the traveller: if they are not vigilant, travellers get sidetracked, led astray, and find themselves lost. And to be a lost traveller is almost as bad as being a bored one.

So, as Sparrowhawk Castle is not on the route to anywhere, we can put it aside and go nowhere with Schiltberger, instead to continue onwards with our proper journey to join the Silk Road(s).

What we now call the Silk Road (largely a twentieth-century term) is not one road but rather a collective noun for the east–west routes, by land and sea, across Eurasia, from Egypt to China, from Turkey to India. Not only silk but much more was traded along these routes: spices for medicine and cookery, jewels, beverages, animals. There are copious records of the silk-route trade in furs and hides, precious stones, dyes, suet, soap, oils, wine, sulphur, rice, alum, sugar, pottery, amber, mercury, caviar, henna. Goods on the Silk Roads travelled both east–west and west–east: English and Scottish wool, French drapery, Italian glass and steelwork, for example, were traded eastwards. The Silk Roads were also the vehicle for human exchange, via missionizing, slavery, sex work and hospitality.

Around 1300, the Silk Roads stretched across an enormous area and had become a well-organized network reaching across Europe and Asia, with guidebooks for merchants in Italian and Catalan. An exemplar of these is Francesco Balducci Pegolotti's *Pratica della mercatura* (*The Practice of Commerce*, c. 1340). Pegolotti was a Florentine merchant and his handbook was designed to enable Europeans (especially Europeans from growing mercantile cities like Florence) to practise business in the east. The *Pratica* was a direct forerunner of a modern business travel manual, focused on international market agility rather than curiosity or religion.

The chronology of Pegolotti's life is hard to reconstruct with precision, but he spent much of his life connected to the great Bardi banking and trading company of Florence. He went to Antwerp in the early fourteenth century to secure privileges for the Florentines there, and then spent some years in London, where he became director of the English office of the Bardi and transacted business with the papacy and with the English monarchy. He sailed from London in 1321 to the then English port of Libourne in Gascony and, via Tuscany, spent about five years in Cyprus, as the Bardi representative in Famagusta. He intermittently returned to Florence, where he had periods of success in Florentine local government, but also seems to have spent time in Armenia, probably dwelling in Ayas (now Yumurtalık), again representing Florentine business interests.

The Silk Roads were configured around mercantilism, and this is reflected in the *Pratica della mercatura*. Pegolotti was partly concerned with safety and local cultures but most of his guidebook is about weights and measures, currency conversion and mints, transit duties and tolls, and lodgings: the emerging practicalities of business travel. Via the Silk Roads we can see the emergence of the 'businessman' and 'business traveller' – a person who travels motivated not by religion or *Wanderlust* but by profit. Yet the Silk Roads were also the stage for pluralistic encounters, the exchange of ideas and engagements with curious novelties. There travellers came into contact with other people and with situations that challenged their ethical bearing and required new ways of engaging with the wider world.

Pegolotti's guide is, among other things, a fascinating glossary of the key language the traveller needed on a journey across the diverse and fluid worlds of the Silk Roads. For instance, he gave word lists in a wide range of languages, from Flemish to Armenian, for terms like 'customs' and 'marketplace', and translated values of coinage. He gave instructions on how to refine gold found in the wild, and very detailed advice on how to avoid being duped by foreign merchants when buying spices and other goods.

It is unlikely that Pegolotti went all the way to China, although his book gestures to the routes across Asia. What is almost entirely missing from his book is a sense of him travelling through interesting or distracting places. He was a diligent and committed merchant, and the Silk Roads, for him and his merchant readers, were a stage for transactions and profits, not curiosity. The vast spectrum of commodities he traded included Persian rose water, Socotran aloes, Bulgarian vair, Sumatran camphor, Tatary shot silks, Egyptian linen, ginger from Arabia and India, Asian rhubarb and Indian spikenard. His sense of place was that of the marketplace.

Pegolotti's book discloses an anxiety about fraud and dishonesty in foreign markets, but it also presupposes a great deal of trust, especially in assumptions about safety when travelling. He largely assumed that Italian merchants had the right to trade and travel through the Near East, and his concern was with providing full details of what taxes should and should not be paid. At Tana, a crucial Venetian entrepôt between the Black Sea and the Volga, he gave a clear account of what duties were due: for instance, gold, silver and pearls attracted no duties, neither the Mongol 'tamunga' (*tamgha*) tax which was charged on the movement of goods and people nor the 'comerchio' levy, a customs or sales tax. Wine, ox hides, saddles and horse hides attracted a 5 per cent duty, except for Genoese and Venetians, who paid 4 per cent. The charging of customs was a way of protecting trades and manipulating prices, but it was also a way of attracting revenue, which could then be spent on improving facilities for traders. Pegolotti is clear that 'pacts', special bargains, could be made with the *doganieri*, customs officers, and there was usually room to negotiate.

Health and safety! If you think you have leprosy, or if you know a leper, you need to know about the wonderful well of Urfa. Its waters heal lepers, as long as they follow this prescription: they must fast for five days, and on each day they must drink the well's water and wash themselves in it. After five days, they should stop washing with it but still drink it up to the tenth or twelfth day.

Like travellers in Europe, those travelling on the Silk Roads were often required to prove their credentials. Italian merchants carried letters of introduction, letters of exchange and safe-conducts, and they relied on written contracts. Pegolotti had a letter of safe-conduct from the King of England when he left the British Isles in 1321. He even gave illustrated information about the merchants' marks stamped in loaves of sugar to protect property and quality.

Pegolotti included information on all the crucial middlemen of Silk Road travel: the *calamancio* (interpreter), *alzatori* (hoisters, who loaded and unloaded freight), *bastagori* (porters), *currattiere* and *sensali* (brokers), *scarsellieri* (couriers), *scrivani* (clerks and scriveners), *vetturali* (carters) and *tantaulli* (guards). By the second quarter of the fourteenth century, business travel was supported by industries that enabled, protected and profited from the people and spaces of the Silk Roads.

Similarly, from the early thirteenth century, Mongol officials, couriers and merchants carried a metal 'passport', a *paiza*, a stamped seal of authority given by the imperial preceptor of the Mongol court. The *paiza* represented an edict of the Mongols' supreme leader, the great khagan or khan, that the bearer should be allowed to travel freely, with unsparing inscriptions such as 'He who has no respect shall be guilty' or 'I am the Great Khan's emissary: if you defy me, you die.' Marco Polo's will refers to such tablets, presented to him by Kublai Khan (reigned 1260–94) to ensure his free movement across the Silk Roads. Polo kept them until his death, apparently as precious, material trophies of the privilege to travel freely.

The main punctuation of a traveller's journey on the Silk Roads was provided by the institution of the caravanserai (sometimes called by its Turkish name, *han*). A caravanserai was similar to the Hanse *Kontor*, Venetian *fondaco* and Jerusalemite Muristan we visited earlier. It was foremost a place for the lodging of a caravan:* a group of travellers, which could comprise merchants, pilgrims, scholars, servants, slaves, vagrants and animals. Some caravanserais were monumental, elegant, built to last, although conditions within them were not necessarily luxurious. Each caravanserai, usually placed a day's travel apart on the main routes, held huge amounts of merchandise and supplies; the twelfth-century historian Geoffrey of Vinsauf described the contents as including everything from spices and silks and 'costly cushions' to armour, medicines, chess sets and barley.

A caravanserai was usually fortified or defensive, built with thick walls, few or no windows and just a single entrance tall enough to allow laden animals – exhausted camels, asses and horses – to enter. Once inside, there was a courtyard or central hall, a kind of hub, in which people socialized and ate, the animals slept and rested, and little stalls were set up to sell things among the travellers: not just spices and silks

* 'Caravanserai' is from the Persian term for a *saray*, 'palace, enclosure', for a caravan.

but also travellers' essentials like horseshoes, new clothes and footwear, vessels for drinks. They sold food for the onward journey too – melons, cheese, all sorts of fruit. There was likely also a well, where everyone could get some fresh water, if they dared. And there were messengers and couriers and sex workers for hire. Some caravanserais had small individual rooms along arcaded aisles, perhaps on a second floor, but it was common for travellers to sleep on the floor, as at the Muristan in Jerusalem, on hastily assembled pallets and mattresses in cell-like side booths.

Pegolotti listed each caravanserai (or *gavazera* as he called it) at which customs fees were charged, and the caravanserai can be seen as the forerunner at once of local government offices, postal networks and roadside rest areas. The caravanserai also in some ways anticipated an international hotel chain, in which the guest could be comforted by the predictable nature of their lodging. But far from being like a luxury palace or international mall, a medieval caravanserai was often more like an ornate barn. In its aisles and precincts, spaces were reserved for the animals' owners and their human servants, where people could bed down on a mattress, not far from the braying asses and ripe dung. Indeed, the pack animals may well have been considered more important than many of the human guests, as the animals were the main means of transport and also represented a significant investment. At Aruch in Armenia the beautiful caravanserai was built around a central hall for housing the animals, with troughs worked into the masonry for their hay and water. The creatures that enabled the journeys were therefore at the centre of the caravanserai.

In the better caravanserais, humans might find lodging in the upstairs arcades. In the various abutments and side rooms, there were sometimes latrines, baths, mosques and chapels, perhaps a slaughterhouse or a laundry, quarters for a physician, a vet, a bath attendant, an imam, a porter or even a small garrison, storerooms full of honey, oil, candles, mead, grain, sometimes a separate section for female guests. Each caravanserai had cats to deter mice from infesting the grain stores.

Remains of caravanserais can be found all along the Silk Roads, from Cyprus to China, but especially in today's Turkey, Armenia, Georgia, Iraq, Iran and Uzbekistan. It was common for a caravanserai to be founded by a local prince or bishop, an act of commercial magnificence and social welfare, all the better to attract people and their trade to the area and connect their territory to places far beyond. At the Orbelyan caravanserai, built in 1332 high in the Armenian Vardenyats Pass, a winged beast and a carved bull decorated the tufa doorway, alongside devout inscriptions mixing Armenian, Persian and Turkish, imploring those who passed by to remember the charity of those who built it. Supporting travel could fulfil the biblical injunction to give food to the hungry and drink to the thirsty, and to welcome the stranger (Matthew 25:35). Or, as St Paul warned, never forget hospitality towards guests because some, 'not aware of it, have entertained angels' (Hebrews 13:2). One never knew who might be in the next caravan.

Pegolotti described numerous caravanserais on the route between Ayas (Yumurtalık) and Tabriz and his itinerary included a stay at what he called the 'Gavazera del Soldano', the 'Sultan's Caravanserai'. This was the lavish Tuzhisar Sultanhan, on an ancient route from Kayseri to Sivas. It was one of several founded, as its name suggests, by the Seljuk sultan Kayqubad I (d. 1237). The exterior was decorated with carved geometric patterns and meandering interwoven stars. Expressive lions' heads frowned from the waterspouts. An impressive crown door suggested that one was passing into the sultan's care and comfort. Elaborate vaulting welcomed the visitor into a canopy of heavenly order.

Upon entry, there were dozens of rooms, and fountains too. Then, stepping through the opening section, the visitor entered a large courtyard, partly covered, decorated with dragons writhing in stone ribbons around the elaborate arches. There was an elevated kiosk mosque – a little adorned hall standing on arches – opposite the entrance. Vaulted eastern and western wings were used for storage and loading, and there was an extremely well-appointed bathhouse with hot and cold areas.

Everything in the caravanserai was configured for travel and mobility. It would usually have been able to house between 50 and 200 guests. In its transience, it was emphatically not a destination but a staging post to elsewhere. Like so many institutions for travellers, the caravanserai was an unpredictable space of social mixing, combining local

customs with people from across Europe and Asia. It was not expensive; indeed, if one didn't have the money, one could often stay for free for up to three days and so the kind of people one encountered there was eclectic, even random.

The merchant-diplomats Giosafat Barbaro and Ambrogio Contarini described in detail what it was like to travel on the late medieval Silk Roads. Both Barbaro and Contarini were Venetian ambassadors to 'Ussuncassan' (Shah Uzun Hassan, d. 1478), ruler of the Aq Qoyunlu state (which covered most of what is today Iran and Iraq). Barbaro made various journeys across Persia and the Caucasus, first as a merchant (from 1436 until about 1452) and later in life as the Venetian ambassador to Persia (from 1472 until 1479). Contarini travelled through Persia and Turkey in 1474–7. As ambassadors, their task was ultimately to ally the Venetian state with the Persians against the Turks. Each left detailed accounts of their journeys. Their writings reveal the well-developed infrastructure for travel across the Silk Roads, but show how progress could be slow, arduous and perilous.

Barbaro described how he and his group travelled from the Black Sea port of Tana using a kind of sled ('zena', from the Russian *sani*), with which to navigate the frozen rivers. It was novel to him that the Tatars preferred to travel in winter, when the ground was frozen, rather than in summer, when they were beset by biting insects. Barbaro's journey with the Tatars included herds of camel and oxen, and massive numbers of horses (he says that one caravan he encountered in Persia included 4,000 horses). In his account, the Silk Roads were busy: 'every route was full of people and beasts following on their way.' Each traveller, he said, brought a two-wheeled cart with them, enclosed with reed matting; wealthier travellers had felt or cloth coverings. On some of these carts travellers carried a timber-hooped 'little house', a yurt, covered with reeds, felt or cloth, 'so that when they lodge they take down these houses to lodge in'. Women in the caravan wore horse-hair facemasks, 'to defend them from the burning sun in clear weather'. Some carried babes-in-arms, the left hand both cradling the baby and holding the horse's bridle, the right hand driving the horse, 'beating him with a whip bound to their little finger'. Barbaro described scouts on the route, travelling anywhere between four and twenty days ahead of the caravan. They carried goatskin bottles full of dry meal to which they would add a little water to make a sustaining paste, supplemented by shooting game on the route or, failing that, eating whatever herbs and roots could be found.

Barbaro stayed at caravanserais and *fondachi*, in lodging houses and in portable yurts when he travelled with a Tatar caravan. At Yazd, he visited the *fondaco*, where the merchants lodged and sold their silks and other wares in little shops, each about 6 foot square. Particularly noteworthy for him were the paper price tags on the merchandise, as paper in Europe was still largely used for luxuries like books.

During his journey, at the hilltop town of Mardin, famous for its silks and fustians, Barbaro stayed in a travellers' hostel founded by the local lord's brother. People here were given food and 'if they seem persons of any estimation they have carpets laid under their feet.' Barbaro was amazed at this profligacy, as the carpets alone seemed to be worth more than the very large sum of 100 ducats a piece.

Sitting alone in the hostel one day, he was suddenly confronted by a naked man. From his goatskin satchel the man, a local sage, produced a little book and began to read prayers.

He inched nearer to Barbaro and asked, 'What are you?'

Barbaro replied, 'I am a stranger.'

To this the man replied, 'I also am a stranger to this world, and so are we all; and so I have left it in order to behave in this manner until my end.'

He told Barbaro to despise the world, comforting him with 'good and eloquent words'. Barbaro called the mystical conversation a 'strange event' and recorded it as a memorable encounter. In the caravanserai and other Silk Road lodgings, such cryptic encounters could take place as diverse worlds were brought together in a transient but intimate community.

At Antalya, Barbaro stayed at a caravanserai which functioned as a customs house (this was not unusual). Here he tried to keep himself aloof, waiting for the caravan to depart, but he was approached by a man who demanded 5 ducats from him, as a customs duty, because he believed Barbaro was going all the way to Jerusalem. Barbaro sought to explain that he was not going to Jerusalem, and a fight broke out between the man who demanded the payment and another man who had vouched for Barbaro. Curses and punches were thrown, and the man who had demanded the payment from Barbaro shouted at him, 'You fool, you'll forever be a fool!' as Barbaro took his horse and fled the caravanserai. He went onwards to Beirut, thence to Cyprus and homewards to Venice. The whole unhappy encounter has the air of an unfortunate set of misunderstandings, where confusions over language and culture escalate rapidly, and the traveller suddenly longs to be anywhere else than where they've found themselves.

Like Barbaro, Contarini stayed in conventional lodgings like caravanserais. But Contarini, a less hardy and less contented traveller than Barbaro, also described the wide variety of accommodation he had to endure. Somewhere near Zhytomyr, he could find no lodging and was forced to sleep in a dangerous forest, 'infested with discontented men', and with no food to eat. In Georgia he likewise frequently had to sleep in the woods.

At a lodging house in Astrakhan, all Contarini's jewels and merchandise were confiscated and a great sum of money extorted from him.

At Qom, he was forced to spend two nights in a tent, suffering from the extreme cold, as he tried to rent a small house to lodge in. Another time at Qom, Contarini and his party became ill in the caravanserai with a fever accompanied by delirium, which made them say 'many insane things' and imperilled their safety.

Contarini also complained repeatedly about the food he had to eat on the Silk Roads: salted sheep tail in Astrakhan, a desperate omelette made from duck eggs and a little butter at Derbent on the Caspian Sea, rancid horsemeat in several places, an unsavoury supper featuring bread, turnips and a little meat at Kutaisi and 'stinking mare's milk' in a Tatar camp. Western visitors to Tatary frequently represented the Mongols (often called Tatars, especially in the western part) as voracious gluttons. Contarini hated the enforced boozing he encountered, where people guzzled strange alcoholic brews and imposed them on their guests. Hospitality – the reception and care of strangers – can often seem to shade into hostility, the stranger received as an enemy.

Towards the end of his journey, when he reached Derbent, Contarini was ragged: his lambskin-lined jacket was all torn, and above it he wore a 'very sorry pelisse' and, on his head, a lambskin cap. People who saw him wondered that he could even afford to buy meat. His companions told him he looked like he had just come from a debtors' prison.

Both Contarini's and Barbaro's accounts made clear that enslaved people and slavery were ubiquitous features of the silk routes from Venice to China.* At the Black Sea port of Poti (known to Venetians and Genoese as Fasso), Contarini stayed on three separate occasions in the house of a Circassian woman named Marta, enslaved by a Genoese man. While Marta gave him a warm welcome, his bed, he complained, consisted of a borrowed 'miserable counterpane' and he grew ill; Marta tended him with an oil and herb poultice. Barbaro was given eight enslaved Russians at Tana by the local emperor's brother-in-law, for which he made a reciprocal gift of some of his merchandise. The fate of these Russians is unclear. Later at Venice, while he was buying wine at the Rialto, Barbaro saw two Tatar men in chains who had been enslaved by Catalans. On trying to escape, they had been 'taken' by the Venetian vintner. Barbaro complained to the notorious *Signori di Notte*, who freed the men. Barbaro took them in for two months and it transpired that they knew people in common from their shared time in Tana; one of the freed men even claimed that Barbaro had inadvertently saved his life during a fire there. The men reminisced about their travels, and the sudden reversals of fortune and extremes of captivity and liberty that characterized their voyages. Barbaro eventually sent them home, on a boat to Tana.

At this time, slavery was endemic in this region, supporting and supported by trade with the west. Barbaro described how a Franciscan named Thermo of Tana used money he'd

* In many languages (e.g. English, French, German, Italian, Portuguese, Spanish, Swedish), the medieval and modern word 'slave' derives from Slav: where and when this originated remains debated, but it reinforces the historical context in which the medieval European slave trade drew most of its human source from eastern Europe and the Caucasus, especially Circassians. Broquière, travelling in the Middle East, was troubled by the slavery he saw, including at Damascus the sale of a young Black girl, not more than fifteen or sixteen years old, led through the streets nearly naked.

made by catching birds to buy a Circassian boy, named him Petriche and made him into a friar. At Poti, Contarini was warned by a certain Bernardino, an Italian, not to go back to Tana, because he himself would be enslaved. At Tabriz, Contarini met two enslaved Slavs who had become Muslim, and who formed a close friendship with Contarini's servants and gave Contarini himself insider information about the shah's movements. Boy slaves, eunuchs, royal slaves, sex slaves, human gifts between rulers, and enslaved prisoners-of-war all feature in Silk Road narratives of this time; Barbaro estimates that in a Tatar encampment there were 1,500 'slaves, herdsmen, couriers and the like'. Travel is often supported by servitude, and to travel is not necessarily to be free.

The journey across the Silk Roads involved vast distances over inhospitable terrain. Wadis growing with tamarisk, broom and oleander gave way to stark plains punctuated by hoofprints, then mountains, then deserts. But along the Silk Roads were distinguished towns and cities, of which one of the most captivating was Tabriz (also called Tauris) in modern-day Iran. Situated on the edge of the Aladaglar Mountains, where colourful oxide slopes met snowy peaks, it was a rapidly growing Georgian and Azeri city in the Middle Ages. It became the capital of the Mongol Ilkhanate dynasty in 1299 and later the capital of what western visitors called 'Persia'.* Tabriz was hugely wealthy, wondrous in its architecture, its gardens and the merchandise in its bazaars.

Marco Polo's father and uncle had been partners in trade partly based in Tabriz, as they sought to expand the reach of

* The Jalayirid, Qara Qoyunlu and Aq Qoyunlu empires of the fourteenth and fifteenth centuries.

their mercantile ventures. Marco himself visited the city in the 1270s on his way to China and spent nine months there on his return journey; he found it 'surrounded by beautiful and luscious orchards' and frequented by Genoese, who visited 'to buy the goods that arrive from foreign lands': from India and Baghdad, Mosul and Hormuz. Mandeville, in the 1350s, described Tabriz as the 'most well known' of the many 'lovely' cities in the vicinity of Armenia.

Tabriz was rebuilt by Mahmud Ghazan (d. 1304), the ruler of the Mongol Ilkhanate that covered what is now Iran, Iraq and most of Syria. Tabriz was furnished with elegant baths, markets and a caravanserai at the city's entrance and exit gates, as well as an adjoining customs house. The city was therefore reconfigured around hospitality for visiting merchants and to maximize the efficiency with which money was drawn from them for that hospitality.

The Spanish diplomat Ruy González de Clavijo was part of the embassy of Henry III of Castile to the Mongol conqueror Timur ('Tamberlaine', 1336–1405). Clavijo spent nearly three months at Timur's court in Samarkand in 1404, and left a long description of his journeys, via Tabriz. On entering Tabriz he was told a story about a group of Genoese merchants. They had bought one of the hills overlooking the city in order to build a castle and trading post there. But once they started building their fortress, the then sultan, Jalayir, reneged and told them that they were welcome to buy and remove as much merchandise as they wanted but merchants were not allowed to build or buy their own castles. The Genoese merchants came to appeal to the sultan, who ordered that they all be beheaded.

Clavijo seems to have kept a diary as he travelled and he gave detailed descriptions of many cities in Persia. He found the great city of Tabriz delightful and enchanting. Its water supply, via irrigation channels and conduits, was of particular interest to him. He noted the public drinking fountains and troughs which even in the summer were cooled with pieces of ice (historically, the region did indeed have magnificent ice houses with upper and lower chambers; ice was gathered in the winter, packed in straw and held underground for the summer months). The caravanserais were built along 'fine roadways, with open spaces well laid out'; inside, they had separate apartments and shops with offices. In the markets wonderful silks were sold in the 'immense concourse of merchants and merchandise'. He described the women coming to the shops to buy perfumes and unguents; they wore a 'white sheet' with their face covered by black masks, so their identity was completely unknown. Clavijo noted this as an interesting custom but passed no comment on it otherwise and did not associate it with Islam. Rather, he was overawed by the lavish mosques, 'beautifully adorned with tiles in blue and gold'.

At the same time, he observed that many of the beautiful civic buildings were in a dilapidated state, pulled down at the command of Miran Shah (1366–1408), the Timurid emperor who had conquered Tabriz (and would, in 1408, after Clavijo's visit, lose the city and have his head impaled in front of Tabriz's walls). After nine days in Tabriz, Clavijo had a favourable impression of the city and left with a group of horses given by Timur himself. He was told about the reliable system of relays and post houses set up by Timur, each a day or half a day apart, each of them containing dozens of horses to serve the high road all the way to Samarkand. The infrastructure of trade and diplomacy conquered space, between geographical, political and religious barriers.

A few decades later, in 1474, Giosafat Barbaro stayed at the caravanserai in Tabriz during his visit to 'King Assambei' (again, Shah Uzun Hassan). On the way there, Barbaro had been attacked twice: first by some Kurds, who had killed four of his companions and stolen their sumpter mules (specially bred pack animals); Barbaro had fled on his horse. Shortly afterwards, a man appeared on the road between Khoy and Tabriz and demanded to see Barbaro's letters of introduction. When he refused this man struck him with 'a blow on the face' that caused Barbaro pain for some four months afterwards. But at the royal court in Tabriz Barbaro was greeted courteously by the monarch who, through an interpreter, promised to redress his losses entirely.

One approached the 'king's' lodge – the sultan's reception chamber – through a gated garden, a mud-walled meadow full of pretty contrivances, including a fountain always brimming with water. The 'king' sat on a cushion made of cloth-of-gold, his scimitar beside him, and the entire lodge was bedecked with carpets. It was decorated too with finely wrought mosaics of different colours. The 'king' was surrounded by his counsellors and singers and musicians, playing harps, lutes, rebecs, cymbals and bagpipes, making an 'agreeable' sound. He presented Barbaro with some luxurious garments: a furred gown, a jacket, a silk girdle and a bombazine headpiece. Barbaro was then instructed to go to the Tabriz maidan, the main marketplace, to watch the weekly games, where wild wolves were brought in to fight with men. Later in his stay in Tabriz, he saw various exotic big cats, elephants, a giraffe and civets. The court seems to have been full of the very wonders of the east: rubies, sandalwood, elegant porcelain and jasperware, pearls, cunning cameos, tents embroidered with gold thread, sugar loaves and delicious confectionery. Barbaro's time in Tabriz, defined by its refinement, pleasure and entertainment, recalls the false paradises that were greedily read about in European travel writing.

Contarini's stay in Tabriz just a short time later could not have been more different and shows how travellers often experience the same place in radically varied ways. He found it a dangerous, expensive city. At the caravanserai, he was greeted with abusive whispers and called 'a dog'. People said he had come to create a schism among the Muslims.

The host told Contarini to keep himself concealed and hide away in the caravanserai. When his party grew hungry and needed provisions, Contarini, his interpreter or a travelling companion named Agustino of Pavia had to sneak out to get them. Contarini glimpsed 'many bazaars' full of silks, 'and merchandise of almost every kind'. However, he was recognized and abused and told that he should be 'cut to pieces'. Eventually, he left the Tabriz caravanserai, as it became engulfed in a local conflict, and sought refuge at the Armenian church in the city, where he obtained lodgings for his groups and their horses.

The pursuit of the Earthly Paradise was at the back of most travellers' minds, even though many accounts of Paradise held that it was inaccessible to mankind. Travel writing and fantasy go hand in hand, as travel is always about being somewhere else, a might-have-been world around the next corner or through the next mountain pass. Mandeville – who frequently described places that he hadn't visited and moreover that didn't exist – wrote laconically, 'I can't really describe Paradise properly, because I haven't been there, and that grieves me.' When writers did describe Paradise, it was sometimes a lush garden (the Edenic and Islamic traditions), sometimes an island (as in the voyage of St Brendan), perhaps a high mountain peak (as we saw in the description of Ethiopia) with a spring from which the great rivers ran. It was said that on a journey to Paradise one was likely to meet Temptation, lying in wait in some coppice or hedgerow, and one would have to hope for Hope and Perseverance to appear on the way, to give the strength and courage to reach the ultimate destination. Some thought Paradise was located towards the 'bottom' of the world – beyond Ethiopia and towards the Antarctic – whereas others held that it was in the east, beyond Cathay. Yet, from biblical writers to Christopher Columbus, it is hard to find agreement where the Earthly Paradise was to be found. For instance, on the 'Beatus' maps that circulated widely in twelfth- and thirteenth-century Europe, Paradise is an enclosure near Mount Lebanon, at the 'top' (east) of the map on the edge of Asia. On the Borgia world map, made in southern Germany or Bohemia about 1430, Paradise is a pretty garden in the far north-east (top-left corner), past China. On Giovanni Leardo's Venetian map of 1442, the 'paradixo teresto' is towards the top of the map, east of India, and depicted as a magnificent city – a city not unlike Venice itself in aspect.

Just as vividly evoked as the Earthly Paradise was its opposite number: the false paradise that could seduce the careless traveller.

The ancient Greek geographer Strabo (63 BCE–23 CE) had located a lost or false paradise in India. He wrote that Alexander the Great had been told of this obscure pleasureland, which was a thing firmly of the past. It had a permanent harvest, springs bubbling with water, milk, honey, wine and olive oil. 'Because of abundance and luxury' the people had become lazy and impious, and so the god Zeus had swept all the pleasures away, turned it to dust and made the people toil ever after. It is often a solace to travellers that those places that provide transitory delights are also bound to poverty and conflict: a false paradise might be somewhere to be visited but one wouldn't want to live there.

From the thirteenth century, the land of Cockayne

(Cockaigne, Cuccagna) was the false paradise most widely represented. Cockayne was on a distant shore, somewhere. Work was forbidden, free sex with willing partners was available to all and sinuous brooks ran with youth-giving liquors. The sun never set and one's clothes were even free from lice. Pigs voluntarily roasted themselves as tasty pies flew through the air. The shingles on Cockayne's pretty church were made of wheaten cakes, and one could tug away the sweet masonry and eat and eat and eat. It was a dreamland of plenty. Cockayne was a place only in poetry, a product of the western imagination, and stories of it often circulated among monastic audiences: the Land of Cockayne was a fantasy for those who could not travel, for people confined to a cloister. Cockayne mocked the simple, austere world in which a medieval monk had to live, a world in which one was expected to avoid the deadly sins of gluttony and luxury at all times. The fantasy of Cockayne turned this upside down, with the idea that somewhere, abroad, there was a place where all appetites could be indulged and even sated: the ultimate, but sinful, resort.

The Silk Roads abounded with similar false paradises. The most famous of these was the pleasure garden built by Hassan Ibn Sabbah (d. 1124), who, in the myths written about him, was called 'the Old Man of the Mountain' and led his sect of Assassins. Historically, the 'Assassins' were an Islamic sect (a branch of the Ismaili) but were represented fancifully in subsequent centuries as isolated heretics whose members undertook suicide missions on behalf of their demigod leader. Marco Polo, as he travelled through Persia to India, was one of the first Europeans to report on the Old Man of the Mountain, saying that he had been told the story 'by many people'. Polo added the historically realistic detail that the 'Sheikh of the Mountain' was overthrown in the year 1262 by a khan of the south-western part of the Mongol empire, Hülegü (d. 1265), who besieged the false paradise for a full three years. This place was usually believed to be somewhere in Syria or Persia and is now identified with the Nizari Ismaili fortress of Alamut in northern Iran (destroyed in 1256 by Mongol forces). The sect was responsible for the deaths of caliphs, Crusaders, emirs and atabegs, and for at least two attempts on the life of Saladin, but was also a sophisticated centre of learning and spiritualism.

The Old Man and his alpine false paradise took on their own imagined, grisly features, which were widely reported by travellers and came to supplant the historic reality of Alamut. Descriptions of the Old Man's garden reveal ideas of paradisiacal plenty and luxury: the world as a fool's paradise. The German historian of the Crusades, Arnold of Lübeck (d. 1212), located the Old Man 'in the territory of Damascus, Antioch and Aleppo'. Here, Arnold wrote, the Old Man, a prince, had built many beautiful palaces, enclosed with the highest walls. 'Many sons of his peasants were brought up from the cradle in these palaces, and they are taught various languages, namely Latin, Greek, Romance, Arabic and many others,' instructed by the prince's teachers until they reached adulthood. Then they were fully convinced that they must obey every word and command of the prince of the land and in return they were promised a place in paradise. In Arnold's telling, the false paradise was a kind of secret military training camp-cum-university in the mountains, a place where young minds were bent to the Old Man's purposes.

In the Old Man's garden, young men were given narcotics (usually hashish, hence the sect's name, Assassins, the hashish eaters). This narcotic would make them fall into a kind of dazed stupor of utter pliancy. At this point, the Old Man would secure the young men's loyalty, promising each man that if he should agree to die he would enter this paradise eternally, and have the young virgins for ever (and as much sex with them as possible and they would still remain virgins). And so each young man who came to visit would make a promise to be loyal to the Old Man and they became unafraid of death, because the beautiful paradise awaited them. Through this trick the Old Man would send the young men into his rivals' territories. The loyal, servile youths, dulled with the Old Man's magic potions and now unafraid of death and looking forward to a posthumous life of endless sex in paradise, would kill the Old Man's rivals, plunder their riches, often sacrificing themselves in the process.

Mandeville, writing c. 1356, delineated a 'sumptuous, well-fortified castle on a mountain' which included 'the prettiest garden'. This contained the sweetest herbs and the loveliest flowers, alongside 'fine fountains and also many pleasant halls and chambers decorated with gold and azure'. Mandeville also included the detail that the Old Man had contrived 'various entertainments and beasts and birds that sang and moved by virtue of clockwork machinery as if they were alive', suggesting both technical ingenuity and the perils of false-seeming.

In Mandeville's description of the garden, there were three virgin girls, not yet aged fifteen, and three rosy-cheeked lads of the same age. They all wore golden clothes and were introduced to visitors as angels. They sat around three pleasant fountains connected to an underground conduit, 'so that whenever [the Old Man] wished one fountain ran with wine, another with milk, another with honey. And he called this place Paradise.'

The story of the Old Man of the Mountain and his false paradise shows a distrust of civilization, violence lurking behind the garden's seductive artifice. The story recognizes travellers' desire for both the Earthly Paradise and its false equivalents. Medieval travellers identified current or former paradises in the lush orchards, sumptuous bowers and arresting brothels they encountered on their route. The Flemish pilgrim Joos van Ghistele, travelling through Egypt in 1481, glimpsed rich merchants indulging themselves in summer-houses and pleasure pavilions near Cairo. These fortunate men enjoyed banquets and orgiastic parties with beautiful women. Van Ghistele commented that it was like the Earthly and Heavenly Paradise rolled into one. As a mere passing traveller he could gaze wonderingly in, relieved to be excluded from its deceitful charms.

The Old Man of the Mountain did not prosper. At some point all the other local lords learned about his ruse. They marched together on his castle, with their armies of archers and elephants, and they killed him and destroyed his false paradise.

Later travellers were unsure about exactly where the Old Man's castle had been, but making their way along the Silk Roads they often passed remnants and ruins, alluring rubble that spoke of lost consequence and faded power. This caused some to wonder if they had stumbled across the last vestiges of the false paradise of the Old Man of the Mountain.

During his travels along the Silk Roads, Giosafat Barbaro learned from a certain Dominican friar named Vincent, a native of Caffa, about violent routs in the year 1486 of the local peoples by fervent Muslims. One such place that had been attacked was 'the country of Gog & Magog', somewhere near the Caspian Mountains. This was a nation, Vincent told him, of Christians who followed the Greek rite and had been violently slain. Barbaro seems to have accepted that there was a land called 'Gog & Magog', a place and a people repeatedly mentioned by travellers but also without fixed coordinates or even a fixed religion.

In the Bible, there is cryptic mention of 'Gog & Magog', at once a person or people, a tribe and a place. In the Apocalypse it is written that, after 1,000 years of tranquillity, Satan will be released to 'seduce the nations . . . over the four quarters of the earth, Gog, and Magog', gathering them all together in battle (Revelation 20:7–9). Then Gog & Magog will spread over 'the breadth of the earth', encompass 'the camp of the saints' and the 'beloved city' (Jerusalem). And a fire will come down from Heaven and devour them. Here Gog & Magog were understood to represent Satan's forces in a last-ditch attempt to overcome Christendom, and were a cornerstone of millennial thinking, of the epic battle to come after 1,000 years.

By the Middle Ages, Gog & Magog had undergone many transformations. As a place (usually a mountain range) or as a people, Gog & Magog were thought to be located somewhere on the Silk Roads: either in the Caucasus Mountains or 'beyond' China. Gog & Magog were sometimes said to be at Derbent on the Caspian Sea. Derbent's name comes from the Persian *dar-band*, 'barred gate': Alexander the Great was said to have trapped the tribes of Gog & Magog here behind closed gates or walls, restraining them from imposing their designs on the rest of the world. The Spanish Franciscan of c. 1350, who claimed to have been in Ethiopia, also said he had resided in the 'castle of Magog', a wonderful fortress built of magnetic iron above the River Magog. It had a counterpart castle of Gog across the valley, and 10,000 men could reside in each. Between the two was a set of iron gates, shutting the entrance to Tatary.

In a complicated and elaborate set of transformations, these enclosed tribes moved eastwards in the western imagination, seeming to reflect developing fears of incursions by the tribal groups across Asia. Alexander's Caspian gates even became the Great Wall of China in some fourteenth-century accounts. Ibn Battuta, an indefatigable traveller from Tangier in north-western Morocco, wrote that the Great Wall of Gog & Magog was sixty days from China. 'This territory', he said, 'is occupied by wandering tribes of heathen, who eat such people as they can catch, and for this reason no one enters their country or attempts to travel there.' He said he had heard about this only from people who had never been there.

The people of Gog & Magog were represented equally variously – either as a group of Hebrew-speaking Jewish cannibals said to be locked within these mountains (waiting for the Antichrist to release them and lead them into Christendom as in the biblical account) or as Tatars. Sometimes they were said to be giants or to practise incest or free love or to poison wells in an effort to spread the plague. A closely related tradition developed, especially in Germany, of a group called the 'Red Jews', who inhabited a land in the east and would one day invade Europe, during the Apocalypse, seeking to overwhelm Christendom.

Mandeville's fourteenth-century travel guide presented a revealing depiction of Gog & Magog. According to him, the Jewish people of ten lost biblical tribes lived there, constrained by walls, mountains and the Caspian Sea. They chose not to escape via the Caspian because they didn't know where it would lead them. In Mandeville's account, they spoke a secret language known to no other men, and for these reasons 'the Jews have no proper land of their own' except this enclosed space between the mountains; and even for this they had to pay tribute to the Queen of Armenia. Mandeville's description of Gog & Magog foregrounds a crucial issue for the traveller: is 'land' or 'nation' a matter of language? Is having a 'proper land' of one's own what makes a people a people? Medieval definitions of 'nation' tended to conjoin language, customs and religion. Gog & Magog can be seen as attempting to think through what it means to be a diaspora, to be a people without a 'proper land', in a world in which cultural identity was derived from land and language.

The changing representation of Gog & Magog displays many features of medieval travel cultures. Places were often extrapolated from vague biblical or historical references. Such places were highly mobile, serving the visitor's needs rather than the specifics of geography. Gog & Magog stood for a dimly apprehended but clearly moralized place; it was a moral landscape waiting for the world to claim it. Fantasies of Gog & Magog were suffused with fantasies of coming to the end of time and to the ends of the world. Gog & Magog also represent the thoroughgoing antisemitism of many medieval Christian travellers who, even when curious and receptive to new cultures and marvels overseas, reserved a vicious hatred for Jewish people wherever they were encountered. It was as if travel across the Silk Roads depended on conjuring warlike adversaries, whose minds were set on the conquest of Europe. Throughout the western history of travel writing, as throughout medieval literature, Jewish residents and visitors tend to function as primal outsiders, represented as inimical to Christian culture and fundamentally threatening. In this form of knowledge, the actual power dynamics of Christian Europe, in which the Jewish communities formed a tiny and embattled minority, were reversed, with a fantasy that saw the Christians as persecuted explorers and gave a threatening agency to imaginary Jewish aggressors, deep within the secretive bounds of the Silk Roads.

The creatures of India

Here follow some of the kinds of monstrous creatures of India:

- Snakes so huge that their diet consists mainly of stags.
- An animal called the leucrocota, with the body of an ass, a stag's haunches, the chest and legs of a lion, horse's hooves, a forked horn and a face that is nearly human.
- Tawny bulls whose hair stands on end in a hideous fashion. They have an immense head and grin open-mouthed from ear to ear. They can extend their horns for battle, and any missile bounces off their tough hides. They cannot be tamed.
- The beast called the manticore is found in India too: it has a human face, three rows of teeth, a lion's body with a scorpion's tail, and burning eyes. It's a blood-red colour and hisses like a snake. It feeds on human flesh and can run faster than a flying bird.
- The unicorn is also found there, with the body of a horse, a stag's head, elephant's feet and a pig's tail. In the middle of its forehead is a single horn, four foot long, gleaming bright and incredibly sharp. The unicorn is very fierce and

has an awful bellow; it transfixes anything in its way with its horn. It can be killed but cannot be tamed.

- There are crabs too, with pincers six cubits long. They can seize elephants and drown them underwater.
- The Indian Ocean produces tortoises, from whose shells people make roomy houses for themselves.

11. From Persia through India

Hormuz – Calicut – Cochin – Maldives – Land of the Brahmins

We now follow the route south-eastwards trailing the vicious hot winds to the great port of Hormuz on the Persian Gulf. This was a popular route from the vastness of the Arabian Desert to the rich wonders of India. If one didn't travel to India and China via land one could take the quicker and arguably safer route by sea. From around 1400, the sea passage became more established than the land route, with the voyage eastwards starting at the Strait of Hormuz, where the Persian Gulf opens into the Arabian Sea.

The ports on the Persian side of the strait – especially Hormuz itself – were the main havens for trade and exchange between India, Arabia and the Indian Ocean. Because of ongoing incursions from Mongol armies, the entire town of Hormuz had been relocated around 1300 from the mainland to the tiny island of Djarun, a harsh peak made of brilliant red-ochre sands and salt. Later medieval 'New Hormuz' was a markedly multicultural city, with merchants and navigators from China, Gujarat and Armenia mingling with Venetian and Genoese brokers, attorneys and missionaries. Around 50,000 people lived densely packed within about five square miles. Hormuz had magnificent bazaars, and hundreds of vessels docked in its harbours, Italian galleys bobbing alongside dhows made out of coconut husks held together by thread and wooden pegs. Marco Polo, visiting Hormuz after travelling through Persia in the 1270s, noted 'all sorts of spices, precious stones and pearls, silk and gold fabrics, elephants' tusks and many other products' being sold there. But he was disturbed by the 'torrid' scorching-hot climate and by the local custom of plunging neck-deep into water to escape from the heat of the summer desert winds. Polo called Hormuz an 'insalubrious' place.

Other visitors likewise felt that Hormuz was best avoided: its sweltering weather seemed to reflect a broader corruption. Odoric of Pordenone was one of the most important travel writers of the European Middle Ages. He was an intrepid and loquacious Franciscan missionary, described by contemporaries as small in stature with a red forked beard; he travelled with another friar, James of Ireland, about whom very little is known. Odoric's world spanned the Friulian village of Pordenone where he grew up, 75 kilometres north-east of Venice, and a three-year stay at the court of the great khan in China. His account of his travels became very widely read and was much imitated. He visited Hormuz in 1318 and said that the heat there was 'incredible' and 'dangerous', and that there were neither trees nor fresh water. He described how the heat caused men's testicles to hang down their legs as far as their knees. In the 1350s John Mandeville elaborated on Odoric's account, saying that the heat made 'men's bollocks hang down to their shins'. This was 'due to their considerable physical degeneracy'. Local people knew how to bind the testicles, smearing them 'with a special ointment to hold them up'. Otherwise these men would die. Some manuscripts of Mandeville's travel guide include pictures of the men of Hormuz, their vast testicles flopping down their legs like extra, shapeless limbs.

Such testicular rumours may simply reflect that age-old licence, via travel, to titter at the absurdities and unreliability of the human body. But the idea that the heat of Hormuz caused men's testicles to sag to their shins came from the encounter of travellers with different versions of 'nature', including climate. While earlier geographers had believed the equatorial torrid zone to be uninhabitable, by Odoric's and Mandeville's time it was understood that, even though people lived there, the tropics existed in a kind of freakish juxtaposition to the temperate lands and 'balanced' civilizations of Europe. Nature did strange things to the inhabitants and the outrageous heat of Hormuz was reflected in the dissolute bodies of its menfolk.

Odoric called Hormuz the 'gateway to India'. The city was also then the gateway to the strange, the marvellous and the frightening. The stuff in its bazaar would make its way to the markets and households of western Europe. Yet at Hormuz the European traveller had left the Holy Land far behind and had left Christendom too. Customs, weather, food, even human bodies, had become unfamiliar and astonishing.

From Hormuz, vessels made their way across the Arabian Sea and to the Indian Ocean, following the main east–west sea route. This route connected Europe and the Middle East to the great territory of India, named after the Indus river running down from the mountains on the subcontinent's north-west side.

The medieval terminology of India embraced the entire subcontinent, from what is today eastern Iran to Myanmar and beyond. India was conventionally divided into three parts. According to Mandeville's definition, these were Lesser India, a temperate region; Greater India, a scorching-hot region; and northern India, a mountainous, icy region. The Venetian traveller Nicolò Conti described the first part of India as being from Persia to the Indus river (today's Afghanistan and Pakistan); the second part from the Indus to the

Ganges (that is, the northern section of India, today's Gujarat, Rajasthan, Punjab, Uttar Pradesh and Nepal); and the third part, 'all that is beyond': the south of the Indian subcontinent, including Sri Lanka, and what are now Bangladesh and Myanmar. For Conti, this third part was the most sumptuous, wealthy, elegant: the people here, he said, 'lead a more refined life, removed from all barbarity and coarseness'. The men were extremely humane, and the merchants very rich.

Each traveller to India had their own idea of how the subcontinent's theoretical geography mapped on to the places they were visiting. India itself was often described as comprising thousands – perhaps 5,000 – 'islands' or territories, a landscape of almost infinite variety and diversity. Despite the familiarity of Indian goods in European markets, 'India' – as an idea – was reported as a place of abundance and strangeness, marvels, idols and natural prodigies, with much to teach the attentive traveller. European travellers had read about the enormous wealth and nibbana-inducing pleasure gardens they were likely to find there. And some travellers' experiences of India seemed to echo or confirm this: they found strange fruit and pungent spices almost freely available, amazing palaces wrought from exotic materials, and non-Christian princes who mulcted dazzling riches and absolute power from huge populations.

In India, nature shocked at every turn. The air was thick with heat; it felt like one was breathing broth. Plump mosquitoes hung lazily in the air, worrying at the neck and wrists and ankles. Reticulated snakes thrice as long as a man crawled through city streets, as elephants went forth caparisoned with castles atop their backs. Wily grinning monkeys and spotted wildcats attacked those travellers foolish enough to take to the roads after dark. In the night sky, the map of the stars was all different, as if the great painted cloth of the firmament had been twisted about. Odoric of Pordenone, visiting India in 1318, said, in summary, 'in the whole world there be no such marvels as in the realm of India.'

The Franciscan missionary Jordan of Sévérac, travelling through India in 1329, repeatedly found that he could not describe what he saw there: the 'perfectly horrible' heat was 'more intolerable to strangers than it is possible to say'. The mango, which he called *aniba* (a version of its Marathi name), was 'a fruit so sweet and delicious as it is impossible to utter in words'. The trees of India were so many and so diverse that 'to describe them would be beyond the comprehension of man.' If travel writing is a form of knowledge, a way of mastering place, then India consistently eluded such mastery: it was impossible to describe.

Indian spices, gems, scent, linen, even parrots and cats, were exported westwards to the Middle East and thence to Europe, staples for wealthy consumers across the world. The medieval documents archived in the Cairo *genizah* (a synagogue storeroom) show an incredibly wide range of objects being traded westwards out of India: waterskins full of pickled fish, coconuts (and coconut scrapers), carpets, rat traps, fishermen's gear, glassware. Not surprisingly, the parts of India best known to travellers from the west were the merchant ports on India's western coast: Khambat in the north, Thane (now a suburb of Mumbai), Calicut (Kozhikode), Cochin and Kollam in the far south.

The Venetian merchant Nicolò Conti left two accounts of his travels in India: the first he gave to the Spanish traveller Pero Tafur when they met in Sinai in 1437 and the second he recounted later to the Italian humanist Poggio Bracciolini (1380–1459) when they met in Rome. Conti spent many years in the Middle East and India, involved in the gold and spice trades. After travelling as far as Java, he stayed for months on the Malabar Coast of south-western India, probably in 1419–20. His account of it, as given by Bracciolini, combines utterly prosaic descriptions of each town's circumference with flights of fancy.

Conti's first observation about Malabar was the wealth of ginger, pepper, brazil wood and cinnamon. These were all rich pickings for the European market. But he immediately also pointed out the enormous snakes ('six ells in length', nearly seven metres), harmless unless irritated, and attracted to little children. While this seems to be a description of a python, the other animals he says he saw there are harder to identify: airborne cats (perhaps colugos or flying lemurs) that flew 'from tree to tree by extending their feet and shaking their wings'; a harmless four-footed serpent with an 'oblong tail' whose meat was prized 'as the best kind of food'; a seven-headed winged serpent that could kill a man with its breath alone, living in the trees.

Be aware: In this region there are hippopotami living both on land and in the water. They are half man, half horse and they love to eat nothing more than men when they can get some.

Conti was particularly impressed by the important port city of Calicut. Calicut was a familiar place for western travellers, mentioned by Pliny and Ptolemy even in ancient times as a source of pepper. Conti found it to be 'a noble emporium for all India', selling paper, ginger, cinnamon, lac (shellac resin), cherry plums and the precious zedoary (white turmeric root, used for stomach medicine in the medieval west). Calicut was India's main western port in the twelfth to fourteenth centuries (and gave the west the unbleached cotton fabric 'calico').

It was at Calicut in 1498 that the Portuguese navigator Vasco da Gama landed, when a 'multitude of people, all dark and naked, flocked to the beach, only covered with cloths halfway down the thigh, with which they concealed their nakedness'. Da Gama's biographer Gaspar Correia (1492–1563) claimed that, for the locals, the Portuguese were something 'they had never before seen'. This tone of wonder, and the self-aggrandizing pose of being the first arrivals, is hard to square with the medieval history of the Malabar Coast, whose ports had a long history of welcoming strangers. By 1400, the area was deeply cosmopolitan. It is inconceivable that the locals had not seen foreign merchants before, as the city had for many years been central to the spice and silk routes.

From the 1340s, Cochin started to rival Calicut as the key western port. Cochin, a promontory on an island, was transformed by a flood in 1341, which both destroyed the nearby ancient port of Kodungallur (Cranganore) and created a deep natural harbour beside the promontory. Cochin always had a diverse population, including many Buddhists, Hindus and Muslims, as well as Christians following the eastern Syriac rite ('Nestorians'), and Jewish worshippers who founded a synagogue in Cochin in 1344. In 1405 the Perumpadappu Swaroopam princely family moved their capital to Cochin and the city flourished. The Portuguese landed there in 1500 and occupied it in 1503; in 1524, Vasco da Gama would be buried there, in the Church of St Francis, often called the first Christian church founded by Europeans in India. The goods traded out of Cochin and from the Malabar Coast were highly prized in the west and made the area dazzlingly wealthy: the plenty there seduced western visitors, although they were more troubled by local customs and religions.

Landing at Cochin around 1400, the visitor would have

been greeted by huge stone statues, round-bellied and garlanded, of Krishna and Shiva, alongside secular reliefs of naked dancers. The ornate, multi-storey buildings were guarded by legions of carved animals, and even the local coins had tiny animals stamped on them. The local statuary had a level of delicacy and intricacy, and was carved in precious materials that were largely unknown in Europe. The temples were worked in local darkwoods, alive with carved leaping tigers. The gables were crowned with a lordly sitting elephant, the peaceful and wise god Ganesha, symbolizing wisdom, comprehension and the removal of obstacles. Other statues called to mind the saints of Europe, carved with their symbolic attributes, but in India they were often boldly naked, nipples and phalli proudly displayed, and with animal parts. On first glance, figures of the mother goddess Varahi, standing upright holding a baby to her breast, looked similar to the Virgin Mary. But Varahi had a sow's head, sometimes tusked, and an aspect of vengeance rather than meekness.

Conti strongly warned Pero Tafur, when they met at Sinai, against going to India. According to Tafur (whose account of Conti differs somewhat from Bracciolini's), Conti had spent some forty years in India and knew it very well: in fact, he had married an Indian woman, a match made by a local prince, and had three children, all born in India. Conti warned against the 'long and troublesome' route between India and Europe (he himself had been forced to convert to Islam in Mecca). In India, the visitor would have to contend with strange races without laws or rulers, the unusual air, the different food and drink, the bestial people (he claimed to have seen cannibalism) who, he said, were unable to govern themselves. Conti seemed to be saying that India was no destination for the curious tourist (Tafur himself longed to go to India

only out of curiosity). According to Tafur, Conti told him, 'You will see heaps of gold and pearls and precious stones, but what shall they profit you since the people are beasts who wear them?'

After listening to Conti's stories of India, Tafur gave up his plans to visit. He wrote resignedly, 'I concluded that if I did not fly there, it was impossible to make the journey.'

Afanasiy Nikitin was a well-connected merchant from the city of Tver, west of Moscow. In the late 1460s, Nikitin left his hometown to travel to the area around the Caucasus and western Persia with a merchant caravan, seeking new markets with the permission of Mikhail (d. 1505), the young Grand Prince of Tver. Nikitin set off with a mixed group of Russian and Persian merchants, travelling through the established trade route of the lower Volga river. But, as with many travellers at the time, circumstances intervened: after stowing away on a moonlit passage to Astrakhan, Nikitin was chased and shot at, his boat ran aground on fish traps, his luggage was plundered, he was shipwrecked in a storm and robbed again. And so, unable to pay for his passage home and led by unhappy providence and a need to recover multiple losses, he went far from his intended route and left his fellow travellers. He visited Baku, where he marvelled at the naphtha fuel burning in the ground with inextinguishable fire. He travelled through Persia for a couple of years. At Jahrom, he wondered at the cattle fed on dates. He reached Hormuz in the spring, probably of 1469; he celebrated Easter there.

Familiar with the cool forests and snowy winters of western Russia, Nikitin found the heat of Hormuz astonishing. There, he said, 'the sun is scorching and burns men.' But he also noted that the city was 'a vast emporium of all the world; you find there people and goods of every description, and whatever thing is produced on earth you find it in Hormuz'. Hormuz was a kind of crossroads of the oceans. Nikitin, alone and unsure but resourceful and entrepreneurial, found himself in bazaars teeming seductively with merchandise.

From Hormuz, Nikitin embarked on an epic and surprising journey which went far beyond the mercantile remit of his initial project and was recorded by him in a disorderly narrative comprising various notes and reminiscences. He sailed across the Arabian Sea, thousands of kilometres, to India. Reaching India later in the year, he settled there for three years, working as a horse dealer. He spent time in Junnar, an ancient town a day's journey from the coast, sited on a stony crag surrounded by forests infested with wildcats. He observed how the Khan of Junnar had elephants and horses to ride, but chose sometimes to ride his male attendants, men who had been captured or bought from the central Asian tribes of Khorosan. At this time, Junnar was part of the Bahmani sultanate, a powerful Muslim kingdom covering much of the west and central region of the Indian subcontinent.

At first, Indian people followed Nikitin about everywhere he went, transfixed by the whiteness of his skin and the clothing covering his whole body. Conversely, Nikitin described the dark-skinned people of India, both shocked and aroused by their nakedness, the women's bare breasts and the 'wicked' harlotry of the Bahmani women.

He described the kind of Indian inn (sometimes called a *dharmasala*, *sarai* or *sattra*) for foreign merchants. Hospices and shelters with food and a bed were often free to travellers as they supported trade. Nikitin says the landlady prepared food, made up the bed and then had sex with the guest. He added that the local women seemed to like white men. They would have sex with their husbands during the day and in the evening go to the foreign men, bringing sweet spiced pastries for the foreigner and sometimes even offering the man money to have sex with them, 'because they like strangers and white people'. At a pilgrimage and trade-fair site dedicated to the Hindu goddess Parvati, Nikitin noted the 'cheap' price of the women, and gave his reader a tariff: 2 *jital* silver coins for intercourse with a woman; 4 *varaha* gold coins for intercourse with a pretty woman; 5 *varaha* for intercourse with what Nikitin seemed to regard as the most attractive woman: a comely, dark-skinned lady, 'all black with small and pretty nipples'. To travel is to ponder sex and sexual discovery: we now call this sex tourism, but a great deal of sightseeing contains an element of lust. Sex tourism supplies travellers' wants and puts the traveller into an intimate set of financial, erotic and exotic relationships with the people among whom they travel. Paying for sex, making money from sex and having kinds of sex not available at home have long been a part of the culture of travel. The 'romance' of travel is often simply a synonym for having a new kind of sex, or feeling sexually alive in new places.

There is a strong sense that Nikitin broadened his own sexual horizons during his journey, rather than just reporting on customs he observed. As his travels went on, he became less censorious of the locals, less upright in his Christian values and less sure of his western, Russian ways. 'He who travels through many countries will fall into many sins, and deprive himself of the Christian faith,' he reflected, self-accusingly, about his time (probably in 1472) at the Muslim court at Bidar, the elegant capital of the Bahmani sultanate.

We might see Nikitin as an early example of the independent traveller who 'goes native', or for whom travel took on elements of assimilation and self-transformation. At first, he tried to avoid eating the local food, surviving on bread and water, but later ate hungrily with local Hindus, Buddhists and Muslims. He wondered at the country's spicery, its pepper, ginger, cloves, cinnamon, aromatic roots, all cheap and tasty and readily available. He got to know the customs and theology of other religions well. Having been robbed of his prayer books early on in his journey, he started to forget when the Christian festivals were, he didn't know when it was Easter or Christmas and he began to lose track of what day of the week it was. He spent most of his time with Muslims, and at one point a local Muslim, Melikh, forcibly converted him to Islam. Nikitin seems to have concealed his Christianity and started to wear Islamic clothing; he took on a Muslim name, Khoza Issuf Khorossani, and declared himself to be 'between the two faiths' of Christianity and Islam. His account finishes with a prayer, in his Arabic, to 'all-hearing, all-seeing Allah', in a clear and apparently voluntary profession of the Islamic faith.

There comes a turning point – it may be hours or it may be months – in each journey when we start to abandon the idea of going home, or at least of going home unchanged. Is there not a moment when every traveller asks themselves, 'What was the point?' What has one got from one's journey? Could one just stay travelling, and never go home? In each new place he visited, in each new foreign experience, Nikitin found new versions of himself that he had not known. The foreignness of the peoples and places he encountered was transmuted into the foreignness of his own past. Travel is often longed for as an escape from the banality and laboriousness of everyday life, but Nikitin went further than this. For if we stay travelling for too long we often feel the need to understand, even to become, the people among whom we travel.

As we pick up new languages abroad, we sometimes also seem to take on new personalities, different selves. Nikitin was an unusually intrepid traveller, and he knew that his journeys were beyond unusual. He sent his account, his Russian punctuated with Arabic and Turkish, back to Russia as a written testimony of what he had become in India. It did not circulate widely, but was copied into several chronicles as the record of a remarkable experience.

In 1472 Nikitin started to make his way back to Tver, and wrote some further parts of his narrative at Caffa on the Black Sea. But he met his death – we are not sure how – near Smolensk in the Grand Duchy of Lithuania. He had travelled so far, survived and engaged with such a variety of experiences and undergone such changes, yet he became another traveller who never returned home.

*

Somewhat similar to Nikitin, but more timid, was the Genoese merchant Jeronimo di Santo Stefano, who went on a 'disastrous journey' to India in the 1490s. Santo Stefano set off with his business partner Jeronimo Adorno on what they thought was going to be a straightforward profitable journey: to buy coral beads and other goods in Cairo and sell them in India, and then bring back goods from India and sell them in Europe.

The pair reached India, sailing in a flimsy *jalba*, a low little craft made of old planks stitched together with cords and driven with cotton sails. It took the two Genoese twenty-five days to get from El Qoseir, on the Egyptian coast of the Red Sea, to India's Malabar Coast.

All went well at first for the two Jeronimos: they found Christians living in the area around Calicut. They learned about the wondrous pepper trees and ginger roots and coconuts. They saw the devotions of the locals, worshipping an ox (cattle are holy in Buddhism, Hinduism and Jainism) or the sun (both Buddhism and Hinduism have significant solar deities) or little home-made 'idols'. They learned excitedly about the local nuptial customs, that each lady could take 'seven or eight' husbands, and that no man wished to marry a virgin.

They then sailed to Sri Lanka, their eyes agog as they came upon highly marketable merchandise. Cinnamon trees grew big as laurels. Precious stones – garnet, jacinth, cat's eye – twinkled everywhere.

Moving on to the Coromandel Coast, on the south-eastern side of India, they saw beautiful red sandalwood, perfect for building handsome houses. After seven months somewhere on that coast, the two men then decided it was time to sell their merchandise. So they set off for a place they had heard about, a land called Ava (which covered the northern and central parts of today's Myanmar), where there were wonderful rubies to be purchased. But a local war meant they couldn't take the route to Ava so instead they travelled to Bago, in the Buddhist kingdoms they called 'Lower India' (now the southern coast of Myanmar). Things started to go badly wrong here for the two Genoese.

They agreed with the Lord of Bago that they would receive 2,000 ducats for their goods. Everything was finalized and contracted and understood, but the Lord of Bago would not release the money. Jeronimo and Jeronimo went daily to his court to request payment. Each day they grew poorer and hungrier, and suffered more from the extremes of heat and cold. And then, after fifty-five days, Jeronimo Adorno died: he'd never been a hardy man, and this finished him off. He passed away on 27 December 1496, and there was not even a priest present to administer the sacraments. Jeronimo di Santo Stefano had his friend's body buried in the grounds of a ruined church, an abandoned place 'frequented by none'. He mourned his friend continually and prayed for his soul. He thought he might die too. But he rallied when at last he got paid by the Lord of Bago for his goods. Then he set sail again.

The Indian Ocean connected a vast trading network, encompassing the east and west coasts of India, Mauritius, the Seychelles, the Maldives, the Andaman and Nicobar Islands and Sumatra. They were connected by trading ginger, sandalwood, pepper and cardamom, coral, paper, arsenic, civet perfume and indigo. On medieval European maps, the landmass of Asia disintegrates into a myriad of tiny islands across the Indian Ocean. Monsoon winds linked the entire area, over distances of thousands of kilometres. Jeronimo di Santo Stefano might have turned back and headed for home when the Lord of Bago had given him the money he was owed, but he decided to sail south-east for Sumatra, attracted by its silks, resins and spicery.

Many travellers are painfully aware of that moment when a purposeful, well-organized and much anticipated trip takes on the heart-sinking character of a fool's errand: every expense incurred, every misfortune encountered, every experience at best a disappointment. And yet the traveller ploughs on, hoping to get something good from the voluntary ordeal. Disasters continued to afflict Jeronimo as he travelled onwards: his property was seized (the local lord claimed it as Adorno's estate as he had died in his jurisdiction) and much of it confiscated. He sailed first to Khambat in Gujarat, and there he sold everything he had for silks and resins that he could trade back home.

Thus Jeronimo di Santo Stefano sailed south, to the palm-fringed shores of the Maldives, due south of Cochin. The Maldives, coral atolls comprising several thousand tiny islands spread over a vast area of cobalt sea, were at this time an Islamic sultanate and a busy entrepôt amid the Indian Ocean trading routes. The archipelago was far from remote, due to its location on the main sea routes from Java and Sumatra to India, Aden and Hormuz. The islands exported ambergris, tortoiseshell and coir rope, but were also a trading post for spices and gems and Chinese silks and pottery. The bad weather forced Jeronimo to spend six months among what he described as the 'black and naked, but healthy and courteous' locals, living on fish and a little imported rice.

The Maldivians had followed Buddhism until their conversion to Islam in 1153; local people held that their conversion was thanks to a visiting sage from the Maghreb who had banished a demon. The islands remained dotted with remnants of their Buddhist past in the form of *hawitta* mounds and *stupa* temples, the sites of which were often converted into mosques. Flying fish made their way purposefully over the waves. Crabs of many sizes scudded everywhere on land. At dusk, giant black fruitbats – winged flying foxes, like foxes in flight – circled the breadfruit trees.

Ibn Battuta visited the Maldives for a period of about eight months, landing at the port of Kinolhas in late 1343. Having travelled enormous distances across Eurasia, he can to some extent be seen as an early explorer; it is not clear what made him visit the islands, although he seemed to go on a touristic whim, saying simply that he had heard about them. The islands, led from the capital at Malé, were then under the sovereignty of Queen Khadija (d. 1380), a sultan's daughter who assassinated her brother (and, later, at least two husbands). Ibn Battuta was welcomed as a sage from north Africa, and appointed chief judge, and he also married a woman from the Maldivian royal family. He found the people 'pious and upright' and sincere, but their devotion lax. He noted the unveiled women's costumes, naked from the waist up. Once he had established himself as a senior judge, he tried and failed to make women including the queen cover themselves. He drove people to mosque with his constable's staff on Fridays. He recorded that his main diet was of coconut: coconut flesh, coconut milk, coconut honey and coconut sap ('oil'). Having married four women, fathered a child and made some enemies in the upper echelons of Maldivian society, Ibn Battuta left in August 1344 for Sri Lanka.

The tiny atolls of the Maldives had a long reach because cowrie shells harvested there and in southern India were the main currency across the Indian Ocean; the tiny shells were also used for jewellery and in religious rituals. Visiting southern China in the 1280s, Marco Polo observed white cowries being used as currency (80 cowries = 2 Venetian groats) alongside gold coinage. Ibn Battuta noted how the Maldivians gathered the beadlike shells from the sea, left them in pits for the flesh to disappear so that they were then ready to be used as currency – at an astonishing rate of 400,000 cowrie shells for 1 gold dinar. He related that the Maldivians bought rice with the shells from the people of Bengal, and that Yemenites used the shells for ship ballast. He also recalled that he had seen the shells being used in Mali and elsewhere in west Africa. Later, similar money cowries were encountered by Portuguese travellers in Senegal in the 1440s.

Jeronimo di Santo Stefano spent six months in the Maldives. Eventually the conditions looked reasonable for setting sail again but, after just eight days, his little vessel was overwhelmed with water. It was impossible to bail it out, and it sank. Some of the men on board drowned. Jeronimo floated overnight, clinging on to a wooden plank, praying desperately for divine mercy, lost in the middle of the traveller's loneliness. What a strange turn of events: a timorous and materialistic Genoese merchant adrift alone in the Laccadive Sea for an entire night, the water streaked with the silver of moonlight and full of unthinkable creatures, stingrays flying soundlessly in the deep, massive shoals of fish clouding the waves.

Eventually a vessel came and rescued Jeronimo. He was returned to Khambat in Gujarat.

Jeronimo di Santo Stefano made his long way back to the west as part of a Silk Road caravan via Hormuz and Isfahan. This caravan, of Armenian and Persian merchants, was 'attacked and plundered', but finally Santo Stefano reached the Ottoman port of Tripoli (now in northern Lebanon) on the Mediterranean coast. Here the Genoese had formed friendly relations with the Ottoman Turks and there was an established community of Genoese merchants. Jeronimo wrote to his friend

Messer Giovan Jacobo Mainer back in Genoa, describing his disastrous travels. He evidently made little or no financial profit on his travels, so he thanked God for the spiritual profit he had made, the 'great mercy' shown to him. He signed off his letter, written in September 1499, intending to return home.

In the accounts of travellers like Nikitin and the two Jeronimos, the whole of India appears as a barely comprehensible fever dream: strange, alarming, a land of promised delights and unknowable perils. If the world was an encyclopaedia for the traveller to peruse, India was its own strange book, hard to read and understand. For Nikitin and Santo Stefano, travelling in India confirmed rather than denied its ever-surprising nature as an immeasurable geographical and social system. India was both an almost indescribable place of wondrous stories and a false paradise where a life of easy luxury could turn to a diseased demise with astonishing speed.

If one were to travel further in India (at least according to Mandeville) one would find a land where the people had feathers on their entire body except their faces and the palms of their hands. These people could move across water just as easily as across dry land. Nearby, there was another country where one would find two oracular trees, the Tree of the Sun and the Tree of the Moon. The trees spoke Indian and Greek, and foretold visitors' futures. It was hard to travel there, however, because of wild animals – dragons and snakes – in the desert. In the nearby isle of Pytan, tiny people lived off the scent of wild apples; they had to carry these apples with them whenever they travelled abroad and died if they were deprived of the scent. There were dozens and dozens of other Indian lands and islands: one where the people had no heads but rather eyes in their shoulders and mouths on their chests; one where an eyeless and headless group of people had mouths in their backs; another where there were flat-faced people without a nose or eyes or lips; another where there were people with one huge lip, which they could use as a sunshade; another land where there were people who were both male and female at the same time, with the genitals of both. John Mandeville even described a kingdom where the king was appointed not because of his wealth or nobility but through something called an 'election', according to whoever is 'morally superior and most righteous and just'. What a different world India was: in Europe, kings usually inherited their thrones or gained them through might and strife!

These peripheral, unencountered people at the threshold of civilization represent the fantastical creativity of the imagination, and the traveller's love of categorization and miscategorization. Yet by constantly depicting India as an exotic wonderland, western visitors often overlooked the everyday humanity of its inhabitants. The motifs of awed discovery and exoticism are touristic ways of *not seeing* similarity, of not really thinking that the people one meets are fully human; and indeed the polytheism of Hinduism remained scandalous to most western visitors. There were two striking points of social difference that almost all western visitors to India noted: *sati* (the ancient Hindu practice of a widow self-immolating on her husband's funeral pyre) and the sect of the Brahmins.

About Malabar, Odoric of Pordenone said that if a dead man left a widow, 'they burn her alive with him, saying that she should abide with her husband in the other world.' He repeated the observation in Champa (Cambodia or Vietnam), saying that after his death a married man was burned, 'and his wife is burnt alive along with him.' This, Odoric was told, was so she could 'keep him company in another world'.

Odoric noted *sati* as a curiosity but also provided the cultural rationale for it, the social and theological reasons behind a religious ritual outside Christianity. The missionary Jordan of Sévérac likewise described how noblemen's wives followed their husbands into the fire; 'for the sake of worldly glory, and for the love of their husbands, and for eternal life, they burn along with them, with as much joy as if they were going to be wedded.' Far from being horrified, Jordan remarked that it was 'wonderful!' He had even seen as many as five living women taking their places on the pyre of one dead man.

Nicolò Conti, the Venetian merchant who visited India in the 1430s, described *sati* as a royal custom: the King of Vijayanagar (Hampi) had, according to Conti, 12,000 wives, of whom between 2,000 and 3,000 had been married on the condition that they would be immolated with their husband on his death. This, they considered, was a great honour which placed them above the other thousands of wives. He also said that in Khambat there was a sect of monogamous vegetarian priests whose wives 'by law' were 'burned with the body of [their] husband'.

For Mandeville, *sati* was practised in a particular Indian territory where social order was topsy-turvy. The women there were sad when their children were born and happy when their children died, when 'they throw them in a large fire and burn them.' The reason for this, they said, was that their children were being born in 'this world of labour and grief and burdens'. This renunciation of life presaged the practice of *sati*: it was a sign of truly loving one's dead husband to throw oneself into the pyre. Mandeville said that widows did this to be cleansed 'of all filth and vice so they will be clean in the next world'.

Jeronimo di Santo Stefano and Jeronimo Adorno observed, to their horrified astonishment, several cases of *sati* during their seven-month stay on the Coromandel Coast. They regularly saw or heard tell of local women who burned themselves alive on their husbands' funeral pyres. Unlike later travellers to India, medieval visitors did not try to stop *sati* when they witnessed it. But, like later visitors, they had a voyeuristic fascination with the burning widows which acknowledged the different ways of believing and behaving (or, to put it another way, a kind of cultural diversity).

Sati wasn't as strange as European visitors made out: after all, they were used to the burning of heretics and criminals, and frequently worshipped images and relics of saints who had voluntarily suffered the most gruesome deaths by fire. St Lawrence had been roasted on a gridiron, the flames of a slow fire licking at his body, as he joked with his tormentors, 'turn me over', as if he were a grilling flank of mutton. *Sati* was another of those odd parallels witnessed by the traveller: shocking because, out of context, violence to which one had become inured became awful in its clarity. *Sati* would, in time, become a mainstay of the colonial perspective on India, a custom that evoked spectacular horror and strange devotion. Upon the Portuguese conquest of Goa in 1510, one of the earliest acts of the first Duke of Goa, Afonso de Albuquerque (1453–1515), was to try to ban *sati*.

In medieval Europe, Alexander the Great (d. 323 BCE) was an exemplary king, soldier, scholar and explorer. He conquered and ruled an empire from Macedonia to India. He was also an exemplar of the transience of worldly power, having died of a fever (or, in some accounts, been poisoned) at the age of thirty-two after building his global empire. The English poet Geoffrey Chaucer (d. 1400) wrote that the story of 'worthy, gentle' Alexander was so well known that 'every person' had heard something of it. Manuscripts of Alexander's life often included technicoloured images of his adventures, such as his descent in a glass submarine during his siege of the city of Tyre, or his flight over Babylon (Baghdad) in an aerial box harnessed by griffins, or the moving death of his loyal horse Bucephalus during a battle in the Punjab.

Histories and romances of Alexander's empire became staples of western fantasies about the east, many of them not even tenuously connected to historical fact or geographical reality. Mandeville told a story about the Brahmins' reaction to an imminent invasion by Alexander. In India, when Alexander came to invade the Brahmins' territory, the gentle people wrote a letter to him. They asked, 'What would be sufficient power for a man for whom the world is not enough? You'll find nothing here for which it is worth waging war against us, because we've got no wealth, and all the goods and chattels in our land are owned communally.' They explained that they had always enjoyed peace until this point, and this was the only thing that Alexander would be able to deprive them of.

The warrior Alexander read this letter and thought to himself that it would be terrible to disturb the Brahmins. And so he replied that they should continue to observe their good customs and not fear him, for he would not invade or molest them.

Mandeville's story is representative of how the Brahmins in India offered curious visitors an arresting lesson in 'natural law' and played a key role in European primitivist ideas of the 'noble savage'. Descended from the Hindu priesthood, the Brahmins were the most elevated social class in central and southern India; their ideals included voluntary poverty, austerity and intellectual endeavour, not unlike a Christian monastic order. By the fourteenth century, Brahmins were no longer only a priestly group, but worked in many professions and held key appointments at the courts of the subcontinent's Islamic sultanates. Western travel writers like Mandeville described them as 'good, honest men who follow a fine faith and lifestyle'. They were not, he noted, Christian but 'by natural law they are full of excellent qualities.' Thus they complied with the Ten Commandments and placed no value in material wealth. In other words, they were like perfect monks but without formal religion: 'they are not jealous, proud or covetous, and they are not lecherous or gluttonous, and they only do unto men as they would have done unto them' (Mandeville strikingly citing Jesus's 'golden rule' in support of a non-Christian group).

Brahmins were not accurately represented in such writing but were rather idealized. They were virtuous pagans, exemplary in their 'natural' perfection. Mandeville placed them in an Indian 'island' called the 'Land of Faith', a bucolic, egalitarian and crimeless society. There was even an absence of storms, thunder, war, hunger, any kind of tribulation.

A long twelfth-century poem about Alexander's deeds in the east, Thomas of Kent's *Roman de toute chevalerie*, described the Brahmins as vegans ('people of a strange doctrine') who ate 'only fruit and herbs and roots', that which the earth destined for them: no meat, fish, bread or flour. In Thomas's account, the Brahmins were at the edge of the world. He approvingly described how their devotion to God led them to self-immolate, in order the sooner to get to Paradise and divine glory – a kind of positive counterpart to the duped Assassins whose pursuit of Paradise was based on an illusion. The Brahmins, conversely, were reported in the west as being sincere, the representatives of natural goodness.

After travelling in India in the mid-fourteenth century, the Italian Franciscan friar Giovanni de'Marignolli told a story about the conversion and baptism of a Brahmin. This happened when Giovanni was staying in the important sea port of 'Columbum' (Kollam) on the Malabar Coast. Here a man 'of majestic stature and snowy white beard, naked from the loins upwards', approached Giovanni. He was a Brahmin of great austerity and sincerity. He prostrated himself in front of him and went to kiss his naked feet. Giovanni demurred. The Brahmin then sat down on the ground and, via an interpreter, gave an account of his life. Strikingly, the interpreter was the Brahmin's own baptized son, who had some time before been abducted by pirates and sold to a Genoese merchant.

The Brahmin man had come from 'the most remote' edge of India. He described his vegetarian life, his habit of fasting for four months a year, his diet of boiled rice, fruit and herbs and his devotion as a priest. He had only had the one child.

In Giovanni's telling, God had recognized the old man and 'enlightened him with wisdom from within'. God had then performed a miracle, by speaking through the priest's idol. The idol told him, against its own will, 'You are now on the path of salvation!' It then instructed him to travel two years by sea to Columbum, where he would find the messenger of God. And so, to Giovanni's mind, it had come to pass – and after three months of instruction, he duly baptized the old man, giving him the name 'Michael', after the archangel, who was particularly associated with mariners, with the weighing of souls on Judgement Day and with the pre-Christian greatness of humankind. 'Michael' returned to his home, to convert the people there.

In Giovanni's moralization, the story 'serves to exemplify that God . . . is no respecter of persons'. Rather 'whosoever keeps the Law . . . is accepted, and is taught the way of salvation.' The story moves seamlessly from praise for the Brahmin's nobility and piety to his conversion – a kind of individual missionizing from a position of admiration that also results in the obliteration of the Brahmin's 'idolatry'. The story is at once believable as an encounter (and foreshadows very many subsequent colonial conversions) and also highly generic – the wise old man, the repudiated idol, the sea voyage through which he is transformed. The Brahmins and similar virtuous pagans offered travellers the possibility that 'nature' in the world beyond Christendom was not hostile. In European travel writing, much was made of the potential of India – or 'India' – to hold within it a kind of 'natural' perfection. India was a sort of laboratory of the imagination, alluring, luxurious, often receptive and of an almost infinite diversity. Giovanni's story of the converted Brahmin suggested that, in the world beyond Europe, there was a receptive audience waiting for the travelling missionaries of Latin Christianity.

Tips for business travellers from Tana to Khanbaliq, c. 1340

1. You must let your beard grow long and not shave.
2. At Tana you should furnish yourself with a dragoman; do not try to save money by taking a bad dragoman instead of a good one.
3. You will do well to take at least two good male servants, who are acquainted with the Tatar tongue.
4. If a merchant wishes to take a woman with him from Tana, he can do so; if he does not like to take one there is no obligation, only if he does take one he will be kept much more comfortably than if he does not take one. However, if he should take one, it will be better that she be acquainted with the Cuman tongue as well as the men.
5. To travel from Tana to Astrakhan take with you twenty-five days' provisions, i.e. flour and salt fish; you will find enough meat at all the places along the route.
6. The route from Tana to Cathay is perfectly safe, whether by day or by night, according to merchants who have used it. Only if the merchant, in going or coming, should die upon the road, everything belonging to him will be sequestered by the lord of the country in

which he dies, and the officers of the lord will take possession of all. And likewise if he should die in Cathay. But if his brother is with him, or an intimate friend and comrade calling himself his brother, then to such a one they will surrender the property of the deceased, and so it will be salvaged.

7. In these parts, they call all the Christians from Romania westward 'Franks'.

12. All Roads Lead to Khanbaliq

Karakorum – Khanbaliq – Yangzhou – Cipangu

In the cool cloisters of St Mary's Abbey in the English city of York, the monks edified themselves by reading about the world beyond their enclosure. The cloister is now a rain-soaked ruin, but in the fourteenth century there were about fifty brothers living there, all following the Benedictine rule. Reading and writing were central to their lives, part of their labour for God; studying their books filled almost every space between services in their great vaulted church. One of the prized volumes in their library was a new manuscript, the *History of the Mongols*, written on vellum in dense black letters with red and blue initials.

The monks of York read about the Mongols with delight, wonder and shock. It was said that each Tatar man could have as many wives as he wished, 'one a hundred, another fifty, another ten'. They learned that the Tatar women had 'a round thing made of twigs or bark' on their heads, which they wore always in the presence of men and to distinguish themselves from other women. It was written too that 'unmarried women and young girls' in Tatary were almost indistinguishable from men, as they all dressed in an identical manner. The Mongol people lived, it was said, in felt tents, built with sticks. They worshipped idols, to whom they offered the first milk of each cow and mare. Where the York monks found something particularly memorable or worthy of note, they marked a little cross or sometimes a pointing finger (a 'manicule') in the book's margin to remind them and future readers to pay special attention to information worth recording.

The York monks' manuscript was new but the text had originally been composed by Brother Giovanni of Plano Carpini, a venerable man who had himself about a hundred years previously visited and met the leader of the Mongols, the great khan himself, Güyük (d. 1248). Brother Giovanni had travelled all the way to the Mongol court at Karakorum, over 9,000 kilometres east of the pope's palace in Rome. He was one of the first westerners known to have reached the court, and wrote the *History of the Mongols* based on his experiences there.* His book brought back to the west a wealth of knowledge about the Mongols, the people who ruled the world east of Europe, from just beyond Kyiv all the way to Beijing.

Brother Giovanni travelled with two other Franciscan friars: Štěpán of Bohemia and Benedykt of Poland. In the year 1245, Giovanni and Štěpán departed from Lyons in France, and met up with Benedykt at Wrocław in Poland. They then travelled east and, within days, had endured hunger, thirst, extremes of cold and heat and various minor personal injuries. The friars had been bidden by Pope Innocent IV 'to examine everything and to look at everything carefully', bringing back a full report on the conditions of the Mongols. They carried a papal bull, requesting the Emperor of the Tatars to 'desist entirely from assaults' on Christian nations and to cease the persecution of Christians. Their mission was mandated in the aftermath of the Mongol invasions of Poland and Hungary, which had, in the early 1240s, reached

* Brother Lourenço, a Portuguese friar, had set out on a similar mission slightly earlier, but his fate is unknown.

as far west as Legnica in Silesia and Trogir on the Dalmatian coast. The friars thus travelled as ambassadors of Christendom, seeking to understand an enemy who, it was widely assumed, was planning a campaign to occupy all of Europe. Giovanni, Štěpán and Benedykt made it only as far as the little town of Kaniv on the River Dnieper before Štěpán fell ill and could not continue.

For almost half a year, Giovanni and Benedykt made their way across the Tatars' land. Giovanni summarized his desolate attitude at the beginning of his book: 'To conclude briefly about this country: it is large, but otherwise – as we saw with our own eyes, for during five and half months we travelled about it – it is more wretched than I can possibly say.' Leaving Europe was, for these men, not pleasurable. But in travel the 'wretched' is the handmaiden to the educative, and Giovanni repeatedly stressed that what he had seen with his own eyes was both veritable and instructive.

Giovanni of Plano Carpini and Benedykt of Poland were indefatigable travellers. They each left a written account of their journey: Giovanni's is expansive, opinionated, political, whereas Benedykt's (as dictated in Cologne upon his return) is brief, discontinuous and less individualistic in its voice. Both accounts are part of a flurry, in the 1240s, of Franciscan and Dominican embassies to the Mongols, during what was evidently a period of panic in Europe about Mongol military strength. In fact, the Mongols were fighting on at least three fronts: not only against the Christian princes of Poland, Moravia and Hungary, but also against the Seljuks of Anatolia and the Abbasid sultans of Egypt and the Middle East. Numerous accounts of this period survive, when the Silk Roads across Asia were busy with merchants, missionaries and ambassadors, all seeking to understand the power dynamics of a rapidly changing world. Giovanni and Benedykt were unusual, but not unique. They mention how they encountered many other people on the move: merchants from Acre, Constantinople, Genoa and Venice, envoys from Baghdad and Korea, and specific kings and princes, like David VI of Georgia (1225–93), Prince Sempad the Constable of Armenia (1209–76) and Grand Duke Yaroslav of Vladimir-Suzdal (1191–1246). Giovanni included an account of how Grand Duke Yaroslav was summoned to meet the great khan and sent home only to turn purple and then die, having been poisoned by the khan's mother.

Giovanni's journey would take him first to Batu Khan (d. 1255), the Mongol founder of the massive khanate known as the Golden Horde and thus ruler of what is now much of Ukraine and southern Russia.* After visiting Batu, Giovanni passed via the Aral Sea, Lake Ulyungur and the Altai Mountains to visit Batu's cousin, the 'Great Emperor' or khan himself, Güyük.

Giovanni and Benedykt planned the journey as they travelled, gaining letters of introduction and safe-conducts from the princes in the hinterland of Christian Europe. These princes also gave them supplies and beaver pelts, as the pair had been told to expect demands for tribute. In Kyiv, the men discussed their intended route with local nobles. They were advised against taking their own horses, due to the deep snow and the scarcity of fodder; they abandoned their horses and instead took pack horses and an escort. Riding across the long heathlands of steppe, beyond the Dnieper and over the Don, they changed their horses between three and seven times a day, travelling from dawn

* The name Golden Horde refers to the wealth and magnificence of the khan's *ordo* (Mongol: 'camp').

until nightfall and often during the night too. The men had to bandage their limbs over and over again, owing to the strain of continual riding. They were sustained during Lent on millet mixed with water and salt. For water, they melted snow in a kettle. In the desert lands of the Kazakhs, they saw the 'skulls and bones of dead men' scattered on the ground like manure, the remnants of unfortunate travellers who had expired as a result of the scarcity of water, or perhaps had met a worse fate. Benedykt tells us that forty beaver skins and eighty badger skins were demanded of them at Saray on the Volga. Giovanni in particular resented being ripped off, as he saw it, for tribute.

At the end of this joyless journey were the splendours of Karakorum, the Mongol capital from 1235 to 1260 and the first Mongol city built in the east. Karakorum was not a city in the western sense but a huge encampment set in lushly pastured valleys in the shadow of the peaks of the Khangai Mountains. When Giovanni visited, Karakorum was in transition from a scattered gathering of yurts to a more permanent urban settlement, with a recently constructed palace. The city's population was not large (perhaps around 20,000 people), but the settlement covered a very large area (about 1,300 hectares in total) around a central walled sector and its adjacent palace complex. The population of Karakorum had been brought from elsewhere – it was an administrative and political centre, and its inhabitants included many Muslim merchants and captives from across the Mongol empire and from places the Mongols had invaded. There were mosques and a Syriac 'Nestorian' church, where eastern Christians (branded schismatics by Rome) worshipped both the human and divine persons of Christ as distinctive, separate essences.

Around this time, an enslaved French goldsmith named Guillaume Boucher, captured in Belgrade and taken to Karakorum, sculpted a metal tree fountain in Karakorum from which silver fruit and leaves hung. For the great khan's entertainment, the tree was adorned with a trumpeting angelic automaton, which could blow its instrument at the command of the khan's butler. The marvellous tree held conduits from which beverages (wine, *kumiss*, mead and rice wine) flowed, to be guzzled in prodigious quantities by the great khan's heavy-drinking court. Boucher's fountain imitated European courtly fashions for finely wrought automata but also articulated the sense of the great khan's power over the natural world, in causing a tree to brim with beverages in the midst of this arid, wind-blown land.

As Giovanni went through western Mongolia, his pace accelerated, his group hurrying to reach Karakorum in time for the long-planned coronation of Güyük Khan. Karakorum was the main court, and the celebrations for the coronation were appropriately eye-catching: Giovanni records that a huge pavilion of white velvet had been erected, big enough to hold 'more than two thousand men'. It was encompassed by a wooden palisade decorated with painted designs. Giovanni marvelled that all the courtiers wore white velvet on the first day, red velvet on the second (when Güyük himself appeared), blue velvet on the third day and the finest brocade on the fourth. The palisade had two gates: one for the great khan alone, and the other for those admitted by armed guards. Everyone else had to stand at a distance. Giovanni's account of the various ceremonies at the khan's court inaugurates a long tradition in western travel writing about China, in which the ruler's courtiers are seen as if acting in a kind of servile unison, brought together through an impersonal bond of unquestioning compliance.

At midday the entire court started to drink a large quantity of *kumiss*. Giovanni and his group refused, and they were offered mead instead, which they drank until they felt utterly sick. How frequently travellers find themselves at parties they would sooner have missed.

And what kind of man did these travellers meet when they finally encountered the great khan? The answer disappoints. None of the early travellers described the khan in individual, human terms; rather they saw him as a metonym for the political and social order of the Mongol court. For Giovanni, Güyük Khan was '40 to 45 years old' (in fact, he was about thirty) and 'of medium height'. The rest of his description focuses on his austere personality: 'very intelligent and extremely shrewd', 'most serious and grave in his manner', 'never seen to laugh for a slight cause nor to indulge in any frivolity'. Giovanni offers no moral interpretation of his physiognomy or complexion, as happened so frequently when Europeans encountered other people. Rather, he saw in Güyük the rigour and order that defined his court and his state.

Likewise, William of Rubruck, a garrulous Flemish missionary who met the great khan about eight years after Giovanni, encountered Güyük's successor, Möngke Khan (reigned 1251–9). William described Möngke as 'a flat-nosed man of medium height, about 45 years old'. In place of appraising the great khan himself, his eye fell on his 'very ugly' grown-up daughter, Shirin, who it was said 'was mistress of all that court'. He also studied the sumptuous decoration of the khan's tent, its cloth-of-gold walls and the khan's own costume of a 'speckled and shiny' pelt like sealskin. William's interview with Möngke became farcical: their interpreter got utterly drunk on rice wine and stopped making sense. In a sign of his imperious majesty, Möngke ordered 'falcons and other birds' to be brought to him and the visitors had to watch, in silence and for a long time, as he inspected them.

William had to request Möngke Khan's permission to stay at the Tatar camp until the winter had passed, but by then the great khan seemed himself to have grown drunk and the interpreter was completely incapacitated, so William and his group left. They were grilled for information about the west by the khan's secretaries, further corroborating William's sense of an attack being plotted. Möngke did eventually allow William to stay at Karakorum, where he met and heard about all kinds of people connected to his life in Europe.

Giovanni of Plano Carpini observed Güyük Khan's splendid coronation, which took place in a tent held up on gold-plated columns and wooden beams fastened with golden nails (the abundance of shimmering gold gave this camp the name Shira Ordo, the 'Yellow Camp'). A huge number of people assembled there and, after midday, everyone started drinking again, non-stop, until the evening. They then ate unsalted roasted meat, sometimes with a salty broth as a sauce. Everywhere he went, the emperor had a little parasol studded with precious gems to shade him from the weather.

After the coronation, Giovanni and his party were effectively imprisoned for a month in the household of the great khan's mother. Giovanni was told that the khan intended 'to raise his banner against the whole of the western world' and wished to keep his papal visitors ignorant of his plans. While they waited, Giovanni (who paid a great deal of attention to how much food he could get) and his companions were given a tiny amount to eat and drink, 'enduring such hunger and thirst that we could scarcely keep alive'. In the end a kindly Russian goldsmith named Kosma, one of several European craftsmen at the khan's court, helped the visitors with a little sustenance.

They were, eventually, freed and given a permit to depart and a letter bearing the emperor's seal. The khan's mother gave them a fox-skin cloak and a bolt of velvet. Her courtiers stole bits of the velvet; Giovanni says, 'This did not escape our notice, but we preferred not to make a fuss about it.' In strange lands, the traveller often has to let things go that would otherwise be cause for serious complaint.

The great khan's letter, dated Jumada 2nd, 644 (late November 1246), was copied into Benedykt's account. In it, the khan reminded the pope that any God was clearly on the Mongols' side for it was they who had 'destroyed the whole earth from the east to the west in the power of God'. How, he asked, could this be contrary to God? He pointed out that Christian princes had not obeyed his predecessors and boldly told the pope to commit to peace with him, a submission he would generously understand. If the pope refused to submit, the khan threatened that he would know him as an enemy: 'after that, we do not know what will happen, God alone knows,' he warned. The long journey had been a success, insofar as the friars had opened a communication with the Mongol court. But the consequence was further threats of violence, and a clear articulation of imperial rivalry.

Travellers to the Mongol east had read of strange rumours about what lay off the beaten track. They were led to believe there were cannibals and rat eaters, dog-headed peoples and axe-wielding warriors, wool-bearing bushes and snow raspberries, millions of mice but an incomprehensible absence of pigs, living, breeding diamonds multiplying in the rocks, customs around death and burial that were unmentionable. Many people identified somewhere in this region a Fountain of Youth, whose waters in some accounts restored youth to the drinker or gave eternal life. The Fountain could also offer beauty and sometimes discriminated by race, turning dark skin white. But these were just travellers' tales.

As he made his way across the Tatar steppe, Benedykt of Poland noticed the huge amount of wormwood growing there, its feathery leaves spreading across the cold flatlands. As he rode he remembered, from reading long before in a frigid cloister somewhere in Europe, a remark by Ovid in his *Epistles*: 'The bitter wormwood shivers in the endless plains.' It seemed to speak directly to Benedykt across time and space. The truth of travel often erupts in such buried memories, where one's past asserts itself in surprising moments, as thoughts from home appear at the ends of the world.

Giovanni of Plano Carpini and Benedykt of Poland were unusually intrepid but, by about 1300, a significant number of Europeans had settled and formed communities in large cities in what we now call China. The papal emissary Giovanni de'Marignolli, who visited from Italy c. 1346, observed three Franciscan churches in Zaytun (Quanzhou) as well as a *fondaco* for the visiting European merchants. Europeans in China were usually there for trade or missionary activity. Far from being an unknown and unknowable empire, China became the destination for a surprisingly large number of European travellers. Key testimonies include those of the Franciscan missionaries William of Rubruck in 1253 and Odoric of Pordenone, the merchant Marco Polo who was in China for much of the 1280s and 1290s, the letters from Giovanni of Montecorvino, sometime Archbishop of Khanbaliq, Peregrine, Bishop of Zaytun (1318) and Andrew of Perugia (c. 1313), as well as the account of the wonders of China and India by the missionary Jordan of Sévérac. As this list suggests, writing and reading about the Far East became an established genre. These accounts were copied into Latin encyclopaedic texts and world histories as western audiences lusted for knowledge about the magnificence of the great khan's court and his almost boundless power.

China was conventionally divided by Europeans into the provinces of Cathay and Manzi: Cathay referred to the 'upper' northern region and Manzi the southern region (confusingly Manzi was also called, by some Europeans, 'Upper India'; it was previously ruled by the Song dynasty). From the 1260s, the Mongol empire fragmented, with various dynasties setting up their own rival khanates. From 1271 to 1368 most of what is now China and Mongolia was ruled by the Yuan regime, a Mongol dynasty that ranked non-Chinese foreigners above Chinese and established a favourable environment for European settlers and visitors. The Yuan dynasty moved the Mongol capital from Karakorum to

Shangdu (Xanadu) and then to Khanbaliq (now Beijing). Khanbaliq served as the winter capital and the Yuan administrative centre.* Buddhism was the de facto religion, although there was considerable religious pluralism. In 1368 the Yuan were conquered by the Ming, a Han Chinese dynasty, and the capital moved to Nanjing ('the southern capital'), although this was demoted to secondary capital in 1403 and Khanbaliq/Dadu's primacy restored. The Ming renamed the city 'Bei-ping', meaning 'the pacified north'.

Behave like a local! As you enter each Tatar lordship or each province of Cathay you'll be expected to give a tribute of food and/or drink. *Kumiss* (fermented mares' milk) and wind-dried smoked meats are generally appreciated. Across Tatary, people wear furs and animal skins. In Cathay it can be extremely cold in April and May and you may want to dress like the great khan's courtiers in sheepskin cloaks, sheepskin trousers and sheepskin shoes.

To western travellers Khanbaliq was more recognizable than Karakorum as a great city, and its splendours were written about in superlative terms. In contrast to Karakorum, Khanbaliq had an identifiable city centre. At its heart was the complex known as the 'Imperial City' (what is now known as the 'Forbidden City', built in the fifteenth century, refers to part of this complex). The Imperial City was an elaborate landscaped parkland of pavilions, towers, halls, barracks, temples, warehouses, artificial mounds and residential palaces set alongside sparkling lakes and bridges. This was,

* The Turkic Mongol name Khanbaliq means something like 'permanent urban settlement', but it was also called Dadu, from Ta-tu, the Mandarin for 'great capital'.

according to the reports sent back to the west, the matchless expression of the great khan's power and wealth, technological sophistication and love of ordered beauty.

Perhaps the most famous traveller of the Middle Ages, and certainly the best-known visitor to pre-Ming China, was Marco Polo, the voluble if pedantic, prosaic and unreliable Venetian merchant. Polo was not an explorer (his famous travels took place across established merchants' networks) and he was less a traveller than an expatriate migrant worker. He first set out for China in 1271 aged seventeen, from his family's house in Venice via Acre, accompanied by his father Niccolò and uncle Maffeo, both of them experienced merchants who had already, in the 1260s, traversed much of Asia. The Polo family were representative of the Venetian world of the Black Sea, trading in jewels and other commodities between Venice and the ascendant, westward-moving Mongol empire. The Polo men spent some seventeen years serving in Kublai Khan's administration. Marco Polo seems to have been a gifted linguist, able to negotiate across the various nations trading with the Mongols, and he was also involved in the salt industry. He returned to Europe in the mid-1290s.

We know about Polo principally through the book he co-wrote, properly called *The Description of the World*. This was composed in French in a Genoese prison, a co-production between Polo and his fellow inmate, the romance writer Rustichello of Pisa (d. c. 1300). Both men were held for ransom in the wars between Genoa and Venice. Polo was released and returned to Venice around 1299, and lived out his years as a wealthy merchant and a famous author-traveller (he died in 1324, around the age of seventy). Despite its wide readership, *The Description of the World* is a work of political geography more than a travel narrative. As a travel guide, it lacks the sense of individual observation or distinctive voice of other early travellers to the Far East. For many pages, Polo's travels are presented in earnest, literal terms, listing currencies, commodities, bureaucratic rules and second-hand miracles. Still, his book was hungrily read in Europe for evidence of the burgeoning world of the east.

By the 1280s, when Polo visited Khanbaliq, it was a well-established city, where Arabs, Persians, Nepalese, Tibetans, Uyghurs and many others worked for the glory of (or in servitude to) the great khan. Polo was kept in the khan's service, an exalted vassal, but Beijing, the city he called 'Taidu' or 'Cambaluc', was, for him, a wonderland which stimulated his capacity for description.

Polo said the Imperial City at Khanbaliq was the largest palace ever seen, a place 'so immense and so finely wrought that there is not man on earth who could imagine improving on its design and construction, even if he had the power to do so'. For Polo the palace was the supreme articulation of the khan's power and sophistication, and his account of it reflects the gawping wonder of an awestruck tourist. The complex was housed within a 'great square wall', a mile long on each side, 'completely white and battlemented'. At each corner were sited large palaces of great beauty and opulence that were used as arsenals for the great khan's munitions. As at Karakorum, there was a gate that opened for none but the khan himself. Internal walls, made of marble two paces thick, formed a kind of terrace where people could stroll and survey the entire area, looking out of the Imperial City at those not allowed in. An exquisite pillared balustrade was a meeting place for the court, and a great flight of marble steps led up to the khan's own palace.

This palace was a feast for hungry eyes, its walls completely covered with gold and silver and decorated with elaborate reliefs: dragons, birds, knights, battles and all kinds of beasts.

The ceiling was similarly dazzling, bearing pictures made in gold. The palace was built round a gigantic hall, 'so vast and wide that more than 6,000 men could easily eat there'. The extent of the palace and its many rooms was, for Polo, 'quite bewildering'. There were treasuries for all the great khan's precious gems and gold, and large houses and halls for his wives and concubines. 'Everything', said Polo, was arranged for the khan's 'comfort and convenience, and outsiders are not admitted' (a sly suggestion that Polo had himself become an insider).

Around the palace were wooded parklands, where beautiful deer and squirrels sported in meadows 'lush with grass'. Paved roads ran through the glades, irrigating and draining the lawns. Just beyond the palace was a manmade hill, 100 paces high (about 75 metres). The hill was planted as the khan's arboretum; Polo reported that 'whenever someone mentions a beautiful tree to the Great Khan, he orders it pulled up with its roots and a quantity of earth and transported by elephants to this mound.' The hill, called the Green Hill, contained 'the most beautiful trees in the world' and was always green. Some said that it was covered in green lapis lazuli, to make it evergreen. The hill had been built by the great khan 'for the sake of the beautiful view' it gave of the Imperial City, an impressive sight for all who were able to experience it. Around the hills were fishponds and conduits, all for the khan's enjoyment, and swans and waterfowl. Polo, an eyewitness and repeated visitor to the court, little appreciated nature but loved contrivance and sophisticated trickery: for him, travel was about noting new technologies and wonders, an account of all that wasn't available at home.

At the northern extent of the new Mongol city were the Drum Tower and the Bell Tower, built by Kublai Khan in

1272. The Drum Tower marked daybreak with a rhythmic beat resounding from its impressive storeys. The Bell Tower rang out the end of the day and marked the point at which an unofficial curfew started. Both towers – high, tiered, ingeniously decorated – used imposing architecture and public music to keep time and order, and to announce the great khan's control over Khanbaliq and its inhabitants' lives.

Polo's account is unusual and important because it also gives a brief description of the city outside the Imperial precincts. Khanbaliq was a new planned city, according to Polo, and the population had been moved there from the old city, except those who harboured rebellious intentions. They were left behind. The new city measured almost 40 kilometres in perimeter, built within a perfect square of crenellated walls. Within, the whole city was laid out as a grid of straight, broad streets, like a chessboard. Palaces, inns and houses were constructed in measured plots, each in a courtyard off the finely built public roads (Polo described here the characteristic *hutong* lanes of old Beijing). The whole place, for Polo, was 'so beautiful and skilfully planned that no description can do it justice'. There is no sense in his account of Khanbaliq of anything other than admiration for the great khan's capital, an articulation of power and order and a place beyond words. Yet, for all his proximity to the khan, Polo was speaking to a western audience, imparting a 'specialist' knowledge based on experience. His account of Khanbaliq holds within it the imprecise but vivid archaeology of a lived memory. The city's status as a hub for 'vast numbers of merchants and foreigners' was reflected, for Polo, in the number of its 'sinful women'; he assured his readers that at least 20,000 sex workers, who discreetly lived in Khanbaliq's suburbs, serviced men for money. 'They are all needed', he said pruriently, 'to satisfy the vast numbers of merchants and foreigners who come and go here every day.' Moreover, they paid no tax, instead offering sexual services to state officials. Polo himself (at once merchant, foreigner and employee of the great khan) may well have had first-hand experience of Khanbaliq's sex workers.

A few generations later, reports of the Imperial City had become the stuff of legend. John Mandeville summarized the European idea of Khanbaliq in his *Book*, itself based on Odoric of Pordenone's description from his three-year stay there in the 1320s. Mandeville called the city 'Cadom' (a corruption of Dadu). It had, he said, walls that were 20 miles in circumference and contained twelve gates. The whole place was so richly arrayed that it defied comparison. The gardens were elegant, and held 'a fine mountain' that was 'the prettiest to be found anywhere'. The palace walls were covered with red panther pelts which exuded a pleasant smell and shimmered in the sun so 'one can hardly look at them'; there were never foul stinks there and these panther skins were valued like gold. The married women wore on their heads the image of a man's foot cleverly crafted in gems and peacock feathers; this signified their subjection to their husbands. The emperor's throne and hall were bedecked with jewels and gems, repetitively listed by Mandeville. He writes that the Mongol court was 'more magnificent and splendid than we had ever heard. We would never have believed it if we hadn't seen it.' There is a tease here, because he hadn't seen it, but the reports of the Imperial City were so impressive that they were, essentially, incredible. By Mandeville's time, the organization of the imperial palace was designed to reflect the western idea of the great khan's potent perfection, a cosmic order in which the palace represented the supreme being of the khan himself.

Some years after Giovanni of Plano Carpini and Benedykt of Poland's journey, on 8 January 1305 Giovanni of

Montecorvino wrote a letter from Khanbaliq to the minister general of the Franciscan Order in Italy. Giovanni was also a Franciscan, born in southern Italy and with a long career as a missionary in Armenia and Tabriz. By 1305 he had constructed a Christian church in Khanbaliq, baptized about 6,000 people into the Christian faith, educated dozens of local boys in Latin and Greek and copied out thirty psalters and two breviaries in manuscript so the local community could perform religious services. He had learned to speak the Mongols' language (and even translated the New Testament into it). It seems to have been a largely solitary existence for him as a Latin Christian in Khanbaliq. In his letter, he called for reinforcements; he needed more books and 'two or three comrades' who could help him missionize. He was confident that he could convert the great khan himself, at this point Temür Khan (d. 1307), the grandson of Kublai Khan and great-great-grandson of Genghis Khan.

Giovanni of Montecorvino had much experience as a missionary and set about converting both the people and the built environment of Khanbaliq. He had built a church with a three-belled campanile and in 1305 was busy trying to establish a second church. He blamed the 'labours and tribulations' of his experiences in Tatary for turning his hair white at the age of fifty-eight. He was evidently committed to his mission, but his letter ends on a familiar awestruck note: 'there is no king or prince in the world who can equal the Great Khan in the extent of his land, and the greatness of the population and wealth.' Time and again, we find in western reports an image of China as truly an awesome empire, with Europe and the Roman Church no match for it. Later, Giovanni of Montecorvino successfully converted a Mongol prince, George, apparently a Nestorian and Confucian who became Catholic (but did not renounce Confucianism) and helped to build a cruciform church in the lost town of Tenduc. Giovanni had no such success with Temür Khan, whose Buddhism (which Giovanni called 'idolatry') was securely established.

Giovanni recommended the safest and quickest route to China: a friar, accompanied by a courier, could make the journey in 'five or six months' if they travelled through the lands of the 'Northern Tatars'. This route started at Tana, passed the Black Sea and went via the western Mongol capital at Saray on the Volga and then across what is now Kazakhstan. The alternative route, Giovanni warned, was 'very long and very dangerous', for it involved two sea voyages; it would take more than two years and was, he said, the equivalent of sailing first from Acre to Provence and then again from Acre to England. The sea route was via Hormuz to the Malabar Coast and then from St Thomas's (Mylapore near Chennai) on the east coast of India to China. And yet the land route he recommended had been closed 'for a considerable time' because of wars taking place and it seems that Giovanni was obliged to go by sea. His letter is part of a body of European knowledge about how best, despite the rigours of the journey, to bridge the space between Europe and the amazing court of the great khan.

A few years later, in 1338, yet another Franciscan friar named Giovanni, Giovanni de'Marignolli, a high-ranking Florentine churchman at the papal court, was sent by the pope to the court of the great khan. Three years after leaving Avignon, and after having passed through the Gobi Desert, Giovanni reached 'Cambalec' in the summer of 1342. Khanbaliq was indescribable: 'Of its incredible size, population and military array we will say nothing.' But it is clear from the brief description he gave that he and his party of thirty-one fellow travellers were treated extremely well by the great khan, given liberal quantities of meat and drink, 'paper for lanterns' and 'costly raiment'. Giovanni received a personal request from the khan that he himself should become Archbishop of Khanbaliq, at the cathedral at the palace's gate, as built by Giovanni of Montecorvino in 1305.

Among the many places visited by Marco Polo was the large and splendid city of Yangzhou (often called Yangchow). Yangzhou, sited on a plain, thrived where the remarkable Grand Canal, running for over 1,000 kilometres from Beijing to Hangzhou, met the wide waters of the Yangtze river. Shallow lakes and slender canals wove through the city. Junks and sampans slipped downstream, fuelled by human sweat. The canals were crossed by carved bridges, each splendidly ornamented. Tiered Buddhist pagodas, with their gently tapering flanks, gave the city an elegant, elaborate skyline. According to his account, Polo did not just pass through Yangzhou but spent three years there. He reported that the residents practised 'idolatry' and spoke the Persian tongue. He then claimed that he had been appointed governor of the city, by the great khan's commission. This, he said, made him one of the khan's 'twelve highest-ranking barons'.

Polo's boast is not to be believed. He is not attested in Chinese sources. It is possible that the word *sejourna* (stayed) became corrupted in manuscripts to *seigneura* (governed); it is not unusual for travellers to think of themselves as being in charge rather than passing visitors. Such travellers' unreliabilities aside – all travellers are subjective – Yangzhou was one of the key destinations for European visitors, and Polo was unlikely to have been the only European there.

When Odoric of Pordenone visited Yangzhou in 1322–3, the city had a Franciscan convent and three other 'Nestorian' churches following the eastern Syriac Christian rite. There had long been a Persian merchant community in Yangzhou, trading between China and Hormuz. At the same time, Genoese and Venetian expatriate merchant communities were established there.

We know that one of the families living in Yangzhou at this time was that of Domenico Ilioni. The Ilioni family, from Genoa, had established itself in Persia, probably at Tabriz, in the thirteenth century and then moved to Yangzhou. Two tombstones unearthed in the city reveal something of the lives and deaths of Domenico's children, Caterina (d. 1342) and Antonio (d. 1344). Caterina's beautifully preserved tombstone is inscribed in Latin in Gothic lettering, with carved line drawings of the martyrdom of her namesake St Catherine of Alexandria, alongside angels and a Madonna and Child. Antonio's less well-preserved stone likewise shows conventional Christian imagery, of the Last Judgement and the martyrdom of his patron saint, St Anthony the Abbot.

These images seem at first to express familiar memories of European religious culture, imported from Italy. However, their style is not European but more like Chinese Buddhist art of the time, and it is possible that the stonemason was a local convert to Christianity or simply a commercial artist. Moreover, the executioner of St Catherine is dressed as a Mongol warrior, retranslating the saint's story from west to east. The Ilioni family had travelled, physically, almost as far from Europe as they could, but remained closely connected to their origins through the trading of goods like silks and spices: from Yangzhou to Tabriz, to the Genoese colony at Pera in Constantinople, and back to Genoa and beyond. Their gravestones reveal the entangled world of a syncretic, global city, linking western Europe with the Far East, via caravanserais of the Silk Roads and merchants' junks across the Indian

Ocean. Through articulating their deaths in stone monuments, Caterina and Antonio Ilioni left a lasting testimony to the interconnected world of which they were part, in which travel and contact over enormous distances kept east and west in constant interplay.

And what was beyond China? To the east lay the realm of Cipangu or Japan, only loosely apprehended by European travellers in our period. On Behaim's Globe of 1491, Cipangu is a long archipelago, illustrated with a regal tent (the sign of a king) and notes on its nutmeg and pepper forests. The description of the archipelago is minimal: Cipangu has a king and its own language; its inhabitants worship idols; there is much gold there and a rich yield of spicery. This information is taken from Marco Polo, usually credited as the bearer of the first account of the Japanese empire to reach the west. Polo's description set the template for European notions of Japan for about 300 years.

Even Polo did not pretend to have travelled to Japan. He had clearly heard about the kingdom during his time in Mongol China, which had launched significant but unsuccessful attacks on Japan in 1274 and 1281. He had been told that Japan was inhabited by 'white, good-looking and courteous' people, 'exceedingly rich in gold' and 'completely independent'. Repeating a rumour that was often made by travellers around Asia, Polo said that the people were cannibals, killing captives and eating their cooked flesh for a family meal. There were yet worse 'exploits of these idolaters' that he had heard of, but they were 'so outlandish and diabolical that they are not fit to be mentioned in our book, because such wickedness would be too much for Christian ears'. This marks the limit of Polo's information. He knew little else about Japan, and his account of the country avoids factual or cultural specificity. Japanese curiosities he noted included a huge palace entirely covered with fine gold and a notable Japanese burial custom, according to which the dead were burned or buried, those that were buried having a local pearl put in their mouth.

The rest of his account comprises a sensationalized story about the calamitous 1281 Mongol invasion of Japan, which occurred during his service at Kublai Khan's court; he would therefore have been on the scene as reports of the failed invasion came back to Khanbaliq. It is also one of the few moments in his book when Polo talks about the practicalities and perils of travel itself.

The Mongol fleet set off from Zayton (Quanzhou) and Xingzai (Hangzhou), two of the most important imperial ports in eastern China (the latter conquered by the Mongols in 1276). The fleet was led by two rival captains, 'Abacan' (the Mongol chief Arakhan) and 'Vonsainchin' (the Song defector Fan Wenhu), whose mutual enmity doomed the expedition from the outset. The fleet reached Japan but, before a single parapet or postern could be taken, a northerly gale blew in. Seeing that they would be wrecked if they remained in harbour, the Mongol fleet put to sea. Once they were out in the turbulent waters, the gale intensified and the ships started to collide and shatter. Thousands drowned, others escaped, if their boat was able to navigate through the awful seas. Some ships, including those that held the two commanders, managed to land at a small, uninhabited island.

Once the storm had abated, the commanders gathered all the officers and captains – that is, the senior noblemen in the fleet – and fled back to China. They left 30,000 mariners abandoned on the small island, shipwrecked and desolate. A short time later, the Japanese invaded this island, planning to seize the miserable shipmen whose own commanders had left them for dead. But, according to the story Polo was told, some of the Chinese men outwitted the Japanese and were able to sneak around a mountain and board the Japanese fleet. They stole the boats, sailed to Japan and were taken for Japanese sailors and welcomed to the 'capital city', which they promptly seized (historically speaking, this would have been Kyoto). They 'chased out all the people except for some good-looking women', whom they kept 'to serve them', and held the city for seven months; they surrendered only when they were guaranteed that their lives would be spared. Meanwhile, the Chinese commanders who had made it back to the great khan's court were executed.

Polo's description of Japan as a place of limitless merchandise ripe for plunder, stuffed with gold and pearls, echoes the other medieval wonderlands of the Far East, a vaguely understood dominion of boundless wealth, ready for the intrepid merchant-traveller to make their fortune. Polo's spirited account – presented as recent news – of the failed Mongol attack has at its centre that most medieval image of changing fortune: the storm or tempest. The tempest was long a favoured image for describing the perils of rapaciousness and the vicissitudes of man's journey in life: the violent sea change which caused the stern to rise and the prow to fall, which plunged powerless mortals into the blinding waves of its depths, which moved the fleet's straight course to chaos through an uncontrollable will. The tempest's squalls caught all, aware or unaware, and they could only curse the power of their gods. In Polo's telling, the storm alone hindered the Chinese, the leveller of ambition and the limiter of travel, and as such was the boundary – a natural boundary – of the great khan's empire, where conflicting winds brought even the greatest of worldly powers to frustration.

Polo's version of events in 1281 is not historically accurate; it reflects face saving on the part of the defeated Chinese, and aspects of his story are directly contradicted in contemporary Chinese and Japanese sources. Arakhan had in fact died before reaching Japan, and was replaced by Ataqai as commander-in-chief. The occupation of Kyoto is fantastical; the Mongol fleet harried Takashima, where the dreadful typhoon struck. The Japanese removed the surviving Chinese to Hakata (Fukuoka), where Mongol, Korean and Han soldiers were executed. Others were imprisoned or enslaved. Three survivors made their way back to Khanbaliq to relate what had befallen the great khan's fleet, and their testimony was used in Fan Wenhu's court martial at Khanbaliq, in which he was found guilty of abandoning his troops on the islands off Kyushu.

Almost all medieval travel writing makes clear that no one has seen the whole world. The truth or reliability of Polo's account of Japan little mattered to his European audience because Japan was *terra nullius* as far as western understanding went. It was yet another abundant place among the strange isles of the east. For all his long-distance travels and his many years spent in Asia, Polo was unsure about the extent of the world, and certain that there remained yet further worlds to be visited, discovered and profited from.

Eating out in Mongol China

Marco Polo is often credited with bringing a range of foods from China to Italy, but there is no evidence he brought recipes back with him. He did note many peculiarities of diet and rituals around food: for example, he described excellent spiced date wine in Hormuz, the exclusive diet of meat and rice in Kashmir, the Tatar habit of eating horse, dog and mongoose, the central Asian offerings of fat and broth to the gods, the rice and millet noodles of China and the wonderful pears and peaches at the Hangzhou market. The encounter with other diets, dining conventions and social taboos around food is a perennial part of travel. In general, travellers focused on curiosities or rules of dining rather than the preparation of food, and were impressed by the great plenty of food in medieval China.

Here follow some medieval rules about dining and hospitality in a *ger* (yurt) in Mongol China.

- When an animal is to be eaten, you should truss its legs up, cut open the belly and squeeze the heart tight in your hand until the animal dies. After this, you can eat the meat. Whoever slaughters an animal in the Muslim fashion will himself be slaughtered.

- Genghis Khan prohibited the dipping of your hands in water; water should instead be scooped with vessels.
- Genghis Khan forbade his subjects to eat food offered by another until the one offering the food had tasted it himself, even if you're an emir and the other a captive. He forbade anyone to eat anything in the presence of another without first having invited him to share the food. He forbade any man to eat more than his comrades and to step over a fire on which food was being cooked or a dish from which people were eating.
- When a traveller passes a group of people eating, he should get down from his horse and eat with them without asking permission, and they must not hinder him in this.
- If *kumiss* is not offered to the thirsty, you shall pay a fine of one sheep.
- If you refuse to offer a traveller shelter for the night, you might be fined a three-year-old mare.
- You must not use a knife to remove meat from a cooking pot, as this will take the head off the flame.
- You must not urinate inside a yurt. If you do this voluntarily, you'll be put to death. If it's accidental, you'll have to pay a sorcerer to cleanse you and the yurt and all that's in it by passing through two fires, and before it's

purified no one should dare enter it or remove anything from it.

- The theft of mare's milk, wine and tea will be punished by a fine of five head of cattle. The theft of grain will be punished by a fine of one horse.
- You must not pour milk or put any other food or drink on the ground.
- A person who chokes on food must be driven out of the yurt and killed at once.
- If a piece of food is given to anyone and he puts it in his mouth but doesn't eat it and spits it out, a hole will be made beneath the yurt and he shall be drawn out into the hole and killed mercilessly.
- If you can't stop drinking alcohol, get drunk only three times a month. If you exceed this, you'll be punished. Getting drunk twice a month is good, and once a month is even better. What could be better than not drinking at all? But who on earth can do that? If such a person were to be found he would be worthy of the highest praise.

13. Visiting the West

Istanbul 1470 – Hormuz and Jeddah 1413–15 – Peterborough 1393 – Jerusalem 1325–7 – Poitiers 1307 – Bordeaux and Paris 1288

Many people outside Europe, if they thought about Europe at all, thought of it as 'the Land of the Romans', 'the Land of the Franks' or 'the Latin empire', far from the main centres of the world's population. In the period 1300 to 1400, the world's biggest cities were likely Beijing and Nanjing, each with over half a million people, compared to Rome's 33,000, London's 50,000 and Paris's 200,000 (all these figures are approximations). So far, this book has largely focused on the touristic eye and 'I' of European travellers going east. It has foregrounded their curiosity, their prejudices, their desires, their tendency to exoticize and the ways their reports and opinions shaped their world. We now rotate the globe a little in order to consider how the west looked to eastern travellers and visitors. To do this topic justice would take many more volumes. Here, I offer a few perspectives as a corrective to the west's dominant gaze, a gaze that did so much to construct the idea of travel with which we now live.

We started our journey with Behaim's Globe, which presented the view of the world from Nuremberg. We now take a different view, from Istanbul, sometime Constantinople, sometime Byzantium, in the 1470s, fifty years after Bertrandon de la Broquière's mission there. Since 1453, the city had come under the rule of the Ottoman emperor Mehmed II

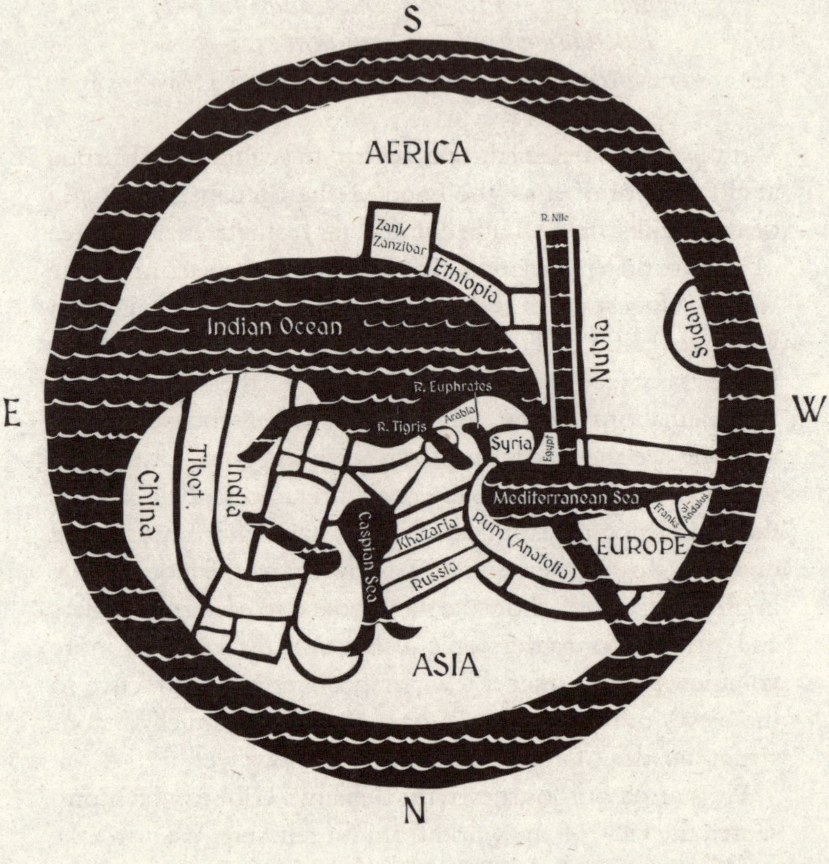
S
AFRICA
Zanj/
Zanzibar
Ethiopia
R. Nile
Nubia
Sudan
Indian Ocean
R. Euphrates
R. Tigris
Arabia
Syria
Egypt
E
W
China
Tibet.
India
Caspian Sea
Khazaria
Russia
Rum (Anatolia)
Mediterranean Sea
Franks
al-Andalus
EUROPE
ASIA
N

(aka Mehmed the Conqueror); its population, its visual aspect and its global orientation had fundamentally changed.

Mehmed II conquered Constantinople in May 1453; he was aged just twenty-one at the time. His forces killed the Byzantine emperor Constantine XI Dragases Palaiologos (1405–53), effectively ending a Christian empire which could be traced back to ancient Rome. All over Europe, kings and churchmen reacted with shock and horror to what they saw as a victory of Islam over Christendom. The Ottoman troops were granted the prize of three days of looting. On the third day, Mehmed held a victory celebration, guaranteed safety to the remaining Christians and set about transforming the city. The Basilica of Hagia Sophia became a mosque and Mehmed swiftly moved his capital from Edirne to Constantinople (which began to be called Istanbul, its popular Turkish name, derived from the Greek *eis ten polin*, 'to [or "in"] the city').

In 1459, Mehmed began having a magnificent palace, Topkapı, built for him. From his private quarters in Topkapı's shaded hilltop precincts, the sultan could look over the Golden Horn, his gaze commanding the sea routes east to the Black Sea and west to the Aegean and the Mediterranean. Mehmed made it no secret that he wished to conquer Rome, just as he had taken the 'New Rome' of Constantinople; from his elaborate palace at Topkapı, he declared himself Kayseri Rum, literally a new 'Caesar of the Romans'.

Sultan Mehmed had cosmopolitan tastes, bridging east and west, part Islamic *fatih* (conqueror), part Renaissance prince. He amassed books and artworks from the territories he conquered, and he wanted to view the world through the eyes of those he had vanquished, the Venetian navigators and merchants who had previously dominated the Mediterranean.

He commissioned a wide range of maps of different perspectives and geographical approaches.

In particular, Mehmed seems to have had Turkish cartographers make a large number of Islamic maps, including several drawn into copies of Abu Ishaq al-Istakhri's *Kitab al-Masalik* (*The Routes of the Realm*, a hugely influential tenth-century geographical work). Mehmed had these maps in his personal possession and put them in Istanbul's mosque libraries too. On these maps, south is at the top. North is at the bottom. What is now Iraq is at the map's centre. Two main continents dominate: Africa in the south (top) half, Asia in the north (bottom). The maps are bisected by the Persian Gulf and the Indian Ocean.

Ottoman territory is marked as the Land of the Rum, the Muslim empire of Anatolia, and most of continental Europe is marked, optimistically, as the Land of Greater Byzantium, a greater Turkey. Christian Europe is just a small slice of the north-west (bottom-right) corner, where a tiny territory is marked as 'Franks', western Europe). To its right (west) is al-Andalus (the Islamic emirates of southern Iberia until Castile's conquest of Granada in 1492). Christian Europe is, according to this worldview, an obscure corner, lacking in detail or notable features. From Istanbul, western Europe was the edge of the world. In other words, in some maps from Mehmed's Istanbul the values and perspectives of European maps are shifted about: a different world, a world of difference.

In the summer of 1480, Ottoman Turkish forces besieged the southern Italian city of Otranto, then part of the kingdom of Naples. The Ottomans were making unprecedented incursions in the west, including their siege of Rhodes (in the same year) and raids and landings throughout the Mediterranean. At the same time, European-style maps were being made for the Ottoman court by one of the most famous cartographers in western Europe, Francesco Berlinghieri (1440–1501) of Florence. Berlinghieri used the ancient *Geographica* of Ptolemy (c. 150 CE), a Greek treatise on world cartography that became widely translated into Latin around 1400. The *Geographica* mapped and described the world from the islands of the Atlantic to the eastern coast of China. Berlinghieri 'updated' Ptolemy by translating the work into Italian poetry and adding cartographic detail. Berlinghieri's maps, dazzlingly decorated in lapis lazuli and gold leaf, show all of Europe, its coasts and rivers and cities. One can see 'Canterborges' (Canterbury), 'Londra' (London) and 'Excestria' (Exeter) in England, 'Rocelle' (La Rochelle), 'Bordeos' (Bordeaux) and 'Baiona' (Bayonne) on the Atlantic coast. The place names on the map tend to be ports or ecclesiastical centres. Scandinavia is largely absent, and the Baltic is crudely sketched, but the Atlantic and Mediterranean littorals are shown in great detail and with startling accuracy.

Berlinghieri's book was designed for Mehmed, but Mehmed died before it could be completed; a magnificent copy of the book with its painted maps was presented in 1482 to Mehmed's son, Bayezid II (r. 1481–1512). Islamic crescents are marked in the elegant margins, where other copies have the Christian cross. This atlas was a curious counterpart to other maps in the Ottoman collection, most of which foregrounded the Persian and Indian Ocean worlds. Berlinghieri's map extended Turkish knowledge of the west, and allowed the new sultan to look west with a 'western' view, using the latest Italian geographical knowledge presented in Italian poetry. Just as Christian Europe had gradually taken an interest in the wider world, the world beyond Europe developed an interest in the west.

Good to know: Camels are used for travel in many parts of the world. Some people say there are two types of camel: the Bactrian and the Arabian. The Arabian camel, or dromedary, has one hump on its back, the Bactrian has two (although some say it's the other way round). People ride, load and eat camels, and one can wear camel skin or use it for leather tenting. 'Cameline' or 'camlet' is a soft Asian wool made from camel hair. The herder of camels is called the 'dromedarius' or cameleer. Camels and dromedaries run fast. They have hot, acrid, thin blood, so their milk is thinner than that of other beasts.

It is clear that China was for a long time connected with the far west, both via the silk routes and by the maritime trade routes to the eastern coast of Africa, the Horn of Africa, and the Arabian peninsula. Medieval Chinese coins have been found as far afield as England and Ethiopia. It was well known by the 1470s that 'men from Cathay have travelled eastwards,' and there were even reports that two 'strange and wonderful' Chinese had appeared in Galway in Ireland, reflecting the belief that there was a direct sea passage between eastern China and western Europe. Such anecdotes can be dismissed as strange rumours and misunderstandings – perhaps these blow-ins in Ireland were from Iceland, Greenland or north America? However, we do have much more detailed and certain records of Chinese travellers in the far west from earlier in the fifteenth century, during precisely that time when European travel was also expanding rapidly.

Zheng He (Cheng Ho; 1371–1435) was a high-ranking eunuch (a castrated official) at the Ming court. Between 1405 and 1433 he undertook seven massive seaborne expeditions, sailing through the oceans to bring back treasure – in the form of tribute, plunder, ambassadors, new merchandise and women for the imperial court. Each of the expeditions led by Zheng He comprised thousands of mariners and traversed the widest extent of the Chinese world, from south-east Asia to east Africa. His fleet, built and maintained in the massive imperial dockyards at Nanjing, comprised stupendously large vessels, at least 90 metres in length and with nine masts. There were horse ships carrying the cavalry, water tankers for holding drinking water, supply ships full of food and dozens of smaller vessels.

On three of his voyages, Zheng He was accompanied by a voluble translator and travel writer named Ma Huan (pen name 'Mountain Woodcutter'). Both Zheng He and Ma Huan were Muslims, and their voyages were partly framed as pilgrimages to 'the land of the Heavenly Square', that is, Mecca. Ma Huan was also an observant and curious travel writer. His first journey with Zheng He, in 1413–15, was a remarkable voyage, comprising sixty-three ships and over 28,500 men, which sailed out of Nanjing to Java, Sri Lanka, the Malabar Coast (including Cochin and Calicut) and as far west as Hormuz and Aden. In his foreword (written in 1416) to his account of that journey, Ma Huan described how his curiosity had initially been piqued by reading a fourteenth-century geographical text, *An Account of the Islands and their Barbarians*. He wrote that, after reading about the various peoples, topographies and climates of the planet, he asked himself, 'How can there be such dissimilarities in the world?'

Like many western travel writers, who set off on their journeys both to research and to confirm what they had already encountered in others' accounts of the world, Ma Huan used the massive voyage to see with his own eyes the places he had read about and to 'walk them in person'. And thus he knew that written descriptions of the world 'were no fabrications, and that even greater wonders existed'. He said little about the practicalities of travel. Rather, his method was to collect notes, on the 'ugliness and handsomeness' of the people he encountered in each country, about local customs, about products and merchandise and about boundaries and jurisdictions. In his foreword, he described himself as 'a mere simpleton', privileged as he was to accompany the imperial envoy on such a journey, and spoke of the voyage as 'a wonderful opportunity', the kind that occurs only once in a thousand years. He finished the foreword with an assurance to the reader that he was 'incapable of literary elegances' and so his 'honest pen' could be trusted. Ma Huan emerges through his account as at once precise and inquisitive, keen to record the world in detail but also full of desire for new wonders – an oscillation between the travel writer's wish to be accurate in what they saw and their desire to convey the world's marvellousness.

One of the tasks of the journey was to capture a usurper to the throne of Semudera, a sultanate on Sumatra's northern tip, but Ma Huan says little about the military logistics of the venture. His enquiring eye and taste for the detail of local cultures is quite at odds with what must have been the shockingly bellicose appearance of the fleet with which he sailed and the assertive expansion which lay behind the Ming dynasty's international journeys.

Ma Huan's extraordinary account of the world covers many pages and includes a great deal of fascinating detail, ranging from a lyrical poem on his great ship's progress 'on the roaring waves of the boundless ocean' to an account of Malaccan weretigers (tigers who turn into men) and to lists of the wines of Sri Lanka and the ten uses of Indian coconuts.*

The north-westernmost point visited by Ma Huan was Jeddah, the port for Mecca, on the western side of the Arabian peninsula. He also visited several ports in east Africa. Jeddah was a major commercial port in its own right and a western terminus of most Indian and Chinese shipping. Ma Huan gave only a brief description of the town, and its 'stalwart and fine-looking' people, their 'very dark purple' skin, and the pacific and admirable customs of the residents: 'there are no poverty-stricken families', he wrote, and 'they all observe the precepts of their religion, and law breakers are few.' Admiringly, he added, 'it is in truth a most happy country,' before making his journey to Mecca and its 'Heavenly Hall', where he gave a description of the wonderfully built mosque. Its walls, he recounted, were 'formed of clay mixed with rose water and ambergris', giving out perpetual fragrance. He described the 'Heavenly Square' of Mecca in the familiar terms of the Earthly Paradise, a place of architectural ingenuity, social ease and natural pleasure.

Ma Huan's account of Hormuz reflects his experience of one of the key places where east met west. Hormuz, by his

* Namely, according to Ma Huan:

1. sweet sap, a beverage
2. wine fermented from the sap
3. coconut oil, from the coconut flesh
4. sugar, from the coconut
5. food, from the flesh
6. coconut fibre, for making rope for shipbuilding
7. coconut shells, for making bowls and cups
8. coconut ash, for inlaying gold or silver
9. coconut trees, for building
10. coconut leaves, for roofing houses

reckoning, was twenty-five days with a fair wind from India's Malabar Coast: this would involve travelling about 61 nautical miles (113 kilometres) per day across the Arabian Sea. Just as western travellers did, Ma Huan defined Hormuz by its status as a global entrepôt: 'Foreign ships from every place and foreign merchants travelling by land all come to this country to attend the market and to trade; hence the people of the country are all rich.' Unlike western travel writers, who complained about Hormuz's heat and commented on the residents' pendular testicles, he admired the city's wealth and the 'reverent, meticulous and sincere' religious and personal conduct of its inhabitants. Devout Muslims, 'refined and fair', 'stalwart and fine-looking', they wore 'handsome, distinctive and elegant' garments. Moreover, the city's civil and military officials, and its physicians and diviners, were 'decidedly superior to those of other places'. He wrote approvingly that it had experts in every kind of art and craft. Ma Huan presents Hormuz as a superbly governed happy world city, pure and honest in its customs. Indeed, if a family fell into poverty, 'everyone gives them clothes and food and capital, and relieves their distress.' He was about as far as he would travel from China, and in the most international and diverse of ports, and it was here that he found an image of a harmonious and desirable urban society.

At Hormuz, he greatly enjoyed watching the performance of a local trick, involving a small white billy goat. In this performance, a man beat a drum, clapped his hands and sang a song to which the billy goat capered about. The creature then climbed a wooden pole and stood on the top of this pole and another, which was just about big enough for its four hooves, and made 'posturing movements like dancing gestures'. The man added extra poles and height, and the little goat continued to move about. The finale was for the man to push the poles away and catch the goat in his hands.

Ma Huan also recorded a set of tricks at Hormuz involving a large black monkey, which was blindfolded and struck on the head by a random member of the crowd. When the blindfold was removed from its eyes, the monkey was nonetheless able to go straight to whoever had struck him; 'it is most strange,' exclaimed Ma Huan.

Another of the wonders of Hormuz was a local cat called the 'fly-o'er-the-grass', apparently a lynx or caracal, with pointed black ears and a tortoiseshell coat. Ma Huan learned that this cat was 'mild, not vicious' and had the power to cause fierce animals, like lions or leopards, to 'prostrate themselves on the ground'. The fly-o'er-the-grass was, according to Ma Huan, 'king among the beasts'. Ma Huan's lynx has an intriguing counterpart in Christian accounts of the panther, a 'gentle animal' with sweet breath and a pacific nature, which symbolized Christ in the medieval bestiary, the popular book of beasts.

The accounts of the billy goat, the monkey and the lynx reveal Ma Huan's eye for the curious, outside his flotilla's ambitions for profit or conquest. His admiration for these animals chimes more generally with his praise of Hormuz: a place of cheap bounty, 'all the precious merchandise from every foreign country', of plentiful carrots and very large melons, pomegranates as large as teacups and fragrant apples as big as a fist. Throughout his account of Hormuz, Ma Huan suggests the harmonious interplay between man and nature, in which the wealth of commerce stemmed from a delightful and propitious natural disposition.

His curious eye stands in stark juxtaposition to the purposes of the journey of which he was part: to intimidate and dominate the trading world of greater Asia, and to exact tribute from each place. As the Chinese boats left Hormuz, they were accompanied by a vessel on which the King of Hormuz had loaded lions, giraffes, horses, pearls, gems and other gifts. He also sent an inscribed golden leaf, evidently showing the insignia and lineage of the Hormuz throne. There was a significant human cargo included too, of various chiefs and ambassadors. Many of them would stay in China for years: some of those who sailed from Hormuz to Khanbaliq in 1415 were only given leave to be conducted back home in 1421.

Zheng He knew that the voyages he commanded were exceptional, for he left a legacy of several monumental stone steles. Two of these, at Nanjing and Nanshan, give thanks to Mazu 'the Celestial Wife', the Chinese sea goddess and protectress of sailors. They represent a lasting monument not only to Zheng He's journeys but also to the Ming dynasty's use of seafaring to display its wealth and power to the wider world.

We previously met Henry of Derby as he prepared to embark on his Crusade-cum-pilgrimage-cum-tour through Prussia, Europe and the Holy Land in the early 1390s. Henry returned from Jerusalem via Famagusta, Rhodes and Venice. He travelled with several souvenirs. These included a leopard (probably presented by the King of Cyprus) for which he had a room made on the galley to Venice. The leopard and his salaried keeper seem to have lived out their days shivering in the royal menagerie of the Tower of London. Henry's return luggage also included four cups made of ostrich eggs, several butts of wine, fine Venetian silks and linens, falcons (with a Milanese glove) and a parrot in a cage hung from a cord.

But his most precious souvenir was a Turk, picked up at Rhodes, converted to Christianity and given the name Henry, like his master-patron. A bed, a pilgrim's cape, a 'toga' (a cloak) and several pairs of shoes were bought for 'Henry Turk' on the way to England. At Troyes, the Turk was separated from Earl Henry's party and sent back to England, with the chaplain Hugh and two other priests and a falcon, boating along the River Seine. 'Henry Turk' is last heard of in the English town of Peterborough, with its imposing Gothic Benedictine abbey rising from the fenland. We have no record of his voice or feelings, or even his original name.

'Henry Turk' was an unusual but not unique figure. For example, an 'Ethiopian' named 'Bartholomew', who had possibly escaped from being enslaved in Sicily, went on the run in England in the 1250s. Later, in 1470, the wealthy Englishman John Paston wrote a letter boasting about a 'new little Turk', a Turkish dwarf, who it was reported had a penis as long as his leg; this Turk seems to have been an attendant in Paston's London house, possibly a Turkish soldier or ransomed captive who had made his way to England via Venice or Genoa. The fleeting presence of such figures in the historical record reminds us of those people for whom western curiosity was not an abstract thought experiment. They were purchased, captured and converted, then brought to remote shores where they were left to prosper, or to fail.

Het'um of Armenia (c. 1245–c. 1315), prince and prior, lived a life at the intersections of place and identity. He was born into the royal family of Cilicia or Little Armenia in what is now south-east Turkey, and his father was Lord of Corycus (Kızkalesi), on the coast due north of Cyprus and in the region of the fabled site of Sparrowhawk Castle. As a youth Het'um was made governor of Corycus and married a cousin, Zabel, of the ruling Cypriot Ibelin family. His uncle was King Het'um I of Armenia, who had successfully negotiated his kingdom's place within the shifting political world of the thirteenth-century Middle East; King Het'um was a skilled diplomat who gained an alliance with the Mongols to guarantee his country's safety. But from the 1260s the Mamluks successfully overwhelmed the Armenian–Mongol pact, and over the following hundred years the kingdom was ravaged and eventually dissolved. Het'um of Armenia appears to have taken part in embassies between England and France. Around 1299 he may have made a pilgrimage to Paris, and by 1305 he had certainly left Armenia to join the monastic Premonstratensian order in their beautiful cliffside abbey at Bellapais in Cyprus. This was a way of absenting himself from vicious dynastic struggles going on in Armenia, which led to two kings, Het'um II and Leon III, being assassinated in December 1307. At this point, Het'um had settled in the French city of Poitiers, where he became prior at the abbey and remained for about eighteen months. He befriended Pope Clement V (1264–1314), who was frequently at Poitiers, and sought western alliances for the Armenian crown and for his kinsman Amalric Lusignan of Tyre (d. 1310), a claimant to Cyprus. At the same time, and apparently at the request of the pope, Het'um composed a geography of Asia, one of the first of the Middle Ages; he dictated the text in French to a scribe, Nicholas Faucon, who then translated it into Latin. It was called *The Flower of Histories of the Orient*, and became an influential account of the world, as seen by an Armenian in exile. *The Flower of Histories* was soon a foundational text in communicating to western Europe knowledge about Armenia and about the Mongol world.

Much of Het'um's narrative concerns the rise of the Mongols, stories of Genghis Khan and the conflicts between the Mongol rulers of the greater Persian region and the sultans of Egypt. Het'um said little about his own travels, although he was clearly an eyewitness to many of the events he described and moved extensively between Armenia, Cyprus and France, and possibly much further afield (members of the Armenian court were certainly at Rome in the west and at Khanbaliq in the east during this period). He summarized the three ways in which he gathered material for his book: first, from 'the histories of the Tatars'; secondly, from the eyewitness oral testimony of his uncle King Het'um, which was then committed to writing; and thirdly, from his own eyewitness recollections – 'I speak as he who was present in person, and what I have seen I have recorded truly.' This neatly summarizes the medieval approach to writing about both travel and geography, as a melange of past memories melded with the individual's voice and perspective.

Het'um's book opens with a description of the realms of the east from Cathay to Turkestan to India to Persia through Armenia and Georgia to Syria. As in western geographies, Jerusalem and its environs are the place at which the world culminates, but for Het'um the realm of Cathay, 'the most noble and rich realm of the world', was the necessary starting point. This was not only because of the contours of Mongol power but also because the Cathayans were, according to Het'um, distinguished by their 'subtle labour and ingenious arts', their inventiveness in art and manual work. In his globe, the centre of gravity had shifted conclusively to the Far East, and ultimately his book sought to encourage European rulers to ally with the Mongols if they were ever to retake Jerusalem and the Holy Land.

It is not surprising that Het'um's tract ends with an exhortation to his western European readers to undertake a 'general passage', an international crusading expedition of 'pilgrims' to recover the Holy Land. He therefore sought to spread knowledge about the east in order that it be reconquered, urging a mass movement of people by three routes: first, through

Barbary (which he did not recommend, given poor knowledge of 'the condition of this country'); secondly, via Constantinople, the route taken by Crusaders of old but perilous because of the Turks in that country (Het'um added that, if this route were to be taken, Mongols would have to be used to 'ensure the way', bringing food to the pilgrims and providing reasonably priced horses). The third route, 'the other way that everybody knows' and preferred by Het'um, was by sea. This route, he said, would need each port to be fully provisioned for the pilgrims, and he recommended especially that they all come to Cyprus 'to rest themselves and their horses' after the labour of crossing the sea. Alternatively, he recommended that the pilgrims go via Armenia, and they could tarry or even winter in the city of 'Tersot' (Tarsus), the capital of Little Armenia, where they would find 'great plenty of waters and pasture for their horses', and from where they could easily occupy the city of Antioch.

Het'um's desire was transparent: to put Cyprus and Armenia at the centre of the changing European world, both 'to conquer the city of Jerusalem with the help of God' and to make an alliance with the Mongols which would ensure the integrity of Cyprus and Armenia against both the Turks and the Mamluks. His hope was that 'the might of the enemies', the Mamluks, would be 'confounded rather by two than by one' – an early statement of the need for alliances.

Written in Poitiers in the first decade of the fourteenth century, Het'um's manifesto turned out to be both nostalgic and naive. Jerusalem was not retaken by Christians. His text, however, became widely read and much copied, as the practicality of crusading was abandoned in favour of misty-eyed romance and fantasies of chivalry. While Het'um's son Oshin (d. 1329) became Lord of Corycus and played an active role in Armenian politics as king regent, Little Armenia collapsed by 1375, caught up in endless power struggles and territorial wars between Cyprus, Turkey, the Tatars and the Mamluks. The last King of Little Armenia, Levon V (1342–93), was one of the main peacemakers between the English and French at a conference in Amiens, hoping to unite them against the Turks who had devastated his kingdom and sent him into exile. Levon died in exile in Paris in 1393, calling in vain for another crusade, as exhorted by Het'um.

As we have seen, the Mongol court at Karakorum and then at Khanbaliq was international, cosmopolitan, diverse in nature. It was centripetal, attracting people from all over the world to it as a centre of power and wealth. It was also centrifugal, sending out ambassadors, diplomats, messengers and pilgrims into the world.

One such Mongol emissary was Rabban Bar Sauma, a Mongol Christian born near Khanbaliq, who recorded his extraordinary travels. In the 1260s, Bar Sauma set out on pilgrimage to Jerusalem with one of his students, Markos. They made their way through central Asia, arriving at the Armenian Silk Road town of Ani: then a thriving city but now a desolate landscape of ruined churches and broken bridges. They were warned that their onward route through Syria was too dangerous, and so went to Persia and visited the Mongol court of Abaqa Khan at Hamadan. During this journey, Markos was elected bishop and then patriarch, taking the name Yahballaha III. He suggested to Abaqa Khan's successor, Arghun Khan, that his wise and venerable teacher and companion Bar Sauma might undertake a mission further west, to build a Franco-Mongol alliance against their common enemy, the Mamluk sultans of Cairo, who then held Jerusalem.

In 1287 Bar Sauma, by now considered to be of a great age

(at least in his mid-sixties), set off from Baghdad for Europe. Arghun Khan gave him 2,000 pieces of gold, a *paiza* (the Mongol bull-cum-passport) and thirty animals for transport. The patriarch gave him permission to depart and a letter of introduction. Bar Sauma's account of his travels is unique and contains some wonderful details. Here we will look briefly at his journey through Europe and his impressions of it.

His journey took him to Constantinople, where he embarked for Italy. Sailing through the Mediterranean, he witnessed the eruption of Mount Etna (on 18 June 1287), 'a mountain from which smoke ascended all the day long', which burned with fire during the night and filled the air with the stench of sulphur. Echoing many who had travelled over these waters, Bar Sauma said that the 'Sea of Italy' was 'a terrible sea', in which thousands of people had perished. He reached Napoli (Naples) 'after two months of toil, and weariness, and exhaustion', reflecting the dismal conditions of medieval sailing, especially awful for Mongols unaccustomed to the rigours of sea travel.

At Naples, he met the monarch 'Shardalo' ('Charles le deux', Charles II, King of Naples, d. 1309) and was well received. On 24 June 1287, Bar Sauma described his pleasure in sitting on the rooftop of his mansion overlooking the Gulf of Naples; the pleasure lay not in the serene view of azure seas, but in admiring the way King Charles's forces attacked those of his enemy, James II of Aragon and Valencia (1267–1327). He wondered at how precise and targeted the battle was, how the enemies managed to kill only combatants and not other people.

He then proceeded to Rome and thence to 'Ginoh' (Genoa), where he spent the winter. He admired the body of St John the Baptist in a silver casket at the Church of 'Sinalornia' (the Cathedral of San Lorenzo) and was shown an emerald paten which was said to be the very plate from which Christ had eaten the Passover meal with his disciples.

He went north through 'Onbar' (Lombardy) to 'Pariz' (Paris) the capital of 'Frangestan' (France), where he met King Philip IV, the Fair (1268–1314). His impression of Paris is touristic. He spent a month there and he and his party 'saw everything there was in it'. He was particularly struck by the number of students – 30,000 – engaged in studying all kinds of books, of biblical commentary and exegesis, of philosophy, rhetoric, medicine, geometry, arithmetic, astronomy. These students were 'engaged constantly in writing' and all of them received grants for their subsistence from the king. He visited the royal mausoleum at Saint-Denis, where gold and silver statues of dead kings decorated their tombs and 500 monks chanted for their departed souls. In sum, Bar Sauma felt that he and his companions 'saw everything which was splendid and renowned'.

He proceeded south-west to 'Kasonia' (Gascony), an English possession, where he met the English king, Edward I, probably at Bordeaux from where the English ruled. He returned to Genoa, where he saw 'a garden which resembled Paradise'. It was temperate all year, full of fruiting trees with green leaves in any season. And there was a vine which yielded a harvest of grapes seven times a year, although the locals didn't make wine from it.

Bar Sauma's tour of Europe culminated in a stay in Rome, where he had a momentous encounter with the newly elected pope, Nicholas IV (d. 1292). Bar Sauma reported that he had addressed the pope directly, with the words 'Now that I have seen your face, my eyes are illumined, and I shall not go away broken-hearted to the countries of the east.' The pope awarded him a 'mansion' in which to stay, with servants on hand to keep him well supplied. Bar Sauma watched the Easter processions in Rome, including Palm Sunday when 'countless thousands and tens of thousands' of people gathered with olive branches. He saw the pope conduct the service in luxurious vestments, a red costume with gold thread running through it, studded down to his sandals with precious gems, jacinth and pearl. Bar Sauma's diplomatic mission was essentially unsuccessful inasmuch as he failed to gather an army against the Mamluks. But the pope did give him relics of Christ's clothing, Mary's kerchief and some small fragments of unidentified (possibly unidentifiable) saints too. The pope also gave him 1,500 gold coins for his journey home.

From Rome, Bar Sauma travelled back over the sea, the way he had come, to Baghdad, where he wrote about his travels. While his account of the west is unique, it is also notably similar to western accounts of the east, a narrative sustained by the perils of seafaring, of warfare, of paradisiacal gardens and unusual relics, of potent rulers and their infinite riches, of observed customs that lay between the strange and the recognizable. For Bar Sauma as for medieval western travel writers, understanding the world meant discovering that it was not everything it had seemed to be. At the same time, Bar Sauma's travels reveal the interplay between pilgrimage, diplomacy, missioning and touristic curiosity, and the way the traveller's gaze could be directed from east to west.

How to find the Fountain of Youth

The Fountain of Youth, inspired by biblical descriptions of the rivers of Paradise and a 'well of living waters' flowing from Lebanon (Canticles 4:12–16), was searched for by many medieval travellers. Most famously the Spanish explorer Juan Ponce de León, in 1512, received a commission from the Holy Roman emperor Charles V (1500–58) to capture the island of Bimini near Hispaniola (Greater Antilles), where health-giving waters were said to flow. Here are a few of the many medieval descriptions of the Fountain:

In the thirteenth-century epic *Huon of Bordeaux* the hero Huon finds a Fountain of Youth by the Nile, in the Emir of Babylon's gardens:

> In the midst of this garden there was a fair fountain coming out of the River Nile that flows from Paradise. This fountain was of such virtue that if any sick man drank thereof, or washed his hands and face, the unchaste should be made chaste, and also if a man had been of great age, he should return again to the age of thirty years, and a woman would become as fresh and lusty as a maid of fifteen years. (This fountain had that

virtue for forty years, but ten years after Huon went there, it was destroyed and broken by the Egyptians, who had made war on the Admiral then in Babylon.)

And when Huon had washed his hands and face in the fountain and drunk its water, he beheld the palace and thought it marvellously fair. And when he had long regarded it, he saw just beside the fountain a great serpent who guarded the fountain, to the end that none should be so hardy to drink or touch the fountain, for if any traitor or heretic touched it he could not escape without death. But when the serpent saw Huon, he inclined himself without appearing to do him any ill.

Sir John Mandeville identified the Well of Youth near Polombe (Colombo) on the island of Serendip (Sri Lanka):

South of the city of Polombe is a hill that people call Polombe, from which the city takes its name. And at the foot of this hill there's a pretty well which has a sweet flavour of all kinds of spices, and it changes its flavour variously at each hour of the day. And whoever drinks three times a day from that well shall be healed from any kind of illness that they have. For I have drunk from that well, and I think I do feel better for it. Some people call it the Well of Youth, because those who drink from it seem eternally young and live

> without severe illness. And it is said that the well comes from Paradise, for it is full of virtues.

The poet and historian Jean Froissart (d. c. 1405) in *The Pretty Bush of Youth* showed that not everyone believed in the Fountain of Youth:

> I have heard talk of the Fountain of Youth and of invisible stones too. But these are impossible things for never, by the faith of St Marcel, have I ever seen anyone who has said 'I have actually been there.'

14. A Rough Guide to the Antipodes and the End of the World

The Antipodes – Sumatra – Java – Panten – The sea of death – Land's End

Medieval travellers, astronomers and merchants were very well prepared for the idea of new landmasses, new continents and new civilizations appearing all over the globe (new in the sense that they were unknown, but old in the sense that they preceded European knowledge). Travel is often said to open the mind, to allow one to have fresh experiences. Yet in medieval Europe the discovery of 'new' places did not necessarily query fixed categories of knowledge, for travel writing had already primed every traveller to expect a world full of prodigies and marvels.

In the fourteenth century, people told a story about a young man from Europe. It appeared in travel guides, chronicles, sermons, geographies and poems. In the story, the young man set off from his home because he wanted to see the world. He was the clever and curious son of farmers who had never travelled far from their small herd of cattle. He went all the way to India, and then he carried on. Using boats, donkeys, horses and his own two feet he travelled 5,000 miles beyond India in the east, into the lower part of the world. He was so far from home and saw so many marvels, he barely knew where he was.

The greatest marvel, however, was the land he encountered where he found people speaking his own language and living as people did in his own village. They were even herding cows using exactly the same words that his own father and mother did. It seemed to him that he could travel no further, so he turned around, intending to travel all the way back home. But after a short while he stumbled across his own house: his mother, his father, their cows, their pastures, all there, at the very end of the world. He had travelled as far from home as he could, yet had, somehow, ended up at home.

At first, the young man thought he had reached the Antipodes, the exact opposite side of the world: the southern region where people were thought to have their feet opposite to the people in the north. Crucial to the theory of the Antipodes – foot to foot, contrary to contrary, pole to pole – was the potential for the two sides of the world to correspond, as direct opposites, as radically alike rather than unlike.

The travelling young man was not uneducated; he had studied a few books about the planets and the firmament, and he knew that the entire world was precisely 20,425 miles in circumference (although others said it was 31,500 Roman miles). It dawned on the young man that he had, in fact, travelled so far that he had gone entirely around the world, across the breadth of the whole thing or perhaps around its entire height, up and down: either way, he had circumnavigated the globe. His journey had taken him around the world, by land and sea, and returned him to his own country.

The young man's parents, educated mostly in tending cows, thought the world had no underside, no bottom; if they thought about it at all, they thought of the world as a kind of line, leading up to Jerusalem, and if one went downwards one might lose one's balance and fall off, into the unknowable expanses of the sky and the stars. If they had seen a map of the world, they assumed that the 'back' of it, the globe's reverse, was full of sea, because they believed the only habitable part of the world was in the northern zone, their zone. And some of the preachers at church believed this too, and they had read in their books that it was foolish to believe in men living on the other side of the world. If one believed that the world had a top (the Arctic), a centre (Jerusalem) and a bottom (the Antarctic, *anti* the Arctic), and if one believed that the Antipodes were directly opposite to Europe, then one had to believe that crops and trees could grow *downwards*, or rain and snow could fall *upwards*. People like the young man's parents couldn't accept this.

But the young man knew differently, and his vast voyage had proved it to him: one could travel all around the world without toppling off into the firmament. So now he knew that there were people on the opposite side of the earth: just as he thought of them underneath him, they thought of him as being underneath them.

And he thought he remembered how God said in the Bible: 'Do not be afraid of me, who hung the earth from nothing' (Job 26:7). The young man considered the round orb of the planet, its people and its seas and its cities and its mountains, all suspended in the air, held up by God's ingenious influence and incomprehensible control.

The story of the young man who traversed the world, all around and up and down, made explicit the controversial proposition that the hot area around the equator, the torrid zone buffeted by scorching seas, was evidently passable. Conventional geographical wisdom had long argued that this torrid zone was a barrier to human travellers. Later medieval scientific certainty about the earth's roundness confirmed that both the biblical world and the known world of three continents (Africa, Asia and Europe) could not fill its entire surface: there had to be more, whether inhabited or not.

Look out for vegetable lambs growing on trees on the island of Caldihe. You might see a kind of gourd or pumpkin that can be cut open when ripe. Within, one will find a little creature made of skin, bone and blood like a little lamb, without wool.*

By the later Middle Ages men, and women, were frequently sailing across the earth from one side to the other. Indeed, the *Malay Annals*, compiled in the fifteenth century to tell the story of the emergence of the Malay monarchy since the eleventh century, begin with the story of 'Raja Iskander', a Muslim version of Alexander the Great, 'a Roman of the country of Macedonia' who 'set out to visit the east' and achieved 'lordship over the whole earth from east to west, from north to south'. Ultimately, Iskander was acclaimed as the originator of the dynasty crowned at Palembang (Indonesia), who founded Singapore and established the sultanate of Melaka (Malacca). Medieval Java, Sumatra and the Malaysian peninsula dictated marine passage over an enormous area, and were always closely connected to global commerce, even as these regions were only haltingly apprehended by Europeans.

The islands of Lamuri (the name given both for the kingdom of Banda Aceh and for all of Sumatra) and Java were the closest place to the Antipodes that Europeans visited in the Middle Ages. These islands were central to the spice trade and

* Caldihe is a distant island, beyond Tatary and Cathay, somewhere on the way to India and the Caspian Sea. These vegetable lambs are actually just like the barnacle geese that are said to grow on logs in Ireland. These barnacle geese initially have soft shells, then they grow and mature, attached at the beak to the log. Once they are covered in feathers, they fly away. Or so people say.

were deeply connected to the Indian Ocean world of commerce and travel. The term 'Java' often covered a galaxy of islands in the Java Sea. Ibn Battuta, in the early fourteenth century, established that 'Java Minor' can be associated with Sumatra, whereas 'Java Major' (or 'Djaouah') referred to what is now Java, Indonesia and/or Borneo and beyond. Descriptions of the territory called Java Major may also have embraced the northern coast of Australia. Both Marco Polo and the Franciscan missionary Odoric of Pordenone described Java Major as 'the largest island in the world', at over 3,000 miles in circumference, a description which cannot help but presage the way in which Australia would be evoked. In any case, locating the precise correspondence between medieval ideas and modern geography is less important than understanding that, long before the recorded first European arrival in Australia (the Dutch trader Willem Janszoon landed there in 1606), the Antipodes were a point of speculation and enquiry, promising a world both of wonders and of tantalizing similarities.

Accounts of the lands of the Antipodes are few, but medieval maps often feature them, if obliquely. As with Behaim's Globe, maps existed in a dynamic interplay with actual discoveries, as sirens, mythical islands and biblical locales jostled for space with newly visited coasts and recently explored interiors. There was a heterogeneous tradition of mapping, including diagrams, charts and sumptuous *mappae mundi*. On many maps, the Antipodes appear as a 'mirror' or counterpart, towards the bottom or 'south' of the map, to the known world at the top or 'north'. On Behaim's Globe, Java (and other islands in the region like 'Pentan' and 'Candyn') are accompanied by a short text about the Antipodes: these are, the Globe says, situated so far south that the Pole Star is invisible and instead the Antarctic star becomes visible. The Globe continues to describe how this country 'lies foot against foot with respect to our land, and when it is day with us they have night, and when the Sun sets with us they have their day'. Moreover 'half of the stars, which are beneath us, and not visible to us, are visible to them.' And Behaim adds his source: 'All this is because God has created the world together with the water of a round shape, as described by John Mandeville.' East of Java, Behaim's Globe shows a huge expanse of water, studded with multicoloured islands, overlaid with text about the rest of the world. The watery, 'round' world was thus made complete on the Globe, a fourth part of the world (before America became known as such) joining Java to Africa via the expanse of the seas.

Other medieval maps vary greatly on how they presented what was beyond India and Java. Some placed the Antipodes at the rim of what they represented, usually in the south-western or south-eastern section of the map. In some cases this suggested that a 'fourth continent' should be inferred as being on the 'back' or 'underneath' the *ecumene* represented on the 'front' of the map. Other maps simply place blank space in the Antipodes, to represent their status as unknown and to suggest their emptiness. The medieval Antipodes thus came into being as a place barely visited but known to exist.

The Mirror of the World, a fifteenth-century retelling of a twelfth-century encyclopaedia, includes a vivid image of two men walking around the world in opposite directions and meeting, foot to foot and face to face, 'below' their point of departure. The accompanying text explains that, 'like a fly goes round about a round apple', a man or beast can go round the entire extent of the earth, all around it, 'so he should arrive under us and it would seem to him that we were under him.' And if he kept going, he would go 'so far that he should return again to the place from whence he first departed'. By this point, it was clear that *theoretically* speaking circumnavigation of the world was possible, in all directions, up and down, east and west, even if hazards and human fallibility always got in the way.

In 1325, before he reached China, Odoric of Pordonone sailed in a junk from India to Sumatra. He visited various ports on the northern coast of the island and travelled around the Malay Archipelago. He also visited Java, Borneo (and probably Brunei) and south-east Asia via the Nicobar Islands.

Odoric understood that he was approaching the Antipodes as he sailed to Lamuri, the north-west tip of the island of Sumatra, then part of the Pasai sultanate, a great trading dynasty. It was a wonder for him to begin to lose sight of the North Star (Polaris, the Pole Star), 'as the earth intercepted it'. Odoric had not only broadened his horizons through

travel but had passed the horizon. The map of the skies waxed unfamiliar, as the lodestar used for navigation by shipmen all over the northern hemisphere fell away, fixed in a different, distant sphere.

For Odoric, Lamuri itself was distinctive on two main counts. First, the people, both men and women, went about completely naked. Not unreasonably, and following a logic Odoric must have understood if not accepted, they told him that God had made Adam naked, so why go against divine will and wear clothes, especially in such fearsome heat? Secondly, the people there ate human flesh just like, said Odoric, Italians eat beef. They even bought children from overseas and sold them for flesh to butchers in the meat market. They had plentiful wheat, rice, camphor, aloes and plantains, but still loved the taste of human flesh.

Europe's fascination with cannibalism is surely as old as European travel; travellers' fancies confront the traveller with behaviours of which they have no personal experience but are led to believe are widespread. It became a self-referential observation that, beyond Europe, cannibalism was rampant and therefore non-Christian people were not fully 'civilized'. Charges of cannibalism tend to occur in ill-defined contact zones, at the further outposts of the known and understood world. Akin to customs like sodomy and polygamy, cannibalism was held to be deeply shameful and yet remarkably common overseas, and travel writing offered a space in which it could be explored (and pruriently enjoyed). Medieval cannibalism was an intriguingly wide category, and the reasons for cannibalism were various: people were eaten by virtue of religion, cruelty, starvation and justice. Odoric may well have heard about cannibals in Sumatra but, even if he hadn't, he would have expected to find cannibalism at the edges of the east, and his journey to novel frontiers would have been more convincing to his audience for the presence of cannibals there. Likewise, Sinbad the Sailor of Baghdad, the figure of the consummate Islamic traveller, was said to have encountered cannibals on his third and fourth voyages to the east. At the 'Mountain of the Apes' (possibly a version of Sumatra, on account of its orangutan-like fauna), Sinbad's crew was devoured by a terrifying giant who roasted the men on coals. On his next voyage, the restless Sinbad was shipwrecked on an eastern island where the ghoulish Magian people rubbed visitors with a special oil which caused them to become foolish and to grow enormously fat; they would then be 'slaughtered, roasted, and fed to the king'. Stories of Sinbad, set in the ninth century but circulating throughout the Middle Ages, similarly point to cannibalism as a key peril which marked out civilized travellers from the savagery of the island kingdoms they visited.

After Sumatra, Odoric described Java as being a large island whose king had seven kings in his dominion. It was, he says, well populated and had an abundance of spices and foods, though not of wine.

Yet after he had called attention to these desirable products, Odoric gave an account of Java that sounded familiar, unexotic, predictable even. The king lived in a marvellous great palace, 'the most beautiful there is', with gold-plated walls, decorated with stories of knights in battle. It could almost have been a royal court in France or Italy.

Beyond Java, according to Odoric, was the island of Panten, seemingly some version of the island of Bintan between Sumatra and Singapore or maybe the Hindu–Buddhist kingdom of Banten on the western side of Java. The trees there produced a beautiful flour for the making of fine white bread. Odoric said that he had eaten this bread, 'for all these things

I have seen with my own eyes.' Possibly recalling the sago tree, he stressed the capacity of God, even here, to offer nature in the service of mankind, in a mundane marvel that suggested holy communion appearing as natural sustenance.

But Panten was also alive with natural danger. Odoric reported a terrible tree that produced the 'most deadly' poison in the world. The only known antidote was human shit diluted with water. This was a much repeated myth of a Javanese poison tree. It shouldn't have been so remarkable to Odoric, because animal droppings were common in western medical remedies: cow and ox turds and goose and dove droppings were frequently used in European medicinal plasters and drinks.

Local people could thrive in Panten only thanks to the enormous canes growing by the seashore, which fruited with precious gems. These gems, when carried on the person, meant one could not be injured by iron or steel blades, and one's blood could not be let or shed. People even carved wounds into their arms in which to place these gems, as nature's talisman in a dangerous place.

Beyond Panten, the oceans raced southwards. Odoric described a 'dead sea', a sea of death, 'a body of water without a bottom'. He warned that if one should have the misfortune to fall into this sea one would never be found again. And if sailors let their boats stray too far from the shore, the waters of this awful sea would carry them down, never to return. Odoric was perhaps repeating what locals had told him, about the Java Sea or the Sunda Strait or the Indian Ocean between Java and Australia. This was the southernmost point of Odoric's epic travels, the furthest into the Antipodes he was able, or dared, to go. He had travelled to the edge of knowledge and to the threshold of death.

European maps likewise suggested the perils of straying

too far towards the edge of the world. The Hereford *mappa mundi* (c. 1300) has the letters M O R S (death) encircling the world, four points on everyman's compass, a reminder of the earthly traveller's mortality. Fra Mauro's Venetian map of c. 1450 bears a legend south-east of India that ships sailing southwards will be carried by currents 'into the Darkness' where, 'through the density of the air, and the tenacious waters, they must perish.' Similarly, Mandeville and others reported 'adamantine rocks' in the eastern oceans, which drew iron towards them in a violent manner (local ships were therefore made without nails or other ironware). Some people even said they had seen a kind of long island and had been told by sailors that it was the remnants of all the ships wrecked by the adamantine. The great vessels had been reduced to a fatal mass of trees and branches sprouting from the wreckage. If travel is a way to feel alive, that might be because in travel we flirt with danger, before the waves of the oceans of oblivion reach out for us.

The torpid seas beyond Panten marked the limits of Odoric's knowledge, for he admitted that no one knew where people carried away by the waters were taken or what became of them. Beyond Panten death encircled the world no matter how far one went. Everything in the *ecumene* – its gold, its spices, its gorgeous palaces and solemn temples – would be swept away. The Antipodean seas became a River Styx, flowing with death, or maybe a Lethe, the waters of oblivion. A vortex, a watery maze, a sea of troubles, the Devil's own ocean.

Odoric's sea of death is entirely in keeping with the medieval Christian understanding of God's creation as too awesome for an individual to apprehend. The sea of death marked the point at which the only option was to turn back. It was on the shores of Panten that Odoric accepted the limitations of his travelling enquiry, bowing to landscapes and forces greater than he. He took a boat north, from Panten to Champa (now Vietnam), thence to Khanbaliq, to places more accessible than Panten's perilous shores.

In fact many medieval travellers turned their thoughts to the ends of the world rather than to homecoming. Marco Polo, like Odoric, described fatal seas at the edges of the known world: between Java and the Andaman Islands, a sea so deep and turbulent that ships could neither anchor there nor sail away, so they were swept forever into its gulf; and south of Madagascar a sea with a continual southwards current, from which any sailor was unlikely to return. Travel may broaden the mind not through limitless discovery but by helping us understand our limits, and the world's limits.

Thus places called Land's End appear all over the globe, representing the limits of the traversable world. Other places, like the Pillars of Hercules at Gibraltar, were held to be the limits of the navigable ocean. Medieval world's ends included the Galician Fisterra (*Finis terrae*, 'land's end'), Finistère in Brittany, Land's End (known as *Inglendesende*, 'England's End', at the south-western edge of England), Pembroke (*Pen Bro*, 'land's end') in Wales, and Ultima Thule ('Thule the Furthermost'), variously identified with Shetland, Iceland, Greenland or somewhere beyond. Johore at the tip of the Malaysian peninsula was known in the Middle Ages as Ujong Medini ('Land's End'), the main island of Singapore was called Pulau Ujong ('The Isle at the End') and the port of Makassar on Sulawesi was known as Ujong Pandang ('Horizon's End'). For Māori, Cape Reinga ('Underworld Cape'), at the northern tip of New Zealand, became the most spiritually significant location, where spirits were said to leave this world to descend to the underworld. These were the ends of the world as we try to know them in a place.

Thule was a kind of northern counterpart to the Antipodes.

The historian and ethnographer Adam of Bremen, writing about 1070, was the first known European to write about north America, in his account of the Norse settlement at Vinland (settled by Leif Erikson around the year 1000). Adam also wrote about Thule, which he said was situated at an immense distance from all other islands and remained 'barely known'. It was called Ultima Thule because it was the last of all the islands in the ocean. At the summer solstice it was never dark there, and at midwinter there was no daylight. Thule was, said Adam, a distance of six days' sailing from Britain.

He tentatively identified Thule with the volcanic island of Iceland. Thule's ice made the sea solid. This black, dry and ancient ice would blaze away if set on fire. The people of Thule lived 'in a holy simplicity' in underground pits, with just livestock to farm and clothing made of animal pelts. 'Instead of towns they have mountains and springs as their delight,' Adam hymned. They would share whatever they have with both foreigners and locals, one of many meritorious customs in their culture. Beyond Thule, there was nothing else.

Gabriel Tetzel, a German patrician travelling from Nuremberg in the 1460s, rode out to Fisterra in Galicia after visiting Santiago de Compostela. He noted that the peasants called the place 'Finster Stern' ('Dark Star' in German), even though its correct name was Finis Terrae ('Land's End'), but both seemed fitting. 'One sees nothing anywhere but sky and water,' said Tetzel. He was told that the seas there became so turbulent that none could cross them. Galleys and ships had set off to discover what was beyond these seas, but none had ever returned.

Further to the south-west too there was another limit to the traversable world: Cabo Não or Cape No, a terminal point and a promontory in west Africa. According to Alvise Cadamosto's account of the navigator and slaver Nuno Tristão's journey to Mauritania in 1443, the cape had gained this name because anyone who rounded it never returned. This was the limit that Prince Henrique the Navigator (1394–1460), Infante of Portugal, longed to cross, and he sent fleets of his best caravels 'to sail everywhere successfully', 'to learn new things' and 'to cause injury to the Moors' living in the region. He was fascinated by Prester John, but was intrigued too by the possibility of deepening Portuguese trade into and beyond the Sahara. His first fleet that passed Cape No by 100 miles found only 'sandy and arid land', 'neither dwellings nor people', so it turned back. A second fleet passed the cape by 150 miles but also found nothing. He kept on sending out his caravels, full of victuals, arms and munitions, until they found something: eventually the Portuguese boats met with 'brownish men' from Berber tribes and then 'at last' they 'discovered . . . the country of the first Blacks' and after that 'other races of these Blacks of varied tongues, customs, and beliefs'.

Curiosity and voracity for land and profit had got the better of these travellers. The development of lateen-sailed caravels that could manage the open seas, the systematic charting of the Atlantic and African coasts and the use of more accurate astronomical methods of navigation all contributed to a sense of a world that could be conquered not by individual travellers but by the nations they represented. By passing Cape No, through the strangely aligned desires both to know more and to wage war, these Portuguese caravels can be seen as representative of a new era of travel: positively called the 'Age of Discovery' but perhaps better called an age of conquest and expropriation, in which travellers refused to accept long-held limits on where they could, or should, travel.

15. Coda: Journey's End

Most travellers feel at some point that they have had enough, that they long for the familiar, that the time for travel has ended. Yet, while many medieval travellers write about the moments of departure and arrival, not all write about the voyage home. For many travellers, one of the first things they did on arriving home was to set about composing an account of the journey they had undertaken. Those who do describe their return give us a glimpse of the indefinite feelings of homecoming and the moment of a journey coming to its close.

Ibn Battuta, for instance, raced home across Asia and north Africa in 1348 and 1349, as plague tore through the world's cities. At Damascus he saw thousands of people dying of the pestilence, Christian, Jewish and Muslim victims weeping together in the streets as they clutched their holy books, imploring God to end their suffering. Ibn Battuta reached his home in the 'glorious land' of Morocco in November 1349 where he temporarily laid down the 'staff of travel'. He found, after his travels around the world, that Morocco was the best of lands, with plentiful fruit, fresh water and nourishment. The Sultan of Morocco embodied and surpassed all the virtues of the rulers Ibn Battuta had encountered from Java to Constantinople. In his hometown of Tangiers, Ibn Battuta visited his mother's tomb, and then he himself grew sick. He was confined with an illness for three months. And then he was on the road again, travelling to al-Andalus via Gibraltar to take part in the wars against the Christians.

Our old friend John Mandeville wrote that he came home via Rome to get his book of travels confirmed and ratified as true by the pope and all the wise men in Rome. This certainly didn't happen (the pope was in Avignon, for a start) and much of the material in Mandeville's *Book* is patently untrue. It's likely that the story of the homecoming via Rome was a monastic joke by the author of Mandeville's *Book*, mocking the idea that physical travel confers some kind of experiential advantage on the traveller, laughing at the notion that wandering around the world might yield true or valuable knowledge. As any cloistered medieval monk knew, one often understood things one had *not* seen, and one saw things one could not understand. The truth of travel as an idea resided in its ability to stimulate reflection on the mysteries and wonders of God's world, and one didn't need to leave the cloister for that.

However, one of Mandeville's readers, the seasoned pilgrim William Wey, marked his homecoming in a radically different fashion. After his second visit to Jerusalem, in 1462, Wey returned to his monastery in the English village of Edington, on the edge of the bleak reaches of Salisbury Plain. Here he constructed a remarkable Jerusalem chapel, a multimedia creation of buildings, books, maps, vestments, images, souvenirs and relics. The building, built off the main choir of his church, included a painted cloth showing scenes of Jerusalem, the Mount of Olives and Bethlehem; a paper crucifix which had been bought in Jerusalem; some stones from Jerusalem and Bethlehem, brought back by Wey; and a replica of the Holy Sepulchre itself made in boards or planks. Wey's installation gives a strong sense of how place was portable – the pilgrim could bring Jerusalem with them – and almost infinitely translatable. Wey's written testament funding the building of the chapel stipulated that nothing should ever be removed from it, but it appears to have been a victim of the English Reformation, swept away by Protestant reformers in the sixteenth century. They did not believe in the holiness of pilgrimage, the value of relics or the pardons and indulgences dispensed to travellers.

The ever-garrulous Felix Fabri included a poetic account of his return to Ulm in January 1484. As he rode through the Iller Valley south of Ulm a torrential downpour soaked him, and this was the worst moment in his entire journey. He felt sad, spineless, shrunken with cold, impatient and anxious: all the turbid feelings of homecoming manifested in a rainstorm. But when he saw Ulm itself, he felt joy, comfort and pleasure at being back in its presence, joy equal to the misery he had felt at being away. He hardly recognized the city, for its splendid new walls had been completed in his nine-month absence.

As Fabri was crossing the Herdbrucker over the Danube, local people started to recognize him, and some ran to the convent to seek a reward for delivering the good news of his return. Fabri got to his convent gate but found that the brothers were at vespers, loudly chanting and singing their evening prayers; he struck the door hard in order to be heard, but in vain. It is always surprising for the traveller to discover that life goes on when they are away, that others' routines have remained intact. The city had changed but the rhythms and habits of everyday life had kept their dependable shape.

Eventually the convent dog, usually an angry barking beast who guarded the gate, sensed Fabri's presence. In Fabri's account, the dog started to emit 'unusual howls and joyful snuffles', and scratched at the gate from inside with his paws and teeth as if trying to break it down. Fabri opened the gate, the impatient dog leaped into his arms, snuffling, his tail wagging, and then hared through the convent at full pelt, whining happily all the time, announcing the arrival of a friend. Mirroring the dog, Fabri's prior, Ludwig Fuchs, ran to Fabri and, forgetting his senior station and great age, leaped on him as if trying to extinguish a fire, clinging to his neck in a friendly embrace. The rest of the brothers gathered round and led Fabri in a procession to the main altar, all falling to the ground in honour of the sacrament and receiving a blessing. The brothers could then spend the rest of the evening chatting amiably about Fabri's experiences: it transpired that they had received false reports that he had died at sea or had been taken captive by Turks.

Fabri's homecoming is a portrait of joyful reunion, completed by his closing description of finally, and reluctantly, shaving off his many-months-old beard. A beard, he said, 'is a natural ornament that beautifies a man's face', but on returning to his profession as a friar he felt he should once again conform to the expectations of his order and look 'venerable' rather than 'strong and fearless'. The beard had marked his temporary identity as a travelling pilgrim; its removal marked his reintroduction into his daily, static life. Nonetheless, Fabri hints that he felt himself changed inside, and through travel had become a better friar and superior preacher.

Meanwhile, the redoubtable Odoric of Pordenone did not describe his journey home, but closed his account of his travels in a terrible valley, somewhere deep in Asia. In this valley, 7 or 8 miles long and carved by a 'River of Delights', was the hideously deafening sound of drumming and other music. And on the valley's floor were littered hundreds of corpses, the bodies of non-Christian men who had perished almost instantly upon entering that fearsome place. In the rock on one side was the 'very great and terrible' face of a man. Here Odoric says his spirit died within him. He began to repeat to himself the words *Verbum caro factum*, 'the Word became flesh' (John 1:14), an incantation that reminded him that he travelled with the spirit and grace of God, and that all created things in this world were part of a divine plan. The supernatural was the counterpart to the miraculous, in a world at once thrumming with omnipresent holiness and extreme ungodliness.

When he finally returned to Europe and the familiarity of his monastery at Padua, Odoric was asked by his superior, Giudotto, to dictate an account of his travels to a fellow friar, Guglielmo of Solagna. So it was that in May 1330 Odoric described where he had been and what he had witnessed. He said he included only that which he had seen with his own eyes or which had been told to him by faithful men. Here the wonder of travel was turned into the storytelling of travel writing. Odoric avoided ornate language, speaking instead in a homely way, so his account could be understood by both the lettered and the unlearned.

A few months later, Odoric set off for Avignon to visit the pope. However, he was not to reach his destination: he was taken ill, and was warned by a wise old man dressed as a pilgrim to turn back and to head for his native province of Friuli. The old man told Odoric to make haste, as he had only ten days left to live. People would later say that this old pilgrim was the spirit of St Francis of Assisi himself.

Odoric died ten days later at Udine, the Friulian capital, in January 1331. He had been to the world's very edges, to the brink of knowledge, but it was at home, near his place of birth, that he met his death. In the months after Odoric's death, healing miracles were reported at his tomb. One visiting woman was said to have tried to cut off his finger to take away with her as a pious souvenir, in the hope that the blessings of travel might continue to accompany her.

Odoric's story bears out the idea that at the end of our exploring we arrive where we started, but we understand that starting point anew. On returning from their journey, the traveller is somehow changed, wise in new ways, having encountered radical difference and wonderful similarity, their home life and prior knowledge thrown into a new relief. Travel forces us to consider the significance of our lives, and to encounter the littleness of the human amid the planet's variety and unknowability.

As he struggled homewards, the dying Odoric may well have felt that the earth he had traversed had itself become tiny, nothing more than a series of points on a small surface, and that the time had come to turn from earthly things to the celestial. This was not to cease roaming, but to search instead for yet other worlds. As the sun set and the blue deepened into night, Odoric received his passport into the skies, to join those released from their bodies and from earthly travels, into the brilliant circles amid the blazing stars, where the soul would begin its mysterious, incorporeal journey towards the horizon of infinity.

Sources

The best way to find out more about travel in the Middle Ages is to read the accounts of travellers themselves. The travellers are listed here by their common names, with a brief biography and the sources consulted.

Adam of Bremen (fl. 1070). Chronicler of Bremen, also spent time at the Danish court; wrote an early account of the islands of the north, including Iceland, 'Thule' and Vinland. Adam of Bremen, *History of the Archbishops of Hamburg-Bremen*, ed. and trans. Francis J. Tschan (New York, 1959).

Adornes, Anselm (d. 1483). Merchant and politician of Bruges, later diplomat at the Scottish court. Undertook a pilgrimage to Jerusalem in 1470, described in a written account by his son Jan. *Itinérarie d'Anselme Adorno en Terre Sainte: 1470-1471*, ed. and trans. Jacques Heers and Georgette de Gröer (Paris, 1978).

al-Istakhri, Abu Ishaq (d. 957). Arab-Persian geographer; author of *The Routes of the Realms*, an illustrated geography of the Persian region. *Kitab al Masalik wa l-mamalik*, ed. M. J. de Goeje (Lyons, 1870; Leiden, 2014).

Anonymous [Anonymous Englishman] (fl. 1344–5). Englishman, author of an account of his journey through the Mediterranean to the Holy Land. Anonymous Englishman, *Pilgrimage to the Holy Land*, trans. Rosalind Lintott, https://rememberedplaces.wordpress.com/anonymous-englishman/

Anonymous [Spanish Franciscan] (c. 1350). Castilian Franciscan friar, who wrote a geographical compendium with unusual descriptions especially of Europe, Africa and the Atlantic. *Book* *of the Knowledge of All the Kingdoms . . . Written by a Spanish Franciscan*, ed. and trans. Clements Markham (London, 1912).

Antony of Cremona (fl. 1330). Franciscan friar, visited the Holy Land 1327–30. Antonius de Cremona, 'Itinerarium ad Sepulchrum Domini', ed. Reinhold Röhricht, *Zeitschrift des Deutschen Palästina-Vereins* 13 (1890), 153–74.

Barbaro, Giosafat (1413–94). Merchant, diplomat and pilgrim from a wealthy Venetian family. Travelled widely in the Golden Horde, Tatary, Persia and elsewhere. Later fought against the Turks and in 1472 was sent as ambassador to Persia. *Travels to Tana and Persia*, ed. Lord Stanley (London, 1873), pp. 1–103.

Battista of Imola (fl. 1480–84). Italian-born Franciscan friar and messenger, later of the Convent of Mount Zion, Jerusalem. He was one of two men who made a missionary journey from Jerusalem to Ethiopia in the early 1480s, and later described his journey to Francesco Suriano; it is included in Suriano, *Il trattato di Terra Santa e dell'Oriente*, ed. Girolamo Golubovich (Milan, 1900).

Benedykt of Poland (fl. 1245–7). Polish Franciscan friar, accompanied Giovanni of Plano Carpini in their mission to Güyük Khan in the 1240s. He dictated chronicles of his journey upon his return. *Mission to Asia*, ed. and trans. Christopher Dawson (New York, 1966; rev. edn Toronto, 1980), pp. 79–84.

Benjamin of Tudela (1130–73). Jewish pilgrim and merchant, who travelled to the Holy Land c. 1165. *The Itinerary of Benjamin of Tudela*, ed. and trans. Marcus Nathan Adler (London, 1907).

Bertrandon de la Broquière (d. 1459). Burgundian diplomat and pilgrim, who travelled to Turkey and the Holy Land in the early 1430s. *Le Voyage d'Outremer*, ed. C. Schefer (Paris, 1892).

Brasca, Santo (fl. 1480). Administrator and politican in the Duchy of Milan. Travelled to Venice and the Holy Land in 1480 and wrote a detailed travel guide. *Viaggio in Terrasanta di Santo Brasca 1480 con l'itinerario di Gabriele Capodilista 1458*, ed. Anna Lepschy (Milan, 1966).

Brewyn, William (fl. 1469). Monk of Canterbury who travelled to Rome in 1469. William Brewyn, *A XVth. Century Guide Book to the Principal Churches of Rome Compiled ca. 1470*, ed. and trans. C. Eveleigh Woodruff (London, 1933).

Breydenbach, Bernhard von (d. 1497). Jurist and churchman of Mainz; later, a celebrated pilgrim. In 1483 Breydenbach travelled to Jerusalem and Egypt, accompanying Count Johann zu Solms (who died at Alexandria on the return journey). Breydenbach's 1486 printed account of his journey, with images by Erhard Reuwich, became a bestseller. *Les Saintes Pérégrinations de Bernard de Breydenbach: extraits relatifs à l'Égypte suivant l'édition de 1490*, ed. and trans. F. Larrivaz (Cairo, 1904); Bernhard de Breydenbach, *Peregrinatio in Terram Sanctam: Eine Pilgerreise ins Heilige Land*, ed. Isolde Mozer (Berlin, 2010).

Brygg, Thomas (fl. 1392). English pilgrim, equerry to Thomas Swynburne, travelled through the Holy Land in 1392. *Western Pilgrims (1322–1392)*, ed. and trans. Eugene Hoade (Jerusalem, 1952).

Buondelmonti, Cristoforo (c. 1385–c. 1430). Florentine Franciscan priest and traveller, author of an influential illustrated description of the eastern Mediterranean and a much copied drawing of Constantinople. Cristoforo Buondelmonti, *Description of the Aegean and Other Islands*, ed. Evelyn Edson (New York, 2018).

Burchard of Mount Zion (fl. 1274–83). Dominican friar, probably from Magdeburg; spent many years in Palestine, as well as travelling widely in the Mediterranean and Asia Minor. Author of the most detailed and much read thirteenth-century guide to the Holy Land. Burchard of Mount Sion, *Descriptio Terrae Sanctae*, ed. John R. Bartlett (Oxford, 2019).

Cadamosto, Alvise (d. 1488). Venetian explorer and slaver, undertook expeditions to west Africa for the Portuguese crown. *The Voyages of Cadamosto*, ed. and trans. G. R. Crone (London, 1937).

Caldwell, Geoffrey, *see* ***Travel Guide to the East***

Capgrave, John (1393–1464). Augustinian monk from Lynn in eastern England; as well as writing popular saints' lives, Capgrave wrote a travel guide for the Rome Jubilee of 1450. John Capgrave, *The Solace of Pilgrimes: Rome 1450: Capgrave's Jubilee Guide*, ed. and trans. Peter J. Lucas (Turnhout, 2021).

Capodilista, Gabriele (d. 1477). Paduan nobleman and lawyer. He wrote an account of his 1458 journey from Venice to the Holy Land. *Viaggio in Terrasanta di Santo Brasca 1480 con l'itinerario di Gabriele Capodilista 1458*, ed. Anna Lepschy (Milan, 1966).

Casola, Pietro (1427–1507). Milanese nobleman and Milanese ambassador to the papal court at Rome. Travelled via Venice to the Holy Land in 1494. *Canon Pietro Casola's Pilgrimage to Jerusalem in the Year 1494*, ed. and trans. Margaret M. Newett (Manchester, 1907).

Clavijo, Ruy González de (d. 1412). Ambassador of King Enrique (Henry) III of Castile to the court of Timur at Samarkand. *Embassy to Tamerlane, 1403–1406*, ed. and trans. Guy Le Strange (London, 1928).

Commines, Philip de (d. 1511). Franco-Burgundian diplomat and memoirist. *The Memoirs of Philip de Commines, Lord of Argenton*, ed. and trans. Andrew Richard Scoble, 2 vols. (London, 1855).

Contarini, Ambrogio (1429–99). Venetian nobleman and diplomat, sent by the Republic of Venice to make an anti-Ottoman alliance with the Aq Qoyunlu khanate in Persia. *Travels to Tana and Persia*, ed. Lord Stanley (London, 1873), pp. 105–73.

Conti, Nicolò (c. 1385–1469). Venetian merchant, whose family was established in Egypt and Syria. He spent thirty-five years travelling in Asia. 'The travels of Nicolò Conti in the East', in *India in the Fifteenth Century*, ed. and trans. Richard Henry Major (Cambridge, 1857; 2010), pp. 1–39.

Cucharmois, Jean de (c. 1465–c. 1531). Lyons-born traveller and writer; made a pilgrimage to Jerusalem in 1490. 'S'ensuyt le sainct voyage de Hierusalem', in *Le premier livre de Guerin Mesquin* (Lyons, 1530).

Daniil of Kyiv (fl. 1107). Pilgrim, first known travel writer of Kyivan Rus'. Travelled through the Holy Land shortly after the success of the First Crusade. *Jerusalem Pilgrimage, 1099–1185*, eds. John Wilkinson, Joyce Hill and W. F. Ryan (London, 1988), pp. 126–39.

Dorothea of Montau (1347–94). Mystic and visionary, born at Montau (Mątowy Wielkie) near Gdańsk; after married life with many children, in 1391 she removed herself to a cell against the wall of Marienwerder (Kwidzyn) Cathedral where she remained for the rest of her life. Canonized in 1976. Johannes von Marienwerder, *The Life of Dorothea von Montau, a Fourteenth-Century Recluse*, ed. and trans. Ute Stargardt (Lewiston, NY, 1997).

Dürer, Albrecht (1471–1528). Celebrated painter and master printmaker. Albrecht Dürer, *Diary of his Journey to the Netherlands, 1520–21*, ed. and trans. W. M. Conway, J. A. Goris and G. Marlier (New York, 1971).

Eptingen, Hans Bernhard von (d. 1484). Nobleman from Pratteln near Basel. In 1460 he undertook a Holy Land pilgrimage in the entourage of Otto II of Pfalz-Mosbach. 'Die Pilgerfahrt Hans Bernhards von Eptingen', *Beiträge zur vaterländischen Geschichte* 12 (1888), 13–75.

Fabri, Felix (c. 1438–1502). Swiss-born friar, who spent most of his adult life in the Dominican priory at Ulm. Travelled to the Holy Land in 1483–4. *The Book of Wanderings in the Holy Land*, ed. and trans. Aubrey Stewart, 2 vols. (London, 1892); *Fratris F. Fabri Evagatorium in Terræ Sanctæ, Arabiæ et Egypti peregrinationem*, ed. Conrad Hassler, 3 vols. (Stuttgart, 1843).

da Gama, Vasco (d. 1524). Portuguese explorer, regarded as the first European to have reached India via the Cape of Good Hope by sea. Various letters written on da Gama's return to Portugal described his expeditions in detail. *A Journal of the First Voyage of Vasco da Gama, 1497–99*, ed. E. G. Ravenstein (London, 1898); Gaspar Correia, *The Three Voyages of Vasco da Gama*, ed. and trans. Henry E. J. Stanley (London, 1869).

van Ghistele, Joos (c. 1446–c. 1525). Ghent-born nobleman who spent several years travelling in the Holy Land and the eastern Mediterranean, Aden and Syria. *Tvoyage van Mher Joos van Ghistele*, ed. R. J. G. A. A. Gaspar (Hilversum, 1998).

Giovanni of Montecorvino (d. 1328). Born in Campania. Franciscan missionary to Armenia, Persia, India and China, and first Archbishop of Khanbaliq. *Mission to Asia*, ed. and trans. Christopher Dawson (New York, 1966; rev. edn Toronto, 1980), pp. 224–31.

Giovanni of Plano Carpini (d. 1252). Born in or near Perugia; companion and early follower of St Francis of Assisi. Chosen by Pope Innocent IV to lead a mission to Güyük Khan, who rejected the pope's invitation, delivered by Giovanni, to become Christian. Giovanni's account of his trip is the oldest western European account of travel to the Mongols. *Mission to Asia*, ed. and trans. Christopher Dawson (New York, 1966; rev. edn Toronto, 1980), pp. 3–72.

Grünemberg, Konrad (d. 1494). Son of the Mayor of Constance; author of books of armorials and in later life controller of Constance's mint. Undertook a pilgrimage to the Holy Land in 1486. *The Story of Sir Konrad Grünemberg's Pilgrimage to the Holy Land in 1486*, ed. and trans. Kristiaan Aercke (Moncalieri, 2004).

Gucci, Giorgio (d. 1392). Florentine wool merchant; took part in a Florentine group pilgrimage and business embassy to the Holy Land 1384–5. *Visit to the Holy Places of Egypt, Sinai, Palestine, and Syria in 1384, by Frescobaldi, Gucci and Sigoli*, ed. and trans. T. Bellorini and E. Hoade (Jerusalem, 1948).

Gumppenberg, Georg von (d. 1515). Bavarian nobleman, wrote a very brief account of his 1483–4 pilgrimage to the Holy Land. *Deutsche Pilgerreisen nach dem heiligen Lande*, ed. Reinhold Röhricht and Heinrich Meisner (Berlin, 1880), pp. 115–19.

Guylforde, Richard (c.1450–1506). English courtier to Henry VII. Travelled from the English port of Rye through Europe to the Holy Land in 1506; he died shortly after arriving at Jerusalem and was buried there. An account of his travels was written by Thomas Larke, his chaplain. *The Pylgrymage of Sir Richard Guylforde to the Holy Land*, ed. Henry Ellis (London, 1851).

Het'um [Hetoum] of Armenia (c. 1245–c. 1315). Cilician Armenian statesman and general, a member of the Armenian royal family. Became a Premonstratensian prior in France later in life. *A Lytell Cronycle: Richard Pynson's Translation (c. 1520) of* La Fleur des histoires de la terre d'Orient *(c. 1307)*, ed. Glenn Burger (Toronto, 1988).

Hieronimo [Jeronimo] di Santo Stefano (fl. 1490s). Genoese merchant, travelled to Asia in the 1490s. 'The Journey of Hieronimo di Santo Stefano', in *India in the Fifteenth Century*, ed. and trans. Richard Henry Major (London, 1857).

Ibn Battuta (1304–68/9). Berber scholar and traveller; travelled across Iberia and Eurasia over about thirty years, including pilgrimages to Mecca and periods as an ambassador of the Delhi sultanate at the Yuan court in Khanbaliq. *The Travels of Ibn Battuta, AD 1325–1354*, ed. and trans. H. A. R. Gibb (London, 1929).

Ibn Jubayr (1145–1217). Traveller and geographer, born in Valencia, al-Andalus. He wrote a chronicle of his travels in the 1180s across the Holy Land to Mecca. *The Travels of Ibn Jubayr*, ed. and trans. Ronald Broadhurst (London, 1952).

Jacopo of Verona (fl. 1335). Augustinian friar and Veronese pilgrim to the Holy Land in 1335. *Liber peregrinationis di Jacopo da Verona*, ed. Ugo Monneret de Villard (Rome, 1950).

Jean de Tournai (d. 1499). Merchant of Valenciennes. Undertook a long journey to the Holy Land via Rome and Loreto in 1488–9. Lucie Polak, 'Un récit de pèlerinage de 1488–1489: Jean de Tournai', *Le Moyen Age* 87 (1981), 71–88.

Jordan of Sévérac (fl. 1280–c. 1330). Catalan Dominican and missionary to India. Appointed first bishop of Kollam (Quilon); wrote an account of the marvels of India. *Mirabilia Descripta: The Wonders of the East*, ed. and trans. Henry Yule (London, 1863).

Kempe, Margery (c. 1373–c. 1439), English businesswoman, mystic and pilgrim. After having fourteen children, Kempe embarked on a journey to Jerusalem and Rome in 1413, and undertook many further pilgrimages. Her devotions were often accompanied by noisy crying; she had her life story written in the 1430s. *The Book of Margery Kempe*, ed. and trans. Anthony Bale (Oxford, 2015).

Lannoy, Guillebert de (1386–1462). Flemish nobleman, became Burgundian diplomat to England, Lithuania and Muscovy among other missions. He was sent by Henry V of England to the Holy Land in 1421–2 to consider reviving the Crusader kingdom of Jerusalem. *Œuvres de Ghillebert de Lannoy, voyageur, diplomate et moraliste*, ed. C. Potvin (Louvain, 1878).

Leo of Rozmital (Jaroslav Lev of Rožmitál and Blatná; d. 1486). Bohemian nobleman and travelling diplomat. *The Travels of Leo of Rozmital*, ed. and trans. Malcolm Letts (Cambridge, 1957).

Le Saige, Jacques (fl. 1518). Silk merchant of Douai, travelled to Jerusalem via Venice and Loreto in 1518. *Voyage de Jacques Le Saige*, ed. H. R. Duthillœul (Douai, 1851).

Ludolph of Suchem (Sudheim; fl. 1336–41). A priest, probably from Lower Saxony, who spent some years in the Holy Land. His travelogue and account of the region after the Crusades was much read and copied in Europe. *Ludolph von Suchem's Description of the Holy Land, and of the Way Thither*, ed. and trans. Aubrey Stewart (London, 1895).

Ma Huan (d. 1460). Voyager and translator who accompanied early Ming dynasty naval expeditions. In 1416 he composed a travelogue of the 1413 expedition to Java and Hormuz; he subsequently revised and expanded his account, to include accounts of the 1421 expedition to Sumatra and Hormuz and the 1431 voyage to Calicut and Mecca. *Ying-yai sheng-lan: The Overall Survey of the Ocean's Shores*, ed. and trans. J. V. G. Mills and Chengjun Feng (London, 1970).

Mandeville, John (fl. 1356). Pseudonymous author of a very prevalent travelogue from England to Jerusalem and through Asia. Mandeville claims to have been a knight from St Albans in England, but is more likely to have been a Flemish or French monk; his true identity remains unclear. Sir John Mandeville, *The Book of Marvels and Travels*, ed. and trans. Anthony Bale (Oxford, 2012).

Marignolli, Giovanni de' (fl. 1338–53). Florentine friar; left Avignon in 1338 to travel to India and China; spent three or four years at Khanbaliq. *Cathay and the Way Thither*, ed. and trans. Henry Yule, 3 vols. (London, 1913–16), vol. 3, pp. 208–69.

Martoni, Nicola de (fl. 1394–5). Notary of Carinola near Naples; made a pilgrimage to the Holy Land in the mid-1390s. 'Relation du pèlerinage a Jérusalem de Nicolas de Martoni, notaire italien (1394–5)', ed. Léon Legrand, *Revue de l'Orient Latin* 3 (1895), 566–669.

Mauro, Fra (d. 1464). Travelled as a youth in Asia, became a Camaldolese monk of Murano and leading Venetian cartographer. His world map, commissioned by the Portuguese crown, is one of the most complete and extensive surviving such maps. 'Fra Mauro's Globe', Museo Galileo, Florence, https://mostre.museogalileo.it/framauro/it/introduzione.html.

Mergenthal, Hans von (fl. 1469–78). Aristocratic pilgrim from Saxony to the Holy Land, accompanying Albrecht Duke of Saxony in 1476. 'De peregrinatione in Palestinam Illustrissimi', in Balthasar Menz, *Itinera sexa diversis Saxoniae Ducibis et Electoribus* . . . (Wittenberg, 1612).

Meshullam of Volterra (d. 1507/8). Tuscan-born gem dealer and traveller; voyaged through the Holy Land and eastern Mediterranean in 1481, often visiting Jewish communities. *Jewish Travelers*, ed. and trans. Elkan Adler (London, 1930), pp. 156–208.

Niccolò da Poggibonsi (fl. 1345–50). Tuscan Franciscan friar. Travelled with a group of companions around the Holy Land for five years in the late 1340s. On his return he wrote a vivid and detailed account of his travels. Niccolò of Poggibonsi, *Libro d'oltramare*, ed. Alberto Bacchi della Lega, 2 vols. (Bologna, 1881).

Nikitin, [Afanasiy] Athanasius (d. 1472). Merchant and traveller from Tver in western Russia. He departed on a commercial voyage in 1466 and, after various misfortunes, lived for three years in the Bahmani sultanate in central India; he seems at least partly to have converted to Islam during his travels. 'The Travels of Athanasius Nikitin', trans. Michael Wielhorsky, in *India in the Fifteenth Century*, ed. and trans. Richard Henry Major (London, 1857).

Odoric de Pordenone (Odorico Mattiuzzi; 1286–1331). Friulian Franciscan friar. In 1318 Odoric was sent as a missionary via Constantinople to Armenia and Persia; he then spent many years in India, China and throughout Asia. He only returned to Europe around 1329 and died shortly after dictating an account of his journeys. His text was extremely popular and influential in medieval Europe. *Les Voyages au XIVe Siècle du Bienheureux Frère Odoric de Pordenone*, ed. Henri Cordier (Paris, 1891); Odoric of Pordenone, *The Travels of Friar Odoric*, ed. Paolo Chiesa, trans. Henry Yule (Grand Rapids, MI, 2002).

Ogier d'Anglure (d. 1412). French knight and courtier. Undertook a pilgrimage to the Holy Land in 1395 and wrote a detailed account of the journey on his return. *Le sainct voyaige de Jherusalem*, ed. F. Bonnardot and A. Longnon (Paris, 1878); *The Holy Jerusalem Voyage of Ogier VIII, Seigneur d'Anglure*, trans. R. A. Browne (Gainesville, FL, 1975).

Pegolotti, Francesco (d. 1347). Florentine merchant, representative of the Bardi company. Wrote a standard glossary and guide to the trade routes across Europe and Asia. Francesco Balducci Pegolotti, *La pratica della mercatura*, ed. Allen Evans (Cambridge, MA, 1936).

Polo, Marco (1254–1324). Celebrated Venetian merchant and traveller. His journeys followed those of his father and uncle, who had travelled to the court of Kublai Khan in the 1260s. Polo left a detailed account of his time in Asia, dictated in prison in the 1290s to fellow prisoner Rustichello da Pisa. Marco Polo, *The Travels*, ed. and trans. Nigel Cliff (London, 2015).

Poloner, John (fl. 1421). Pilgrim, probably from Prussia or Poland, who visited the Holy Land in 1422. *John Poloner's Description of the Holy Land*, ed. and trans. Aubrey Stewart (London, 1894).

Richard of Lincoln (fl. 1454). Medical practitioner and pilgrim, of Lincoln or possibly London, who wrote a Middle English account of his pilgrimage to the Holy Land. *Richard of Lincoln: A Medieval Doctor Travels to Jerusalem*, ed. and trans. Francis Davey (Exeter, 2013).

Robert of Clari (fl. 1202–4). Picard knight and Crusader. Wrote a chronicle of the events of the Fourth Crusade (which include the sack and conquest of Constantinople). Robert de Claris, *La Conquête de Constantinople*, ed. and trans. Peter Noble (Edinburgh, 2005).

Rot, Peter (d. 1487). Burgher of Basel. Undertook two pilgrimages to the Holy Land with his father Hans (d. 1452), details of which they recorded in a small manuscript book. 'Hans und Peter Rot's Pilgerreisen', *Beiträge zur vaterländischen Geschichte* 11 (1882), 331–408.

Rubruck, William of (fl. 1248–55). Flemish Crusader and missionary; was sent by Louis IX of France to convert the Tatars and undertook a mission to the Mongols at the command of Emperor Baldwin II. *Mission to Asia*, ed. and trans. Christopher Dawson (New York, 1966; rev. edn Toronto, 1980), pp. 89–223.

Sanseverino, Roberto da (1418–87). Man-of-arms and nobleman, the nephew of Francesco Sforza, Duke of Milan. He wrote a detailed diary of his 1458 pilgrimage to the Holy Land. *Felice et divoto ad Terrasancta viagio facto per Roberto de Sancto Severino*, ed. M. Cavaglià and A. Rossebastiano (Alessandria, 1999).

Sauma, Rabban Bar (d. 1294). Monk and ambassador. In the 1280s and early 1290s he undertook a remarkable pilgrimage from Yuan

China, visiting Paris, Rome and Constantinople. *The Monks of Kublai Khan, Emperor of China*, ed. E. A. Wallis Budge (London, 1928).

Schiltberger, Johann (1380–c. 1440). Nobleman, of Hollern near Munich. Taken prisoner in 1396, Schiltberger spent many years as a captive and mercenary in Timurid Asia. His colourful account of his journey and eventual escape was widely read in medieval Germany. *The Bondage and Travels of Johann Schiltberger, a Native of Bavaria, in Europe, Asia, and Africa, 1396–1427*, ed. and trans. J. Telfer (London, 1879).

Sigoli, Simone (fl. 1384–9). Florentine merchant and pilgrim who travelled to the Holy Land in 1384–5. *Visit to the Holy Places of Egypt, Sinai, Palestine, and Syria in 1384, by Frescobaldi, Gucci and Sigoli*, ed. and trans. T. Bellorini and E. Hoade (Jerusalem, 1948).

Spanish Franciscan, *see* **Anonymous**

Suriano, Francesco (d. c. 1529). Venice-born Franciscan friar and scribe, who spent time in the convents at Alexandria, Beirut and Jerusalem. His detailed and zealous description of the Holy Land, *A Treatise on the Holy Land*, is often stridently aggressive towards non-Christians. *Il trattato di Terra Santa e dell'Oriente di Frate Francesco Suriano*, ed. Girolamo Golubovich (Milan, 1900).

Swynburne, Thomas (c. 1357–1412). English military captain, diplomat and pilgrim. Visited the Holy Land in 1392. Later captain of Calais and mayor of Bordeaux. *Western Pilgrims (1322–1392)*, ed. and trans. Eugene Hoade (Jerusalem, 1952).

Tafur, Pero (c. 1410–c. 1484). Born in Córdoba, travelled as a diplomat, soldier and pilgrim between 1436 and 1439. Visited north Africa and the Black Sea, and travelled across Europe. *Pero Tafur: Travels and Adventures, 1435–1439*, ed. and trans. Malcolm Letts (London, 1926).

Tetzel, Gabriel (d. 1479). Patrician of Nuremberg, who travelled with Leo of Rozmital as part of his 1460s diplomatic mission. *The Travels of Leo of Rozmital*, ed. and trans. Malcolm Letts (Cambridge, 1957).

Travel Guide to the East. A late fifteenth-century travel guide, giving a great deal of detail about what the traveller should buy in Venice. Possibly written by one Geoffrey Caldwell of London. BL Cotton MS Appendix VIII.

Villehardouin, Geoffrey of (c. 1150–1213). Nobleman from Champagne and participant in the Fourth Crusade (1199–1204); subsequently wrote a chronicle in French. 'Villehardouin's Chronicle of the Fourth Crusade and the Conquest of Constantinople', in *Memoirs, or Chronicle of The Fourth Crusade and The Conquest of Constantinople*, ed. and trans. Frank T. Marzials (London, 1908).

Voisins, Philippe de (fl. 1490). Nobleman, Lord of Couffoulens in Languedoc and Montaut in Gascony. Set out on a voyage to the Holy Land in 1490. *Voyage à Jérusalem de Philippe de Voisins*, ed. Philippe Tamizey de Larroque (Paris, 1883).

Walther [von Guglingen], Paul (fl. 1482–3). Franciscan friar of Heidelberg who travelled to the Holy Land in 1482–4; on his return he created an illustrated travelogue, *Fratris Pauli Walteri Gugliensis: Itinerarium in Terram Sanctam et ad Sanctam Catharinam*, ed. Matthis Sollweck (Tübingen, 1892).

Wey, William (d. 1476). Administrator and monk, undertook journeys to Santiago de Compostela (1456), and twice to Jerusalem (1458, 1462). He wrote a voluminous account of his travels, *The Matter of Jerusalem. The Itineraries of William Wey*, ed. Bulkeley Bandinel (Edinburgh, 1857); *Itineraries*, ed. and trans. Francis Davey (Oxford, 2010).

Zosima the Deacon (fl. 1419–22). Monk-deacon of the Monastery of the Trinity of St Sergius near Moscow. Travelled widely in Kyiv, the Holy Land and Constantinople (1419–22) as both a pilgrim and a member of the Muscovite royal entourage, recorded in his *Xenos* ('Wanderer'), written on his return. *Russian Travelers to Constantinople in the Fourteenth and Fifteenth Centuries*, ed. and trans. George P. Majeska (Washington, DC, 1984), pp. 166–98.

References and Further Reading

Abbreviations

BL = The British Library, London
DPR = Bartholomeus Anglicus, *De proprietatibus rerum*, from M. C. Seymour et al. (eds.), *On the Properties of Things: John Trevisa's Translation of Bartholomaeus Anglicus, De proprietatibus rerum*, 3 vols. (Oxford, 1975–88)
TNA = The National Archives, Kew, London

Population estimates throughout are taken from Tertius Chandler, *Four Thousand Years of Urban History: An Historical Census* (Lewiston, NY, 1987).

Preface

On the culture of medieval travel I recommend Mary B. Campbell, *The Witness and the Other World: Exotic European Travel Writing, 400–1600* (Ithaca, NY, 1988); Michel Huynh et al., *Voyager au Moyen Age* (Paris, 2014); Shirin A. Khanmohamadi, *In Light of Another's Word: European Ethnography in the Middle Ages* (Philadelphia, 2013); Shayne Legassie, *The Medieval Invention of Travel* (Chicago, 2017); and, on elite travellers, Margaret Wade Labarge, *Medieval Travellers: The Rich and the Restless* (London, 1982). For an overview of travel writing as a genre see Tim Youngs and Nandini Das (eds.), *The Cambridge History of Travel Writing* (Cambridge, 2019). My thoughts on the nature of travel have been stimulated by Pierre Bayard,

How to Talk about Places You've Never Been, trans. Michele Hutchison (New York, 2016); Alain de Botton, *The Art of Travel* (London, 2002; the 'midwives of thought' quotation at p. 57); Paul Fussell, *Abroad: British Literary Travelling between the Wars* (Oxford, 1980); and Emily Thomas, *The Meaning of Travel* (Oxford, 2020).

For the *Codex Calixtinus* see Annie Shaver-Crandell, Paula Gerson and Alison Stones, *The Pilgrim's Guide to Santiago de Compostela: A Gazetteer* (London, 1995). Elizabeth Bishop's 'Questions of Travel' appears in her collection *Questions of Travel* (New York, 1965).

Chapter 1: The Shape of the World in 1491; or, A Preamble with Martin Behaim

On Behaim see the facsimile in E. G. Ravenstein, *Martin Behaim: His Life and his Globe* (London, 1908), supplemented by Rui Manuel Loureiro, 'Searching the East by the West', *RiMe: Rivista dell'Istituto di Storia dell'Europa Mediterranea* 9 (2021), 105–25. For an incisive account of European ideas of the world in Behaim's day, see Valerie Flint, *The Imaginative Landscape of Christopher Columbus* (Princeton, 1992).

On the medieval Antipodes see Alfred Hiatt, *Terra Incognita: Mapping the Antipodes before 1600* (London, 2008; the quotation from Fillastre at p. 158). On John of Holywood see Lynn Thorndike, *The Sphere of Sacrobosco and its Commentators* (Chicago, 1949), including an English translation of Holywood's treatise (pp. 118–42). For Cicero and Macrobius see Marcus Tullius Cicero, *Scipio's Dream* (Macrobius, *Commentary on the Dream on Scipio*, ed. and trans. William Harris Stahl (New York and London, 1966), VI. 1–3, pp. 74–5). On the voyage and Isle of St Brendan see John R. Gillis, 'Taking history offshore: Atlantic islands in European minds, 1400–1800', in Rod Edmond and Vanessa Smith (eds.),

Islands in History and Representation (London, 2003; 2020), pp. 19–31. The maxim from Egbert of Liège is in *The Well-Laden Ship*, ed. and trans. Robert Babcock (Cambridge, MA, 2013), p. 223.

The currency exchange table is taken from William Brewyn's travel guide of c. 1470.

Chapter 2: The Point of Departure, with Beatrice, Henry and Thomas

On the phenomenon of pilgrimage in medieval Europe see Diana Webb, *Pilgrims and Pilgrimage in the Medieval West* (London, 1999); Jonathan Sumption, *Pilgrimage: An Image of Mediaeval Religion* (London, 1975); and Simon Coleman and John Elsner, *Pilgrimage, Past and Present* (London, 1995).

Beatrice Luttrell, *née* Scrope, of Irnham (Lincolnshire), submitted her petition for pilgrimage in the second half of 1350 (TNA SC 8/246/12265) and her permission was granted by Edward III's court on 18 October 1350; her belongings reflect those found in later medieval wills (see *The Fifty Earliest English Wills in the Court of Probate, 1387–1439,* ed. F. J. Furnivall (London, 1882)) and depicted in her family's famous book, *The Luttrell Psalter* (BL Add. MS 42130), which also includes a picture of her. See too the discussion of her father-in-law in Michael Camille, *Mirror in Parchment* (London, 1998), pp. 122–51, describing the family's pilgrimages and religiosity. Her ring is based on a French ring in the British Museum (Londesborough #53). See too Janet Backhouse, *Medieval Rural Life in the Luttrell Psalter* (London, 2000).

Details of Earl Henry's journey are taken from his remarkable expense accounts; Henry was later Henry IV, King of England; see *Expeditions to Prussia and the Holy Land*, ed. Lucy T. Smith (London, 1894).

Thomas Dane, sub-prior of the Austin Friars, London, requested a year's leave of absence to go on pilgrimage in 1440 (TNA C270/31/19). His travel guide is based on the *Travel Guide to the East* in a fifteenth-century manuscript (BL Cotton MS Appendix VIII). For contemporaneous scenes of departure on a pilgrimage, see *The Beauchamp Pageants* (BL Cotton MS Julius E IV/3), showing the Earl of Warwick's journey from England to Jerusalem via Venice, at https://www.bl.uk/manuscripts/FullDisplay.aspx?ref=Cotton_MS_Julius_E_IV/3

On inns in medieval England see John Hare, 'Inns, innkeepers and the society of later medieval England, 1350–1600', *Journal of Medieval History* 39 (2013), 477–97, and Martha Carlin, 'Why stay at the Tabard? Public inns and their amenities c. 1400', *Studies in the Age of Chaucer* 40 (2018), 413–21. Some of the details of my travellers are based on the archaeological evidence furnished by the 'Worcester Pilgrim', a corpse analysed in the 1980s; see Katherine Lack, 'A dyer on the road to Saint James: an identity for "The Worcester Pilgrim"?', *Midland History* 30 (2005), 112–28.

Those interested in knowing more about the historical reality of medieval shipping from Rye and similar ports are directed to Gillian Draper et al., *Rye: A History of a Sussex Cinque Port to 1660* (Chichester, 2009), and to the website *The Merchant Fleet of Late Medieval and Tudor England* at http://www.medievalandtudorships.org/

The prognostication and spell are edited from BL MS Sloane 965, ff. 6v–7v, a miscellany of c. 1450 including texts on humours, elements, urines, complexions and lunaries.

Chapter 3: From Aachen to Bolzano

For Petrarch's mountain aesthetics see Petrarch, 'The ascent of Mont Ventoux', trans. Hans Nachod, in Ernst Cassirer, Paul

Oskar Kristeller and John Herman Randall (eds.), *The Renaissance Philosophy of Man* (Chicago, 1948), pp. 36–46.

Dorothea of Montau's life is told in *The Life of Dorothea von Montau, a Fourteenth-Century Recluse*, ed. and trans. Ute Stargardt (Lewiston, NY 1997).

On Aachen see Walter Maas and Pit Siebigs, *Der Aachener Dom* (Regensburg, 2013); the figures of numbers of pilgrims are taken from J. Stopford, 'Some approaches to the archaeology of Christian pilgrimage', *World Archaeology* 26 (1994), 57–72, p. 57.

On St Ursula see Jane Cartwright (ed.), *The Cult of St Ursula and the 11,000 Virgins* (Cardiff, 2016). On pilgrim badges, see Brian Spencer, *Pilgrim Souvenirs and Secular Badges* (London, 1988), and the excellent kunera.nl website.

On Felix Fabri and his Ulm context see Kathryne Beebe, *Pilgrim & Preacher: The Audiences and Observant Spirituality of Friar Felix Fabri* (Oxford, 2014); Herbert Wiegandt, *Ulm: Geschichte einer Stadt* (Weissenhorn, 1977). On hospitality in medieval Ulm I consulted Franz Müller, *Die Geschichte des Wirtsgewerbes in Ulm* (Ulm, 1930). On Richental, see *The Council of Constance*, ed. and trans. Louise Ropes Loomis (New York, 1961).

The instructions for good table manners are taken from *John Russells Boke of Nurture*, ed. Frederick J. Furnivall (London, 1894), pp. 18–21, reflecting etiquette for an aristocrat's valet from c. 1450.

For information on medieval routes and tolls see the Viabundus project (https://www.landesgeschichte.uni-goettingen.de/handelsstrassen/index.php).

The bedtime conversation from *La Manière de langage* is my translation from Oxford, All Souls College MS 182, ff. 321r–v, a manuscript dating from c. 1413.

Chapter 4: A Stay in Venice, and Onwards to Rome

For a historical account of aspects of medieval Venice see Joanne M. Ferraro, *Venice: History of the Floating City* (Cambridge, 2012). I found the following especially useful in terms of Venice and travel: Franca Semi, *Gli 'Ospizi' di Venezia* (Venice, 1983); Guido Ruggiero, *The Boundaries of Eros: Sex Crime and Sexuality in Renaissance Venice* (Oxford, 1985); Frederic C. Lane, *Venice: A Maritime Republic* (Baltimore, 1973); Paula C. Clarke, 'The business of prostitution in early Renaissance Venice', *Renaissance Quarterly* 68 (2015), 419–64; Jane L. Stevens Crawshaw, *Plague Hospitals: Public Health for the City in Early Modern Venice* (Aldershot, 2016). Florence Edler, *Glossary of Mediaeval Terms of Business: Italian Series, 1200–1600* (Cambridge, MA, 1934) remains an indispensable resource.

On the pathogens of skeletons from Lazzaretto Vecchio I consulted Thi-Nguyen-Ny Tran et al., 'High throughput, multiplexed pathogen detection authenticates plague waves in medieval Venice, Italy', *PLoS One* 6 (2011), e16735, and for a more general account of public health in the city see Jo Wheeler, 'Stench in Sixteenth-Century Venice', in Alexander Cowan and Jill Seward (eds.), *The City and the Senses* (Aldershot, 2007), pp. 25–38.

I took details of the Venetian landscape from paintings in the Gallerie dell'Accademia di Venezia, especially Bellini's *Procession in St Mark's Square* (1496) and Carpaccio's *Legend of St Ursula* (1497–8).

On early passports see Valentin Gröbner, *Who Are You? Identification, Deception, and Surveillance in Early Modern Europe* (New York, 2007), and Patrick Bixby, *License to Travel: A Cultural History of the Passport* (Berkeley and Los Angeles, 2022).

On Rome see C. David Benson, *Imagined Romes: The Ancient City and its Stories in Middle English Poetry* (University Park, PA, 2019); Hendrik Dey, *The Making of Medieval Rome: A New Profile of the City, 400–1420* (Cambridge, 2021). Giotto's altarpiece from St Peter's is now in the Vatican Museum.

The Rome indulgences are from Capgrave, *The Solace of Pilgrimes*.

Chapter 5: Across the Great Sea: From Venice to Cyprus

The information on mermaids and sirens brings together various medieval myths about them, including those gathered in *DPR*.

A crucial survey of the experience of being on a Venetian galley is Benjamin Arbel, 'Daily life on board Venetian ships: The evidence of Renaissance travelogues and diaries', in Gherardo Ortalli and Alessio Sopracasa (eds.), *Rapporti mediterranei, pratiche documentarie, presenze veneziane* (Venice, 2017), pp. 183–219. See also Renard Gluzman, *Venetian Shipping: From the Days of Glory to Decline, 1453–1571* (Leiden, 2021), and Antonio Musarra, *Medioevo marinaro: prendere il mare nell'Italia medievale* (Bologna, 2021).

On the devotional sites that sprang up to serve the travellers, see Michele Bacci et al., 'Marian cult-sites along the Venetian sea-routes to the Holy Land in the Late Middle Ages', in Maria Stella Calò Mariani and Anna Trono (eds.), *The Ways of Mercy: Arts, Culture, and Marian Routes between East and West* (Salento, 2017), pp. 81–106.

The quotation from Machaut is from Guillaume de Machaut, *The Capture of Alexandria*, ed. and trans. Janet Shirley and Peter W. Edbury (London, 2001). On Gilbert the Englishman I consulted Robin Ward, 'Mediaeval advice on the avoidance and treatment of seasickness', *The Northern Mariner/Le marin du nord* 14 (2004), 69–72.

On the *Cog Anne* see E. M. Carus-Wilson, 'The Merchant Adventurers of Bristol in the fifteenth century', *Transactions of the Royal Historical Society* 11 (1928), 61–82.

On laws and regulation of the Venetian colonies see Freddy Thiriet, *Délibérations des assemblées vénitiennes concernant la Romanie, 1364–1463* (Paris, 1971). On Venetian Modon I am indebted to Panagiotis Foutakis, *I Methóni kai i istoría: i Venetía kai i exousía*

(Athens, 2017); also M. Mollat, *La Vie quotidienne des gens de mer en Atlantique, IXe–XVI siècle* (Paris, 1983).

On medieval Famagusta and brawling in bars I am indebted to Nicholas S. H. Coureas, 'Taverns in medieval Famagusta', in Michael Walsh, Peter Edbury and Nicholas Coureas (eds.), *Medieval and Renaissance Famagusta* (Farnham, 2012), pp. 65–72, and S. Bliznyuk, *Die Genuesen auf Zypern: Ende 14. und im 15. Jahrhundert* (Frankfurt, 2005).

I travelled in Cyprus with George Jeffery's *Historic Monuments of Cyprus* (Nicosia, 1918), the outdatedness of which proved essential in reconstructing the vanished places of Cyprus's past; likewise on Stavrovouni, John Hackett, *A History of the Orthodox Church of Cyprus* (London, 1901), pp. 442–52.

For Nicole Louve's original poem see Alain-Julien Surdel, 'Cinq semaines en galère', *Le Pays Lorrain* 100 (2019), 107–10; I also consulted the poem's original manuscript (Épinal, Bibliothèque Municipale MS 59(217), ff. 89r–90v).

Chapter 6: A Walking Tour of Constantinople

For general accounts of Byzantine Constantinople see Jonathan Harris, *Constantinople: Capital of Byzantium* (London, 2007); Jonathan Harris, *The Lost World of Byzantium* (New Haven, 2015); Judith Herrin, *Byzantium: The Surprising Life of a Medieval Empire* (London, 2007); and Nike Koutrakou, 'Medieval travellers to Constantinople: wonders and wonder', in Sarah Bassett (ed.), *The Cambridge Companion to Constantinople* (Cambridge, 2022), pp. 295–309. On the Fourth Crusade see Thomas F. Madden, 'The Venetian version of the Fourth Crusade: Memory and the conquest of Constantinople in medieval Venice', *Speculum* 87 (2012), 311–44. On the persistence of crusading as an idea long after the First Crusade see Aziz Suryal Atiya, *The Crusade in the Later Middle Ages* (London, 1938).

On Bertrandon's biography I am particularly indebted to Jaroslav Svátek, *Prier, combattre et voir le monde* (Rennes, 2021), pp. 50–53.

On the animals of the Hippodrome, including al-Marwazi's observations, see Nancy Ševčenko, 'Wild animals in the Byzantine park', in Antony Littlewood, Henry Maguire and Joachim Wolschke-Bulmahn (eds.), *Byzantine Garden Culture* (Washington, DC, 2002), pp. 69–86. On the statue of the horseman, see its recent very full 'biography' by Elena Boeck, *The Bronze Horseman of Justinian in Constantinople* (Cambridge, 2021). On the changing idea of the 'wonders of the world' see Kai Brodersen, *Die sieben Weltwunder. Legendäre Kunst- und Bauwerke* (Munich, 1996; 2006).

The advice for travellers on getting a guide and on the Hodegetria is taken from Stephen of Novgorod's visit to the city in 1348/9; see Georg P. Majeska, *Russian Travelers to Constantinople in the Fourteenth and Fifteenth Centuries* (Washington, DC, 1984), pp. 15–47.

The list of travellers' costs in the Holy Land is taken from Thomas Brygg's account of his 1392 pilgrimage. For a comparative list of prices see 'List of Price[s] of Medieval Items' at http://medieval.ucdavis.edu/120D/Money.html, and Ugo Tucci, *Mercanti, navi, monete nel Cinquecento veneziano* (Bologna, 1921), pp. 200–201, although precise correspondences in value are hard to make, especially across foreign currencies.

Chapter 7: Through the Holy Land to Babylon

On the medieval Holy Land, especially in terms of various kinds of travel see Nicole Chareyron, *Pilgrims to Jerusalem in the Middle Ages*, trans. W. Donald Wilson (New York, 2005); Christopher MacEavitt, *The Crusades and the Christian Worlds of the East: Rough Tolerance*

(Philadelphia, 2008); Elizabeth Ross, *Picturing Experience in the Early Printed Book: Breydenbach's* Peregrinatio *from Venice to Jerusalem* (University Park, PA, 2014); Sylvia Schein, *Fideles crucis: The Papacy, the West, and the Recovery of the Holy Land, 1274–1314* (Oxford, 1991).

The Sabbatory river is described by Mandeville and by many others. See further Daniel Stein Kokin, 'Toward the source of the Sambatyon: Shabbat discourse and the origins of the Sabbatical river legend', *AJS Review* 37 (2013), 1–28.

On Acre and medieval travellers see Anthony Bale, 'Reading and writing in Outremer', in Anthony Bale (ed.), *The Cambridge Companion to the Literature of the Crusades* (Cambridge, 2018), pp. 85–101, and Laura Morreale, *Pilgrims and Writing in Crusader Acre*, https://scalar.lauramorreale.com/pilgrims-and-writing-in-crusader-acre/dynamic-map-of-the-pardouns-dacre?path=pilgrimage-path. The record of Jewish drinkers in Acre's taverns is at https://rb.gy/35c3.

On Islam and Muhammad in medieval Europe see Suzanne Conklin Akbari, *Idols in the East: European Representations of Islam and the Orient, 1100–1450* (Ithaca, NY, 2009); Nicholas Morton, *Encountering Islam on the First Crusade* (Cambridge, 2016); John Tolan, 'European accounts of Muhammad's life', in Jonathan E. Brockopp (ed.), *The Cambridge Companion to Muhammad* (Cambridge, 2010), pp. 226–50. On Embrico of Mainz and Muhammad's flying coffin see John Tolan, *Faces of Muhammad: Western Perceptions of the Prophet of Islam from the Middle Ages to Today* (Princeton, NJ, 2019), pp. 69–72.

The best description of what medieval pilgrims would have encountered at Sinai is in Denys Pringle, *The Churches of the Crusader Kingdom of Jerusalem: A Corpus*, 4 vols. (Cambridge, 1993–2009), vol. 2, pp. 49–62. The visitors' graffiti at Sinai is described in Hyacinth Rabino, 'Le monastère de Sainte-Catherine (Mont-Sinaï)', *Bulletin de la Société Royale de Géographie d'Égypte* 19 (1935), 21–126. On balsam, see Elly R. Truitt, 'The virtues of balm in late medieval literature', *Early Science and Medicine* 14 (2009), 711–36, and in the context of late medieval pilgrimages see Marianne

P. Ritsema van Eck, 'Encounters with the Levant: the late medieval illustrated Jerusalem Travelogue by Paul Walter von Guglingen', *Mediterranean Historical Review* 32 (2017), 153–88.

The advice on how to cross the desert is taken from Meshullam of Volterra's account of the Sinai.

Chapter 8: A Walking Tour of Jerusalem

For an overview of the status of medieval Jerusalem for travellers see Chareyron, *Pilgrims to Jerusalem*. Dan Bahat, *The Illustrated Atlas of Jerusalem* (New York, 1990), pp. 108–17, provides a visual overview. To understand the built environment of medieval Jerusalem see Denys Pringle's remarkable archaeological studies, *Secular Buildings in the Crusader Kingdom of Jerusalem: An Archaeological Gazetteer* (Cambridge, 1997) and *The Churches of the Crusader Kingdom*. Martin Biddle's *The Tomb of Christ* (Stroud, 1999), pp. 28–40, gives a full account of the Holy Sepulchre itself; Colin Morris, *The Sepulchre of Christ and the Medieval West: From the Beginning to 1600* (Oxford, 2005) is an engaging story of the tomb's many forms.

On the dating of the olive trees at Gethsemane, I consulted Mauro Bernabei, 'The age of the olive trees in the Garden of Gethsemane', *Journal of Archaeological Science* 53 (2015), 43–8.

On holy footsteps in Jerusalem, I recommend Jean-Marie Fritz, 'Empreintes et vestiges dans les récits de pèlerinage: quand la pierre devient cire', *Le Moyen Age* 118 (2012), 9–40.

The phrases in foreign languages are taken from William Wey (Greek), Arnold von Harff (Albanian and Arabic) and Anonymous/Wynkyn de Worde, *Information for Pilgrims* (Turkish) (London, c. 1498).

Chapter 9: A Detour to Ethiopia

I recommend François-Xavier Fauvelle, *The Golden Rhinoceros: Histories of the African Middle Ages*, trans. Troy Tice (Princeton, 2018), for an overview of Africa and its relationship with the wider world in medieval culture. On the Horn of Africa, the material gathered in Samantha Kelly (ed.), *A Companion to Medieval Ethiopia and Eritrea* (Leiden, 2020) is very useful. On Ethiopia and travel writing see *Ethiopia through Writers' Eyes*, ed. and trans. Yves-Marie Stranger (London, 2016). On Lalibela I recommend Jacques Mercier and Claude Lepage, *Lalibela: Wonder of Ethiopia; The Monolithic Churches and their Treasures*, trans. Jennifer White-Thévenot and Jane Degeorges (London, 2012).

The diplomatic correspondence between Rome and Ethiopia is published in Osvaldo Raineri, *Lettere tra i pontefici romani e i principi etiopici (secoli xii–xx)* (Vatican, 2003), and the relevant material is surveyed in Matteo Salvadore, *The African Prester John and the Birth of Ethiopian–European Relations, 1402–1555* (London, 2017), and Verena Krebs, *Medieval Ethiopian Kingship, Craft, and Diplomacy with Latin Europe* (Cham, 2021), the latter being especially valuable on Battista of Imola (pp. 136–9). On the location of Barara see Hartwig Breternitz and Richard Pankhurst, 'Barara, the royal city of 15th and early 16th century Ethiopia, *Annales d'Éthiopie* 24 (2009), 209–49.

The sources on Prester John are usefully gathered in Keagan Brewer (ed.), *Prester John: The Legend and its Sources* (Farnham, 2015).

On the mobile location of the Kong mountains, see Thomas J. Bassett and Phillip W. Porter, '"From the best authorities": The Mountains of Kong in the cartography of West Africa', *Journal of African History* 32 (1991), 367–413.

The mythical Ethiopian diet of smoked honeysuckle is taken from *DPR*.

John of Gaddesden's medical advice is summarized from H. P. Cholmeley, *John of Gaddesden and the Rosa Medicinae* (Oxford, 1912), pp. 52–5.

Chapter 10: On the Silk Roads

For a stimulating overview of the history and culture of the Silk Roads see Peter Frankopan, *The Silk Roads: A New History of the World* (London, 2015). On the caravanserai see Kate Franklin, *Everyday Cosmopolitanisms: Living the Silk Road in Medieval Armenia* (Berkeley and Los Angeles, 2021). Geoffrey of Vinsauf's description of a caravanserai is taken from his account of Richard I of England's looting of a convoy in 1192, in Roy C. Cave and Herbert H. Coulson, *A Source Book for Medieval Economic History* (Milwaukee, 1936; repr. New York, 1965), p. 155. See too Gül Asatekin and Georges Charlier et al., *Along Ancient Trade Routes: Seljuk Caravanserais and Landscapes in Central Anatolia* (Rekem-Lanaken, 1996). On European slavery in the context of the Silk Roads see Hannah Barker, *That Most Precious Merchandise: The Mediterranean Trade in Black Sea Slaves, 1260–1500* (Philadelphia, 2019).

On Pegolotti's context see Lorenzo Pubblici, *Mongol Caucasia: Invasions, Conquests, and Government of a Frontier Region in Thirteenth-Century Eurasia (1204–1295)* (London, 2022).

On the Old Man of the Mountain Dorothee Metlitzki, *The Matter of Araby in Medieval England* (New Haven, 1977), pp. 222–31 remains incisive, and can be supplemented by Freya Stark's atmospheric *The Valley of the Assassins and Other Persian Travels* (London, 1934). The Islamic history of the Old Man is described in Shafique N. Virani, 'An old man, a garden, and an assembly of Assassins: Legends and realities of the Nizari Ismaili Muslims', *Iran: Journal of the British Institute of Persian Studies* (2021), https://doi.org/10.1080/05786967.2021.1901062

On Cockayne see Herman Pleij, *Dreaming of Cockaigne: Medieval Fantasies of the Perfect Life*, trans. Diane Webb (New York, 2001). Accounts of the leprosy-healing well of Urfa (formerly Edessa) appear in several travel guides, here taken from the anonymous 1507 'Travels of a Merchant in Persia' in *Travels to Tana and Persia*, ed. Stanley, p. 144.

The quotation from Arnold of Lübeck is from *The Chronicle of Arnold of Lübeck*, ed. Graham A. Loud (London, 2019). I. de Rachewiltz's *Papal Envoys to the Great Khans* (London, 1971) collects early accounts of European travellers on the Silk Roads on religious business. For an example of a Mongol safe-conduct (*paiza*) see the one from c. 1240 now at the Metropolitan Museum in New York: https://www.metmuseum.org/art/collection/search/60006641; the *paiza* inscriptions given are from this specimen and from a private collection. For context, see Bixby, *License to Travel.*

On Gog & Magog, I recommend Victor I. Scherb, 'Assimilating giants: The appropriation of Gog & Magog in medieval and early modern England', *Journal of Medieval and Early Modern Studies* 32 (2002), 59–84; and Andrew Gow, *The Red Jews: Antisemitism in an Apocalyptic Age, 1200–1600* (Leiden, 1995).

On medieval locations and depictions of Paradise, including Leardo's, see Alessandro Scafi, *Mapping Paradise: A History of Heaven on Earth* (London, 2006); for the lost paradise of Strabo see *The Geography of Strabo*, ed. and trans. Duane W. Roller (Cambridge, 2014), p. 670.

The information on the creatures of India is taken from Gervase of Tilbury's early thirteenth-century *Otia Imperalia*, ed. and trans. S. E. Banks and J. W. Binns (Oxford, 2002), pp. 188–91.

Chapter 11: From Persia through India

A useful summary of the history of medieval Hormuz is given in Ralph Kauz and Roderich Ptak, 'Hormuz in Yuan and Ming sources', *Bulletin de l'École Française d'Extrême-Orient* 88 (2001), 27–75.

On India and late medieval travel writing see Joan-Pau Rubiés, *Travel and Ethnology in the Renaissance: South India through European Eyes, 1250–1625* (Cambridge, 2002). Jagjeet Lally, *India and the Silk Roads: The History of a Trading World* (London, 2021), and Elizabeth A. Lambourn, *Abraham's Luggage: A Social Life of Things in the Medieval Indian Ocean World* (Cambridge, 2019) put the Eurasian merchant worlds of Nikitin and Santo Stefano in useful historical perspectives. See also the chapter, 'The Indian subcontinent: on the way to everywhere', in Janet L. Abu-Lughod, *Before European Hegemony: The World System, AD 1250–1350* (Oxford, 1989), pp. 261–90.

On Nikitin see especially Gail D. Lenhoff and Janet L. B. Martin, 'The commercial and cultural context of Afanasij Nikitin's journey beyond three seas', *Jahrbücher für Geschichte Osteuropas* 37/3 (1989), 321–44; Mary Jane Maxwell, 'Afanasii Nikitin: An Orthodox Russian's spiritual voyage in the Dar al-Islam, 1468–1475', *Journal of World History* 17 (2006), 243–66; Gail Lenhoff, 'Beyond three seas: Afanasij Nikitin's journey from orthodoxy to apostasy', *East European Quarterly* 13 (1979), 431–47.

Thomas of Kent's account of Alexander in India is taken from his *The Anglo-Norman Alexander (The Roman de Toute Chevalrie)*, ed. Brian Foster and Ian Short (London, 1976). On *sati*, I recommend Ania Loomba, 'Dead women tell no tales: Issues of female subjectivity, subaltern agency and tradition in colonial and post-colonial writings on widow immolation in India', *History Workshop* 36 (1993), 209–27.

The tips for a business traveller are taken from Pegolotti, *Pratica.*

Chapter 12: All Roads Lead to Khanbaliq

For a crucial account of the world of trade and the Mongol empire see Abu-Lughod, *Before European Hegemony*.

The York manuscript of Giovanni of Plano Carpini is now Cambridge, Corpus Christi College MS 181 (which also contains parts of William of Rubruck's travel account). For Giovanni of Plano Carpini, Benedykt the Pole and William of Rubruck, see Christopher Dawson, *Mission to Asia* (Toronto, 1980) originally published as *The Mongol Mission* (London, 1955) and de Rachewiltz, *Papal Envoys to the Great Khans*. Peter Jackson, *The Mongols and the West, 1221–1410* (Harlow, 2005), offers an excellent summary of conflict, trade and missionizing between Europe and Mongol China.

On the historical circumstances of vanished Karakorum, I found Jan Bemmann et al., 'Mapping Karakorum, the capital of the Mongol empire', *Antiquity* 96 (2022), 159–78, and K. Sagaster, 'Die mongolische Hauptstadt Karakorum', *Beiträge zur Allgemeinen und Vergleichenden Archäologie* 19 (1999), 113–28, extremely useful. On Guillaume Boucher and other western captives at the khan's court, see Leonardo Olschki, *Guillaume Boucher: A French Artist at the Court of the Khans* (Baltimore, 1946). On the history of the Imperial City from 1368, I recommend Geremie R. Barmé, *The Forbidden City* (London, 2008).

On the Ilioni tombstones see Francis A. Rouleau, 'The Yangchow Latin tombstone as a landmark of medieval Christianity in China', *Harvard Journal of Asiatic Studies* 17 (1954), 346–65, and Jennifer Purtle, 'The far side: Expatriate medieval art and its languages in Sino-Mongol China', in Jill Caskey, Adam S. Cohen and Linda Safran (eds.), *Confronting the Borders of Medieval Art* (Leiden, 2011), pp. 167–97.

On Marco Polo see John Larner, *Marco Polo and the Discovery of the World* (New Haven, 1999) and Simon Gaunt, *Marco Polo's* Le Devisement du Monde: *Narrative Voice, Language and Diversity* (Woodbridge, 2013). For compelling accounts of the historicity of Polo's travels see Stephen G. Haw, *Marco Polo's China: A Venetian in the Realm of Khubilai Khan* (London, 2009) and Hans Ulrich Vogel, *Marco Polo* Was *in China* (Leiden, 2013). See too Kim Phillips, *Before Orientalism: Asian Peoples and Cultures in European Travel Writing, 1245–1510* (Philadelphia, 2013) for an insightful overview of medieval travel writing about the east. I also found much useful information in Jonathan Clements, *An Armchair Traveller's History of Beijing* (London, 2016).

For historical accounts of the 1281 Mongol invasion of Japan, see Jung-pang Lo, *China as a Sea Power, 1127–1368*, ed. with commentary by Bruce A. Elleman (Singapore, 2012).

The information on dining at Genghis Khan's court is taken from V. A. Riasanovsky, *Fundamental Principles of Mongol Law* (Tientsin (Tianjin), 1937), and Plano Carpini; the main source from the former is Genghis Khan's *Great Law* (*Yasa* or *Ikh Yasag*), which covered Mongol subjects' behaviour, includes a wide range of food- and drink-related commandments and taboos. The *Yasa* was followed across Asia but no original manuscript of it survives so its contents are speculative, partly based on travellers' accounts. Plano Carpini's *History of the Mongols* includes information on Mongol dining habits which both chimes with and adds to the *Yasa*'s laws.

Chapter 13: Visiting the West

Two crucial studies of medieval Islamic understandings of Europe, including some accounts of travel to Europe, are Bernard Lewis, *The Muslim Discovery of Europe* (New York, 1982) and Daniel König, *Arabic-Islamic Views of the Latin West* (Oxford, 2015). I also recommend Nancy Bisaha, *Creating East and West: Renaissance Humanists and the Ottoman Turks* (Philadelphia, 2004), on the changing idea of the Turk in Europe around 1453, and Giancarlo Casale, *The Ottoman Age of Exploration* (Oxford, 2010).

Mehmed's maps are well described and summarized in Karen Pinto, 'The maps are the message: Mehmet II's patronage of an "Ottoman Cluster"', *Imago Mundi* 63 (2011), 155–79. I consulted the manuscripts at Topkapı in summer 2017; the *Geographia* in *terza rima* of Francesco Berlinghieri is Topkapı MS GI (A84). On Berlinghieri, I recommend Sean Roberts, 'Poet and "world painter": Francesco Berlinghieri's *Geographia* (1482)', *Imago Mundi* 62 (2010), 145–60.

The anecdote about the Chinese in Ireland appears in a manuscript of Aeneas Piccolomini (Pope Pius II), the *Historia Rerum Ibuque Gestarum*; the story was known to Christopher Columbus. See Flint, *Imaginative Landscape of Christopher Columbus*, p. 59.

On the Chinese goddess Mazu see Y. Zhang, 'The state canonization of Mazu: Bringing the notion of Imperial metaphor into conversation with the personal model', *Religions* 10 (2019), 151–73.

On the interconnected worlds of medieval Europe and the Near East see Atiya, *The Crusade in the Later Middle Ages*. On Bartholomew the Ethiopian see Michael Ray, 'A Black slave on the run in thirteenth-century England', *Nottingham Medieval Studies* 51 (2007), 111–19; Paston's Turk is referred to in *Paston Letters & Papers*, ed. Norman Davis, 3 vols. (Oxford, 2004), vol. 1, p. 415.

The Fountain of Youth narratives are from *The Ancient, Honorable, Famous, and Delightfull Historie of Huon of Bordeaux* (London, 1601); Mandeville; and Jean Froissart, *Le Joli Buisson de Jonece*, ed. Anthime Fourrier (Geneva, 1975), my translations.

Chapter 14: A Rough Guide to the Antipodes and the End of the World

On the medieval Antipodes see Hiatt, *Terra Incognita*; Matthew Boyd Goldie, *The Idea of the Antipodes* (London, 2010); William D. McCready, 'Isidore, the Antipodeans, and the shape of the earth', *Isis* 87 (1996), 108–27; and Marcia Kupfer, 'Mappaemundi: image, artefact, social practice', in P. D. A. Harvey (ed.), *The Hereford World Map: Medieval World Maps and their Context* (London, 2006), pp. 253–69. Various versions circulated of the story of the man who walked round the world or visited a subterranean 'other world'; those given here are taken from Mandeville's *Book of Marvels and Travels*. See too Gervase of Tilbury's account of the 'Devil's Arse' (Castleton, Derbyshire), an entry point to the Antipodes, as narrated in his *Otia Imperialia*, ed. Banks and Binns, pp. 642–5. The description of the Antipodes in Cicero is from *Scipio's Dream*, in Macrobius, *Commentary on the Dream of Scipio*, ed. and trans. Stahl, VI.3, p. 74; the quotation from Augustine is from *City of God*, ed. and trans. Henry Bettenson (London, 2003), p. 664.

See Abu-Lughod, 'The strait and narrow', in *Before European Hegemony*, pp. 291–315, for an overview of medieval Java and its environs. For the stories of Sinbad the Sailor, who repeatedly 'yearned for travel and traffic', see *The Annotated Arabian Nights*, ed. Paulo Lemos Horta, trans. Yasmine Seale (New York, 2021), pp. 201–62.

For the *Malay Annals* see *Sejarah Melayu or Malay Annals*, ed. and trans. C. C. Brown, rev. R. Roolvink (London, 1953; rev. Oxford, 1970).

The Mirror of the World (Westminster, 1481) is available in a digital facsimile at https://dpul.princeton.edu/scheide/catalog/r781wk70m.

On poison trees see Michael R. Dove, 'Dangerous plants in the colonial imagination: Rumphius and the Poison Tree', *Allertonia* 13 (2013), 29–46; Tim Hannigan, 'Beyond control: Orientalist tensions and the history of the "upas tree" myth', *Journal of Commonwealth Literature* 55 (2020), 173–89.

A Note on Quotations

Medieval travel writing combined eyewitness reportage with 'borrowings', often unattributed, from previous accounts. At various points in this book I have likewise pirated phrasing from travellers, real and imagined, medieval and post-medieval. Some of the most obvious borrowings are as follows:

p. 15 'The hospitality is pitiless'. Beverley Nichols, *The Sun in My Eyes, Or, How Not to Go Around the World* (London, 1969), p. 24.

pp. 15, 28 'To be a tourist is to escape accountability. Errors and failings don't cling to you the way they do back home. You're able to drift across continents and languages, suspending the operation of sound thought.' Don DeLillo, *The Names* (New York, 1982), pp. 50–51.

p. 16 'We are drugged to forget how little our strides carry, however stretched they may be; the real position remains almost unchanged since the yardstick is infinity.' Freya Stark, *Ionia: A Quest* (London, 1954), p. 68.

p. 24 'the rain, and the crows, and the rabbits, and the deer, and the partridges and pheasants'. Charles Dickens, *Bleak House* (London, 1866), p. 9.

p. 25 'the fanaticism one spends on the trivial'. Dilys Powell, *An Affair of the Heart* (London, 2019), p. 130.

pp. 32, 38 'The beckoning counts, and not the clicking latch behind you: and all through life the actual moment of emancipation still holds that delight, of the whole world coming to meet you like a wave.' Freya Stark, *Traveller's Prelude* (London, 1950), p. 37.

p. 49 'uninterrupted wave of the pious carillon of vespers'. Stefan Zweig, *Journeys*, trans. Will Stone (London, 2010), p. 8.

p. 62 'ultimate and unbroken'. Patrick Leigh Fermor, *A Time of Gifts: On Foot to Constantinople* (London, 1977), p. 56.

p. 73 'there is no use pretending that the tourist Venice is not the real Venice.' Mary McCarthy, *Venice Observed* (Lausanne, 1956), p. 15.

p. 104 'the stark horrors of boredom'. Evelyn Waugh, *Remote People* (London, 2011), p. 139.

p. 104 'The man who has criss-crossed every ocean has merely criss-crossed the monotony of his self.' Fernando Pessoa, *The Book of Disquiet*, trans. Iain Watson (London, 1988), p. 144.

p. 109 'grey, melancholy woods, and wild stone spires'. Robert Louis Stevenson, *Treasure Island*, ed. Peter Hunt (Oxford, 2011), p. 71.

p. 110 'The air settled into an agitated silence.' DeLillo, *The Names*, p. 121.

p. 125 'dusty purlieus'. Lawrence Durrell, *Bitter Lemons* (London, 1957), p. 153.

p. 138 'transformed into a tumble of terraces, a play of light and shade.' Stark, *Ionia*, p. 174.

p. 159 'the feeling that one's foreignness is the crucial element of one's character'. Vikram Seth, *From Heaven Lake: Travels through Sinkiang and Tibet* (London, 1983), p. 10.

p. 185 'Even the light was hot.' Geoff Dyer, *Out of Sheer Rage* (Edinburgh, 1997), p. 15.

p. 187 'There are towns where one is never present for the first time.' Zweig, *Journeys*, p. 30.

p. 195 'an atmosphere of cultured bric-a-brac', Stark, *Traveller's Prelude*, p. 45.

p. 195 'When you get there you feel something final. There is an arrival.' D. H. Lawrence, 'Taos', in *Mornings in Mexico and Other Essays*, ed. Virginia Crosswhite Hyde (Cambridge, 2009), p. 125.

p. 205 'the print of a man's naked foot'. Daniel Defoe, *Robinson Crusoe*, ed. John Richetti (Harmondsworth, 2001), p. 122.

p. 215 'some improbable land of violence and piety, courtesy and treachery, barrenness and fertility'. Dervla Murphy, *In Ethiopia with a Mule* (London, 1968), p. 1.

p. 216 'Sometimes we lurched along a narrow track with cliffs rising on one side and a precipice falling away on the other; sometimes we picked our way on broad ledges among great volcanic boulders; sometimes we grated between narrow rock walls.' Waugh, *Remote People*, p. 124.

p. 222 'One's first entry into a war-stricken country as a neutral observer is bound to be dream-like, unreal.' W. H. Auden and Christopher Isherwood, *Journey to a War* (London, 1939), p. 28.

p. 255 'The allure of lost consequence and faded power is seducing me, the passing of time, the passing of friends, the scrapping of great ships!' Jan Morris, *Trieste and the Meaning of Nowhere* (London, 2001), p. 3.

p. 273 'But what was the point? What had he gained from all this commotion? What had he got out of his journey?' Jules Verne, *Around the World in 80 Days*, ed. and trans. William Butcher (Oxford, 1995), p. 202.

p. 308 'the Yangtze is a river of junks and sampans, fuelled by human sweat.' Paul Theroux, *Sailing through China* (London, 1983), p. 21.

p. 308 'gently tapering flanks'. Jan Morris, *Last Letters from Hav* (London, 1989), p. 96.

p. 312 'the tempest which causes the stern to rise and the prow to fall, which plunges powerless mortals into the blinding waves of its depths, which moves the fleet's straight course to chaos through an uncontrollable will'. Paraphrasing Dante, *Divine Comedy*, *Inferno* V:28–40; *Paradiso* XXVII:122–49; *Purgatorio* V: 109–30.

p. 350 'a sea of troubles'. William Shakespeare, *Hamlet* III.i.

p. 350 'the gorgeous palaces. The solemn temples'. William Shakespeare, *The Tempest* IV.i.

p. 354 'the turgid, indefinite feelings of homecoming'. Evelyn Waugh, *Labels: A Mediterranean Journal* (London, 2011), p. 205.

p. 359 'We shall not cease from exploration, / And the end of all our exploring / Will be to arrive where we started / And know the place for the first time.' Paraphrasing T. S. Eliot, 'Little Gidding'.

p. 359 'your passport into the sky, to a union with those who have finished their lives on earth'; 'the small earth he had traversed seemed newly tiny, nothing more than a series of points on a small surface'; 'the brilliant circles amid the blazing stars', paraphrasing Cicero, *Scipio's Dream*, in Macrobius, *Commentary on the Dream of Scipio*, ed. and trans. Stahl, III.6–7, IV.1, pp. 72–3.

A Note on Illustrations

The illustrations here are based on and inspired by medieval sources. Like illustrations in a medieval manuscript, they may not always exactly portray the source image.

1. A windrose. Based on BL Royal MS 17.C.38, an English copy of Mandeville; the owner (possibly one William Osborne) had travelled from England to Florence and written their itinerary in their manuscript.
2. Behaim's Globe. Nuremberg, Germanisches Nationalmuseum, WI1826.
3. Fra Angelico's Christ Child, holding the orb of the world. From the *Madonna della Ombre*, Florence, Museo di San Marco dell'Angelico.
4. Aachen Cathedral, interior.
5. Pilgrims' badges: St Ursula with some of the 11,000 virgins in a boat (Cologne, c. 1350–1400); based on a badge found at Dordrecht; now Rotterdam, Museum Boijmans Van Beuningen, Collectie Familie van Beuningen 1682. Ambulant vulva with pilgrim's hat, rosary and phallic pilgrim's staff (France, 1400–1500); based on a badge found at Paris; now Prague, Uměleckoprůmyslové muzeum v Praze, UPM5774(1894).
6. The pillars at Venice of St Mark and St Theodore.
7. Constantinople, after Buondelmonti's 1420s maps.

8. The animals of the Holy Land, after Erhard Reuwich's image in Bernhard von Breydenbach, *Peregrinatio in Terram Sanctam* (Mainz, 1486).
9. The Church of the Holy Sepulchre, Jerusalem, after the image in a German translation of Niccolò da Poggibonsi's *Book of Outremer*, BL, Egerton MS 1900, f. 12v (Nuremberg, c. 1465).
10. The cold well of Ethiopia and a sciapod. From a manuscript of Mandeville's *Book of Marvels and Travels*, BL, Royal MS 17.C.38, f. 36v (southern England, c. 1400–25).
11. The kiosk mosque at Tuzhisar Sultanhan caravanserai, Turkey.
12. The goddess Varahi, based on a sandstone sculpture, Mumbai, Chhatrapati Shivaji Maharaj Vastu Sangrahalaya S74.2 (Madhya Pradesh, c. 1000).
13. The automaton and fountain at Karakorum, based on the description given by William of Rubruck.
14. Simplified Islamic world map, following the kinds of Arabic and Persianate maps read at the Ottoman court, after Istanbul, Süleymaniye Kütüphanesi MS AS 2971a, f. 3r, and Topkapi Sarayi Müzesi Kütüphanesi MS A.2380, f. 4r.
15. The men who walked around the world, after *The Mirror of the World* (Westminster, 1481).

Acknowledgements

My father was a geographer, and it was in his study that I learned to love maps and atlases. It was childhood travel with my family that opened my eyes to the possibilities of geography, to other worlds and to curiosity about place. So it is to my brilliant dad, Professor John Bale, that this book is dedicated.

I would like warmly to thank my editors; at Viking Penguin, Tom Killingbeck and Alpana Sajip, and Amy Cherry at Norton, for their vision, encouragement and input; and also Daniel Crewe, Charlotte Daniels, Giles Herman and Peter James. My agent Veronique Baxter at David Higham Associates helped me to shape the book and always gives the best advice and support.

Thanks especially to Roderick Bale, Ruth Bale, Annie Crombie, Barbara Davidson, James Francken, Molly Murray, Timothy Phillips, Vic Sowerby, Nikki Vousden and Harry Wallop for immensely helpful feedback on drafts. Thanks too to Heike Bauer, Mark Blacklock, Carolyn Burdett, Isabel Davis, Jonathan Fruoco, Daniela Giosuè, Claire Harman, Seda Ilter, Elliot Kendall, Joanne Leal, Lisa Liddy, Gudrun Litz, Nimrod Luz, Assaf Pinkus, Alison Pyatt, Marina Toumpouri, Marion Turner and staff at the London Library. Robert Rouse, Jarrah Sastrawan, Soon-Tzu Speechley and Christopher Tan added to my knowledge of the ends of the earth. I am grateful too for the thoughtful engagement of my students on my MA course at Birkbeck, University of London, on 'Medieval Worlds', co-taught with Kate Franklin. The translation and transcription of the 'Anonymous Englishman of 1344–5' was funded by the Leverhulme Trust 'Pilgrim Libraries' project (IM-2015-041) and undertaken by Rosalind Lintott, for which warm thanks.

Doing fieldwork, I benefited from many kindnesses around the world, in German hospitals and Maldivian speedboats, from Aachen to Zurich, from Acre to Beijing. I'm grateful to an array of apartment hosts, airline and hotel staff, archivists and librarians, taxi drivers and medical workers who assisted me as I travelled, often in very difficult circumstances, to research this book.

Timothy Phillips has been my constant and loving support, my ideal reader and favourite travelling companion. Both he and Benny, the sleepy black cat, are this particular traveller's reminder that one of the pleasures of travel is the joy of returning home.

Index Locorum

Index Generalis

Page references in *italics* indicate images.